SPRING 2025
Tiny Terrors
VOL.1

GRAVESIDE PRESS

CONTENT NOTES

Please note: because this is a horror anthology, it should be assumed that the basic horror tropes will apply.
These include death, gore, and violence.

For a list of potentially triggering subjects, please refer to page 474.

DREAM EATER FOR SALE

CAROLINE BARNARD-SMITH

Brightest blessings, Dearest Seeker. I extend to you an invitation to browse Starlight Collections Boutique, your one-stop shop for Dream Eaters (also Spirit Companions and Angelic Helpers—ask about my 2-for-1 sale!). Do you struggle to reach the Astral Plane? Do you feel Hexed, Cheated, or Blocked in some way when you try to lucid dream? Perhaps you simply suffer from debilitating nightmares? My Dream Eaters can syphon all negative energies from the dreaming world and return your dreams to peace and equilibrium. My captured Dream Eaters are AUTHENTIC! As per Sweet Dreamz seller regs, you will receive a tangible item upon receipt of payment. I am an experienced Witch, Medium, Paranormal Investigator, and Keeper of Dream Eaters with more than 25 years' experience. Thank you so much for your interest… Perhaps you were meant to find your way here. If you feel this post speaks to you, visit my website or feel free to message me. I'm always honoured to hear from true-hearted Seekers!

THE COLD FLICKERING emanating from the TV pulled at the edges of Molly's smile, made it appear warped and feral. She severely doubted she could call herself a true-hearted Seeker, but the website had stoked a small ember of joy she hadn't felt in months. The antiquated forum was an eye-straining mishmash of purples and pinks. A garish title floating at the top proclaimed this glorious relic of the early noughties to be The Sweet Dreamz Club.

Molly expected the site to be abandoned, left to float at the shadowy recesses of the interwebs like a barnacled ghost ship. She was surprised to find the posts were recent. People were discussing lucid dreams and how to trigger them. Others calling themselves dream-walkers offered to provide a link between your dreams and those of another for a modest fee.

Walk in another's head, they promised. *See the world through their dreaming eyes.*

Molly had been about to click away when she saw the post titled, *Dream Eaters for Sale*, written by a self-proclaimed witch from Kent who called herself Lucretia.

Maybe it was the lack of sleep. Maybe it was the aftereffects of running on coffee and fear for weeks, but something made Molly click the private message button.

Molly: Do these dream eaters really work?

The seller responded almost immediately.

Lucretia: Yes, they really work. I have several entities for sale. They are extremely powerful and not to be used as toys. Are you sure you're serious, Dearest Seeker?

Molly sat up straighter on the sofa, torn between goading the woman on or inquiring why she was awake and eager to chat at such a late hour. If she wasn't peddling bullshit, surely she should be soundly ensconced within her own lucid dream, flying around the lost city of Atlantis or chilling with movie stars.

She lifted a hesitant finger to her phone screen and typed, *I'm not sure if I believe in this sort of thing.*

The witch's second reply took longer to materialise. Molly rubbed at the back of her neck, massaging away an uncomfortable prickling sensation. Lucretia: It doesn't matter that you believe, it only matters that you Seek. You found your way to me for a reason.

Molly supposed that was true, the reason being she was bored and sad and had absolutely no intention of forcing herself to sleep just yet. Her gaze wandered to the empty double bed floating below the ceiling. It was fixed between two walls, the sagging mattress caged by repurposed stair railings, the only access provided by a long splintering ladder. The bed was both a marvel of invention and an ugly monument to the squalling meanness of her landlord, a man who had wrested a student apartment from a damp garage with barely functional heating.

Lucretia: You are having nightmares.

It wasn't a question, but a statement. Molly frowned down at the small, bright screen in her hand.

Molly: What makes you think that?

Lucretia: I gather impressions from people. Their passions and fears. Your fear is a scarlet blade that weeps as it cuts. Tell me about your nightmares, Dearest Seeker.

Molly's first impulse was to close the site and turn off her phone. This overly familiar internet stranger was prying a bit too close to home. Her finger hovered over the screen. Finally, she typed, *Why do you need to know about my nightmares?*

Lucretia: So that I can establish which Dream Eater will be the most suitable. They each have unique personalities and temperaments. No two are alike, just as no two dreams are alike. Some Dream Eaters are skilled at softening dreams of death and dying. Some are able to vanquish monsters. Some merely provide a comforting presence in a bleak landscape.

This couldn't be real. Surely the woman was nothing more than a grifter, trading hope and restful slumber to the desperate and REM-deprived.

Lucretia: Perhaps we could start with something simpler and work back from there. Why do you think you're having nightmares?

This was turning into a bizarre late-night counselling session. Despite Molly's misgivings, it was comforting to talk to somebody. Even an internet witch who sold dream eaters for a living. She was tempted to engage, but where would she even start? Grandmother's death? Ryan's swift exit? The baby? Ryan's last communication before he disappeared was a text message. In the long grey hours before dawn, Molly would stare at that sad little missive and wonder how she would ever explain it to their daughter.

Here's all I have left of Daddy—a one-line text with no punctuation. But he signed off with a winky face, so it's all okay.

In Ryan's absence, thinking about the baby made Molly feel nauseous in a way that ran deeper than morning sickness. She imagined the life knitting itself together inside her—a tiny wad of jelly forming skin and tender organs in the warm dark at the centre of her body—and immediately pushed the image away.

I'm pregnant and my boyfriend's left me, she typed, pressing send before she could second guess herself.

If she had bothered to make any real friends, she was sure they would have advised her against having a child so young. She was only halfway through her art history course, still living in student accommodation. But when she'd peed on that little plastic stick and watched the second line appear with a trepidation that verged on horror, she had been in love and her grandmother had still been alive.

> **Lucretia:** Yes, I can feel your grief. You do not grieve for your broken relationship though, not truly. Perhaps a buried, vital part of your psyche knew this man would not make a good life-mate. You knew you could raise this child alone, and make a better job of it. You grieve in a deeper way, for a different person.

Molly found herself nodding along as she read Lucretia's words—small, neat text blinking within the fuchsia shell of the Sweet Dreamz Club website. Staring at the background for too long made her feel as if she was being slowly enveloped in pink and purple flesh. She blinked and began typing her reply.

> **Molly:** You're right. Ryan was a prick.

Ryan urged her to end the pregnancy shortly after announcing he was leaving her. Leaving her for someone at work, he'd said. Someone called Lana. In the small privacy of her thoughts, Molly had started spelling the hateful name backward.

"What about your degree?" he'd said. "You have to put yourself first, Moll."

Then her grandmother passed and the thought of termination seemed impossible. The baby was a hazy, amorphous object floating on the horizon, projecting uncertainty and fear, but it was too soon for more loss.

Lucretia: Are you ready to tell me about your nightmares, Dearest Seeker?

Molly allowed the message to fester in its glaring pink-flesh cocoon, unanswered for several minutes as she contemplated putting the nightmare into words.

It always started with the noise—that terrible, dry slithering on the ladder fixed to the bed. The noise, and then a shadow hauling itself over the brink to stare at her from across the mattress. Even though she'd had the nightmare many times, that first moment of recognition always shook Molly. It was her grandmother, dragged from the grave and bristling with cold malice. She was forced to watch, gagged and paralysed, as the old woman's mouth fell open beneath flinty eyes, dripping with a black, oily substance. Shadow-Grandmother's face was a waxy mask, the skin pulled back so tightly across her brittle skull it looked as though it would split and flake.

Then long, clawing hands reached for Molly, aching to rake and crush and dig. They clamped onto her legs. Beat after dreadful beat, hand over hand in time with the raging of her ratcheting heartbeat, Shadow-Grandmother climbed her prostrate body. All Molly could cling to was the knowledge that when her grandmother's face finally loomed over her own, fingers sharp as winter branches clutching at the soft folds of her throat, it would end. When she woke, she'd inevitably find herself strangled in her blanket, the feel of her grandmother's dust-dry fingers still on her neck.

Molly could almost feel Lucretia's impatience leaking from the phone screen.

Molly: The dreams are about my grandmother, she typed. But in the dream, she's not my real grandmother.

The thing that came at night—the Shadow-Grandmother—felt real though. It moved with venom and purpose, leaving behind a tangible sense of presence upon waking.

Molly: I know it's not my real grandmother. She was always soft and warm. When I held her, she smelled like baking. Shadow-Grandmother is something else. Something ancient and spiteful that means me harm.

Molly stared at her own message, not quite believing she had been the one to write it. She hadn't realised she believed those things until she'd punched them stark and clear into the luminous square of the chat box.

Lucretia: I am so sorry to hear that! It sounds as though some particularly nasty energy has attached itself to you, drawn by your raw grief. I do wonder if you've always had such vivid dreams? I'm getting the impression of talent from you. Have you ever dreamwalked?

Molly: I don't think so, but I did used to dream about a town.

Before her grandmother's death, before the pregnancy and Ryan's affair, Molly had dreamed good dreams. Most of them were half-remembered ghosts, foggy and incomplete, but one was a recurring dream about a familiar town made up from scraps of her own life. During the long, numb months after her parents' accident, she had often met her mother there. In the night-town, her mother always smiled. She always wore her sea green coat, and she always had tiny blue daisies woven through her hair.

Molly hadn't visited the night-town since the nightmares began. There was no comfort now in waking or sleeping. She wondered if she'd ever go back to the pub she'd conjured when she grew older, a place where she'd met old friends and lovers and where once she'd watched her grandmother mixing cocktails behind the bar in a purple and gold shaker.

Lucretia: Thank you for being so honest with me, Dearest One. I believe I can help. The entity I feel drawn to for you has been in my possession for a long time, waiting for a very special companion.

Molly: Where do you get them from? The dream eaters, I mean.

Molly imagined a vast metaphysical auction house, the shelves lined with Ouija boards and jewel-encrusted skulls. Sitting at the front, waiting on every word from the auctioneer, she pictured Lucretia, her hair a wild auburn tangle that rose high enough to annoy onlookers straining to see past it three rows behind.

Lucretia: Some I entice and trap myself. Some I procure from other collectors. Dreams are the entry and exit points for our souls and a Dream Eater can be your soul's companion. Do you wish to take control of your dreams, Dearest Seeker? undefined

Molly flashed back to her nightmare. The rasping footsteps on the rungs of the ladder, the stiff legs raking across her body. The leaf-dry hands holding her down.

She paid the ridiculously hefty two hundred and fifty pounds asking price before she could talk herself out of it.

Three days later, a small, plain parcel arrived. Molly parted the copious amounts of bubble wrap and pulled out a squat, clear jar wrapped in muslin. It came with instructions written on a thick piece of card in pin-neat handwriting. The penmanship surprised her. She had expected Lucretia's handwriting to be a messy scrawl, replete with wild flourishes and heartfelt doodles.

Apparently, she had to perform a ritual.

The idea was ridiculous, but her only plan for that evening was another congealed food delivery with a side of reality TV. Molly read the instructions again and went to hunt for salt in the kitchen.

The ritual itself was vastly disappointing. She followed the instructions, placing the jar inside a ring of carefully laid salt and then—and this was the part that made her feel truly ludicrous—addressing the jar. The instructions informed her the entity trapped inside was called Jaspar. Had it introduced itself to Lucretia and offered this name, or did the witch make that up on the fly? But she'd come this far, she might as well continue the charade.

"Welcome, Jaspar," she intoned. "I brought you here to aid me. I humbly offer you my nightmares. Please accept my offering, then pass back through the dreaming veil from whence you came."

Having to say, "whence", was almost too much. Molly finally unscrewed the lid and peered inside the jar.

She wasn't sure what she'd been expecting, but she wasn't entirely surprised to find it empty. A grey residue clung to the sides and when she lifted it to her face, the sweet-sharp smell of dried vomit wafted back at her. Molly removed the entire thing to the bin and swept up the salt.

That night, the nightmare returned. Even in her sleep, Molly berated herself for wasting her inheritance money on an empty jar that stank like week-old throw-up. No wonder Shadow-Grandmother was so angry with her. She shrank into the corner where her bed intersected with the cold press of the damp wall and watched the figure loom in its usual place at the top of the ladder, fixated by the deep lines carved into either side of its downturned mouth. Molly braced herself, hoping she would wake quickly this time.

But something was different. There was movement to her left, something flickering between the bed railings. A second entity had entered the chat.

Gripped so hard by fear she could barely turn her head, Molly followed the thing's progress as it squeezed between two wooden bars and poured through like pooling smoke to stand on the mattress beside her. No more than half a foot high, the shape was so black it looked like a jagged tear in space. Twin fire pits flamed in what she assumed was a face.

The creature studied her for a moment. More solid now, its damp-velvet skin stretched across a compact, muscular frame built for leaping and scurrying. It fixed eyes hot and pitiless as the lit ends of cigarettes on Shadow-Grandmother and sucked in breath until its chest swelled to a pulsing, misshapen tumour.

"Molly."

Her grandmother's voice, thin as reeds scraping a dry riverbed. Molly looked back at her, eyes grinding in their sockets as she forced them to move, to witness. The creature wasn't sucking in breath, it was sucking in her grandmother, devouring her. Shadow-Grandmother thinned and warped, coming apart in smoky tendrils to be consumed by the black hole with the brimstone eyes. The last thing Molly saw before waking was the look of surprise and despair plastered across her grandmother's bleached-corpse face.

Molly was almost full term when she saw the dream eater again, her stomach swollen like hard fruit. The nightmares, the ritual, even the dream eater itself, had receded until all that was left was foggy, soft-edged reminiscence. She was handing in her essays on time. She remembered to take her folic acid supplements and had started searching for new apartments. Then her night-town returned in joyful, jumbled-up pieces, and one night after being lulled to sleep by her daughter's fluttering kicks, she made it back to the pub on the waterfront.

It was unchanged. The same golden lights swam through their canopy of palm fronds. The same dimly illuminated interior beckoned her inside to a warm, cushioned place where her grandmother was waiting. Molly walked with her, following a coastal path studded with sea thrift and red campion. Gulls called to each other overhead, racing between stars the colour of liquid sapphires.

"Can you see the baby?" Molly asked, knowing that Grandmother absolutely could see the baby because in dreams, everyone knows everything.

When she didn't reply, Molly turned to see her grandmother's smiling face waver and disappear. She was alone on the empty path, the sky grown cold and quiet. The night-town shuddered.

Molly became aware of an unwelcome presence, an intrusion in her private oasis. The waves on her right had been lapping across a softly sloping beach, reflecting back starlight. Now they raged a dirty grey, growing so high and fierce they threatened to break over her head.

Then she saw it.

The dream eater stared back at her from a ledge on the cliff. It glowered, mouth set in a grim line, long hands curled to feathery fists at its sides.

The baby kicked Molly awake. She rolled onto her side, breathless and shaking, the taste of brine and blood in her mouth.

She would have explained the dream away. She would have resumed packing up the apartment and planning for her baby's imminent arrival if it wasn't for the hard and brutal fact that when Molly next saw the dream eater, she was awake.

Bored and sleepy at the launderette one dreary Thursday afternoon, sitting on a hard plastic chair and waiting patiently for her machine's last spin cycle to grind to a halt, she saw him creeping against the wall.

He materialised at the edge of her vision, a smudgy rip in reality. When she turned to face him, he should have disappeared. He didn't. The dream eater was flesh, or what passed for flesh in his world. Molly could count the tufts of hair erupting from his face like scrubby strands of coarse black grass. His grey muzzle twisted into a snarl, the filmy orbs of his eyes undulating like rising magma. The edges of the dream eater's body were smoky and inconsistent and at the centre of him yawned a meaty pot belly, raw and tender as steak.

One of the machines spluttered to a stop, tearing Molly's attention away. When she turned back, the demon was gone.

Jaspar began to torment her. She saw him at her doctor's office, side-eying her from behind the water cooler. He skulked amongst boxes of fruit at the supermarket. He curled like a suckling pig in a crib at the baby store, long hooked thumb jammed in his mouth, lava eyes moving behind slitted lids as he feigned dreaming sleep. He was a wisp of black smoke curling back around a corner, a pair of burning coal eyes glinting from the depths of a badly lit stairwell.

Molly dredged the Sweet Dreamz website from her memory, found Lucretia, and tried to message her. She received an automated reply in response:

I do not accept returns or offer refunds. This is NON-NEGOTIABLE! If you are having problems with your Dream Eater, Dear Seeker, please remember that nothing in this realm or theirs is ever given freely. The Dream Eater expects a toll and will get angry when it isn't paid. Brightest blessings. Lucretia

Molly was quite sure this particular piece of earnest advice had not been included in the instructions.

When the dream eater invaded her night-town again, Molly realised what the toll was.

He was sat on a barstool, long grey tongue plunging suggestively into a glass of whiskey.

"What do you want?"

Molly's voice sounded hollow and desperate inside the dream, like a scream echoing from inside a well.

"Why won't you leave me alone?"

The dream eater leered at her, unfurled a long velvet-smoke hand, and gestured at the pub.

He wanted her town, her night world. Her comfort and escape. That was the price for sucking Shadow-Grandmother into his inky oblivion.

Molly looked around the bar, wondering if she could give it up. Grandmother was sitting in a corner with her knitting needles. It was her real-world grandmother, radiant as she had been in life. The corners of her translucent blue eyes crinkled when she smiled, one needle falling to her lap as she raised her hand in a half-wave.

Molly looked back at the dream eater and silently mouthed, *"No."*

The baby came the next Saturday morning. Molly woke cramping in the night and called herself a taxi. She spent the next twelve hours terrified the dream eater would leap into her delivery room and show himself to the brusquely mannered midwife encouraging her to push.

That was the last time she thought about Jaspar for a while. When Sophie entered the world, she stared up at Molly with large blue eyes the colour of summer cornflowers, and all thoughts of nightmares and demons scattered from her mind.

The new apartment was warm and full of light. After a week at home with baby Sophie, Molly had almost convinced herself the dream eater was banished from this place. Then she woke in the night to hear Sophie screaming like the world had shaken loose.

She knew this was normal. She'd read the literature. But the screams were panicked, a shrill alarm honed sharp by fear.

Molly rolled over to face the Moses basket beside her bed and scrambled to a sitting position, horror like biting poison swelling so fast and dense in her chest she thought she would vomit.

The dream eater was balanced on the edge of the basket.

The demon was an expanding shadow crouched over her daughter, expelling something rank and amorphous into her mouth. Sophie was still fast asleep, her tiny face red and wrinkled, eyes closed tight against her tears. She was screaming in her dreams, choking on inherited nightmares.

For the first time, anger replaced Molly's terror. She lunged at the creature, but he jumped to the other side of the basket and resumed his task, mouth stretching grotesquely wide. When Sophie's cries pitched higher, Molly threw back the duvet and stood to face him.

"I know what you want."

One glowing eye, sharp and faceted as a ruby, rolled around to look at her. Great gouts of stinking vapour clouded Sophie's face. It swirled around her snub nose and pale lips before draining into her tiny body like foul grey water emptying into a plughole.

"You can take it," Molly screamed. "Take the dream, just leave her alone."

The gushing smoke stopped, dissipating into the air and leaving only a fine, ashy mesh hanging between the dream eater and her baby. The demon crouched and leaped, landing heavily on Molly's bed. It locked its flaming eyes with hers, drew a deep breath. Molly felt something shift and tug inside her. A wrenching movement like a worm waking in the ground. The thing reared within her, questing up and out, searching for an exit.

It burst from her mouth.

She tasted blood and the acrid burn of rank vinegar. A thick white haze undulated in front of her face, overlaid with a golden gauze that flickered like sunlight breaking across waves.

The dream eater sucked it all away, devoured every last smokey tendril, every lingering delectable morsel until his expanding chest bulged, the skin pulling thin as though he might burst like a fetid balloon. Finally satiated, he bowed and blinked out of existence.

Molly leaned over the Moses basket and gathered Sophie into her arms. She pressed her baby tight to her chest and sank back onto the bed, one hand smoothing the back of Sophie's downy head. She tried to recreate her night-town, tried to remember what had been there and who she had seen. She knew something vital was missing, but the details were an icy hole, a ragged gouge in a deep whorl of her mind where she supposed the dream used to nestle.

She looked down at her daughter, calm now, her mouth moving languidly around a tiny thumb.

It seemed a fair trade.

LAWYER, CAPTAIN, COOK

DEVIN OLDHAM

WHAT I REMEMBER most is the way the gentleman smelled as he stirred his pot in the galley kitchen; like moist earth, tilled of fresh grave it overpowered the stew. He was, bewilderingly enough, the only passenger aboard the vessel to whom I had not been properly introduced.

The crew, as rowdy as freebooters are, seemed friendly enough. They had found my coinage sufficient, at least. And once I emptied my satchel and pulled out my pockets to show I had nothing more of value, they left me be. Some even seemed warm and sought companionship.

One such individual was a man known as Dog-Wailer Jim; he took it upon himself to deliver to my chamber a folded piece of burlap containing dried fruit. He'd revealed that he was store master of the ship and, for reasons that will forever remain a mystery, he took a shining to me.

Over the following weeks, we had many long conversations into the night. One such night, I asked after the cook and seemingly from nowhere, Dog-Wailer Jim produced a half-drunk bottle of grog. At first, I assumed the drink to be in lieu of an answer, but after we each downed our cup, he spoke like the conversation had never lulled. I noted a delicate, well hidden fright forming as a tightness at the edges of Jim's lips.

"The French fella?" he asked.

I only nodded, not knowing if he was French at all. As I said, I simply knew him to be the vessel's cook and nothing more.

"He never sleeps, he hardly leaves the kitchen. His stew tastes like raw onion and he has a dark spot on the back of his shirt." He shuddered. "It seeps and drips. I try not to eat what he cooks." He held up a handful of the nuts and fruits that had become our favourite shared meal and threw it into his opened mouth. "He stinks, too."

"Like a mouldy tomb," I added.

Sadly, That was the last meal we shared.

They found Jim's body in the cargo hold, where he'd been ripped to shreds, as if by wild animals

But it was no animal; we all knew this because his keys had been pilfered. Keys that opened all locks aboard the ship, save the captain's quarters.

Briefly, I was the primary suspect of the grizzly murder, but Jim's fellows vouched for me. It seemed during the near month at sea, many of the pirates had grown to accept me as an honorary member of their crew. At some drunken gathering below deck, they even spoke openly about their criminal exploits. I, having trained as a lawyer in what felt like another lifetime, began giving them advice on how best to avoid the rope if ever they found themselves captured by one of the myriad British naval ships infesting the Caribbean this fine and hot summer.

Jim's vigil was held above deck, and even the ill-often seen captain stood with respect as the burlap covered body was heaved overboard. What a statue of a man the captain was. He wore boots nearly to his knees, and despite his dark and brooding features, he carried the appearance of a heroic legend like Lancelot. His jacket, long and tailored entirely for another man, flapped loudly in the wind. He caught me looking at him, and I returned my gaze to the bizarre funerary rite. The cook was the only notable absence of the affair.

The very night of the funeral, be it from true hunger or a nostalgia for Jim's company, I craved so strongly a handful of dried apricots that I crept from my quarters and made my way to the dry storage. Expecting only to find a locked room, to which the keys had been stolen, I instead came upon an opened door.

Grunts and growls came from inside, and I crouched low in the darkness of the lanternless midnight. The moon spilled in from the porthole and drenched the storeroom in a pale blue light. In that light, I saw the cook. He crouched over a pile of supplies, once belonging to a merchant, now property of our captain and his men.

The cook was shirtless, and the entire sheet of skin that had once covered the ropey muscles of his back had been flayed away. The tear looked old, yet had no evidence of scarring. The white bone of his spine could be seen through the black ichor and gangrenous mould covering the wound; it shifted and contracted like an albino snake. As he stood straight, the columns that made up his vertebrae squished thick, black jelly to the floor. It splunked loudly and with such a gruesome stink that I could not help but let out a whimper of disgust.

The man, though I believed at the time he was no man at all, turned. And, be it a trick of the moon or some otherness of his aspect, his eyes shone bright, like those of some night-born vermin.

I awoke facedown on the storeroom floor with a splitting headache. It seemed my good favour had run its course, and no amount of fraternization over spilled cups of grog could dissuade the crew of my guilt when they found me there. Admittedly, I had no good excuse for being in the center of the previously locked storeroom, unconscious, with Jim's only keys in my pocket.

Thankfully, they took mercy on me and I ended up a prisoner in the ship's brig: a tiny cell tucked away in the lower part of the cargo hold.

At first I proclaimed my innocence to anyone who entered the cell, but soon, I heard my own voice ranting of monsters and the cook being a half-man. I would awaken in cold sweats nightly, my throat hoarse from shrieking in my sleep. I dreamt of the black jelly, I dreamt of the smell. And in those horrid dreams, in only the way dreams could manage, the captain stood and looked at me, and he, too, had those same luminous eyes. I slept as little as I could manage.

They fed me scantly and gave me only enough water to keep me alive. I was feverish and delirious one night when, as the moon crested half-full and whiter than a carnation, a silhouette came to the chamber. Hunched and snarling, it leaned against the bars. I knew by its scent that it was the cook. Drool dripped from its slavering maw, and in the lunatic glow of my tiny glass porthole, his teeth were razor-sharp shards, and they numbered in the hundreds.

He spoke then, and his ethereal voice carried itself upon the air slowly, like molasses coating my ears.

"Pity, pity little English," it said.

I tried to call for help, but I had no saliva to form the vowels.

It leaned in close and pressed its face in between the bars until its eyes bulged unnaturally; they were a simulacrum of the moon themselves. "I can free you, if you wish."

"In exchange for what?" I asked in a whisper. A deal with this monster seemed dire, but the prospect of dying, thirsty and alone in the brig of a pirate ship, seemed infinitely worse. After all, even he showed me a degree of mercy, more than he had extended to poor Jim.

He gripped one of the bars. His fingers ended in yellow, gnarled claws. With an inconsequential amount of effort he twisted the bar, and to my amazement the iron, bolted to the thick wood above, came loose. He twirled it like a baton.

"Anything," I said, ashamed by the sound of my own weakness.

"The captain, though tough he is, wears a coat that isn't his." He twisted another bar free from the cell door. "Get it, give it, before the full moon." With a final twist, he wrenched away a third bar, leaving a space wide enough for me to squeeze through. "Hurry, English, it's coming soon!"

And with that, he was gone. Only the shadow of his odour remained.

Bewildered and moon-drunk, I collapsed again; I do not know how long I slept, but when I awoke nightfall had come and gone and come again. I squeezed myself through the gap in the bars, realizing with a deadening finality that no more food or water was coming; the brig was intended to become my tomb. So I had only one option, even if it may have been delivered by a vapourous nightmare that I had little doubt was an hallucinated fantom.

I stumbled as silently as I could through the tight passages of the lower decks. Finally, in the darkness, I found my way to the stairs leading to the deck proper. Terror loomed when I saw the moon, large and ominous, like a lidless eye which never blinked, but only ever watched me round and full. His moon. His full moon. The deadline had come.

I sneaked past the skeleton crew that patrolled the area and manned the sails. But they were few, and the task was easier than I thought it would be.

The door to the captain's quarters was a cabin accessible only from above deck. A window made from many stained glass panels glowed yellow from the candlelight within; I loomed over it and pressed my cupped hands against the glass. The dark form of the captain sat in a chair facing the door, as if waiting for someone. He held a pistol and was naked save for his thick, strange-leather coat.

Then he rose like a spark of lightning. I ducked, but was slow and sick. The door opened and his flint-powdered hand beckoned me inside. Apparently, I was not whatever threat he was expecting.

The first thing I noticed about his chamber, as its warmth welcomed me from the doorway, was how ornate and beautifully dressed it appeared. Furniture with suede finishings and a gallery wall adorned with fine works of obviously stolen art. The captain had a higher level of taste than many of my now incredibly successful schoolmates from Cambridge. A pot of tea brewed on the hob of his private oil stove and the peppery scent tickled my nose, filling me with a painful longing for England again.

He spoke without looking up, only checking the firing mechanism of his pistol, scraping away a black buildup with his thumbnail. "I have killed so many men." He spoke slowly and with a thick Spanish accent. It was an educated voice, and though he wore only a long-coat and nothing else, he commanded from me an uncanny degree of respect.

I said nothing in return, but hearing the shanty-songs of the crew as they checked the aft roping above us, I shut the door and stepped inside.

"Tell me, English, how many men have you killed?" he asked as he placed the pistol, loaded and ready to fire, on the high table beside the stove. "Hm?" And he made his way to the other side of the room, back towards the chair he'd pulled out to face the door.

"I have killed one man, and one child," I said, honestly.

He perked up at this admission. With an incredible flourish, he spun to face me and sat himself in his lounge chair in one fluid motion. "Please, sit."

I did not. I stood awkwardly, avoiding eye contact with the man and his nude body, now shamelessly spread.

"Hm, the killing of a child, that is a cold practice for an English lawyer," he said.

I must have had a shocked look on my face, because he laughed.

"I know who you are. At least, I know who you purported once to be." He leaned forward. "But tell me—who are you, really?"

I shifted uncomfortably and gestured to the tea. He nodded and I creeped over. I poured a cup and sipped. It filled me with a warmth that began in my stomach but found its way through my entire body, my mind, my soul.

"A man…dishonoured me," I began. I made my way to the fainting couch that laid straight across from the captain's favourite chair. "We agreed to duel with pistols. But I had…once had…*do* have," I corrected, "a deep and ravenous rage within."

The captain smiled; he reveled in my admission, his penis twitching at the thought of violence. I knew then that this was indeed a pirate, and the wall dressings were, in fact, only dressings. This man was an animal, this man was a cage that held a beast: like the cook…like myself.

"I turned quickly, and instead of firing upon the man, instead of playing by the silly rules of his…his stupid mind-games, I directed my shot to his eight-year-old son who watched from the crowd." I relived the moment as I told it. "In the panic, I—well, I ran off, didn't I?" My posture relaxed, and I now stared openly at his confidently exposed body. And he shrunk, ever so slightly; the dynamic of power had shifted a tiny bit in that moment. "That was the boy. I heard the father hung himself from grief." I laughed. "I guess I won."

"Fascinating," he said. "You did not kill Jim."

I shook my head.

"You wept at his funeral. I thought maybe they were tears of guilt. But no, you loved him." He waved his hand, desperately trying to regain control of the situation. Trying to regain control of me. "You are a killer. Like us all."

I shrugged. "When I shot that boy, I killed him as a man. I made the choice; I saw hell, and I stepped over the threshold," I said. "In that way, we are alike."

"But one of my men is different," he added. And I knew exactly who.

"We are all doomed," I said, "but him…" I paused. For the first time, I took notice of the details of the captain's jacket. Its light, tanned leather was slick and black around the edges. The seams glittered and I swear the thread that patched the pieces together was woven of silver. Despite being treated and hardened, it had a thin layer of fur covering it entirely, as though it still grew from a beast's hide. And in some places, it still bore pale blue veins, pulsing with living blood.

"He *is* doom," he said, continuing my trailed thought.

"Right," was all I could manage through my disgust.

Bang, bang, bang!

Something rattled the door and the moonlit silhouette of a hunching monster loomed across the warbly glass of the window.

The captain rose with a flourish. The time of talk had ended. We were leaving my realm and entering his own.

"I have faced down doom before, Englishman!" he cried. In a flamboyant twirl, he went for his pistol.

Except it was gone.

All the bravado slunk away, and he groaned a sigh of defeat. I'd robbed him of the fight.

When he turned back to me, I had his own loaded pistol pointed straight at him.

"You side with a monster?" he asked. Not the voice of a man who was afraid, but that of a man who hated to lose.

I fired the shot.

At that moment, I knew that thus far it had been too easy. He dipped as soon as the trigger clicked. Gunpowder and smoke filled the air, and I was blinded.

He rushed me without hesitation.

Bang. Bang. Bang.

The door splinted as the massive, hunched beast from the storeroom barreled itself through.

No—the monster was not the same. It was as if, since the last full moon, he'd undergone some sort of metamorphosis.

The skin that had once been the cook drooped to the side and the black, skeletal jelly-thing emerged from the blanket. Its head rose from the mess of flesh, out of the blood and organs, up like a flower. The top was a thousand chomping teeth. Its head was black bone, slick with wet, foul ichor.

The captain had pinned me and, to my bewilderment, he was laughing in my face. He kissed me on the cheek and, with no effort at all, grabbed the pistol. As the beast tucked its too large body under the threshold, the captain loaded a bead with the incredible speed of…well, of a pirate.

A second shot rang out, but even the noise was different from my own. The precision of the blast was a marvel and shards of the stained black skull of the demon shattered in a brilliant fireworks display.

I grabbed his coat by the tails and yanked, attempting to free the man from the item the creature so desperately seemed to want. I pulled with all my strength and the captain howled in undignified pain. The coat had attached itself to him, like new skin healing over a bad burn. Again I heaved; the ripping sound was terrible. The cook, only half a face now, the hole in his skull pouring with gelatinous clots, let out the howl of a deranged wolf.

The captain was bleeding severely, as if removing the coat was no different from flaying the man's own back. But still, with alacrity, despite the agony, he reloaded the pistol.

The monster ignored me. For a brief second of clarity, I realized it thought I was helping it. I suppose, to some degree, I had been.

The captain turned to me once the pistol was loaded and smiled. "A fitting end," he said, and placed the gun to his temple.

"*No!*" I cried. But the shot never happened. The night-thing was upon him with incredible speed.

The gun fell beside me, still loaded, ready to fire. I never lifted it. I only watched, aghast, as the demon tore the jacket free from its wearer. Blood covered every inch of the room and me. I observed the entire rite, knowing that I was too much a coward to pick up the pistol and shoot at the beast. What good would it have done? I was adept only at killing the innocent, the tiny and confused.

When it was finished, the cook adorned his prize, and it knitted itself to his back, healing his black, festering wounds and reforming the approximate likeness of a man. He reached over his shoulders and as he tore out the silver strings that bound the garment together, his fingers sizzling at the touch. The most gruesome part was when he was nearly finished, he pulled free the captain's remaining skin and threw it over his head like a cursed hood. That reformed his face, though it was a bit different from before. He possessed a fraction of the captain's handsome guile.

When the affair had finished, the sun crested over the blue, waveless ocean. The monster trotted from the quarters and stood above deck, drawing a deep breath.

Unsurprisingly, with the newly gained charisma of the former captain, the cook had taken charge of the vessel in only a few weeks.

He had become the captain.

He had become *my* captain, and I sailed at his side as his first mate.

Over years of plunder and chaos, I grew not to like him, but to revere him, and even upon my deathbed, when asked, I had called him a great and terrible *man*.

APOSTOLNIK

J C LEE

On such a perfect morning, Lewis might have easily forgotten that he was here primarily for work, not leisure. The warm May sunshine tempered by the cool of the shade; the scents of locally grown oregano, rosemary, and basil that drifted from the small shops to his right and left; everything seemed designed to pleasure his senses as he strolled between the tall buildings bordering the narrow streets of the ancient city.

Occasionally, he glimpsed a picturesque courtyard down a narrow cobbled alley, the delicious fragrance of roasted meats and Mediterranean spices tempting him to take an early lunch at one of the many small restaurants. However, when he finally gave into temptation and sat at a quiet table under the shade of an olive tree, he took out his sketchbook and decided to make do with a strong coffee. Food at this hour would only dull his senses.

His artist's eye could not help but be fascinated by the juxtaposition of ancient beauty and modern tawdriness in this, the oldest part of town. From where he was sitting, he could see renovated terraces whose yellow stone facades shone tastefully in the intense sunlight. The doorways retained the traditional, attractively carved double doors framed within a Roman arch, painted green—always the same shade of moss or sage, he mused.

Shifting his gaze only a little, he was struck by the sight of a ruined dwelling: sealed off, gutted and crumbling, still displaying the ravages of war. Behind it there loomed a modern apartment block, probably no more than ten years old, whose dirty white paint was already flaking to reveal the dull, grey concrete underneath.

Did people really live in buildings as ugly as this? He shook his head in disgust and made a series of rapid sketches, more out of habit than intent, before paying the bill and continuing on his way.

There was no need to rush. He knew his destination was nearby, if tricky to locate. The route led him past a number of tourist shops marketing the same over-priced trinkets and the occasional colourful displays of local artwork. Here he might halt to amuse himself at the expense of the old shopkeepers who mistook his browsing for genuine interest.

He had a particular strategy—his "mockegy" as he called it. He would pick up one painting after another, pretending to scrutinise them, listening in silence to the broken English of the store holders as they muttered their praises for the artist. He silenced them with a sneer and lectured them loudly on artistic taste, ridiculing the crudity of line and colour in each, the mundanity of the content, and the dishonesty of the images. Landscapes, townscapes, old men and women in traditional costume—they might appeal to the uneducated tourist but never to anyone blessed with an artistic eye such as himself. He had particularly harsh words for the garishly painted wooden icons and their asking prices of thirty or forty euros.

"I'll tell you what they're worth," he said to one frail old woman. "This one is fifty cents; this larger one maybe one euro. And that's for the wood, not the paintings, which are worthless. Tell you what, I'll take them back to my apartment and use them as kindling for my wood burner. Winters are freezing in New York, did you know that? So what do you say, huh?"

He left her red-faced and tearful, and winked at the small group of tourists skulking nearby, who appeared embarrassed but also fascinated by his diatribe.

But he was here to work, he reminded himself, not to have fun. Leaving the trashy art behind, he made his way along a series of narrowing alley ways, away from the tourist trail, into an ever more ruined and silent townscape where barbed wire stretched along the top of pock-marked walls. Although the civil war had ended decades before, this part of town bordered the green line that still divided the city. These ruins had none of the morbid beauty of the gothic that he was hoping to find in the ancient nunnery of Agia Varvara.

◆———————————————————◆

For Lewis, art wasn't a hobby but a gainful career. At first he'd struggled, barely able to survive on the few paintings he sold. That is, until he'd found his particular niche: fantasised sexual violence, stylistic enough not to be pornographic (although many critics disputed this claim) but sufficiently weird and lurid to appeal to wealthy clients with specialist tastes. Ones willing to pay well to see their bizarre fantasies captured on canvas.

Although there were a few gay women among his client list, most were men with imaginations as creative as his own, where women—young and slender, beautiful, virginal and vulnerable—were always the victims, raped, tortured and impaled by a bizarre range of male predators, ranging from depraved aristocrats to lascivious monks, from leering dwarves to voracious vampires. He had discovered the greater the flow of blood and bodily fluids in his paintings, the faster the dollars flew into his bank account. For as well as charging thousands of dollars for special commissions, his income was boosted by the hundreds of clients who subscribed worldwide to his private website, where they could view his gallery and purchase prints at lucrative prices.

Lately, he'd used actual historical events as inspiration for his work, with sadistic soldiers in colourful uniforms committing their atrocities in a range of imaginatively brutal ways. And now, excited by the potential of adding religion to his particular mix of sex and sadism, Lewis was visiting this particular site for the first in a series of paintings that would feature the rape and torture of nuns.

He'd come across the story of the destruction of the convent of Agia Varvara early in his research. In 1204, while returning from the sacking of Constantinople, a group of Venetian crusaders had pillaged any Greek Orthodox monasteries they could find in the name of western Christendom. The convent of Agia Varvara had been home to over a hundred nuns, mostly young novices, all of whom they had subjected to horrific acts of sexual torture before locking them in the chapel and setting it alight.

Lewis had become fascinated by visions of knights in crusader uniform stripping and brutally raping young nuns, so much so that feverishly lurid images had infected his dreams, one of which he'd found particularly inspirational. In a series of initial sketches, he had drawn a young novice strapped to an altar table, naked apart from a long black veil covering her head, neck, and shoulders, a sword piercing her breast as she was raped by a masked crusader in full body armour. The sacrilegious nature of the image would, he was sure, enhance its lurid sensuality.

He did not usually find it necessary to visit historical sites for his paintings as the internet normally provided images enough. However, on none of the search engines had he been able to discover a single image of Agia Varvara and he'd felt a sudden urge to visit the actual site. Spring in New York had been cloudy and dull and he knew he deserved a holiday. And now that he was finally here, his excitement was mounting as he approached the site, anticipating the inspiration he would gain from actually standing within it, absorbing its atmosphere as well as visually studying it.

◆———————————————◆

Initially, however, he was greatly disappointed. It was smaller than he imagined, located along a dark, deserted back street, opposite a stretch of empty industrial buildings long since abandoned. Access was through a rusty metal gate enclosed inside a low wall, obviously added at a much later date when historical ruins had begun to be valued, especially those that lent themselves to narratives of cultural or religious nationalism.

Yet the ruins were neither charming nor particularly picturesque and, now that he was here, he could understand why it was devoid of tourists or, indeed, of religious worshippers. Severed columns, broken arches, a haphazard scattering of cracked walls and foundation stones conveyed little sense of what the original buildings might have looked like. Nor were there the usual written signs, in either English or Greek, to offer the visitor any guidance or information. In the centre was a small chapel with a domed roof in the traditional orthodox style, probably no more than two or three hundred years old, Lewis estimated. It, like the ruins themselves, had no architectural merit. He sighed as he took out his camera, cursing out loud but determined to find ways to make the site work for him as an artist.

He began by snapping various images of ruin and desolation, some from a distance, others from close range. A brief check on his camera reassured him it was capturing the details well, even the shape and pattern of those ruins cast deep within shadow. When he entered the chapel, he was immediately struck by how dark and empty it was. And cold, too, genuinely cold. *It must be a boon to visit in the scorching summer months*, he thought, and actually shivered as he tried to steady his camera while videoing the interior in its entirety—the uneven paved flooring, the vaulted roof, the walls stained with age, the half-open doorway that afforded him his only light, and finally the stone altar table in the centre, open to view as there was no sign of the usual altar screen. Clearly, this chapel was no longer in use and had not been for some time.

By now he was uncomfortably cold, but before leaving, he approached the altar. It seemed far more ancient than the chapel itself, so much so that he wondered whether it might be the original, somehow spared from the conflagration that had consumed the convent. *Yes,* he thought, this would be the perfect model for his first painting, the rape of the beautiful novice. Wishing to capture the sensation of its uneven texture, he closed his eyes and ran his hands across its surface.

Strangely, it seemed to soften to his touch as he did so, growing warmer and more malleable, more like a coarse woollen cloth than stone. He opened his eyes and let out a sharp gasp as he swiftly withdrew his hand; for there, in front of him, spread across the altar, was the semi naked nun of his dream. He had been caressing her veil and she had been staring into his eyes, a look of terror on her face, as though he were her assailant. Stumbling backwards, he tripped awkwardly over an uneven paving stone, almost falling to the ground. By the time he steadied himself and looked again at the altar, the vision of the nun had disappeared. Greatly unnerved, he left the building quickly, relieved to find himself back in the relative comfort of the shade outside and perched himself on one of the large, random stones to recover his equilibrium. Clearly, he had absorbed the atmosphere of the site all too well. He'd intended to make a series of sketches to complement his photographic record, but quickly abandoned the idea. His hands were too unsteady and everywhere he looked about him he seemed to see the figure of the nun, naked apart from her veil, lurking in the shadows and watching him. He would have to return to his hotel and come again tomorrow, when he had fully recovered from his shock.

His heart still pounding in his chest, he left the site and retraced his steps back to the tourist trail. But this proved to be more difficult than he had expected. Soon he found himself in a street he didn't recognise, full of empty and abandoned buildings, even more desolate than the streets he had walked down just an hour or so before. He turned into cul de sacs and ever narrowing alley ways, with no sign of life anywhere and was on the verge of panic when, suddenly, unexpectedly, he caught sight of a small shop ahead to his left. There were no other signs of commerce or habitation nearby. It was, indeed, a strange place to have a business. With some relief, Lewis stopped and gazed through the shop's cavernous opening into its shadowy interior and stepped inside.

It was yet another venue selling artwork. But as his eyes became accustomed to the dim light, he quickly realised the art on display here was not for tourists. All of its subjects appeared to be religious. There were icons, but of much greater quality than those he had so far seen, with evidence of what looked like gold leaf in the haloes surrounding the heads of saints, Madonna and child. And they were painted on blackened pieces of wood of various shapes and sizes. As he looked closer, he felt sure much of the usual black colouring that bordered the images had the charred appearance of fire damage.

"Wood rescued from sacred sites."

Startled, Lewis turned and glimpsed a small figure seated in a corner at the rear of the shop. It leaned forward into the light to reveal the ancient face of an old man, wrinkled and toothless, with glazed eyes gazing in his direction.

"They're impressive," said Lewis truthfully. "But I can't see you selling many. Why hide away here? Don't you want the tourists to find you?"

"I don't," came the reply. "I cater for more serious custom. Those who know and value my work know where I am."

The old man's English was good, if heavily accented. Lewis smiled ruefully. He and the old man shared something in common.

"I'm lost, I'm afraid."

He stopped as the old man leant further forward into the light, and he saw how his eyes were, viscous, cloudy and discoloured. But he was able to give Lewis some precise directions.

Calmer now, Lewis looked about the shop. There was no need to rush away and there were multiple art works of reasonable quality hung on all three walls. To his right, at the back of the cave—for it truly seemed like a cave—there was a narrow wooden staircase leading up to an even narrower balcony. It would be so easy to rob the old fool, thought Lewis. And he was intrigued by something the old man had said earlier.

"Wood from sacred sites, you said. Tell me, did any of this wood come from the ruins of Agia Varvara?"

Something seemed to flash in the old man's sightless eyes.

"Why do you ask?"

"I'm an artist. I'm interested in religious sites for a series of works I am planning." This was true enough.

"You know something of the site's history, then?"

"Only a little."

"But you are intrigued by it."

Lewis said nothing but watched the old man intently as he seemed to be making a decision.

"I have one such piece. Very, very old." He paused. "It is said to be painted on a scrap of the original altar screen retrieved from the ruins after the crusaders left to continue their diabolical mission. No one knows by whom. It came to me quite by chance and I had to promise to keep it safe, never to sell it. I have it here, hidden away."

"It must be priceless!" Lewis immediately cursed himself silently as he saw the old man's expression harden.

"It is more than priceless. It is sacred…powerful. And as I said, it is not for sale."

"Of course, of course, I understand."

In the silence that ensued, Lewis looked about him. What if the old man was speaking the truth about its age and origin? A plan was already forming in his mind.

"This one here. It's very beautiful."

He picked up a sizeable piece depicting the usual Madonna and child painted against a background of gold leaf. It was a decent piece of work, but in no way outstanding.

"I'd like to buy it," he said.

The old man took it from him, holding it only inches from his face as he studied it, finally offering a price that seemed reasonable enough. Lewis took out the money, then asked, "If it is really here, could I take a quick look at this sacred work before I leave? It would honestly mean a lot to me."

The old man didn't seem surprised by this request. His face remained expressionless as he scrutinised Lewis through his clouded eyes.

"It is at the top of the wooden staircase," he said, finally. "On the balcony above my head. You will find it on an easel, under the apostolnik."

"I'm sorry?"

"The apostolnik. The black veil worn by nuns still in their novitiate."

"Ah, yes." Lewis recalled the name from his research.

He paid for his painting and, refusing the old man's offer to wrap it, made his way up the stairs to the balcony, holding his purchase carefully under his arm.

He found the easel in a narrow alcove at the top of the stairs to the right. It was completely invisible from the floor below. He smiled at his luck when he saw its size, but screwed up his face at the musty smell. Carefully, he placed his own painting on the wooden floor, against the wall next to the easel, and picked up the apostolnik, immediately letting it fall to his feet. Not only was this the apparent source of the unpleasant smell, but its texture, its whole feel, was identical to the one he had imagined so realistically in the chapel. Breathing heavily, he withdrew his cell phone from his pocket and shone the torch on to the painting, scarcely able to stifle a gasp of surprise. For, staring out at him, was an image of a young woman, a nun, who could have been the same novice he had seen in his vision—albeit from earlier, happier times. Her face was placid, serene, with a gentle smile and beautiful, generous eyes.

"Stunning, isn't she? So pure and yet so sad."

Lewis remained staring at her, speechless. Sad? He looked again into those eyes and, yes, he could see a hint of sadness there. The more he looked at the painting, the more it captivated him. "Yes," he said finally. "Yes, she is."

"Legend has it that only one young novice escaped death at the hands of the crusaders. Though not rape. She spent the remainder of her brief life fasting and praying to God for revenge. And her prayers were indeed answered when the ship carrying the crusaders home to Venice disappeared during a storm. On hearing the news, she died with a smile on her lips, her final words being a request to be buried in an unmarked grave among the ruins of the convent."

"And this is her?" Lewis's throat was dry with excitement.

"Oh yes, I am sure of it." He paused, then added, "Sometimes I feel her ghost comes to visit, as if to remember what she once looked like in life. Making the short pilgrimage from her grave—that was never discovered, by the way."

It proved to be a quick and easy job to swap the two paintings and drape the apostolnik quietly over the Madonna and child. Lewis called out a word of thanks as he descended the staircase, confident that the blind old fool would fail to notice the switch, especially as the dimensions of the two paintings were almost identical. He was right. "I will expect you back here soon!" was all he said as Lewis stepped out into the street. Unable to refrain from laughing, he followed the directions he had been given and hurried back to his hotel to study his prize.

His was one of the more expensive rooms; spacious, tastefully decorated, with matching mahogany furniture throughout. In one corner, there was a desk with a solid wooden chair; opposite, by the french windows that led out on to a small balcony, stood a large dresser. Lewis placed the painting there, carefully balancing it against the mirror, before opening the windows and shutters that kept the room in shade and stepping through them to enjoy the breeze outside. The third floor room was pleasant and airy and looked out over a maze of terracotta rooftops beyond the quiet street below. A neat, narrow garden ran around the entire hotel, protected by a low wall and pointed railings that gleamed in the afternoon sunlight. Slipping back inside, he smiled to see this same sunlight casting a bright halo around the face of the nun that had previously been in shadow.

Dragging the chair over from the desk, he placed it a few feet in front of the painting and studied it closely. Leaning back in the cushions, he stared, once again amazed at the clarity of the image in front of him, fascinated by a technique that was evidently far more highly developed than that displayed in any icons or other early religious art he had seen before. And so realistic, almost photographic in its intensity. Yet the wood upon which it was painted was obviously so very, very old. Could it be an elaborate hoax, he wondered, like the famous Turin shroud? But such doubts soon disappeared from his mind as he gazed into the eyes of the nun. They were, indeed, very sad, beautiful eyes. Hypnotic, too. He continued to stare into them, unwilling or perhaps unable to look away as his mind began to empty and unwittingly he drifted into sleep.

The dream came upon him suddenly, like a physical shock, and was as vividly realistic as the painting itself. Lewis felt as if he were awake but inside a body and at a time that was not his own. There was noise— the screams of women, the raucous shouting and laughter of men, a whimpering and panting of breath that he knew to be his own as he fled in terror along stone floors, down narrow corridors, below vaulted ceilings. The smell of fear was all about him—in piss, faeces, vomit and blood. And beyond that, behind him, the smell of burning and the pungent stink of male sweat.

He was aware of figures fleeing in all directions—young women dressed in black, faces streaked with the grime of smoke and tears and distorted in terror. With a sudden shock he realised he was one of them, clutching a veil tightly around his frail, female form as he squeezed himself inside a dark alcove, holding his breath, hoping against hope that the darkness would hide him from discovery. But he felt the flow of warm piss trickling down the inside of his thighs as he heard the clink of armour and smelled the rank sweat of a crusader approaching, calling out mockingly in a strange language, cajoling him to show himself, as though he were a child in some innocent game. But there was nothing innocent in his voice, only menace and lust. Fear and disgust—intense, physical disgust—overwhelmed Lewis as he realised what lay in store for him, in this young female body, if he were discovered. And as he looked up, he caught the eye of the soldier leering at him, his smile revealing rotten teeth, letting out putrid breath as, sword in hand, he leant down to grab his veil, his apostolnik, and drag him by the neck from the hiding place.

Lewis awoke from the dream as suddenly as he had fallen into it to find himself crouching in a corner of the room, his arms clasped around his knees, rocking back and forth and whimpering like a frightened child. Gradually, he became conscious of knocking at his door. It opened, and a maid entered. The room was once again in deep shadow. Without seeing him, she walked over to the balcony and threw open the shutters, which had evidently blown shut. The wind outside was fierce, much stronger now than earlier in the day.

The maid turned and let out a shriek of surprise as she caught sight of him. Her look was one of concern as she spoke in Greek, asking a question he could not understand but whose meaning he could readily guess. Quickly he tried to pull himself together, rising shakily to his feet, forcing a smile and attempting to mime a stomach ache. She was young and pretty and had a small box of candy in her hand. He smiled again—this time, he hoped, more convincingly. She hesitated for an instant; then, still frowning, she turned and placed the box on a corner of the dressing table, when she caught sight of the picture of the nun. With a gasp, she drew back, placing her hands together, as if in prayer. Then, crossing herself several times, she turned and spoke to Lewis, once again in Greek, urgency in her voice as she performed some kind of mime, placing her hands together at the top of the painting then drawing them down slowly in front of it. He had no idea what she meant but wanted rid of her, so he nodded, saying "Nai, nai,"—"Yes, yes," practically the only Greek word he knew. She scrutinised him, her expression serious, before nodding and turning to leave, pausing to cross herself once more as she shut the door behind her.

Lewis closed his eyes and let out a deep sigh. He was relieved at being alone once more, but, more profoundly, relieved at having escaped from the terror of his dream. Most troubling of all, however, was the lingering disgust he felt at having been in the body of a woman, and one who had been on the point of being raped.

He looked again at the painting. The image of the nun couldn't have changed, of course, but it *looked* different. Whereas before he had seen beauty and sadness in her eyes, now he detected a glint of mockery. On an impulse, he stretched out his arm to touch the contours of her face, but drew back suddenly as his fingers felt it give out an unnatural heat, as if the figure were alive. Instinctively, he stepped away from the painting, his heart pounding inside his chest. He thought of turning it to face the wall, but that would've required touching it again. He looked at his watch. It was still only late afternoon. The old man *had* said there was something powerful about this painting. He had also, somewhat cryptically, suggested he would soon be seeing Lewis again. Bewildered, disconcerted, Lewis mused the old fool had been right on both counts.

The sun was sinking and the shadows in the streets lengthening as Lewis hurried back to the shop. The excited anticipation from earlier in the day on approaching Agia Varvara had been replaced by a sense of mounting anxiety. Sweat dripped from his forehead and his whole body trembled as he passed by the ruins, recalling despite himself the vividness of the dream in all its horror. By the time he approached the old man's shop, he was still shaken. Relieved to find the door wide open still, he was nonetheless bewildered when he stepped across its threshold.

Instead of hanging on the walls, the paintings were now stacked in untidy piles on the floor. There was no sign of the old man. Instead, when Lewis called out, the figure of a young woman loomed into view at the top of the wooden staircase. At first, he mistook her for the nun and his blood froze. He would have fled in terror if she hadn't called out "Kali spera!" to him, descending the staircase in quick strides that made it creak under her weight.

"Good evening," she repeated, this time in English, as her face came into view. "Grandfather told me to expect you."

Lewis let out a long breath. She was much stockier than the nun, and although dressed in black, wore work clothes, with a headscarf nothing like an apostolnik. He felt foolish as she looked at him, evidently puzzled by his disquiet.

"You are the man who took the painting today, yes?"

"Y-yes, I am," he stammered. "I was hoping to ask the old…your grandfather… some questions about it. It…it is quite an extraordinary work."

"I am afraid I can't help you with that," she replied, wiping her hands on her apron. "I know nothing about these paintings. I am only here to help pack up the shop. For good."

"Oh. Is he all right?"

"No, he hasn't been well for some time. But he always insisted he couldn't retire. Not yet. Then today, he came home early and went straight to his bed. When I asked what the matter was, he told me that the moment had come. He said he would always know when, and it had arrived."

Lewis frowned, as perplexed as he was disappointed.

"What did he mean?"

The woman answered with a shrug of her shoulders. She had the air of someone who was always too busy to think too deeply about anything. "He asked me to come here and wait for you, to give you this when you arrived."

From the back of the store, she picked up a black bundle.

"He said you would recognise it."

She held it out to him. He did, in fact, recognise it. But he sure as hell didn't want to take it.

"The apostolnik." His voice was little more than a whisper.

"Yes. You must hang it over the painting, he said. I am to tell you that unless you cover her face with this veil, she will not rest. He said you would know what he meant."

Lewis hesitated, pondering with a sense of dread the words of the old man. Only this morning, he would have laughed them off. But now, deeply troubled by the strange power of the painting and that nightmarish dream…

"Could you…could you put it in a bag for me, please?"

The woman let out a sigh of annoyance before fetching a used plastic bag from a drawer in the old man's desk and bundling the apostolnik unceremoniously into it.

"And now I must ask you to go," she said impatiently as she thrust the bag into his arms. "It will be dark soon and I still have work to do before I lock up."

She turned away from him and, for a few moments, he watched her busy herself, appalled by the rough manner in which she treated the paintings, scraping the stacks roughly across the stone floor as she threw sacking over them. When she paused and gave him a rather hostile look, as though she could read his thoughts, he left.

It was dark by the time he was back at the hotel. Whereas earlier the railings outside the entrance had been gleaming in the sunshine, now they were backlit by light pouring out of the hotel windows, their shadows etched along the walls at the opposite side of the narrow street. As he entered the building, he was struck by the powerful aroma of cooked food coming from the restaurant area. He suddenly realised that he hadn't eaten since breakfast. But, despite the pangs of hunger in his stomach, his nerves were so on edge that he had no appetite and could not face a meal. He remembered the box of candy left by the maid earlier. That would do him.

As he walked past reception, the hotel manager called out his name. Reluctantly, he approached the desk, and was puzzled to be reminded of the hotel's policy regarding non-paying guests in rooms. Impatiently, Lewis gave assurances he had no intention of entertaining a guest of either sex and was turning to leave when the manager called him back.

"Mr. Lewis." The manager seemed hesitant, embarrassed. "I am afraid your guest has been seen."

"What do you mean?"

"The gardener came to see me about an hour ago." He paused. "He came in some distress. Apparently, a young woman had been staring at him, her face pressed against your window. Such a pale face, he said, Such an evil stare he said, so evil he refused to carry on working."

Lewis had seen the gardener—a big, ugly bruiser of a man with dirty, crooked teeth and appalling BO. He couldn't imagine him being frightened of anything or anyone, let alone a face at a window. "This is absurd," he said, completely nonplussed.

The manager carried on. "Fortunately, when I accompanied him back outside, she had evidently retreated away from the window. He returned to work but at the rear of the hotel. And now I must request that you ask her to leave."

Instead of protesting, Lewis invited the manager to accompany him up to his room.

"If you can find a woman in there, you're very welcome to throw her down the stairs." His tone was more than a little aggressive. "Believe me, I won't try to stop you!"

Once in his room, Lewis turned on all the lamps and stood aside, inviting the hotel manager to search wherever he wished—under the bed, inside the wardrobe. When no woman was found, he offered Lewis an embarrassed apology and promised to have another word with the gardener. As he was leaving, he paused to look at the painting, which was still on the dresser where Lewis had left it earlier.

"Your painting, tell me. Is it worth a lot of money?"

"Yes. Why do you ask?"

"Then may I suggest you keep it somewhere secure for the rest of your stay? Unfortunately, the hotel safe is not large enough to accommodate such a work. But I can put you in touch tomorrow with a security firm nearby who will lock it away for you at a very reasonable price."

Lewis nodded. The idea of removing the painting from his room while he considered how best to sell it off appealed to him. They agreed to meet after breakfast to make the arrangement. With an apologetic bow, the manager left.

Lewis glanced over at the painting, but only briefly. It frightened him. Yes, he had to acknowledge that his fear, however irrational, was real. He thought of the old man's advice. *Cover her or she will grow restless. Cover her face with the apostolnik.*

His hand shaking, he helped himself to a candy from the box the maid had left earlier before tipping the apostolnik from the bag on to his bed, unfastening the string around it and, with a shudder, spreading it in front of him. The unpleasant smell from the shop was far more powerful now as he unfolded it, a stink of must and dust, as though he were handling something recently locked away in a crypt or stolen from a tomb. The sudden image of a skull's gaping eye sockets staring out at him through the folds of the veil made him break into a sweat while the acrid smell mingled with the sugary taste of the candy made him retch.

Spitting the candy on to the floor, he screwed his eyes tightly shut and rubbed them hard. Was he going mad? Looking over once again at the painting, he was sure the nun's appearance had indeed changed. She was smiling now, but it wasn't a pleasant smile. And her eyes. The mockery he had noted earlier had hardened. They were now glaring at him, full of malevolence and hatred. He was being ridiculous, he knew, but he crossed himself as he picked up the apostolnik and threw it over the painting, swiftly backing away as if he were dealing with a wasps' nest. With great relief, he saw the veil get caught over the back of the mirror and, although not covering the painting in its entirety, it still hid from sight the central figure of the nun herself.

But the *smell*. He couldn't sleep with that smell.

Throwing open the balcony doors, he stepped into the cool evening air, breathing steadily as he sought to calm himself. There was a full moon and the shadow it cast of the railings onto the wall below reminded him of prison bars. He smiled grimly. Tomorrow, he would imprison the nun and not see her again until he'd sold her for a good price. The thought lifted his spirits. As for the stench in his room, well, he would sleep with the windows and shutters wide open tonight.

Several hours later, Lewis was snoring gently and the breeze blew cool, fresh air from the balcony into his room. A flood of moonlight illuminated the apostolnik, draped as it was over the mirror, and the corners of the painting it had failed to cover. A scene of peace, of beauty, perhaps, disturbed only by a sudden stronger gust that ruffled the folds of the veil. This was followed by another, then another, each one growing in strength yet strangely silent, lifting the veil further and further away from what lay beneath it.

Lewis slept on, dreamless, unaware of what was happening so close to the foot of his bed. His regular breathing was undisturbed by the constant fluttering of the apostolnik, each flutter more violent than the one before, each time revealing more of the painting, until the face of the nun appeared, lit by a halo of moonlight. As if she herself were exhaling a hot breath, the fabric now lifted away from the mirror. Tossed by air blowing from two opposing sources, it twisted upward, upward, finally breaking free from the mirror's hold, folding and unfolding, changing form and shape with increased rapidity as the gusts grew stronger and as the sleeper slept on.

Then all was still and silent again.

But the room was not quite as it had been. If Lewis had been awake, he would surely have noticed the drop in temperature; he would have seen that the painting was now uncovered and the apostolnik had found a new form, one that still covered the nun but in the fashion for which it had been intended when first woven. The painting had emptied, it seemed, and become a sculpture, a sculpture for which the apostolnik appeared to add a final touch of realism.

No, wait. Surely a sculpture could not move, could not glide from the shadows in this manner. Surely it could not approach the foot of the bed and shift its gaze downwards. A sculpture, however realistic, could not twist its face and express such burning malevolence, and it could not float into the air and hover over a sleeping figure, the figure of a man who had begun to stir in some discomfort, as though trying to awaken himself from some dreadful nightmare.

But when his eyes opened, what awaited him was infinitely more terrifying.

For now the veiled figure hovered just inches above him, her face almost pressed against his own, her lips apart, breathing mist—or was it smoke?—into his mouth, the rank taste of which made him cough and retch and squirm away from her. As he spluttered and gasped for air, he tumbled out of the bed onto the floor. Naked, he drew away from the bed toward the balcony, gasping for air. But the figure was as swift as it was silent. She had an airy, almost transparent quality; apart from her veil that gave material solidity to her form, which was now erect, drifting purposefully towards the naked man.

His eyes were wide with fear, his face a mask of horror which seemed to have rendered him speechless. For there were no screams, no pleadings, just a low, helpless whimpering as he backed out onto the balcony. His hands grasped for the shutters, as if they might protect him from the malevolent figure moving relentlessly towards him. He scrabbled in panic for the handles, but it was useless. In the blink of an eye, she was once more pressing her face against his, the folds of the apostolnik twisting like tentacles in the wind, encircling his head. The more he struggled, the tighter the knot became .

He bent backwards over the rails of the balcony, leaning as far as he was able, when the tentacles released him from their hold. But this was no act of mercy, for he had been using all his strength to push himself away from the appalling spectre, to escape from the deathly stink of the apostolnik, and the reverse momentum now flipped him over the rails and into the air. As his body somersaulted and fell, he saw, for an instant of horror, that he was plummeting directly on to the sharp points of the railings below. There, he was impaled through neck, chest, stomach, and groin, before he could let out a scream.

The night porter discovered the body. By the time an ambulance arrived, it was clear nothing could be done to save him. Police sealed off the area, hotel guests and staff were questioned, his room thoroughly examined. The hotel manager provided the clearest explanation for what must have happened. A mysterious guest, a woman, had earlier been seen in the American's room. She must have overheard a discussion about the value of a painting he had just purchased. The manager had seen it earlier that day, but now it had vanished. Evidently she had tried to steal it and there had been a scuffle that ended in this gruesome tragedy. But who this woman might have been and how she had made off with her prize without being seen remained a mystery. In the weeks that followed, neither were found.

A few days after the horrific event, one of the young maids employed at the hotel handed in her notice, so traumatised, she said, that she could no longer continue working there. Like everyone else, she did not know what had happened to the troubled American, the man she had found crouching in a corner of his room, but she did know where the painting was—safely hidden somewhere where only she could find it.

She had been sleeping that night in the attic room set aside for those maids on the early morning shift. A strange dream had awoken her, a dream in which a young nun whom she recognised begged for her help. The maid had felt compelled to go to her aid immediately. She had found the American's room empty and seen the face of her nun glowing brightly in a shaft of heavenly moonlight. Crossing herself, she had wrapped her in the apostolnik that lay on the floor in front of the dresser, slipped out of the hotel's rear entrance and walked through the dark, empty streets to her apartment. Early the following morning, she had made her way to an abandoned building near the ruins of Agia Varvara where both painting and apostolnik were now securely stored. She felt no guilt in this, quite the contrary, for she had prayed in front of her nun and been given clear guidance. The commotion surrounding the death of the American would soon die down and eventually be forgotten, and her nun would let her know when a suitable new owner had been found. A man who would pay a large price indeed to own her.

Meanwhile, she, the maid, was to be patient, and wait, just as her nun had been waiting patiently for centuries, and would continue to do so for centuries to come.

A MASK FOR OSIRIS

NORMAN GARY THOMSON

THE PRIEST HAZUMER gathers linen wrap to dress the prepared body of Santek, Master embalmer. Runs his fingers over the red incision curving under Santek's left rib cage, exit wound for his organs, and lengthy cords of intestine. Heart remains in place, he notes. Shrunken, cold and indifferent, as in life. But necessary for Ma'at's inspection and judgement for Santek's new existence.

Hazumer's breathing quickens, as it does whenever he thinks of stepping into Santek's position of principal palace embalmer. With a rush of satisfaction, he whispers in Santek's left ear: "What kept you going, you old schemer, far beyond the years the gods allot? Pride and ambition, in part, I reckon. A lofty eagerness to dress the Pharoah himself one day for his journey into the Deadlands. An honour beyond measure. A crowning epitaph for a lifetime of skill and dedication to your chosen art. Adulation of several generations of colleagues and apprentices.

"But look at you now: dead as yesterday's morning breezes. And who will remember you by next flooding of Mother Nile? Still, not to worry. I'll more than capably stand in for you. Was always an attentive student, no? Eager, open to learning, compliant. It's a fitting tribute that I'll be ready to direct our ailing Lord's journey towards the Guardians of the Dead in spectacular fashion. And you, departed fraudster, will only evoke a memory to passing travellers who glance at the glyphs on your tomb entrance."

He nods approvingly. Santek's face is painted in realistic flesh tones. The cheeks are full and lifelike, firmed with cotton wadding. Hazumer places his jackal-headed Anubis mask close to Santek's head, checking the fit. Dark, hollow eyes reflect the impenetrable mystery of death and absence. The painted ears stand erect and alert, as if probing for acts of disrespect done to this body, or disparaging comments from the workers in the mortuary. A loyal and steadfast protector of the community of the dead.

"Your tribute badge for Osiris, departed friend. Eternal House awaits, however you might be arrayed. You should hope the god will show lenience towards your many sins, overlook your frequent swindling of your own clients, rich or poor alike. We saw it often here in the workshop—sawdust in the cavities when they, too, paid for linen."

Hazumer presses against the chest cavity: firm and full, packed with bootlegged blocks of horse hair sold out the back door of the royal stables. Sure, Santek left a sizeable legacy to purchase quality products, including new linen stuffing, but he'll never know the difference, will he?

He pats his hand along Santek's ribs. "I trust you'll forgive my shorting you expensive myrrh and cassia? The market vendors are in supply crisis, and prices have soared beyond reasonable since the wars in the north and the blockades of trade routes. Really, you chose an awkward moment to let go. Our associates here haven't noticed the lack, and your…*contribution*…pays my gambling debts twice over."

A young worker appears at his side. Kheti, a simple country lad, apprentice now in Hazumer's company of embalmers for three years. Gentle in manner and outlook, Kheti showed from his first days of employment a flair for dramatic colour in painting country scenes, border design, and animals. Earlier, Hazumer recalls complimenting the lad on his strong rendition of hieroglyphics along the front of one of Santek's canopic jars. An earnest promise of sustenance in the afterlife from the protective deity to the deceased, painted over slats of polished Lebanese cedar: *Beer and honey shall laden thy table. Dates and pomegranates shall laden thy table.*

Now Kheti is holding that same jar, dedicated to the god Hapi, one of the four sons of Horus, protector of the dead man's lungs for use in the afterlife. Kheti's hands are shaking, his shoulders shivering. The baboon-like mask of the god over the lid of the jar nods in sympathy with the lad's trembling hands, as if he were in silent, cynical agreement with some unspoken conspiracy.

For a moment, Hazumer fears the jar will drive crashing to the floor. "Steady on, lad. There's no time to make suitable another jar. You're acting like you've seen a ghost."

"No phantom, Master. But a strange occurrence still." He reaches a hand toward the lid of the jar, brushes the snout of Hapi. "Please, see for yourself, tell me the gods of Chaos are not at work among us, laughing at our efforts, seeking to ruin our present readiness."

"Tell us, then. And quickly, so you might save yourself from some approaching sickness, no doubt self-inflicted. The truth now, Kheti. Were you too much into the drink last night?"

"No drink, Master. Though I might have benefitted from a tavern visit. Stayed unmoved by this fearful unravelling."

Haltingly, Kheti removes the wooden lid from the jar. The baboon's mouth seems to smile at the lad's vacillation. "Sire, I was careful to follow procedure with Santek's lungs for their interment with his body. I kept close observation over their bath in the natron solution, handled them with the gentlest of touch, never rushed the drying period. I took especial care in wrapping them in new linen from our stores. Recited the prescribed prayers for their fitting in the jar." Kheti bows his head and trembles in confusion. "I acted with honour and respect through the whole process of preparation, as the sacred texts demand we should."

"This was well done, Kheti. As your training dictates. Continue so, and you'll always keep a place among us."

"But never was I prepared for what followed. Come, sire, look you here." Kheti leans the canopic jar forward so that Hazumer can see its contents: a clean white linen wrap about the size of a sofa cushion. The fabric is swelling and falling in slow, rhythmic pulses.

The same rhythm as a man at rest breathing.

A shock like a hammer blow slams along his shoulders. He reaches a tentative hand toward the bundle. A slight warmth pervades the fabric.

Hazumer stifles a gasp. He turns toward the preparation table, grips the edge to steady himself. How can he still the cold fear rising in his throat? What black magic has the dead priest been practising, unbeknownst to his colleagues and friends? Where did he hide any secret texts with the inscribed prayers to the gods to assure his immortality?

In a halting voice, he cautions Kheti. "I thank you for this warning. But not a word to anyone, lest we incite a panic that disrupts this whole procedure, perhaps halting Santek's burial completely. Can you do that? Control your fear, and carry on as normal. Until we find an answer?"

"Yes, sire. But please you—indeed, please the company—we shall rid ourselves of this monstrous task in short order."

"Leave the jar with me, Kheti. I can assure you, no harm will come to your person."

"I can join Sennenmut's work crew, he has lost two workers to sickness—and he has a backlog of tasks needing assistance."

"Do you know, have the keepers of the other jars, the liver, intestines, stomach, found any strange anomalies in their contents?"

"None they have told me, sire. My friend Iset is keeper of Santek's jar for his stomach. But his recent behaviours show nothing unusual or cause to worry. He's happy with his evening beer and amorous nuzzling with his sweetheart from the village." Kheti gazes on the jar lid and the sombre mask of Hapi. The baboon's lips are curled in a jeering line. "It seems we're facing a horror with no easy explanation. Fortunately, no one has been hurt with it."

"So far, may the gods be thanked," Hazumer says. "And I want to keep it that way, get this necromancer in his tomb straightaway. Seal the door and walk far from its presence. Let its existence be completely erased from memory."

Hazumer watches Kheti depart quickly without a backward glance. He stares at the painted face of Santek, the dried lips, spidery lines alongside the eyes, pale forehead. Can he find behind this human death mask an explanation—or even a hint—for this unearthly incident?

He sighs his frustration at the unyielding solemnity of the aged body. Thinks: *You will carry the secret of the breathing lungs to your grave. Alongside your conniving and deceptions and thieving.*

He lifts away the Anubis mask from beside the dead man's neck and carries it with him across the workshop to an apprentice painting the final hieroglyphs on Santek's wooden coffin. The images of Isis and Nephthys, guardians of the dead, in gleaming gilt, emerald and carnelian, adorn the box's head and foot. A horizontal inscription records Santek's name and office; also a list of food offerings—wine, honey, wheat cakes—and grave goods. Beneath this list, a written charm to Osiris implores the god to secure the wellbeing of Santek's *ka*, his eternal soul. Hazumer skims the charm, welcomes the return of cynicism towards his former master. Thinks: *They got you in the end, just so. You charlatan, always praying you'd live forever, trusting in the power of secret spells and incantations to secure your immortality. I daresay, some poor sods in your employ thought you might succeed, taking so long to give it up.*

Hazumer holds forth the mask to a waiting apprentice painter. "The feather of Ma'at needs finishing—here, over the forehead. The sketch is ready for you. Do that image up clean, then we can think of packing him in."

"We're almost there, sire," the painter answers. He leans toward the mask, relaxes the brush in his hand. His brow furrows. Alarm sharpens his voice. "Trouble is, I tried filling the outline with paint this morning. Gave me constant frustration, it did. That one sign."

Hazumer glances back to the preparation table and the body, then turns toward the charms to Osiris inscribed on the coffin box. "What is it? Let's have a look."

"Ma'at's sacred feather. I told you. The outline sketch won't hold the red paint. Look here, I colour along the vanes but it soaks away into the plaster coating. All that's left is a foggy outline. But no true tint."

A chill of apprehension surges in Hazumer's chest. The symbol is crucial to Santek's journey to the Other House, where Osiris weighs his heart against the feather. A light heart assures his entry to the Field of Reeds and eternal peace; too heavy and it's a ready meal for Ammit, the soul-eating monster. But the weighing must be done. For a judgement. *And for my promotion*, Hazumer reminds himself.

"How many times?" he asks.

"I've tried four, five infills." Apprentice shrugs. "Nothing. Yet the other strokes came up flawless on the first application, as you can see. Gilt edges over Jackal's ears. Black liner around his eyes. I've never seen a failure like this before."

Hazumer grasps the brush from the lad's limp hand. "Let me have a go. There has to be a reason." He dips the bristles in the paint pot, then runs the brush along the feather's barbs. For a moment, the gleaming liquid holds firm and vibrant. Then the thin lines grow pale and indistinct. Hazumer studies the image, perplexed. Perhaps an imperfection in the plaster over the board?

Then a low moan grows in his throat. Fleetingly, he sees again in his mind the rising and falling bundle in the canopic jar. Is it possible Santek has found in his dark charms and prayers a guide to immortality? His eyes widen in fear and disbelief. A red viscous liquid outlines the feather's vane and barbs. It swells and leaks in rivulets into the afterfeather, then drips from the hollow shaft.

Hazumer gathers a droplet of the liquid on his fingertip and dabs his tongue. He tastes the bitter iron flavour of blood.

He glances to the mortuary slab…and the waiting corpse.

Santek's wizened brown fingers are drumming along the table boards.

ONE IN THE BED

KATHERINE TRAYLOR

SHE DIDN'T KNOW how long it had been happening. It felt like years since she'd gotten any rest, but as she lay there wrapped in darkness and terror, time had no meaning. All she knew was that she was haunted, and that it always came at night.

Every morning, she woke to a fresh memory of the horror, unable to think of anything else. Waking life was a dream that faded with the coming of night. Waiting paralyzed for the next visitation, she swore she'd never sleep in this bed again. She'd move, beg shelter if she had to, anything to get away.

But night after night, hour after hour, she woke alone there, waiting for the thing to join her. Again and again, when she began to think she was safe and the thing would not come, there it was, sinking into the bed beside her.

Now she felt it coming again. Pleas bubbled into her throat and stopped behind her teeth, prayers to a force she couldn't name that tonight would break the pattern. If she could only *get up,* push herself out of bed, she might finally escape.

But it was impossible. Her nerves seemed loosened from her muscles. No act of will would let her move. She could only lie terrified as it came, finding her unerringly in the darkness though she longed to disappear.

Slowly, the covers lifted. Cool air bathed her skin. The mattress sank as a heavy weight lowered itself onto the bed beside her.

The ceiling was a distant void, blurring in the dark. Matt blinked, his eyes the only part of him that dared move. Everything else lay rigid, screaming in silence, as the thing beside him breathed against his pillow.

This didn't always happen—or if it did, he wasn't aware of it. Sometimes, exhausted from working overtime, he fell asleep in seconds and was aware of nothing at all.

But more and more often since he'd moved there, he'd unwittingly crawled into an occupied bed. The half-heard sound of breathing grew louder every time, the presence of the thing more undeniable.

The first time something had crawled in beside him, he'd nearly had a heart attack. After he'd stopped screaming, he'd turned on the lights and searched the bed from top to bottom, staring for a long time into the dark space underneath. But there had been nothing hiding, nothing at all in the room except the stained walls, the clumpy greige carpet, and the pile of cardboard boxes he had yet to unpack. As his heartbeat slowed, he'd realized he'd imagined it, and after a moment he'd spread the blankets out again and climbed back into bed.

Then he'd felt it: not warmth, but waiting coolness, an unseen presence on the mattress beside him. It wasn't visible under the fluorescent lights when he turned them on again, but Matt had known in his shaking heart that it was there.

When nothing happened, he'd concluded that he was overtired. *Miss enough sleep and you'll start imagining things.* Curling himself gingerly into the empty half of the bed, he'd lain shivering until exhaustion had claimed him.

But he'd felt the thing again and again since then.

Two nights ago had been the worst. Aching from an all-day inventory at work, he'd finally stretched out in bed, allowing his hand to slide bare inches past the meridian.

Something had *gasped*, though he hadn't heard it with his ears, exactly. In that cool space reserved for the unseen, his hand had brushed against another body.

The feeling had vanished immediately, the presence retreating like a snail sucked back into its shell. But Matt had leapt shrieking from the bed and turned on the light to see what had disturbed him.

Again, there had been nothing there. He'd stripped the bed bare but found only clean white sheets, the space beneath the bed as empty as ever. Leaving the light on (and turning on every other light in the house), he'd closed the door and gone to sleep on the floor of the unfurnished living room.

At first he'd resolved to sleep there permanently, going into the bedroom only to dress and keeping the door shut the rest of the time. But after a few nights, he'd given up. The living room's huge windows let in too much noise and light from the parking lot, and he slept badly on the floor even without considering the questionable carpet he was lying on.

And he *had* to sleep. His job was exhausting, the hours long, and he needed a good night's rest every once in a while to recover. So there he was, huddled at the left edge of the bed like a peeled-black blanket, holding his breath in hopes that the thing in the dark wouldn't notice him.

Nothing happened for a long time. Matt began to slip into sleep, dreams building in flashes in the corners of his mind.

Then a weight beside him shifted and sighed, sliding unseen feet further down the mattress.

In an instant, he was up again, heading to the living room for another sleepless night.

He couldn't do this much longer. He'd barely had a full night's sleep since moving there. But there was no way out: he had nowhere to go. After his former roommates had left him in the lurch, he'd had to move with very little notice. The fine for breaking that lease, plus an unexpected car repair he'd been stuck with a week later, had stripped his savings to the bone. He could barely afford this place as it was. Moving again this soon would ruin him completely.

But whenever he looked at the closed bedroom door, he was sure he heard the sound of quiet breathing.

Whenever she woke to breathing in the dark, she moved closer to the edge of the bed. She couldn't forget when those fingers had brushed her hand—how her whole body had recoiled from the touch. Now, clinging to the side of the mattress, she tried to lie still as a ragged quilt, a wrinkled sheet, something it wouldn't notice.

But the thing in the dark took more space in return. Soon, there was almost no room left for her.

A few nights ago been the worst. For an instant, defiant, she'd decided to reclaim her bed. Before the visitor had come, she'd gathered her boldness and slid herself towards the middle of the bed, daring the presence to evict her.

It had done worse. When the sheet had lifted, a heavy weight had lain *on top of her,* crushing the breath from her body.

The suffocating pressure had lasted only an instant. Then the thing had retreated, tearing off the covers as it went. It had stayed gone all night, and it hadn't been back since then. But the memory of that bruising weight, the heat of unseen muscles pressed against her, was embedded in her mind. Somehow she kept lying there, despite everything, sleepless in a cursed, infested bed.

But she never moved towards the center again.

Now, paralyzed, furious, she waited for the next invasion. Again she felt it sink into the mattress, heard it grunting and turning, seeking comfort in its stolen bed.

It lay still for a while (perhaps sleeping, lulled by whatever obscene visions kept a nightmare company at night). Then, just as she started to relax, it rolled towards her, heavy as a rotting log in water. Under the sheets, she could feel its unseen fingers sliding towards her.

She couldn't move. Frozen by whatever uncanny reflex possessed her, she swallowed helpless tears and listened to it breathe, wondering for the thousandth time, *Why am I still here?*

The next day, wobbling with exhaustion, Matt knocked on his neighbor's door. Not long ago, he would have died before doing this. Even now, the thought of what he was about to ask made him cringe. But he hadn't had a full night's sleep in weeks. His eyes were raw. His hands shook. At work, he kept dropping things, forgetting orders. It was only a matter of time until he got fired, or fell asleep at the wheel and killed someone.

So when his neighbor opened the door, Matt pasted on his most normal smile and said, "Hey, man. This is going to sound crazy, but…do you think there's any chance my apartment could be haunted?"

Jayden, who was his age and worked at the next factory over, looked surprised—but not scornful. In fact, he looked strangely *guilty*. "Um… I wouldn't swear it's *not?* A lady died there a few months before you moved in."

Bile rose in Matt's throat. He swallowed convulsively, fighting full-body shudders. "Are you fucking kidding me?" He hadn't expected a *yes*. He'd expected Jayden to laugh at him and tell him he was hearing things. At that point, his next step (after selling some plasma) would have been a psychiatrist's office. "You're serious? Somebody actually died there?"

"Yeah, man." Jayden shrugged awkwardly. "Sorry."

"Why wouldn't you say anything?" They always said hello and had hung out a few times. Matt had always thought they'd gotten along. He rubbed his arms nervously, thinking of the abandoned dishes he'd found in the kitchen, the Garfield mug he drank his coffee from, the old pair of women's flip-flops he'd been shoving his feet into to take the garbage out. He'd thought it was all regular apartment detritus. But were these a dead woman's things?

"This is why I didn't tell you," Jayden said as Matt tried not to hyperventilate. "The last three people who lived there were all shitty neighbors, and they all moved out in like a month or two. I didn't want you to move, too. You're way better than they were."

Matt scoffed. "If I had money to move, I wouldn't be here in the first place." He sighed, realizing there was no point in being angry. Knowing about the dead woman wouldn't have made him happy, but it wouldn't have changed his decision to move in, either. This apartment complex, with its crumbling parking lot and musty living rooms and blue lights flashing outside almost every night, was the only place he'd found that he could afford. At least he knew he wasn't imagining things. "Anyway," he continued gruffly, "how did she die?"

Jayden looked relieved, seizing on the new topic. "Don't worry, man, it wasn't gross or anything. She had an aneurysm or something. Died in her sleep. And they found her right away, so it wasn't like there was a smell..." Seeing Matt's wince, he quickly changed the subject again. "She was a super nice lady. I didn't know her well, but she always smiled and asked me how my day was. One time she gave me cookies." He smiled wistfully. "Damn, they were *good*, too."

Matt raised an eyebrow. "You think the ghost is going to make me cookies?"

Jayden rolled his eyes. "No. I'm just saying, like, if she's haunting you or something, it's probably fine. I doubt she's going to hurt you."

Remembering the cool, shrinking presence—how it had flinched away from him—Matt felt a stab of guilt. "She's probably as scared of me as I—wait." His eyes widened. "You said she died in *bed?*"

"That's a perfectly good bed!" his landlord snapped over the phone. "It's barely two years old. I already put a new mattress on there. That's required by law." His voice held a note of complaint: Mr. Colson hated hearing that he was 'required by law' to do anything. "If you're squeamish about the bedframe, you're going to have to man up and deal with it, because I'm not replacing it."

Matt clenched his teeth. "So you've just been letting people move in and sleep there, not telling anyone someone *died* in that bed?"

"There's no legal requirement for me to report that," Mr. Colson said primly. "Not like California, where it's stigmatized property if anyone's died there in the last three years. You want to be superstitious about something that happened months ago, that's on you."

Matt swallowed his first response, then his second. He'd known his landlord was scum when he'd signed the contract, but every conversation was a fresh reminder. "Could you at least switch the bed out?" he asked tightly. "You've got to have another one in storage."

"Sure, but it's on your dime. Somebody has to open the storage shed, haul out the new bed, drive it here, switch it, and put the other one back in storage. Including labor and cleaning fees, that's...say, four hundred dollars."

Matt choked on a laugh. "Damn, maybe I should quit my job, start moving furniture. Sounds like it pays real good."

"Sure thing, smart guy. So, shall I call the movers?"

"Nope. Thanks." Biting back a final comment, Matt hung up.

That night, he stood in the quiet bedroom for a long time, staring at the bed. His muscles buzzed. He wasn't even a tiny bit sleepy. But this had to end, and he could only see one way to do it.

He'd slept in a death-bed for weeks. There was no way around that. But from here, it looked perfectly normal. There was nothing left of its former owner: the mattress and linens were new, and there wasn't a headboard for fingerprints to cling to. He'd turned the mattress over twice, checked every inch of the bedframe, and hadn't found a single hair that wasn't his. Perhaps the lost spirit wasn't clinging so much to objects as it was to impressions, a general memory of 'bed.' Short of hiring an exorcist, there was likely no way Matt was going to get rid of her.

And no matter how much the situation skeeved him out, he'd slept much better in this haunted bed than he ever had in the living room. Mr. Colson was scum, but he was right: it was a perfectly good bed.

He took a deep breath. Then he took several more. Finally, aware it wasn't getting any earlier, he turned off the light, tiptoed across the room, and crawled beneath the blankets.

She was awake when it crept under the covers. She'd had several nights alone, a brief span of peace. But she viscerally knew the presence of this body when it came, the heat that spread under the sheets as it settled in to rest.

It was closer this time. She'd been sleeping nearer the middle, lulled by the phantom's absence. Now she couldn't move for fear—could only lie and wonder: was it going to climb on her again?

Why am I still here? If she had any willpower, she'd leave the house and run into the streets, abandoning the possessed bed to whatever wanted it. But whatever drove her by daylight was gone. She felt bound to this house, this room, this *bed*. Her waking mind was trapped under a veil, and all hope of escape was trapped with it.

Minutes passed.

The thing shifted under the covers, redistributing its weight. There was something strangely careful in its movements tonight, as if it were trying to move without jostling her. Could it possibly think she wasn't aware of it, when she'd known it was there since the bedcovers twitched?

She was suddenly angry. She wanted to tell it off. What did it think it was doing? What was it trying to get away with in the dark? She opened her mouth, all the terror of the last few weeks bubbling into words, ready to flood out with the next breath.

But the thing spoke first.

"Excuse me." It was a quiet voice, polite given the circumstances. "Would you mind moving over just a little bit?"

For a moment, she was too shocked to respond.

The presence waited quietly.

Too bewildered to do anything else, she finally edged a little to the side.

The presence sighed softly. She felt it relax, settling deeper into the mattress. "Thank you," it murmured, already sounding half asleep. "Good night."

She took a deep breath, gathering her nerve. "Good night," she whispered.

It didn't answer. In the darkness, she heard it breathing: slow and soft, falling gently into whatever rest awaited dreams.

Gradually, her breathing slowed, too, and soon her worry faded into sleep.

Bitter Harvest

JACQUELINE K GOLDBLATT

Judy Boy was on his way to the bone orchard[1] I knew it. He knew it. The whole damn accommodation[2] knew it, but we still fought to keep him around, pouring whisky down his throat to help him stay warm. Despite our lack of manners, morals, and hygiene, we could all agree it was in bad taste to kick a dying man out of a train car in the middle of a summer storm. That is, if you could even really call Jude a man. He was more of a kid, to be honest. Still wet behind the ears, a greenhorn rookie in the art of traveling the rails. Heard he ran away from home so his family could afford to eat. Others would call that stupid, but me? I call it noble.

It was quiet in the car save for the pounding of the rain outside, the crash of thunder, Doc's soft murmurings of comfort and the boy's labored breathing. In the low lamplight, I could still see his chest fighting to rise and fall, like a message in a bottle bobbing on the waves. Jude never was good at reading messages. I'd told him not to go into that yard. I told him the sign meant Bad Dog[3], that even though it looked a bit like a sideways thermometer, no warmth was to come from a place like that, only cold fangs and claws. Even now I can hear the "Crunch!" as the hound sunk its teeth into his side, still hear him scream out my name, howling, "Booker, Booker help! Get it offa me!" I'd gotten it off

---

1   **bone orchard:** graveyard.

2   **accommodation:** freight train car

3   **Bad Dog:** Hobos often left little symbols for each other that signified different things. They communicated important information to each other through these codes and symbols.

of him, beaten the beast with my bindle[4] 'til its brains, like pink mashed potatoes, plopped to the ground, 'til I was sweaty and my hands were covered in blood. But by then it was too late. The wound was too deep, and infection set in quick. Now, all we could do was comfort him best we could.

We were all fond of the kid, 'cept for Arch. Then again, that man wasn't fond of anything other than his flask, to be frank. But that's besides the point. The majority of us thought him a friend. He always shared his grub and was quick to notice when the railroad bulls[5] were on our trail. His shoulder was always available for Wells to cry on when he got into one of his maudlin states, which was often enough. Heh, considering the amount Wells cried, I always wonder how Jude kept his shirts dry.

Any cigarettes he managed to get his hot little hands on he traded to Foy in exchange for stories read off of stolen Dick Tracey comics and Little Orphan Annie strips in the paper. Foy had a great talent for voices, y'see. I always thought he'd do well on the radio, if he ever got the chance. He wasn't all that obliging to entertain without a little incentive, so we all looked forward to when Jude and him had one of their little trades and we could hear him imitate Flattop Jones and Daddy Warbucks. I suspect even Arch liked those nights, though he never let it show much aside from holding off his sharp tongue and sitting still awhile.

Doc thought the kid had potential, what with his gentle nature and steady hands. Whenever one of us got cut up or caught a chill, Doc would get Jude to help with the bandages and such. No one could bandage nearly as well as Doc, but Jude was giving him a run for his money. Sometimes I could barely tell their handiwork apart, that's how similar they were. Bard, one of our newer additions who played guitar and sang with a voice that reminded me of chocolate chip cookies and all things warm and comforting, was always getting injured in some way or another. The man was a natural pain magnet. Really, out of all of us, he seemed the one most likely to kick the bucket, but life wasn't fair. In retrospect, neither was death, apparently.

---

4   **bindle:** a bundle, bag, bedroll, or backpack carried by a hobo
5   **railroad bulls:** railway guards noted for their brutality

Planter and Jude were…well, let's just say they were real good friends. It's not my place to judge what a man does in his spare time with someone he's partial to. Jude *was* nineteen, after all, and Planter wasn't that much older. As long as they weren't hurting anyone, I didn't give a damn. Besides, the two made a buffalo nickel when they went out and played chuck-a-dummy[6] or gut-plunge**gut-plunge:** begging at the butcher for meat to put in Mulligan Stew, so who was complaining?

As for me, there wasn't much to say. I'd seen a lot riding the rails, met a lot of miserable, rotten people who'd sell out their mother to make a quick buck. Jude wasn't one of them. He had a good heart. A heart that was stuttering, straining to go on. One that'd save the boy a lot of pain if it just stopped fighting.

"Waste of good liquor." A voice like a creaky door in need of oil shattered the relative stillness. "Goddamn waste of good liquor. Kid's dying anyway. Why should I give what's mine to that punk[7]?"

Planter, standing beside me, instantly tensed, his shoulders stiffening into two stony bridges under his windcheater[8] as we turned to face the voice's owner. Simeon Arch, body bent like a grey and white candy cane, stared back at us, beady green eyes shot with red veins like a mockery of a Christmas wreath.

I sighed. "Arch, siddown. You've got nothing to complain about. Yer gut's full and so's yer bag. Bet ya could bum a nice bottle offa some baldy[9] man at the next stop."

His scowl deepened, sinking into his face like a toad in a barrel of cream. "I earned that liquor! I earned it and yer takin' it away from me to save this snot-nosed cat[10] who's headed to the orchard! It'd be better if he jumped and greased the track[11]! Least there'd be some dignity in that!"

Planter began to step forward with clenched fists, but I held him back, giving Doc and the others a helpless look. But they ignored me. Doc continued to wipe the sweat from Judy Boy's chalk-white face,

---

6   **chuck-a-dummy:** faking a fainting spell to get sympathy

7   **punk:** a young hobo

8   **windcheater:** a burlap bag, feed sack, etc., worn for protection against the elements

9   **baldy:** an old

10   **snot-nosed cat:** a young tramp or hobo, new to the roads

11   **greased the track:** suicide by leaping in front of a train

murmuring soothing nonsense all the while Foy bundled him up and Wells looked away, tears dripping down his cheeks and shaking his head sadly. "Won't be long now," he kept whispering, wiping the drops from his wrinkled jowls. "Won't be long now."

All of these responses were predictable ones, but Bard's was the one that stuck out the most. Bard, who was normally full of cheer and song no matter the circumstances, just sat there holding the guitar on his lap without strumming it, eerily silent and grim. The man always played that thing no matter what, and oftentimes one or more of us would yell at him to shut the hell up. Now that he actually had shut his yap and stopped his strumming, I missed it more than ever.

As I shepherded Planter along, I could feel Arch's smirk burning into our backs as we walked, hear him calling Planter a coward. "Just try to ignore him," I whispered into Planter's ear, leading him to the other side of the car as quietly as I could, all the while listening as Arch's shouts of "Yeah, you run away! The only reason you want to save this cat is cause' he'll let you rut him, ya dirty jocker[12]!" echoed behind.

I could tell Planter was tempted to rise to the bait, so I quickened my pace and my words. "You're a good man, Planter, and you got morals. You're no lush with a chip on his shoulder. Fisticuffs ain't gonna settle nothing, no sir. Even if it did, you don't want Jude's last memory to be of you clobberin' Arch." I yammered on and on like an old gossip, but Planter's eyes burned with a fire I hadn't seen in a long time as he hushed me with a look sharp as flint.

"He's breaking the code, Booker. He's breaking the code that's been in place since eighteen-eighty nineAn ethical code created by Tourist Union #63 during its National Hobo Convention in St. Louis, Missouri. The code was voted upon and established as a concrete set of laws to govern the Nationwide Hobo Body just so he can get some extra hooch. He's breaking the code. No! Not just the code, Booker, he's breaking the laws of human decency!" He was shaking now, shaking with a white hot rage so palpable I could feel it rolling off of him, rising up from his skin and filling the car with an intense heat that seemed to evaporate the damp

---

12 **dirty jocker:** an experienced hobo who taught minors the way of life; the relationship was often sexual

from my shirt. Then suddenly he went still, staring behind me where the group was. My gaze followed his, and I held back a gasp before biting my knuckles to keep from roaring in outrage.

While the others were tending to Jude, Arch had started digging through the dying boy's bindle. He wasn't quiet about it either. No doubt everyone heard him; Doc's frown deepened, Foy's grip on his box of matches tightened, but they were all too busy dealing with the situation to do anything. My ears started to ring, and I could practically hear Arch's creaky, cawing voice laughing in my head, singing, "It's a dog eat dog world. Or in this case, a dog eat Jude world! Ha ha! More southern comfort for me! Hee hee hee!"

The blood in my veins started to flow like a roaring river, the words JUSTICE JUSTICE JUSTICE ringing like bells beating in my heart, letting the river rush forward in a torrent. I looked at Planter. He looked at me. We nodded. It was in bad taste to kick a dying man out of a train car in the midst of a summer storm, but a live, cheating bastard? That was another story. Still, it would have to wait. The time wasn't right yet.

The hour was close to midnight now, and Jude was fading fast. Planter knelt on the floor, head bowed in prayer. Arch was snoring, fingers wrapped around the cross he always kept round his neck in order to trick religious old ladies. All was silent. Then, suddenly, the beginnings of a song drifted through the air, carried by a raspy, thin voice as everyone turned into statues.

"*Ooh Death. Whooooah death*"*"Oh Death"* or "*A Conversation with Death*" is a traditional Appalachian folk song that is still performed today. The author recommends both the more authentic Ralph Stanley Version and the modernized Jen Titus version, as well as the Amy Van Roekel and Jeff Grace version featured in the popular video game, "*Until Dawn*" …"

Slowly, I looked over at Bard, but his lips were sealed tight, and his hands were locked in place, his old six-string seated securely on his lap. Wells' watery eyes bulged wide as oceans as he shook his head, salty drops pooling into the jowls of his cheeks.

"*Whooooah death. Won't you spare me over 'til another year?*"

The rain began to thunder against the roof of the car as Foy, lantern rattling in his grip, pointed at the bundled figure lying below him. Jude. The boy's face was incredibly pale, his feverish eyes unfocused as they drifted around the room before finally settling on Bard, who wordlessly pointed at the old six-string. Jude rocked his head up and down in a slow nod that reminded me of cattails blowing in a river breeze, loose and disjointed. A warm look of understanding settled itself on the musician's face, one I'd never before had the privilege of seeing. One that, in retrospect, I never wanted to see again. With his long, pale fingers Bard began to pick the strings, plucking out a melody that was all at once foreign and familiar, a tune that passed by and penetrated all who were in its presence. The boy took a rattling breath, then opened his mouth once more.

"Well what is this that I can't see, with ice-cold hands taking hold of me?"

Bard, still concentrating on his strings, replied in a voice that wasn't his own. *"Well I am Death, none can excel, I'll open the door to heaven or hell."*

With a strength he did not and could not have possessed in his current state, Jude wrestled himself from Doc's arms and sat up, Bard's playing growing louder as he rose. The music swelled, rich and haunting, and we all listened, paralyzed by the sound.

Then Arch woke up, and it all went to hell.

"What in blazes is all that racket? Can't a man get some sleep around here?" he hissed as he stumbled to his feet, the cross round his neck swinging wildly. The grating sound of his voice snapped us all out of our respective trances, and I made a hasty grab for Planter. He was quicker than I was, though, slipping from my side and stalking silently up to the other man like a big cat.

"You never do know when to shut up, do ya, Arch?" he whispered, hands twitching oddly.

"I could say the same of you lot, what with all the noise yer making!" Arch snapped in reply, flushed cheeks growing redder by the second.

Planter smiled thinly and spitefully. "Bard," he said without turning around, "keep playing." A leering grin stretched itself across the musician's face as he obeyed, the song picking up where it left off just as easily as a wind-up gramophone. Jude, who had hushed up quick when Arch opened his trap, began to sing once more, glassy eyes staring blindly. *"The children prayed, the preacher preached, time and mercy is out of your reach."*

Bard, still leering, answered in turn, singing, "*I'll fix your feet so you can't walk, I'll lock your jaw so you can't talk.*"

Arch, who looked mad enough to spit, stamped his foot, shaking the car violently. "Did you not hear me the first time, you idiots?! I told ya to quit it! Lock my jaw. Yeah right! I'll lock yours if you don't let up!"

At that, Bard let out a throaty chuckle that sent chills down my spine, fingers never stopping their dance across the guitar's frets. "Mine's been locked since the day I first came into this world, son. Your threats mean nothing to me." His lips peeled back into a smile, and his teeth reminded me of two neat rows of tombstones, well-tended and white as a corpse. "'Sides," he whispered, rising to his feet with uncanny grace, "who takes stock in the threats of dead men?"

At these words, the lantern light flickered out, enveloping the car in alarmed cries and a cloak of darkness. "Foy," I hissed desperately, "Light a match! For chrissakes, light a match!" But Foy's hands musta been trembling, 'cause all I saw were brief flashes of a match before it struck out.

"You absolute idiots!" Arch griped. "Can't even light a goddam—"

The sound of the six-string interrupted him, along with a voice that butterfly fluttered and cut like razor wire. A voice of barren deserts and carrion crows, of sweet release and slick red slaughter.

"*I'll close your eyes so you can't see, this very hour come away with me.*"

There came a rattling gasp, followed by a low moan and a bloodcurdling wail that ripped through my very soul. In the inky blackness, I saw a flash of tombstone teeth and the glint of guitar strings.

"*Death I come to take the soul, leave the body and leave. It. Cold.*"

Thunder roared across the sky, drowning out the music as the lantern re-lit itself. I blinked, letting my eyes adjust, then held back a scream. Lying on the floor in a crumpled heap was Arch, the chain of his necklace twisted tight around his throat, his terrified face a ghoulish purple. The cross pendant was missing, though I didn't have to look far to find it. A few feet away lay Jude, the cross placed between his folded, lifeless hands. A peaceful look of contentment graced his still features Where Bard once stood, only empty space and silence remained.

We all stood there, numb and dumb, not saying a word. Before I knew it, I was laughing. I laughed until I couldn't catch my breath, 'til my face burned hot and flushed and my gut ached. Planter grabbed me by the shirt and practically lifted me off the ground with one hand, eyes wild with panic. "The hell's so funny?!"

My gaze met his and my laughter hitched in my throat before slowly turning to sobs. "P-Planter, we were wrong. Jude wasn't headed to the bone orchard. It was headed towards him, and decided another one of its crops was ready for harvest along the way!"

CITATIONS

"OHNS: A Dictionary of Old Hobo Slang – by Stephen P. Alpert." Original Hobo Nickel Society. Accessed May 28, 2018. http://www.hobonickels.org/alpert04.htm.

FROM BOTH SIDES OF YOUR MOUTH

ALEX LAUREL LANZ

MY SISTER'S MOUTH is in the back of my head. She's hidden underneath my hair. Gapped teeth and a long tongue nestled between my ears.

We were born together, her mouth gaping with mine when we were brought into this world. She always whispers to me, a voice that only echoes inside my skull. My earliest memories are tinged with her.

Terrible, pathetic.

She lashes through my thoughts; we fight over who can think. *Tie a rope around your neck*—Two, three, five, seven. Thinking of something different is all I can do to quiet her. Let something else fill my brain. Today it's prime numbers. Concentrate on counting, force her to stay silent. Smoke swirls over my face after taking a drag off my cigarette. Raindrops patter against the asphalt, and I cradle my half-broken umbrella against my shoulder.

"You shouldn't be smoking."

The voice shakes me back to reality. It's a man, spindles of rain gliding off his black poncho.

Eleven, thirteen—*Terrible*—seventeen. I take another drag to spite him.

"That stuff'll kill you, and I think you should live." His nose scrunches up. His grin sends a prickling chill down my body, even under my heavy gloves and jacket.

"You don't know that." I hate it when people make up things. He doesn't know me. His beady eyes squint like he wants something, hoping

I'll put my guard down. *Stab your neck, cut your throat.* He's breaking my concentration; I have to start over. Two, three, five.

"You can come over to my place where it's dry."

"I'm good." He's getting too close. I back up, scanning the park for a quick exit. Something is behind me: a chain-link fence. Shit.

"Aw c'mon, you can play that guitar." He nods to the case hanging from my shoulders.

Peeling my glove off, I shake my head. *Jump off a bridge. Break your legs, you lay gasping and dying. Jump.*

"Leave me alone." The weak words are buried under the rain.

He comes closer. He isn't going to leave. *Cut your wrists and bleed out. Jump off a bridge.*

My cigarette drops, hissing as it extinguishes in a puddle.

My hand clasps over his.

You're so special, you're so strong. Your muscles are so big. Your cock is so big. Janice thinks you're so funny, she loves the way you smell.

My sister's voice is a flurry, words clashing and tumbling over each other. His mouth goes slack as they burrow into him. All her whispers pour through me and into him. Ecstasy widens his eyes with all the things he wants to hear. All the thoughts he wants to have. All the validation he needs.

Relief tingles up my spine. After all the build-up, her whispers finally cleanse themselves. A purge.

Moaning, his knees buckle, and his muscles loosen.

My head is light, swimming. I stumble, and my umbrella clatters onto the ground next to him. Rain slips down my face. He goes silent, his eyes unfocused.

A burst of adrenaline and I run, skidding between trees. My guitar case bangs against my back with every step.

My sister is quiet, content.

I've scrounged up enough money from strangers to buy lunch and a bus ticket out of here. Money from people kind enough to drop change in my open guitar case while I play on the sidewalk. These moments are so short. This is the only time I can play, the only time I'm free and it's like

I don't have a sister. When she finally sleeps under my hair, empty and still. I can sit in front of shops and make up music, play the notes I hear in the traces of my mind when I'm my whole self.

This old guitar is the sole gift I've ever been given. I found it leaning up against a table at a garage sale, and I begged and pleaded and promised my mother I'd never want another thing in my entire life. And when she haggled it down another twenty dollars, my heart swelled so big it almost burst.

Mother had handed me the case and I clutched it like a life-raft. I plucked on the strings and twisted the knobs like I had seen others do. Until the notes sang. And of course, my sister would begin to whisper. *Stupid, dumb, bad music. Stupid, dumb.*

Whenever I'd get comfortable, Mom would come in, bending over with her hands on her knees, her giant eyes hovering over me. "Beth-Anne, you have to be good to your sister." She would then take my guitar and lay it in the case. "She doesn't get her own body. You must be mindful of what Grace wants."

Grace. They'd named her Grace. Before I was born, my mother had another girl. Small and gray, too feeble to cry out. With a yawning mouth, the baby took in a single breath and then died, having never lived. My mother wept from the time they buried Grace until the time she swelled with me. But when my sister's mouth gaped on the back of my head, my mother said she cried tears of joy. From the minute she held me, she knew Grace had come back from heaven, come back to be reborn. Come back for *her.* Grace returned and would live again, and my body would be her vessel.

I hated Grace with every part of me that wasn't touched by her. Every cell uncorrupted by her presence. No one heard her like I did. No one saw her under my hair. No one knew. But they all wasted away from her, anyway. Every year, Mom grew thinner, paler, dark spots dotted across her skin.

Why couldn't Grace have stayed dead?

Anger festered whenever I looked at the black guitar case against the wall. *Stick a knife in your neck. Terrible. Bad music. Knife in your neck.* My fists beat against the side of my head while I screamed for her to stop. I'd dig my nails into my skin, trying to find where she began and I ended so I could dig her out of me forever. Rip every piece of her out.

I stop at a small diner to order coffee before making my way to the station. A place with plastic chairs and metal tables, a place that isn't so fancy they won't stare if a filthy beggar like me pays in change.

The coffee is burnt and bitter, but I savor it all the same. Leaning against the counter, my guitar heavy on my back and my backpack on my lap, everything I own I carry like a burden.

A rare moment, where I can sip on watery coffee and watch people laugh and make small-talk as they absent-mindedly stare at the muted TV. The times I can let the world whirl around me without having to constantly push Grace away grow fewer and fewer.

Someone is watching me. At the edges of my vision, I sense them. I hunch my shoulders down as if I could shrink myself until I disappeared..

They're coming closer. My pulse quickens.

A woman. She slides onto the stool next to mine. Her sharp face is like a crescent moon, locked onto me. The dozens of rings on her fingers clink against the counter.

I fumble at the strap of my guitar case, preparing to flee.

Her mouth curves into a long smile, eyes bouncing over me in excitement.

"Hey, there." Her singsong voice rings through everything.

My mouth is filled with too much coffee to say anything; I've forgotten how to swallow. Why can't people leave me be?

The TV flashes to a news anchor.

BODY FOUND IN MOSSWOOD PARK

My heart hammers against my chest. Grace stirs. Her lips move, mouthing underneath my hair. *You idiot. You stupid idiot.* The woman follows my gaze, jewelry jangling with every motion. She makes a *hm* sound like she realizes something.

I want more time before Grace wakes up again. More time to strum the guitar, to leave this town on a bus and sleep in the stiff seats while the trees drag past the fogged-up windows.

"I have to go." The stool squeals under me.

Clunk.

My umbrella. On the counter, right between us. The same tattered edge, the same dent in the metal handle. My stomach plummets.

She saw me. She saw that man in the park.

Stick a knife in your neck. You stupid fucking idiot. You did this. This is your fault. It's all your fault—Eleven, thirteen, seventeen. The whole room buzzes. Everything is so loud. Grace, the TV, the laughter, her voice, so loud it crushes me down into a pulp.

"What do—what…" is all that manages to come out.

"You wanna get out of here?"

Yes, more than anything. But I sit, slack-jawed, all of my worldly possessions jumbled in my lap.

The woman shoves the umbrella into a canvas bag, her stare unwavering. She nods sharply towards the door.

"C'mon, we have a lot to talk about."

She towers when she stands, and I'm a pebble in her shadow. But I follow anyway.

She leads me down a quiet street, cradling that canvas bag. I keep my head down, afraid to look at anything head on.

"I'm Zsuzsanna, by the way."

"Oh." I chew on the dry skin on my lips. Two, three, five, seven—*Jump in front of that truck, splat!*—eleven, thirteen.

She gives me a sideways, expectant look. Waiting for me to return the custom and provide my name. I swallow, trying to figure out where we're going, why we're going there. *Drink bleach, fill yourself with poison*—Two, three, five.

If I had to, I could purge again. She'd become another victim, another body trailing behind me as I ran towards the next town. The next state. The option is always there and knowing that makes my throat tight. Palms sweating and itching under my gloves, I resist letting my mind circle around that possibility.

We cross a parking lot and approach a single gray door cut into the back of a brick building. I know better than to ask what this place is.

Zsuzsanna fishes out a lanyard from under her shirt, worn cards dangling from the end. She holds it up to the card reader, and there is a beep before the door clicks open.

"C'mon." She makes a flapping motion for me to follow. "Don't worry, there are no cameras or anything."

Artificial lemon and rot. Too sterile, too cold. The smell pummels my lungs. Nineteen, twenty-three. Someone moans in the distance. The door sighs shut behind us, and the place feels so desolate and dark. Almost out of instinct, I clasp my hands together, readying myself in case I have to use Grace. *Bash your head in*—Eleven, fifteen.

The hall is lined with numbered doors. Mechanical beeps muffled by thin walls.

Finally, she opens one of the doors and nods for me to enter.

A man lays in bed, his mouth gasping open, thin skin stretched over his cheekbones. Skinny, pale arms hang like broken antennae at his sides. *Break the window and cut your throat. Cut your wrists.* Seventeen. Shit, lost track.

Zsuzsanna stands at the end of his bed, curling her fingers over the plastic frame.

"Who is that? What is this?" The door shuts behind me with a groan. The walls are bare, nothing. Three, five, seven.

"His name is Alfred. He liked to garden."

His lips quiver, and I realize he's awake. His eyes are half-open, crusted over. It's too hard to look at him, so I stare at the back of the woman's head. *Punch the window and take the glass*—Five, seven, eleven.

"Why did you bring me here?"

"Alfred suffered a stroke two months ago. He's lost his ability to speak. Before that, he struggled but didn't show it. He doesn't have any family, not anymore. He couldn't work. And I guess that means you end up here, forgotten and alone."

Pity swells in my stomach.

Zsuzsanna looks back at me, her eyebrows lowered into a hard line.

"I saw you in the park."

Cold chills shiver over my skin and I clutch my hands together, ready. My backpack thumps at my feet.

"I don't... I don't know wha—"

"It's okay." Her face softens. "I saw what happened to that body they found."

You stupid bitch, of course you're caught. Put your head under a tire and let it smash your stupid brains out. Smash all over the asphalt. Dumb bitch—Two, three, seven, two, three.

The soles of my shoes squeak against the floor as I back away. *No point in running, jump out the window. Splat on the pavement. Blood.*

"Stop, wait." She grabs my arm, catching a fistful of flannel, and I jerk so hard I almost tumble into the wall. "Don't worry, I'm not going to say anything."

"Then what the fuck do you want?"

"How did you do it? It was so fast."

"What—I can't—"

"It was quick, though, right?" She looms over me, the smell of her lavender perfume burning my nostrils. A monolith that stretches into the sky.

"I—yeah—I don't know." I can't watch when I purge Grace. I can't watch how the color drains and they go limp. It makes acid creep up my throat. Glazed eyes, staring into the beyond while their skin puckers and decays.

"Will you do it for Alfred?"

Everything stops. The stale air is too thick to breathe. My mouth flaps open and shut, silent. *Take the glass and jam it into your jugular. Jump out the window*—Two, three...four. I can't remember.

"You want me to..."

She nods, eyes sparkling.

"That's... No, that's horrible," I spit, a rush of anger overtaking me.

"Look at him," she says. I don't know why I do, why I look back at his vacant stare. "He didn't have anyone before. He has no one now. It would be kind. Let it be over quick. The world has left him in the gutter, and this is the biggest gift he'll ever be given. Wouldn't you want that?"

Stab your eye. Slash your throat. Pathetic.

"You want to *kill* him? What is wrong with you?" I hiss.

"Why did you kill that guy in the park?"

"I-I didn't mean to."

"This isn't murder, it's mercy." Her voice drops to a husky whisper. "It's the right thing. Would you want to live like that?"

Alfred makes a noise between a cough and a croak. *Pathetic waste. Shoot yourself. Dumb bitch*—Two, three, five.

"I don't want to, but I'll go to the police." Her eyes narrow. "Tell them what I saw in the park."

"And say what? You saw some random person touch a guy and now he's dead?" I twist out of her grasp. "You'll get thrown in the loony bin yourself."

"Then why are you running?"

A screen door banging against its frame comes unbidden into my mind. The floor screeching under every step. How I ran out of that house, the door flapping behind me in the wind. The empty shell of my mother laying on the floor. A simulacrum of who she ever was, collecting dust. I ran across the dead grass, Grace quiet and sleeping, hot tears streaming down my face. I'd finally grabbed my mother's hand and let Grace speak to her again. *You're such a good mother. God forgives you, God loves you. You were always meant to be a mother. Grace came back because you're such a good mother.* She had smiled as she sunk to the floor, the happiest I'd ever seen her. Joy traced over her face as her skin withered, as she deteriorated.

I never turned back to see what else I'd left behind.

Alfred's fingers twitch, tangling in the thin blanket. He makes a gasping sound, flakes of skin sticking to his lips. My shadow stretches over his chest; I'm drifting closer to him.

"It's okay, Alfred. It's going to be okay." I pull off my glove, my palm slick with sweat.

I clasp my hand over his.

You've made so many people happy. You're so funny, you're so clever. Your nose isn't big. You make everyone smile. You aren't a burden.

Grace's words barrel through me and pierce into him. All at once, a flurry so powerful he trembles under me.

Until she's done and purged, my mind quiet, and Alfred lays there, skin gray and waxy, motionless. Shriveled, gone. His lips peel back, exposing long yellow teeth.

Sweet silence fills my skull. I let his fragile hand drop onto his chest. Turn.

"My name is Beth-Anne. Do you have any cigarettes?"

Zsuzsanna lives in a small apartment overlooking the park. We sit on the balcony, sucking down nicotine under the orange sky.

"What's it like?" She idly tugs a wayward thread from her shirt.

"I don't know. It…it's nice because it's so quiet afterwards." Shame plunges through me as soon as the words leave my lips. I stare at my mud-caked sneakers. It's such a horrible thing to think, let alone say. "Sorry. I don't mean that."

"It's okay. I think I know what you mean."

She can't possibly know. It's just one of those things people tell each other to feel better. White lies. A sequence of words to keep up the illusion that we aren't alone. That we aren't afraid all the time. Smoke plumes from my lips and I press my back against the wall.

"My dad got into a car accident when I was twelve. Major bleeding in his brain." She clears her throat, her shoulders shuddering.

"I'm sorry."

"He lived for a while but never walked again. He was…different. I guess. Or maybe that really was the core of him. Like certain parts of him were erased and what was left was this mishmash."

I nod, taking another inhale of cigarette so I don't have to say anything.

"Before the accident, he was brilliant. An engineer. He read a lot, helped me build those dioramas for school. Like ones of the solar system and stuff."

"He sounds nice."

"Yeah. But then he lived for seven years without the nice parts of him. Is it even living if it's just pieces of you breathing?" She shakes her head, ripping that thread in two. "He forgot my name, forgot who I was. He'd call me by his sister's name. He swelled up all the time. My mom was so stressed trying to care for him that she started losing weight."

"What happened to her?"

Zsuzsanna leans against the banister, the orange light of the sunset highlighting her straight nose. "After he was gone, she had a heart attack and died. I think it was…all the pain. You know?"

"Yeah."

"I went into nursing because I wanted to help people like my mom did. Be brave like her. Make it easier on people."

I stub out the cigarette. Zsuzsanna looks up at the nothingness above, hugging herself.

"What *you* can do, Beth-Anne, actually helps."

Grace stirs, her lips twitch. I don't have much time before she speaks again. We sit in the shared silence for a while, watching the sky darken above.

Everything about this place is worse at night. The creaking in the walls, the murmurs of the patients. That horrid smell of rot and citrus that burns up my nose.

You terrible bitch. You murderer, end yourself and save everyone. You—Two, three, five, seven. I keep trying to remember that poster of prime numbers from middle school math class, keep trying to remember every detail about that room so I can squeeze out Grace. All the trivial details about the desks, the smell, the water stain bruising the ceiling. *Jump out the window*—It doesn't work.

Tonight, Zsuzsanna leads me to the top floor of that place, reassuring me that no one ever notices.

"How did you know you could do…it?" she asks, tucking her hair behind her ears.

"I always knew. I don't know how to explain."

"I think I get it."

She doesn't, but it's nice to say. A lie that makes people feel connected, understood. *No one wants to get you, fucking freak. Murderer. Disgusting*—Two, three, five,—*pathetic freak, cut your*—seven, eleven, thirteen.

The door is already ajar when Zsuzsanna ushers me in.

A woman sits up in the bed, staring into the dark window. Drool dangles from her lip, thin white wisps of hair sticking to her sweaty forehead. She doesn't notice we're here. *Fucking bitch you awful fucking bitch*—Two, three, five.

"Hi, Edith." Zsuzsanna's steps are soft against the beige floor. "Remember me? I saw you last week."

I shouldn't have come here—*Jump out the window*—I should've run for the bus stop. Should've taken the precious little time I had away from Grace to get me to the next town, away from her, away from this stench.

Edith's rheumy eyes look past us.

"Where's Morris?" Each word, a splinter crack.

"He'll be here soon." Zsuzsanna slips into the bedside chair and fidgets with the bracelets lining her wrist. Sighing, she nods to the photograph on the nightstand. It's of a couple, the picture wrinkled in the corners. A man and a woman sit together wearing formal clothes and big smiles. "That's Morris and her. When they were young. He died decades ago."

The Edith in that picture wears a polka dot dress and has hair coiffed like a halo. Clutching the hands of the suited man next to her, both of them bright eyed. She still wears the ring from this photo, two silver bands joined together by a single diamond. But now it's tarnished, digging into her swollen red flesh.

I wonder what the woman in the picture would do if she saw herself in this room. Would she be afraid? Sad? *Hold your head underwater until you drown*—Eleven, thirteen.

"She has Alzheimer's. She always asks for Morris when she talks at all. No other family. She had to live in a van when Morris died. Now…"

Spit drips onto Edith's thigh, dotting her stained nightgown. *Stupid murdering bitch*—Two, three, five.

Grace is restless, eager. Cool air stings as I peel off my wool glove.

I lace my fingers between Edith's, and her wedding ring is cold against my skin. *Morris always loved you. You never bothered anyone, everyone thought you were so elegant, so beautiful, so smart. You made Morris so happy. He never blamed you for what happened.*

Edith's stiff hand jerks in mine. Bliss stretches out her mouth, tears slipping over her weathered cheek. Skin puckers until she's wilted.

My head swims in the quiet, in the calm; I float in it for a while, listening to the dense silence.

"You're an angel," Zsuzsanna whispers.

"I'm not."

"You are. There isn't anything better than the peace you give."

It must be nice to not know about Grace. To not know about that hidden mouth. To not hear all the things that aren't true. What if she knew? Would she turn away in disgust, or would she stare into that cavernous mouth?

I take the picture off the nightstand. Edith's face full of life, hope, this one moment in time carved out and set in amber. I place it on her chest, over her heart.

Zsuzsanna says I can sleep on the couch and lays out some old clothes for me. I try to protest, saying that I had to get going, but I can't resist the offer of a hot shower. At least she won't mind if I play guitar.

Steam blankets the mirror when I get out of the shower. I raise my hand to rub some of it away but then recoil at the thought of looking at myself.

When I was younger, I realized I had never seen Grace. She was this entity, always behind me, always right out of view. Someone I felt but always crawled away from my sight. After tracing my fingertips over her lips, I dug through our bathroom until I found the hand mirror.

I sat with my back to the mirror on the wall and held up the one in my hand, moving it to reveal the back of my head. My heart stuttered, somehow afraid of what she really looked like. A grim smile, a thousand teeth, worm-like lips? All the attributes I had given her over the years.

She's an abyss that went through me. A black hole. Endless darkness. My heart froze with the truth: —there was no ripping her out. Pulling out a hole is just digging a bigger one.

The humid air settling on my arms reminds me of how exposed I am without gloves and oversized sleeves. Cold anxiety knots in the pit of my stomach. Without fabric protecting everyone from my accidental touch, from feeling my skin against theirs and hearing the sound of Grace's voice, I am so frail and weak.

A cloud of wet air leaves the bathroom with me, my pant legs dragging on the floor with every step I take. Zsuzsanna sits at the kitchen table. She jerks her head up when I approach, startled, like I shook her awake from a dream.

"Oh, Beth-Anne!" She shoves her hands behind her back. Something is wrong with the way she looks at me. Her eyes are too focused, too wide.

"What is that?"

"Nothing." She squirms like I won't notice whatever she is hiding behind her.

"Then show me."

"No—"

"Let me see!" My hand whips forward, stopping within an inch. Hovering over her skin, trembling, a jolt away from grabbing her.

Flinching, her mouth opens wordlessly; we're so close that we share a breath. Her eyes scan over me like she'll find the right thing to say. The silent threat of my touch makes her cower. Careful and slow, she pulls out her hand, balled up into a fist. She uncurls each finger like a flower trying to bloom.

A tarnished silver ring.

Two bands, united by one diamond.

"That's Edith's." Red-hot rage burns my cheeks, and a boiling anger churns in my gut so fast that it's dizzying.

"I can explain," she squeaks.

"That is *Edith's*."

She backs up against the wall, trying to slip away from my outstretched hand. Words come out of her, but I can't hear them over the blood pumping in my ears.

"Is that what this is?! You fucking *liar*. How many times did you fucking lie to me?"

"No, it wasn't a lie, Beth-Anne—"

"Shut up!" *You murdering bitch, kill yourself, murderer.* I can't think of numbers. I only see Zsuzsanna. Her pleading eyes, her shivering palms.

"Don't you get it?" she asks. "She had no one, she died alone. No one cares, no one is coming for this. You're giving them what they want. What everyone wants."

"No one would've wanted this." It hits me all at once. A drop in my chest. The guilt. Mercy doesn't leave the world better off.

"No, really. You are an angel, Beth-Anne, please. It's quick and painless—wait—"

But I don't wait.

I grab her hand.

You are doing the right thing. In heaven, everyone will treat you like an angel. No one understands you, the pain you see, only you're strong enough. You are a good person. A moral person.

All the words blur, a frenzy, jabbing into her. Mouth open wide, eyes rolling back. The weight of Grace being erased. A sweet release.

Her hand drops from mine and she curls on the floor. Skin gray, her mouth stuck in a smile. A withered husk of who she ever was.

My heart clamors in my chest. Guilt sinks through my gut so hard I think I'm going to drop straight to hell. I clutch Edith's ring so tight that it leaves an imprint.

It's not right to leave Zsuzsanna like this. The fleece blanket with the butterfly print will have to do. I cover her with it, though it's too short and doesn't reach her feet. *Light a match and set yourself on fire*—Grace is so loud, it's like a knife carving into my skull.

She lied to me. Was this all a ploy? My thoughts trip over each other, one after the other. Someone will come looking for her soon, someone will notice she's missing. *Murderer, burn your skin off.* There's no point in trying to push Grace out.

The ring.

I still have it, that delicate little thing. In my palm, it looks so small, a lost piece of someone. A nauseous jerk in my gut almost makes me puke when I see it.

Something dangles on the coat rack: the lanyard. The card at the end of it has a picture of Zsuzsanna. I push it into my pocket with the ring.

A low, hot wind kicks stray leaves across the parking lot. The night buzzes with an oncoming storm.

Something yearns in me, pulling me back there to the gray door in the back of that building. *Murderer, put a gun in your mouth. Eat the gun, bullet through your brain.* I keep seeing their faces, how their mouths teetered from hushed shock to smiling. Was this ever kind?

I dig out the lanyard I took from Zsuzsanna. The door beeps open and I slip in. Dark and dank. Too clean, too artificial, too familiar.

Cut your wrists, tie a rope around your neck.

I let her talk. Let every word stab through my heart. No reciting anything will hold her back, and it doesn't matter. I deserve it.

I stand in front of Edith's room.

The door creaks open.

A rasping breath. Long and drawn out.

Tie the rope tight, choke yourself, you fucking bitch.

It's not Edith. It's a man. A plastic mask wraps around his face, tubes hanging between him and the machine that lets out slow and soft beeps.

You dumb murdering bitch, gouge out your eye—Of course it's not Edith; she's gone. More sick guilt stirs in my stomach. I can't return this ring. This room is filled with another man in his dwindling days.

He stirs. Bony hands clutch the white blanket, his eyes open.

"I'm sorry." It's a pathetic squeak out of my mouth. *Slash your wrists.*

My body feels so far away, so slow and sluggish as I try to back out.

The man lifts his head high enough to stare into me with milky eyes. His eyebrows wrinkle like he's trying to digest a million thoughts at once.

A lump grows in my throat. Hot stinging smears my vision.

"I'm sorry." I don't know why I keep saying it, why my tongue keeps retracing those words. "I think I wanted it to be true. That what I did matters. It was better for them. When Grace talks, it hurts so bad."

Finding every ounce of bravery I could muster, I drop the ring onto the nightstand. The same nightstand, naked without that portrait.

"It's not yours, but I can't keep it."

The shadows pool into the wrinkles on his face, dark blotches barely making out a person. Still, the horrible feeling clinging to my heart makes me want to give him something. Like I owe this stranger.

"I'm sorry. It's… She won't stop. She tells everyone else nice things until they die, and then she tells *me* to die. She tells me to kill myself, to cut myself. Because isn't that what I should do?" Grace's words become mine. Grace speaks with my tongue. "Kill yourself, jump, pathetic. It's too much. It's all the time. I want it to be out of me, even if it's for a little bit. I know it's wrong. I fucking *know* that."

Tears stream down my face; I clutch my shirt like it's too hot. I realize I'm sobbing, how much it hurts to say what I hear. All the poison bleeding out of me.

And it's quiet.

Grace doesn't say a word.

I'm crying at the foot of a dying man's bed. Sobbing until my chest feels like it's been carved out and hollowed. We lock eyes, and in his sympathetic gaze, I want to cry again. But instead, we share the silence.

There isn't anything more I can say. Anything more Grace can say. I slide into the chair next to the bed, taking out my guitar. There isn't much I can give, there isn't much that I have. But it's everything I can do.

There's another long, shuddering breath, and the machines sigh with him. We're both alone together here. Two dust motes that happened to collide.

I strum out a tune that I heard on the edges of my mind. Notes I can hear only in the pauses of Grace. It's better than talking, explaining. The notes are soft in this small room, but they're comforting to us both.

The muscles of his face relax. A peacefulness sweeps over him and calms his rasping breaths. Letting the music carry him off into the great unknown.

It isn't all the things he'd ever want, whoever he is. Or all the lies Grace says that make those last moments euphoric. It's only me, a lonely song played by one lost soul to another.

But maybe, just maybe, this time it's enough.

SYMPHONY IN WHITE

VICKY POINTING

WHEN I WAS eight, my mother left me at some gathering of girls my age that she said Would Be Good For Me. It was winter, dark when I arrived. The church hall was dimly lit, its stale scent overlaid with polish. There was a short period of game-playing, during which I did my best to blend into the walls. We had juice and biscuits, then they settled us at tables, gave us cards and paper, glitter, scissors, and glue. I cut and stuck happily enough, absorbed by my work. When I paused to savour peeling the dry glue from my fingers, I noticed the other girls whispering. I leaned in and held my breath, better to hear the story they told.

A ghost had been seen around the church: a white-clad woman, her dress a bright smudge in a dark night. If glimpsed from a distance, she stood her ground, raising her arms towards those who witnessed her. If she appeared close up, her hands tore at you, her mouth ripping open to scream, blood spilling from it. Such an encounter could only lead to madness if you didn't drop dead from fright.

◆———————————————◆

We walk through the village of my childhood, each familiar place passing like a badly taken photograph: blurred, the angle not quite right. Your hand puppets me from the small of my back, my heels scratching on the tarmac as we turn. I'm only half-pretending. I sank my wine for courage and for show, after switching it for the drink you'd doctored.

The air snaps with cold, ready for frost. I'm thankful my coat is fastened tightly, thankful I know where I'm going.

We had returned to visit family at Christmas, June and I, and had gone with them to a cosy pub. Where you waited.

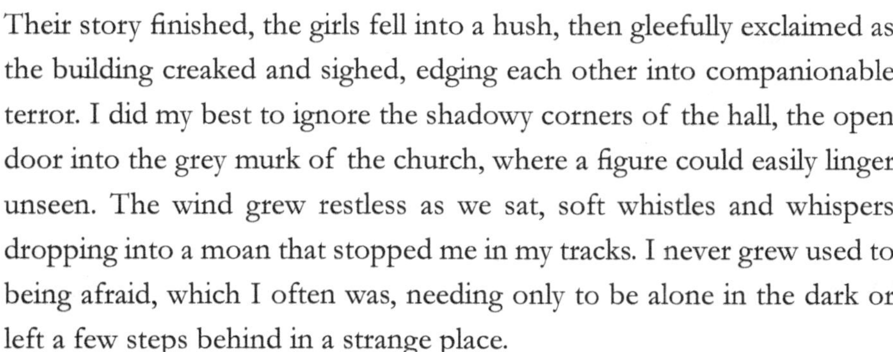

Their story finished, the girls fell into a hush, then gleefully exclaimed as the building creaked and sighed, edging each other into companionable terror. I did my best to ignore the shadowy corners of the hall, the open door into the grey murk of the church, where a figure could easily linger unseen. The wind grew restless as we sat, soft whistles and whispers dropping into a moan that stopped me in my tracks. I never grew used to being afraid, which I often was, needing only to be alone in the dark or left a few steps behind in a strange place.

A movement at my side made me jump; a pony-tailed girl reached for a glue stick. During the games, I'd learnt her name was June. She smiled her apology, sitting back. Sticking done, she watched me, fingers twisting the end of her hair.

"Are you okay?" Her voice was soft, but not quiet enough.

The other girls looked at me. "You're not scared, are you?" one of them said, sounding delighted.

"Of course not."

I glared at June until she went back to her glitter. But I was terrified and, even worse, desperate for the toilet. I didn't dare leave the hall, step out of the side door into the night, traipse across the yard at the back of the church. There'd be nothing but moonlight or maybe the weak glow of a distant lamppost until I reached the concrete toilet block. I'd have to open its door wide, lean deep into the darkness, groping blindly for the pull cord. What if my hand met pale, cold fingers that tore at mine, dragging me into the shadows?

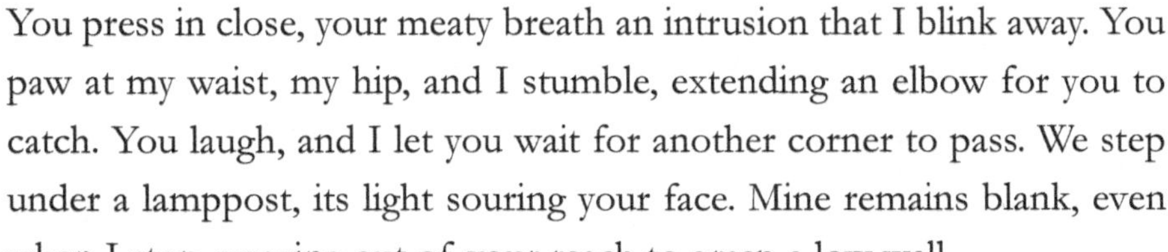

You press in close, your meaty breath an intrusion that I blink away. You paw at my waist, my hip, and I stumble, extending an elbow for you to catch. You laugh, and I let you wait for another corner to pass. We step under a lamppost, its light souring your face. Mine remains blank, even when I stop, swaying out of your reach to grasp a low wall.

"I need to pee," I say, and flop onto the arched stones that top the brick, digging my nails into moss and grit.

"Can't it wait?" you say.

I shake my head, glance over my shoulder at the Baptist church and hall that lies beyond the blank square of grass, beyond the wall.

No, I wasn't going to that toilet block. Instead, when all the adults were occupied, I edged out of another door, and hurried to the room we'd left our coats in. It was brightly lit and half-filled with stacked chairs. Overlapping wooden legs poked skywards and I climbed between them, heart beating hard, until I reached a corner where I couldn't be easily seen. I pulled my tights and knickers down enough to squat. The relief was immense, the warmth of the spreading damp patch on the carpet only lightly scented, but threatening my sensible shoes, so I got up and out quickly.

I'd just reached the edge of the chairs when the lights went out. There were screams from the hall, then irritated adult voices. Black shapes swam as I swung my head, panic rising. Then a creak to my left, a blinding flash, and something heavy knocked me over. I heard its furious groan as my knees slammed into the floor. I shrieked and scrambled up, but it gripped my shoulder, rasping and wheezing.

It hissed, cold fingers shifting to my neck, mouth close to my ear, a sudden smell of dirt and sweat and old things rotting. I twisted away, throwing myself across the room, faint grey light from a small window not enough to avoid knocking my knees and hips into heavy wooden limbs. I flung the door open and stumbled out when a bright light swung into my face. Hands up, I squinted at June.

"It's alright," she said, as I heard another creak behind me.

"In there," I said, and tried to explain between shuddering breaths. She swept the light of her torch across the open cloakroom door, but nothing slithered out. No woman in white was caught in the torch beam.

"Come on," I say, pushing the gate open before you can stop me. "There's toilets here."

"Is that a church?" you say.

"Why? You a vampire?"

You don't laugh, only follow me across the grass to the yard at the back and the concrete block. I think that you will like this place. The only neighbours are the dead, pressed up against the church. The toilet block walls are thick enough to muffle screams. I take care to stay ahead of you.

"It'll be locked," you say, but I know it isn't.

June handed me another torch like hers, so large it took both of my hands to hold it.

"Where'd you get it?" I said, gripping it tightly, shining it into every corner.

"My dad helps out here sometimes." She shrugged. "He's good at gardens."

Then the lights blinked back on, and we squinted and grinned at each other. We turned to go back to the hall, but with every step, my skirt slapped against the back of my tights, sodden. I stopped, horrified. June's grin faded.

"This way," she said. "Quick."

She led me to a silent kitchen, leaving the light off. Cups and saucers loomed in precarious stacks, urns squatting on worktops, their dull skin striped silver by moonlight. June went straight for a cardboard box tucked under a shelf, pulling it out.

"Lost property," she said, starting to dig through its contents.

"Perfect." She handed me a plain black top and purple skirt. "I'll keep watch." She turned her back, facing the door as I changed. I scrunched my dress into a ball, hiding its shameful wet centre.

"What about this?" I said.

June chewed her lower lip, then rummaged in a draw for a plastic bag. I didn't take it, only felt a pinch in my nose, and I blinked to stop the blurring of my vision.

"My mum," I said. "She'll be cross."

June nodded, put the dress in the bag, tucked it under her arm. "We'll think of a plan. Come on."

There's no moon tonight, and you fumble for your phone. Its light throws my dancing shadow onto the toilet block.

"People thought this place was haunted," I say.

"Right." You're not listening, too busy groping for me, your fingers tightening on my arm.

I think of the bruises June had after you hurt her, holding her down in the dirt and the dark. I think of her face when we found her, hours after she'd disappeared, dragged into the cold night by you. And I'm not afraid as I push open the door and step into the pitch black.

I took June's hand and we went back to the others. A strange man stood with the adults as they thanked him for fixing the lights, waving away the apology he tried to make. June ran to him.

"Dad. I got the torches."

"Clever girl," he said.

When my mother arrived to collect me, I asked if June could come over.

"It's nice that you've made a friend," she said, smiling at June and her father as though they were only humouring me. She didn't comment on my clothes until we got home and I took my coat off.

"Me and June swapped," I said as she frowned. "It was a game."

She breathed out heavily through her nose.

"I can't find the light switch," I say.

You huff, but follow me into the toilet block, your silhouette framed for a moment in the paler grey of the doorway. One more step, two, and I dart aside. The blow knocks you into the wall, and you fall to your knees. We prize open your mouth and slip a gift onto your tongue.

"From June," I say.

A second blow and you're out.

I stare at your slack face, remember that June still dreams of you and wakes shrieking, fingers clawed in the bedsheets. Now I can offer you the same. We only have to wait.

Our parents arranged for June to visit one Saturday, and by the time the date came around, I'd almost forgotten about my ill-fated dress. When my mother told me to answer June's knock at the door, June's father stood there as well. He smiled down at me, passing over my dress, washed, ironed, neatly folded. I caught again the gentle scent of earth and rain and vegetation. I stared up at him, recalibrating, the effort leaving me open-mouthed.

"Thank you for lending this to me," June said.

Her father's slight nod confirmed he understood, protecting me from my mother's wrath as he guarded his own daughter from the unkindness of the world. As I would guard her, too, from then on, as best I could.

You wake slowly, our gift making you sweat and tremble. I smile, eager to see what you make of me now. When I hiss, your eyes focus on the pale blur of my dress, the tangle of hair draped over my face. I take my time raising my head until my gaze meets yours. I jerk towards you, and you flinch back in your chair, crying out, tugging against the ropes binding your wrists, your ankles, your chest. I move closer, letting my mouth drop open, the liquid I've been holding spilling down my chin. My face is close enough to yours to feel your ragged breath on my cold skin, see how wide your eyes are as you whimper.

I look briefly to the shadows, where a man waits, dirt and fury ingrained into his skin. Returning my face to yours, I raise myself to my full height, fling my arms wide, and scream.

MOUSE-CLOWN

Z. C. LOKI

THE FIRST TIME any of us spoke about the Mouse-clown was on a Wednesday, out in the courtyard behind the dormitory, next to the playground what stood so very close to the edge of the Woods. Jonesy sat beside Smith out on the bench, and he said to her, "You just would not believe what little Robbie said he saw."

And Smith asked, "Lord, what could it be this time?"

So Jonesy said, "Right there, near those monkey-bars, he said he seen some sorta weird Mouse-clown tryna wave him over into the Woods."

And Smith said, "Boy, he's a wild thing, ain't he?"

As they said these things, some of our kids overheard the conversation and made no efforts in pretending as if they weren't eavesdropping. When Smith noticed them all staring at her and Jonesy, she shushed him and told him not to let the kids overhear what they were saying—she didn't want them getting spooked.

But it was too late. Our kids had heard enough. The mythos had begun; its genesis, then.

By the time they had all come back home from school the next day, every single one of them had heard about the mysterious monster, and by the time supper rolled around, each of them had their own personalized tall-tale of the dread Mouse-clown.

"I saw him sleeping in the Woods!" one said.

"Well, I seen him waiting around in the rain!" another said.

All that day, our kids ran around and in and out and between and to and from each of the six rooms of the dormitory, sharing imaginations and exchanging mythologies. Up the stairs, into 2-C where the bipolar poet Smith still hadn't stopped grieving the death of her girlfriend, where she raised her daughter and goddaughter alone. Zipping over to 2-B, where the perfidious Hernandez and his three adopted boys lived, forever in legal limbo. Striking right past 2-A, which sat empty. Down the stairs towards 1-A, where the craven Mills stayed with his three sons, never leaving home without his gun. Further, further, passing 1-B, which had been home to McCumbers before her untimely death. Running by 1-C, where Jonesy raised two boys and one girl, such a promising dactyloscopist he was. Onwards, onwards, spilling out into the backyard, past the smoking area what none of us used, past the parking lot what none of us could afford. Finally arriving at the playground what stood at the cusp of the courtyard so very close to the edge of the Woods, the edge of their world and all they knew to be safe, the precipice of the domain of all monsters.

In the beginning, we were mostly dismissive of the elusive Mouse-clown, despite how powerfully the stories of it were gripping our children. In fact, Mills even thought it was almost funny how riled-up his kids were getting over such a silly cryptid. But by Friday, the humor and half-charm had worn away. Our kids were becoming so terribly, awfully scared, they weren't just exchanging mere ghost stories by that point; no, they were starting to genuinely fear for one another's lives.

By the next day, the concerns over the looming threat of the malevolent Mouse-clown had expanded into all sorts of precautions a kid needed to take in order to ensure that they wouldn't be stolen into the Woods. Extensive rules had been laid out, and every single one of our kids wholly believed in the dire implications of what breaking those rules would entail. They'd grown too afraid of playing on the playground, having forbidden themselves from even going outside at all. So, in turn, we forbid our kids from ever speaking about the ridiculous Mouse-clown again. Enough had been enough; they were whirl-winding themselves into dangerous paranoia.

However, our attempts had come far too late. Their rules were set. Their doctrines were defined. The sublime fear of the Mouse-clown was enshrined into their minds.

Whatever we tried, it never mattered, for our kids had become stalwarts of anxiety. They barred themselves from being children, grounded themselves from their favorite activities, punished themselves for their own perceived safety. All just to avoid the dread Mouse-clown.

By Sunday, even Hernandez started feeding into the hysteria. He told us, "It just don't make no damn sense that *all* our kids would be so scared about some freak in the Woods for five whole days if there weren't actually some freak that's been in the Woods for five whole days!"

We tried telling him he was being ridiculous, that he was a grown man who shouldn't be holding any stock in children's make-believe. But still, he said he was more than happy to let all his kids remain indoors, just in case. Later that night, and you wouldn't believe this, but Jonesy said, that night, as he was taking out the trash, he could see the lights on in Hernandez's room; the blinds were parted, and fat little fingers held them open, as if the fearful father himself were peeking out into the Woods in search of the monster.

That very next day, hell was nearing eruption. Mills, frantic, almost manic, had us all examine the arm of his eldest boy, Tommy. A large bruise circumnavigated the boy's wrist, and we all agreed it looked *kinda sorta just like* the handprint of an adult. Mills said his boy swore up and down that it'd been the one-and-only Mouse-clown—that he'd fallen on the ground while taking out the trash because the Mouse-clown had tried dragging him behind the dumpsters. And before any of us had come to any sort of consensus on what to do next, Hernandez went and dialed the Law and told them plumb near everything. The Law reprimanded him over the phone for wasting their time with a ghost story, and later, Jonesy reprimanded him for acting so hastily.

On Tuesday, right at around 8pm, an ice storm hit and the power fell out black like a winter solstice. At that very moment, most of our kids began screaming, and those that didn't scream just cried to themselves, feebly, silently, afraid of even their own voices. Since we were all just as strung-out and tensed-up as our kids, we agreed to hunker down in Smith's room for that night. After we got the kids corralled up and moved and somewhat calmed, Mills and Jonesy went through the halls to ensure all the doors and windows were locked. With the others gone,

Hernandez confessed to Smith that he felt a lot safer up on the second floor. Smith replied it might calm the kids down quite a bit if they could trick them into believing the whole thing was a sleepover, like they were all on an adventure back through time, back to the old days, back to Abraham Lincoln times.

But we never did get to try that.

Smith had just started lighting the candles when, from out of nowhere, Jonesy hollered from down on the first floor, "I see him! I see the son-of-a-bitch right there! He's creeping around in the Woods! Right there!"

Jonesy grabbed a baseball bat from underneath one of the sofas, and he bolted out the door, screaming at whatever it was he'd seen. Mills tried to hold him back, tried to reason with him, tried to beg him not to act so hastily, but his pleas fell on ears deafened by adrenaline. So, instead, Mills started screaming for Hernandez to come and help him restrain Jonesy. However, by the time Hernandez had made it downstairs, Jonesy broke free from Mills's grip and ran off, splashing through the freezing rain. So, Mills ran off after Jonesy, after which Hernandez ran off after Mills, and Smith was left alone with eleven frantic children, over half of whom were now in mortal fear for the safety of their fathers.

Our kids were stolen into panic, swallowed by hysteria. A mob mentality of insane adrenaline united them into oblivion when suddenly CLONK! a tree branch fell and smacked against the window and CRACKA-CRACK-BOOM! a lightning bolt struck a little too close to the dormitory and HWOO-HWOO! there in the distance HWOO-HWOO! a train screamed into the air and HWOO-HWOO! that was that.

Chaos reigned supreme on that most unfortunate night, and all our little children fought against Smith as she so desperately fought to hold the bedroom door closed. But our kids knew the ravenous Mouse-clown was in that very room, and they knew they needed to escape it. They knew the impending monster was the one who'd cut the power! It was the one banging on the window! It was the one throwing thunder at the building! It was the one screaming into the air, voraciously, starving for the souls and the flesh and the bones of children! So they battled against Smith, harder, more violent, and they threw themselves at her like a cackle of hyenas dismantling a solitary lion, biting, scratching, clawing at her eyes, and she screamed when her very own girls leapt upon her and beat their fists against her face. She screamed when the door was flung open, when the kids tore her grip from the handle and dragged her away by her feet and then spilled out into the hallway as gushingly as the storm outside.

Chaos claimed sovereignty over the halls of our dormitory, and all our terrified kids ran to hide in any other room—any room except for *that* room. Pulling, shoving, pushing, they fought to be the first down the stairs, the furthest away from the pursuing monster, until one of them tumbled down the steps and cracked open his poor little head wide across the banister. They all ran past him, and they trampled his corpse, and they bumped into one another and cried in that supreme darkness, "Mouse-clown! Mouse-clown!" They screamed its name in the blind of the dark as they did battle with the night itself. In everything, they saw their doom and torture and sufferance and death.

Chaos showed no mercy, and POW! …POW! POW! the unmistakable noise of three gunshots terrified everyone's ears— from the backyard, where three of us had given chase to that abominable apparition. Smith screamed and crawled until finding that corded landline phone, and alone, in the bleeding dark, she dialed the Law. In the background of her call, the dispatchers could hear the cacophonous war-cry of ten murderous children and the desperate weeping of a broken woman.

And this time, they took the call seriously.

This time, they came to see the matter.

By daybreak, the entire dormitory and its surrounding properties had been designated as an active crime scene. Smith had been diagnosed with a severe nervous breakdown along with several wounds of varying severity. Our kids were all seen by officers, therapists, and doctors alike, and all of them shared their god-fearing worries about the blood-starved deity known only as the Mouse-clown.

In the Woods, some forty to forty-five feet in, they found Hernandez dead with a gunshot wound to the head. Half-a-mile west of him, they found Mills, also dead, with a gunshot wound to the pelvis. By the dirt on his knees and the trail of blood from Hernandez's body to his own, it was determined that he'd crawled around for some time after being shot, panicking, trying to navigate his way out of the Woods before eventually bleeding out. Just a few yards north of his body, they came across a pool of Jonesy's blood. Elsewhere, scattered at various points further north, were his wallet, then his keys, then his shirt, then his shoes. But that's all they ever found regarding Jonesy, and he's remained missing all these years since.

Tales of the dread Mouse-clown have since become indelibly woven into the fabric of our community's history. A spirit of mass destruction, having ridden in on that hellacious storm. A peculiar shade of the night, having come to witness bloodshed. A figment of panicked minds, of insanity, of broken streams of consciousness. A monstrous person, possessed with vile ambitions. A devil, what once haunted our eleven young children, now haunts a city of thousands.

Few things have made as considerable excitement as our story from a campus near the Woods, and the excitement generated from the cursed outcomes of that night has ruined our children forever. For them, the mystery will never be solved. The horrors, never over. The memories, never cured.

THE ECHO AND THE ALTAR

P. N. HARRISON

My dad was fresh back from Vietnam when he started shouting about the hum. It started with half-lucid mutters in the middle of the night. At first, my mom didn't think much of it; the doctors had told her that a lot of guys have "trouble coming back from the war." That's how Mom always said it, anyway. It was never PTSD or even an outdated term, like shell-shocked. As a reporter, I've talked to a lot of veterans and their families over the years, and they all use the same phrase: "trouble coming back from the war."

So that's what Mom thought was happening when Dad got louder at night, his murmurings slowly turning into full-throated sentences and, finally, shouts. But what really got her concerned, and what ultimately led to him going away, was when the screams started to come during the day. I'm not old enough to remember it, but when I eventually got courage enough to ask what had happened to Dad, she said we'd be eating as a family or sitting in front of the TV for the nightly news, and he would just carry on. He was never violent, neither to us nor to himself, but his *episodes*—that's the term she used—became more and more common. Exactly what he would say changed, but the topic never did.

Through the screams, he always mentioned the hum.

I have no memory of when Dad went into the hospital, but he was there for most of my life. Mom and I visited him at first, up until the "episodes" got so frequent we couldn't even really talk to him. Then we stopped. We wrote letters to him, and Mom would go to see him herself (I remember staying with Grandma and Grandpa when she did), but she never took us back after I was about three. I felt guilty about it when I was a kid, and that feeling only got worse when I was a teenager.

Finally, when I was in college, I decided to go see him myself. I lived across the state by then in West Texas, so it was a bit of a trip, but I felt like if I was going to be my own person, I needed to see the truth about my father. I called the hospital, and the doctors were reluctant to let me visit. He was "a unique and fragile" case, they told me. But I had it in my head, and I wasn't about to be given the bum's rush. He wasn't listed as dangerous in any capacity, so they didn't have any real room to keep me away.

Still, I wasn't ready for the man I saw.

My mom had told me a lot about my dad and what he was like before the war. He'd been a reporter like I am now and, the way she put it, as sharp as they come. She'd shown me pictures, and it was always of the same whip-thin man, short and healthy with a gummy smile and what seemed to be a perpetually cocked head. That's a weird thing to remember, but it's what I noticed. It was like every photo had caught him right as he was mulling over a quote from his latest interview. That expression is still how I think of him, when I can think about him.

They let me know on the phone before I got there I wouldn't be able to talk to him. "His condition isn't conducive to those kinds of visits," is how they described it. Again, they used that word: "condition." It was just as well. He hadn't seen me in nearly twenty years, and I didn't want to agitate him or cause any stress. Instead, if he was having a good day, the doctors told me I could observe him during some of his structured free time. I agreed.

I arrived at the hospital, and the staff led me to a large room. I was taken aback at how nice it was and how much it looked like what I imagined it would. There were scattered round tables and patients sitting in plastic chairs, keeping themselves busy. They were talking and playing checkers, chess, and cards with each other. Honestly, they might have looked like they were at a Saturday morning social gathering at the VA, if it weren't for the hospital gowns.

One of the doctors directed me to a specific patient. I could tell right off it was my dad. Even though he was older, he still had the same slight, wiry build, and he had his head angled in the same inquisitive way I'd seen all my life in photographs. He sat in front of a picture window that spanned a large part of the wall and overlooked a modest courtyard. His head was facing downward as he read through a book: *The Coastal Castles of Northern England.* The doctors told me the window was his favorite spot, and that he loved to read. This made me smile. Mom had said he was a voracious reader, and I was glad to see that the years and the "episodes" hadn't taken this away from him.

So, I stood there and watched him read for a while, and it was nice at first. I honestly couldn't see why he had stayed there all these years.

But it didn't last.

It began subtly. He closed his book and tugged at his ears. He started shaking his head, slowly at first, then more vigorously. Then the shouting started. It wasn't words, and it wasn't like any screams I had ever heard before. It was like something visceral had welled up inside him and exploded out. Something guttural. Anguished. The orderlies flanked him with rehearsed precision. If this was a movie, there would have been a struggle, and someone would have come running with a syringe full of sedative. Instead, the staff simply lead him away. But, the whole time, he kept on yelling. As the howls grew louder, I could make out a few words.

"The hum! Stop! It won't stop!"

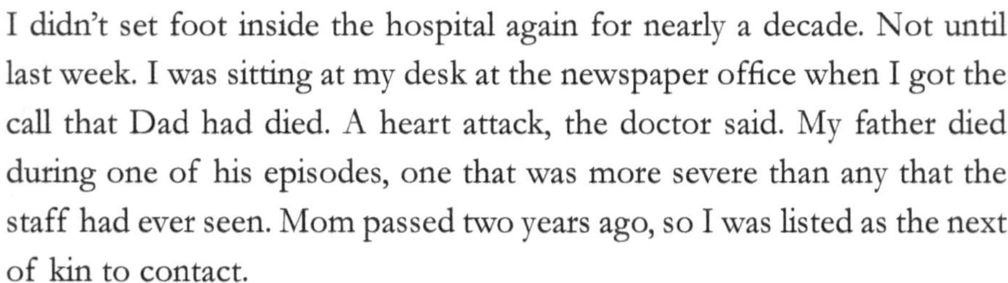

I didn't set foot inside the hospital again for nearly a decade. Not until last week. I was sitting at my desk at the newspaper office when I got the call that Dad had died. A heart attack, the doctor said. My father died during one of his episodes, one that was more severe than any that the staff had ever seen. Mom passed two years ago, so I was listed as the next of kin to contact.

I'd moved to Kansas by then, so it took a full day to drive down to Texas to close out the last of the business with the hospital. It was strange, putting the final marks on a life that I had barely known, but that had been such a large part of my own life, all the same. I finished up the paperwork, and they placed a plastic bag on the table in front of me: Dad's possessions. Every testament to the last twenty-five years of my dad's life, right there in a mid-sized trash bag. I didn't dig through it at the hospital; I don't think I had it in me, truth be told. At the moment, the whole situation felt too abstract, too immaterial. Sifting through that bag was something concrete and final.

I spent the next ten days arranging for Dad's gravesite and getting him buried. Dad, of course, didn't really have anyone close to him left aside from a brother and a sister, so we just had a small graveside service. And, just like that, it was over. I hugged my goodbyes with what remained of my family, and I got in my car to go back to Kansas.

Even after I got back, I still wasn't ready to go through the bag the hospital had given me. It's funny: when I was little, Mom had always put "from Mom and Dad" on my birthday and Christmas presents. But this bag…well, it was the first thing I could remember I had ever actually gotten from my dad. I let it sit on my writing desk, greeting me every time I walked into my apartment. It remained there, unopened, for weeks. Until yesterday.

There wasn't much inside to go through. Mom and I had gotten rid of all his clothes years ago, and I had his service medal—a Bronze Star— inside a shadowbox in a storage room across town. What the bag held were the possessions he'd accumulated over the course of twenty-five years of life inside East Texas State Mental Hospital. There were several books, mostly about travel and writing, with decades-old publication dates. Mom must have sent them to him not long after he went into the institution. I turned these books over in my hands and sighed. Travel… During those early days, Mom must have still thought he would come home, ready to tour the world with her. I guess some part of Dad never let go of the idea, either. One by one, I picked through these misplaced hopes and placed them to the side until I got to the bottom of the bag.

That's when I first saw the journal. It was a beige composition book, the kind that I saw all the time when I was a student in the late seventies and early eighties. The pages and the cover had browned around the edges, but it was in remarkably good shape for something that was more than twenty years old.

I opened it up—the crease along the side cracked and a bit of paper-dust fell off as the corners tore. I had never seen Dad's writing and was surprised at how much it looked like my own. Jagged and messy, a reporter's handwriting. It was obvious pretty quickly this was some kind of therapeutic journaling. It was a single, extended entry, dated from not long after Dad went into the hospital.

My hands shook. I didn't know why then, but I think I get it now. Aside from my visit almost ten years prior, I hadn't heard or read a word from my dad since I was three years old. And there I was, about to dive into his private thoughts. Reading this was the closest thing to a conversation I had ever—would ever—have with my dad. I ran my fingers over the words, and I started to read.

◆———————————◆

November 24, 1976

Dr. Hendrix has me making this journal. I have trouble talking about what happened to me because of my condition. But he thinks that, since I'm a writer and all, it might help me to write things out instead. I guess that makes sense. If I have one of my screaming fits, I can always just pick back up where I was after I stop. So here I am, with a pen in my hand, sitting at a desk like a medieval monk. I miss the typewriter I had in the newsroom. I miss a goddamn lot of things.

Anyway, it all happened back in 1972. My platoon was set up at the base of the mountains in Quảng Ngãi. The scenery was honestly a nice change of pace, or as close to a "nice" as things can get during a war. We had been in Cu Chi before this, searching out tunnel locations and making our way through that bomb-scarred wasteland. The whole place looked like the damned moon landing after all the ordnance runs had leveled the place. After that, the mountains and the forests at the foot of them were, objectively, downright beautiful. Hell, in the evenings me and the other guys used to sit in the shade with the big blocks of ice they'd send us. I never understood how they got those blocks out there without melting. They'd just show up, wrapped in those big rice leaves. We'd spin our beers on the blocks and shoot the shit in the shadow of the mountain. It would have been idyllic if the whole place wasn't trying to kill us.

Well, it was early one morning, before the day really got started. A bunch of us were watching the mountain fog roll in when our lieutenant, a pretty decent guy named Nash, came over with our orders. There had been reports, he said, of Viet Cong clusters up in the mountains. They were coming down at night and causing problems for the GI platoons based at the foot. But it wasn't the normal kind of harassment bullshit, like snipers and sabotage. No, Nash said that people were straight up going missing. The VC would sneak in past the lookouts at night, grab someone, and then disappear back up into the hills before anyone could notice. There weren't mass disappearances or anything, but it was enough to spook command.

Our orders were to go up into the mountains and track down the troublemakers. I won't lie, none of us were very keen on the idea. We'd been doing search and destroy duty on tunnels for a long time and, while it was hell, it was at least a devil we knew. The mountains were something different. They were huge, and the fog made it impossible to navigate. Seriously, if you've ever been in a whiteout snowstorm, it was just like that; you'd have trouble seeing the other guys in your platoon, much less a VC or a booby-trap. On top of that, there were caves all over the place. I've heard some people say they're some of the most beautiful caves in the world, but we all knew some Charlie could slip into one of them after an ambush, and we wouldn't have a snowball's chance in hell of finding them.

Still, we had our orders, so we were going to march up into the lowest parts of the mountains and poke around like good little soldiers. All seventeen of us gathered up our gear, and off we trekked.

As expected, we couldn't see shit. It was just mist and white and the faint outline of Corporal Venn's backpack for hours. He was our maps expert, and I could see the spots where the map rolls bulged against the green canvas sides of his pack. Luckily, Charlie must not have seen us either, because we traipsed around all day and didn't find a trace of the VC. I wouldn't call it a relaxing hike in the hills, but at least we all made it back down safe and sound.

But not all of us made it back up the next day.

When roll-call came around that morning, Venn didn't. The lookouts hadn't seen a thing. We searched all over for him but didn't find a goddamn trace. No struggle, no blood, no nothing. Just gone, vanished like piss in the rain. Lieutenant Nash radioed in the disappearance.

Still, we had a job to do, and we were a little more eager to do it than the day before. Venn wasn't exactly a pleasant guy to be around, all piss and vinegar and a talker, but he was one of our own, and we wanted to know what happened to him, or at least get a little payback. We packed up our gear—Franklin's pack was a little heavier because he had to carry Venn's maps—and we made our way up the trail on the mountainside again. Whoever had snatched Venn had a head start on us, so we weren't exactly confident we'd catch up. That is, unless they *wanted* us to catch up. We were a little spooked from what had happened to Venn, and we were all more than a little wary that this whole thing was a trap to lead us to an ambush up in the mists.

We didn't have to wait too long to find out. After searching for a little over two hours, the first shots came at us. Luckily, whoever was shooting at us couldn't see through the fog much better than we could, and within seconds, we all hit the ground and returned fire. With the visibility, it was all sound and fury and not a whole lot to show for it. We didn't hit a thing, and neither did they. Without surprise on their side, the ambushers retreated pretty quick.

We gathered our wits and surveyed the scene. It was obvious where the shots had come from. By the number of spent rifle shells on the ground, there'd been only a couple of shooters, and they'd retreated to the north. We followed the scuffed soil and bullet casings, searching for where they rushed off to. The investigation eventually found the start of a small side trail, camouflaged in the fog. Usually, these kinds of trailheads were booby-trapped or had snipers stationed not far off, so we were damn careful as we started down the path.

But we came to the end of the trail with no resistance. It was just a sheer rock face, too high to scale with no handholds. We fanned out and looked around, trying to find if there was another side trail or something we had missed. As for me, I was trained to keep my eyes low and search for marks on the ground that might clue us in on tunnel entrances. That's how I found the cave.

It was a small opening, rounded and only about two feet at its highest. I might not have even noticed it was the entrance to a cave if it hadn't been for the scratched soil from people crawling in and out of it. We all—myself especially—knew what it meant; one of us was going to have to go down there. Everyone glanced at the cave, then back over at me and Perkins. Thin and short, we were the usual "tunnel rats" for the group.

Perkins and I had both been in more holes than a sailor on shore leave, but this one was different. All the tunnels down in Cu Chi were underground, and while they never stopped being the most dangerous part of our job, we were at least used to them. They all had common features, things we could expect. This cave, though? It was different. Unfamiliar. Perkins, the crazy bastard, always got excited when it came time to shimmy down a tunnel. But as we looked at each other and then back at the tiny opening, I could see the worry in his face, and he sure as hell could see it in mine. One of us was heading in there, and neither of us wanted the job.

I've heard some platoons—ones with a lot of littler guys—drew straws to see who got stuck with tunneling duty. Since it's just me and Perkins, we settled for a game of rock-paper-scissors. Loser goes into the hole. We sighed, then counted off: one, two, three. I looked down at his two splayed fingers, then at my flattened palm. Scissors beat paper.

I began my usual pre-descent ritual, stripping off my helmet, flak jacket, and fatigue shirt. Holes were too small for our rifles, so I set aside my M-16, and Lieutenant Nash handed me the Colt M1911 pistol alongside the flashlight he kept in his pack for situations like this. Franklin got down in the prone position and fired a rifle volley into the entrance to make sure the way was clear. Then I got down on my own belly and started to squeeze through the entrance.

Rats like me call the inside of the tunnels the "black echo". The "black" part may seem obvious, but there's nothing normal about how absolute the darkness is in these passageways. Once you get just a little past the entrance, you can't see anything without a flashlight, and even that only does a little to cut through that blackness, just enough that you can see what's right in front of you. The "echo" part? It's hard to explain to someone who hasn't been down there. You would think it would be total quiet, all cut off from the surface like it is. And in a way, it is. From the instant you go down into a hole, you can't hear anything from the outside. But you hear everything that happens on the inside. Every scrape against the walls, every shuffle of your pants' fabric, every little thing reverberates through the tunnels. It seems like it's coming from all around you.

The echo in this cave was worse than any I'd gone down into before. From the second I blocked the hole with my body and started crawling, the resonance was everywhere. Nothing loud, at least not at first, just a constant shuffling and thumping that filled up the space all around me.

I wriggled through about ten feet of entry tunnel, then it turned gradually to the right. At this point, the path broadened out and the ceiling raised a little, and I could kneel and do a kind of uncomfortable crouch-walk. I kept the flashlight and my pistol pointed forward and crept my way along, scanning the floor and walls. The VC love to booby-trap passages like this with captured US grenades. A grenade blast in such an enclosed space turns a body into paste. Not long after I started going down below, I had stumbled across what remained of a Vietnamese guerrilla whose booby-trap had detonated early. He was all over the tunnel. The walls, the floor, the ceiling,. Ever since then, I'd walked slower and been a little more careful in my tunnel ratting.

That's about when I first heard it—the hum. Normal cave echoes are irregular, and the sounds range from subtle rustling to heavier footfalls. This hum, it was soft and steady, like the sound my Dad's old ham radio used to make when it was searching for a signal. Except someone tuned every rock in this tunnel to the same frequency. It was all around me, the constant buzzing.

It was weird, but I honestly thought nothing about it at first. I assumed it actually was a radio, part of a VC encampment resonating from deep inside the cave. This thought made me make sure I could reach my grenades. If there was some kind of base or outpost, I would be outnumbered, but I could just roll one of those in and clear the whole thing out. I kept creeping forward, following the gently curving walls of the tunnels.

In underground passages, there were always turnarounds dug into the walls to help the VC with maneuverability and ambushes. So far, I hadn't seen anything like that here. It's like the place hadn't been designed with combat in mind. Even creepier, I didn't notice any signs of recent shovel work. There were marks on the ceilings and on the walls, sure, but they weren't fresh. Whatever this cave was, it had been here a long time, way longer than the US had been in the war. It might have even been there since before the revolt started against the French. I tried to tell myself none of that was important, that the only thing that mattered was clearing out the cave and getting back into the open alive.

The deeper into the cave I went, the louder the hum became. It still wasn't loud, by any stretch, but it was getting hard to ignore. It was behind me, above me. I could even feel a soft vibration in the soles of my boots. Like the whole fucking mountain was tuning up for its big number at a recital.

The humming was so distracting that I almost didn't notice the Vietnamese guy round the corner of the tunnel and level his pistol at me. I fell back at the last second, and his bullets hit the ceiling. Luckily for me, this guy must have been pretty green, because a more experienced enemy would have rolled a grenade around the corner, and I would have been a pile of slop. I hit my spine and the back of my head hard, but I leaned forward and fired my Colt where I thought his head was. I pulled myself back to a crouch, gun still raised, and I swept my flashlight over the tunnel.

My would-be assassin laid on the ground, gurgling, weakly thrashing around. The bullet had torn into his throat. He was older than me, probably fifty years old, and he wasn't dressed like any VC I had ever seen. It's not like Charlie have standard issue uniforms or anything, but this guy wasn't in normal villagers' clothing, either. His outfit was tight-fitting, and he wore makeshift knee pads made from old tire rubber. But there was an element of formality to it, too, almost like a religious vestment. The fabric of his top was supple, and there was an unfamiliar design sown into the sleeves. The same symbol, a kind of hollow diamond shape, was on a pendant around his wrist. Gradually, the burbling in his throat stopped, and his darting eyes were still.

This wasn't the first time I'd killed a man in the tunnels, and while I've certainly had my fair share of nightmares about what I've done, I'd rather kill than die. It was the next part that never set right with me—picking over a fresh corpse like a crow for booby-traps and gear. Still, it was the only way to make sure I wouldn't wind up dripping from the walls from a jerry-rigged grenade. I unloaded his pistol and tucked the magazine into the back of my pants. The gunfire had left my ears ringing. But, even then, I could still hear the hum as though the rocks were broadcasting it directly into my skull. And, deafened as I was, the sound only kept getting louder as I made my way further into the cavern.

I don't know how long I went down that path, but by the time it started to widen, the humming was all I could hear. The roof of the tunnel sloped upwards, gradually allowing me to rise out of my uncomfortable half-squat. Up ahead, the end of the tunnel curved and, around it, came a faint glow of light. I pressed myself against the wall and slid along as quietly as I could. I poked the barrel of my gun around the corner first; I just knew some VC was waiting to paint the wall with the insides of my skull as soon as I peeked my head around. I just hoped the humming was as loud for anyone else up ahead as it was for me. That way, they might have at least missed the gunfire from the previous exchange, and I could have some element of surprise on my side. I pocketed my flashlight and pulled out a grenade; I was going to be ready to lob it and fall back around the corner the second I saw there was too much for me to handle. Both my eyes and my pistol edged around the corner.

The chamber the tunnel opened into was massive, way bigger than anything I had seen underground and far too spacious to cover with a single grenade's blast. It was almost cube-shaped, like someone had carved out a giant box inside the mountain, but the walls were too high to have been made by hand. The few electric lanterns hanging from nails weren't nearly enough to light the whole room, but I wasn't about to let go of my grenade or lower my Colt to reach for my flashlight. I had expected it to be swarming with VC. I scanned the room, pistol raised, ready to fire at the first sign of movement. Except there wasn't any movement. Just a big, still room and an unexplainable racket in my ears. I was having a hard time concentrating, but I still recognized that in cases such as these, stillness is profoundly bad. It's like all the potential energy in the war coils up, ready to spring out at the first idiot who makes a sudden move. Still, I had to clear the place and find out what had happened to Venn. I took a wary step into the room.

The hum detonated, for lack of a better word. All the gunfire and ordnance explosions I'd heard since arriving in Vietnam eighteen months ago, none of it was as loud as the humming. The sound was sudden and intense enough to knock me on my ass. I scrambled, sure I was going to look up to see every Charlie in the cave pointing guns at me. I'd have just enough time to give a dumb smile before they perforated me.

But there weren't any guns or VC. Just a wide-open chamber with shadows covering half of its space. I lay there, halfway sitting up and my gun raised as I tried to pull my thoughts together. My head ached by this point, and my eyes weren't processing what I saw. I'd have to stare for four of five seconds at a time to really know if there was actually anything in front of me. And it was with these slow, stupid eyes that I first spotted it—the altar.

It's been more than three years, and I still have trouble explaining what I saw. I've started to draw it out half a dozen times, but I stop myself every time. Two dimensions can't really contain the thing. Still, I'll try to describe it the best I can. It was an altar in the manner that it sat atop a table-like block of stone. That was the only familiar thing about it. A figure carved from the same stone as the walls of the mountain stood on top of the slab. It was human-like in the sense that it had our shape—a head and two legs and two arms—but it was angular in a way that didn't seem possible. Two spindly arms reached upwards toward the ceiling of the cavern, and four long fingers crooked outwards at right angles from its hands. The head sat atop a freakishly slender neck, and those fingers hooked inside the face's gaping mouth and stretched it open in a way that made the toothless maw cover most of its visage. The torso split into a "Y" at its pelvis then reconverged at its neck, creating a kind of hollow, diamond shape. And inside the empty spot in the diamond was a blackness, deeper than anything I've ever seen before, darker than even the black echo of the tunnels. Yet, somehow this emptiness pulsated and throbbed, like a gargantuan throat swallowing in all the lantern light of the room.

I don't know how long I stared at the thing, but suddenly I could see movement out of the corner of my eye. A Vietnamese man, dressed in the same garments as the one I had encountered before, was dragging something across the room. I raised my pistol at the movement, but stopped short. In his arms was another Vietnamese man, dressed in villager's garb. A flow of fresh blood trickled down his forehead, the telltale sign of a recent blow to the head. He stirred weakly in his captor's arms, but he was clearly disoriented, and his arms and legs were bound. But what struck me was that I could see a combat knife tucked into a makeshift holster on his leg.

This man was a VC. His abductors were something else entirely.

I should have opened fire right then, but they still hadn't seen me, and I was too dumbstruck by the humming and that altar to think clearly. I observed as he dragged the VC toward the table. Then he hoisted the body up and held him to the altar. Tendrils, as impossibly black as the maw itself, probed out of the shadows at the center of the statue and seized the Viet Cong. At first, they prodded at the man before snaking around his limbs and torso. Then, the orifice pulsating rhythmically, they began to pull the body into the void.

Something about the room changed as the VC vanished. The hum grew in intensity. Once again, I winced involuntarily and nearly stumbled as the vibrations beneath my feet strengthened.

Despite the turmoil, the man who had offered forth the body simply knelt down in front of the altar, still as the mountain's stone. I didn't move either. Not until I saw a second man dragging Venn across the room.

I couldn't tell if he was alive or dead. He had the same kind of blunt force wound on his head that the Vietnamese captive had, but he wasn't stirring. The man carrying Venn was smaller than his comrade, and he struggled to manage Venn's bound bodyweight as he made his way toward the altar.

Something happened inside me when I saw Venn like that. Like I said, I didn't really like the guy, but the idea of him being pushed inside that…thing…didn't sit right with me. I raised my pistol and started firing at the Vietnamese man as he wrestled with Venn's bulk. The shots tore through him; I barely missed Venn. Yet, he kept on pulling the body across the room. I fired another volley into him, but he just kept on. My clip ran dry, and I fumbled in my belt to grab a new one. The whole time, he moved closer to the altar. He reached the front of it just about the time I was able to slide my spare magazine into my Colt.

He turned to smile at me. Then, still holding Venn in his arms, he jumped into the darkness.

The hum grew all around me as their two forms vanished. The sound was devastating, louder than ever before. I took staggering steps forward, my balance upset both by disbelief and the trembling in the ground. In front of me, the man who had cast in the first offering still knelt. I pushed the barrel of my pistol into the back of his head and asked him what had happened to Venn. He didn't move. I told him I was going to paint the ground with his brains. He still didn't even look up.

I made good on my promise.

My last sight of the chamber as I scurried away was of the tendrils creeping out again to drag themselves across the brain-wet stone of the altar.

When I got back outside, I told the rest of the platoon that I hadn't found Venn. Instead, I said that I had stumbled upon a major VC outpost in the mountain and retreated. I insisted that we needed to call in major ordnance, pronto. I think the Lieutenant could tell how frantic I was, and when we got back to camp, he got on the radio and called in the order. I still didn't tell them what had happened to Venn. Until today, I've never told anybody.

Later that night, me and the rest of the boys spun beers on the ice. They drank and talked about Venn as the bombs lit up the mountainside. But I couldn't bring myself to talk. All I could do was hope the bombs did their job and that the entrance I used to get into the cave was the only way into that chamber. I prayed that whatever it was inside that mountain was gone for good.

But I know better now. Even after I left the tunnels, the hum has never gone away. Somewhere in that mountain, the offerings are still being made. Sometimes the hum gets stronger, the same debilitating intensity that I felt when Venn fell through that lightless abyss.

The journal closed with these words, and I rubbed my eyes as I shut the book and stared across out the window at the courtyard outside

my apartment. For more than two decades, the echoes of what he had seen—what he had heard—had lived within my father's mind. I hoped he'd finally found quiet inside the Texas soil. But, more than anything, I was struck by a singular fear.

When he died, my dad experienced an "episode" that was stronger than any he had ever felt. Something different had been sacrificed. Something massive. Something powerful.

Just what had those tendrils pulled into the darkness?

BLABBERMOUTH

LANE BLEVINS

THE ODOR OF the Bonneville's interior was made from a compilation of oils. French fry grease stained the upholstery, and the air vents gusted the earthy smell of burnt Pennzoil that leaked from a busted gasket under the hood. The singed synthetic material of the ceiling fabric where a smattering of cigarette burns formed a yellowed constellation, along with the musky aftermath of the smoke itself, added to the white trash bouquet.

Patty didn't mind it. The smell of the rainbow face paint glistening on her skin bugged her instead. A white base coat shined like gloopy sunscreen, pink lollipop circles sat on her cheeks, and a hungry red mouth stretched towards her ears. Her eyelids were painted blue and yellow above the red nose, the dizzying asymmetry of primary colors creating Patty Grinter's alter-ego: Blabbermouth the Clown.

With one hand on the peeling leather of the Bonneville's steering wheel and the other hand desperately scratching underneath the orange Raggedy Ann wig on her head, Patty cursed when the traffic light switched from green to yellow. She stomped on the gas pedal, the mud from her floppy, oversized shoes plopping onto the floor mat.

Heck, she said to herself. *Blabbermouth can't be late to sing Happy Fucking Birthday to little Conner Bellamy, can she?*

She wouldn't be skirmishing with the clock at all if she hadn't made a little pit stop at her ex-husband's shoddy gravestone. Maybe "estranged" was more accurate than "ex"; he'd bailed and gone into hiding to drink himself to death before ever signing the divorce proceedings. These days, Patty's greatest sense of joy was standing at his grave, drinking his favorite brand of beer, and smiling from the fact that he'd never get to taste it ever again. Never get to tug the belt from his saggy Wranglers with the *thwip* sound he savored almost as much as he savored the look in her eyes when she heard it.

Then, after she set the empty beer bottle next to his tombstone, she'd pop a squat in the general vicinity of where his face might be six feet below and release her aching bladder. She'd blow him a hateful kiss and laugh at the thought of those piss-soaked worms wriggling down to infiltrate his casket and slide into his nostrils.

Fuck you, Dwayne. He'd never had any appreciation for Blabbermouth, anyway.

She popped another blister capsule of her Nicorette pack and chewed on gum that tasted like half-remembered mint and ashtray.

She sometimes mourned the math, though it was clear: Blabbermouth made quite a bit more money each week than Patty did. But then, Blabbermouth's expense reports were much simpler. Gas money (to and from the sort of neighborhoods that could afford to hire clowns and magicians and catering and miniature ponies for a nine-year-old's birthday), some long balloons, a new gag or trick every few months, and a smile were all it cost Blabbermouth to exist.

Patty, on the other hand, had utilities and mobile home rent and groceries and medical debt from a rough case of kidney stones a year back and enough Nicorette gum to rot her teeth.

Luckily for Patty, Blabbermouth was always down to hand over her paychecks.

Patty reached into the glove box for an aluminum can of aerosolized deodorant and sprayed it in the general vicinity of her armpits, which leaked profusely in the desert heat. She knew her sweat muddied her makeup, the squiggly trails of it rivering down her temples towards the pillowy roll of fat beneath her chin.

Barely paying attention to her route, Patty cursed again as she made a sharp turn onto the street that held her destination. She reconfirmed the address written on the index card tucked between her thighs. "Hacienda" was the name of the housing development. *4270 Painted Desert Court, Cottonwood, Arizona*, her uncharacteristically neat penmanship read.

The neighborhood looked half-finished and mostly abandoned. Some of the houses were still in the wooden frame stage of construction. Others had paper covering their walls and stacks of shingles and sod waiting to be put in place, but it seemed no one was in any real rush to get around to it. Plastic sheeting fluttered in the wind from open window frames.

The home where she was scheduled to perform—a narrow, butterscotch-colored, two-storied house with Spanish rooftops and a dozen windchimes glittering in the sunlight—was situated like the crowning jewel in the cul-de-sac. No other streets or construction or homes existed behind it. The two neighboring homes had no signs of life, either. No cars in the freshly laid driveways, no bird baths or welcome mats or lacy curtains in front of the gleaming windows.

The backyards weren't fenced, yet. Just a wild expanse of brittlebush, acacia, and jojoba peppering red clay for miles of uninterrupted wild.

Once she put the car in park and popped one last piece of gum into her mouth, and once she adjusted the wig and gave her red nose a ritualistic squeeze so it squeaked like a dog's chew toy, she took on the task of peeling Patty away and becoming Blabbermouth. Blabbermouth wasn't a foul-mouthed widow with worsening vision, oniony body odor, pre-diabetes, and an inexplicable hatred of birds. Blabbermouth had never snorted oxy or slept with a man she knew was wanted for arson.

Blabbermouth was reborn sinless as an infant every time she smiled at the litter of children who offered their gap-toothed grins back at her, reflecting that same purity that insulated Blabbermouth from Patty's unsmiling world: mirrors facing mirrors, a Droste effect of teeth.

The first thing Patty noticed after she opened the driver's side door and set her gigantic shoes on the driveway—after she adjusted her poofy collar until its loose threads stopped itching so goddamn much—was the utter quiet. It made her stomach bubble with an anxious expectation. Like her gut felt certain that the entire street would be sucked into a sinkhole if she took one step further.

Some fucking party, Patty thought, forcing herself to twist her cheeks up into a dimpled chuckle in case the parents watched her from the window—they always did that, always peeked from the curtains as if to make sure she looked at least somewhat reputable.

She looked at the home. Really took it in. Tried to picture herself leaning on the porch railing with a bottle of Dwayne's brand of beer in her hands. She liked the sun-catchers suction-cupped to the windows and the wrought-iron porch swing swaying in the wind, its chains creaking in time with the tinkling windchimes. That part of the house felt real and lived in, but that silence—that very un-birthday-party silence—still unsettled her.

"Where are all the people?" Patty wondered aloud as she absently reached into her backseat for her polka-dotted bag of activities and prizes for the birthday boy.

Her Bonneville was the only car on the street. *Am I early? Did I get the date wrong?*

But no. Above the front door, a banner read "Happy Birthday" with cartoon dinosaurs hugging each letter.

"Their car must be in the garage." She decided this with a firm nod, followed by a strange sadness in her belly at the thought of this boy having a party with no one but little old Blabbermouth showing up. *Probably handed out invitations to everyone in class. Probably sitting there with his birthday boy hat on, his hands in his lap, wondering where all his friends are.*

An inconvenient lump lodged in her throat. She tightened her molars down on the gum to chase that feeling away before she clod-hopped towards the front porch. As much as she wanted to get back in her rust-bucket car and drive back to neighborhoods that'd been completed long ago, she couldn't bring herself to abandon this poor imagined version of a boy she had yet to meet. *After all, you only turn nine once.*

Patty tapped the brass door knocker three times before stepping back behind the pristine welcome mat that had probably seen very little traffic thus far. She plastered a smile on her face and placed her white-gloved index fingers on the pink lollipops painted on her cheeks like she wanted to push her dimples deeper into the layers of fat and muscle beneath. It was her signature greeting. It made her teeth ache every time.

A tall, lithe woman opened the front door, her hair cut in a fashionable bob and her clothes elegant in a way that made Patty want to run her knuckles over the fabric. Little tan splotches were scattered along the woman's cheekbones—not freckles, but a discoloration mothers sometimes got courtesy of pregnancy hormones, a speckled war paint that marked them forever. The woman smelled distinctly of orange rind. Her eyes were wide and brown. Patty thought they looked just as warm as the roof of her camel metallic Bonneville shining out there under the sunlight.

"Mrs. Bellamy," Patty guessed with the high-pitched baby voice she affected when she was in character. "So nice to meet you! I'm Blabbermouth the Clown, and I hear there's a birthday boy in there who could use a good chuckle!"

The woman—presumably Mrs. Bellamy—rested her hand on the door frame like she touched an antique piano. A gentle, tentative touch. "Yes, it's nice to meet you, Blabbermouth."

She held the clown's name between her teeth a half-second too long, like she hated how ridiculous it sounded, hated that she couldn't just speak to the regular woman underneath the paint for a while before services were rendered.

Part of Patty—the part that was sad and unfulfilled and sick all the time with the stink of the world—would love nothing more than to sit across from Mrs. Bellamy at the kitchen table and sip some of her fancy wine and, as soon as the bottle was empty, smash the glass into the woman's face.

Patty, not Blabbermouth, cupped one hand beside her mouth as if to tell a secret. "Am I early for the party? It didn't look like there was anyone else here right now."

Mrs. Bellamy appeared caught off guard by the question. "Yes," she replied, breathless. "Yes, but everyone should be here any minute now. Would you like to come meet Conner?"

"Of course, let's see the birthday boy!" Patty said.

"Please, come in."

Mrs. Bellamy stepped back from the entryway, giving space for Blabbermouth to pass with her big polka-dot bag dragging behind her.

Patty wasn't sure if she'd ever seen a more beautiful house. All the lights inside gave off an amber glow. Every corner looked candlelit, as if Conner's nine birthday candles followed her wherever she went. She couldn't help but let a hushed *wow* escape her lips. What she would do in a house like that. Shit, it wouldn't stay this nice for long. She had no illusions there: she'd drag in her cigarette burns and French fry grease and oil face-paint, and she'd dirty every exquisite surface.

Photographs of landscapes at night decorated the walls, with many of them appearing to have been shot locally, judging by the flora and a few recognizable landmarks, including the Community Clubhouse with its smooth river-rock exterior.

A stocky man with thick, black-framed glasses stood in the kitchen, an old manual Minolta camera draped around his neck. His arms drooped loosely at his sides and his shoulders rolled forward in a way Patty found a bit odd. He almost looked like a child on the verge of a great big sulk. When he saw her, though, it's like someone had turned the wind-up key on his back. He suddenly stood straight, a shaky smile doing its best to brighten his face.

"You must be Mrs. Blabbermouth! Welcome! Conner will be so excited. He loves clowns. This year, at least—last year it was magicians!" Mr. Bellamy chuckled heartily at his own statement. "Mind if I snap a photo? Always saving memories!"

Patty nodded at him, posing with her fingertips jammed back into the lollipops painted on her cheeks; she held that painfully wide smile until Mr. Bellamy lifted the camera to his eye and snapped a photo.

She couldn't help but feel vines of dread spreading throughout her gut. *So, I'm early, that's why there aren't any people here. But what about the decorations, the food, the gifts?*

What kind of birthday party is this?

"The party will be in the attic, Blabbermouth," Mrs. Bellamy said. She gently placed a cupped hand on the clown's elbow, as if guiding a blind woman through the halls. "Conner insisted. We turned it into his playroom when we first moved in, so it has all his toys, all the things he wants his friends to see."

"An attic playroom? That sounds so nifty!" Patty had a hard time convincing even herself with that silly fucking voice.

"It is! He calls it his circus. He has his little troupe of circus animals and his big top tent and his clown dolls. You know how kids are: they go through their phases so intensely, it's like each one hijacks their personality for a bit."

"Oh, I know! But then they find the one that really fits, and they never look back!" Patty said. "That's how it was for me! I was obsessed with the Bozo show. Cooky was my favorite! He was always such a prankster."

If she closed her eyes, Patty could envision her eight-year-old self with her blond braid and pink overalls laying on her soft belly in front of the television, her face cradled in her hands, her sandals dangling from her dirty feet, giggling at Cooky the Clown's antics. She could almost smell the bubblegum stretched across her tongue.

No one came to that girl's birthday parties, either.

The pair walked up the stairs. Through the railing, Patty caught one final glimpse of Mr. Bellamy. His smile lingered on his lips, but it had no mirth, no joy. His eyes held the fear of a man with a gun to his head.

Her oversized shoes squeaking on the hardwood floor, Patty suddenly felt the urge to pee, but she refused to mention it until after she met the birthday boy. She also wasn't entirely convinced the urge came from a full bladder and not a skittish mind.

Though the house was beautiful and the furnishings looked old and lived in, the dim lights and the nocturnal landscapes of increasingly familiar places started to make her stomach churn like one of those old-fashioned washing machines. There's the Chase bank ATM where she pulled out the rest of her savings the week prior to fix whatever the hell was going on with the Bonneville. There's the antique shop housed in a metal shack speckled with old gas station signs where she'd dumped all of her late husband's things because the Goodwill was too out of the way. It felt like a museum exhibit of every place where her life had gone wrong in some way, every place in Cottonwood where she had lost some new crumb of her dreams.

Some part of her feared that the very last picture she'd see affixed to the wall in its plain black frame would be Dwayne's gravestone.

This house was so quiet. So lifelessly quiet. She was desperate for the sound of children giggling and the scamper of little feet. Her mouth watered for a cigarette.

Mrs. Bellamy reached up towards a cord dangling from the ceiling. She gripped the plastic knob and slowly lowered the ladder to the attic, the new metal hinges shrieking.

Multicolored light filtered through the entryway to the attic—reds and greens and blues and golds; she guessed there were a few hundred bulbs of Christmas lights strung up around the room, giving off an otherworldly glimmer. The smell of cotton candy wafted down to her. Gossamer strands of sweetness gathered in a wasps' nest of pink or blue or purple. There was also another smell, though, slinking beneath the sugar. Rich peat, fresh pine. Some other bitterness she couldn't name.

"I just climb on up there?" Patty asked, voice folded smaller than she'd ever heard it before. That mint and ashtray taste overwhelmed her mouth before it was joined with subtle hints of bile. She set her hand on the wood of the ladder, splinters weaving into the threads of her white gloves.

Her right brow spasming from a smile held too long, Mrs. Bellamy said, "Yes. He's waiting."

Patty nodded, placing her foot on the lowest rung and slinging her bag of party favors over her shoulder. The wood from each subsequent step creaked as she set her weight upon it, the sound heralding her arrival. Happy birthday, Conner.

When she reached the top step, she hefted the bag from her torso and set it on the dusty floorboards of the attic. She looked around at the playroom. *Half a playroom,* she corrected. Everything behind her held the typical attic trappings: heirloom furniture and covered paintings and totes full of useless junk no one could bring themselves to throw away or donate (Mr. Bellamy's high school wrestling trophy, Patty would bet, or Mrs. Bellamy's forays into pottery). The shadows clung to those spaces.

In front of her rose a tent made of striped red and white canvas, its peak touching the ceiling of the attic and its entrance flaps pulled back by ropes with golden fringe. Darkness lay beyond.

Fifty stuffed animals flanked the tent. Their black beaded eyes shined with the multicolored Christmas lights strung up along the ceiling beams. From inside the tent came the sound of a music box, eerie little notes tripping over "Entry of the Gladiators" at quarter-time.

"Conner?" Patty asked as she approached the tent.

The pull-down ladder for the attic slammed shut behind her. Patty halfway convinced herself it was an accident—maybe Mrs. Bellamy had just bumped into the ladder and its overzealous springs retracted under the slightest nudge. Maybe she had lifted it because she needed to sweep the hallway of the bits of drywall that loosed from the ceiling each time the ladder was used.

But really, Patty knew. No other cars. No birthday decorations. And little Conner's parents each wore their very own flop, sweat beading above their lips and along their collars.

For a moment, Patty almost decided that Conner did not exist at all—that maybe she'd just been lured into the trap of psychotic cannibal murderers aiming to slash her throat and roast her in the earth like a pig.

The music box cranked faster inside the tent. Patty could feel the grease paint sliding off her face from the sweat. Even the adhesive fixing the red ball to her nose was melting. It felt almost like desertion. Like Blabbermouth the Clown had assessed the wrongness of everything and had promptly fled, leaving Patty behind.

"Conner?" she asked again, her large shoes compelling her one more inch towards the tent, then another, then another. Like they had a mind of their own, those blue bastards, like Patty couldn't get them to listen to her in a million years.

"Blabbermouth," said a voice from inside the tent. The word sounded forced out of a mouth filled with oil or blood, a viscous bubbling to the syllables followed by a few scattered *plops* onto the wooden floorboards. The voice belonged, unmistakably, to a child.

Patty crouched down and slowly fished around in her pocket. Even though she'd been fighting her damnedest to quit her pack of Pall Malls per day habit, she still kept a Bic just in case.

Once her cotton-gloved fingers grazed its smooth surface, she gripped it in her fist like a talisman, pulling the disposable lighter from her billowy striped pants.

Holding the lighter at arm's length from her face in a quivering rebuke of the darkness inside the tent, Patty listened to the sound of the boy's breathing. It crackled like grease in a frying pan.

Patty flicked the wheel of the lighter until the flints scuffed each other into sparking. Like the flaps of the tent, the darkness parted in front of her.

What she assumed was Conner Bellamy stood hunchbacked inside the tent wearing an oversized magician's get-up—the top-hat, the cloak, the cummerbund, and bowtie. He had white gloves, too, only his were sporadically stained with rusty brown.

The boy's eyes, a wild map of red veins that held neither pupil nor iris, bulged from their sockets. His skin was the grayish purple of a full-body bruise. His mouth, agape and slanted to the right, was full of wriggling maggots.

The image of Dwayne's corpse in his grave—the image of the worms eating his eyeballs, which used to make her giggle—filled her mind. She no longer found it very funny.

Patty gasped so hard the Nicorette sucked to the back of her throat, forcing a violent coughing fit. She dropped the lighter and tripped backward, stumbling away from the thing in the tent called Conner, her giant shoes catching on the gaps between floorboards. She felt her balance slip, felt her equilibrium tilt, her broad torso suddenly horizontal as she fell. As her luck would have it, she landed directly on the retractable ladder.

The last thing Patty saw as she fell to the floor below was the flaps of the circus tent opening wider.

Patty woke in a dark room. The orange wig was crusted with dried blood. The back of her head throbbed with staticky pain. She smelled smoke and rot and dirt.

Seemingly from a great distance, Mrs. Bellamy rambled. "Last year it was magicians, this year he wanted to be a clown. And when you have a miracle like Conner, you do everything you can to keep him happy, every little thing you can. When he was born, the doctors said there was no heartbeat, but he was still crying, he was still moving around and crying, so what did they know? He was meant to be here."

Pain needled in her belly now, and Patty forced her eyes open again despite the blurry vision and head-splitting ache of what was either a concussion or a skull fracture. She looked down at her torso. A birthday candle shaped like the number nine jutted from her abdomen, likely attached to a bamboo skewer. Its orange flickering flame cast a dim light around her.

She saw the red and white stripes of Conner's circus tent surrounding her. Directly above her, a framed black-and-white photograph stared back: a middle-aged man in a top hat and magician's coat, a deck of cards splayed between his gloved hands. Below, a layer of rich topsoil coated the floor, filled with the writhing movement of a thousand worms.

Mr. and Mrs. Bellamy kneeled beside her, their fine clothes smeared black with the dirt and brown with Patty's blood; their fingers were woven so tightly together, the blood had fled their knuckles entirely, leaving them bone white. Their smile held the warmth of a parents' purest love, a love Patty had never experienced herself, but maybe she could've if she'd made more effort to be a bit more like Blabbermouth.

On the other side of the Bellamys stood the thing with the empty eyes and the crooked top hat and the mouth full of larvae. Born without a heartbeat but moving all the same. The thing called Conner hunched over Patty. Maggots fell from his cracked lips and stuck to the wide red smile painted on her face. He reached his purplish fingers out towards her face and plucked the red nose away. Patty whimpered, the movement of her cries jostling the skewer in her belly, increasing her pain, which only prompted more whimpers, on and on.

Conner held the red nose up to his face and smiled a wormy smile.

"Blow out your candle and make a wish, sweetie," Mrs. Bellamy said.

"No!" Patty cried. The prospect of being jettisoned back into the darkness terrified her enough for her to finally release her bladder. She screamed and thrashed, but all of her fight dribbled out into the potting soil.

The thing called Conner leaned forward again, pinched her lips shut, and sputtered a breath that smelled exactly how Patty figured a coffin-birth would smell—a breath brewed from equal parts pus and black ichor heaved from two dead sacks where lungs should be. The flame bent away from that gust, then hissed as it was extinguished.

She was swallowed back into the dark. She desperately missed the smell of the Bonneville and the taste of the Nicorette gum and all the other minute details she'd taken for granted, all filed away as more useless and shitty pieces of the shitty puzzle that was her life. She wondered what they would do with the old car. She wondered if they would park it somewhere in the desert beside a magician's black Town Car.

"Happy birthday, Conner," she heard within the void of her grave, right before the boy's teeth bit into the birthday cake of her face.

CEMETERY WHALE

LARRY HODGES

Smeg counted the other ten orcas in his pod over and over as they sang and chased down sea lions, avoiding eye contact whenever one came near. The screaming creatures in the jaws of his pod-mates made him anxious; they were so loud and messy. Counting calmed him down. He did not join in their hunt. Later, he would forage carrion for himself and nibble the sweet seaweeds from the ocean floor.

Something nudged him from below. Smeg pulled away, hoping it was not Darm. It was not; it was his mother, making eye contact and offering him a writhing sea lion in her jaws. In a panic, Smeg looked away and dove for the depths, where no one would look him in the eye or try to put struggling sea lions in his mouth. She whistled after him, but he ignored whatever she was saying. He was fully grown, and yet his mother was still trying to turn him into a "normal" whale.

A school of fish passed by as he dove. After making sure Darm was not lurking nearby, Smeg counted them by sonar with the numbering system he had invented—243—before they disappeared into the silent depths. He did not like the silence, preferring the songs on the surface. He, too, liked to sing, but the other whales did not appreciate the intricate melodies he had copied from humpback whales and passing human ships. The thought of humans—the source of the still painful harpoon scar on his side—made him shudder. How could the same animal that created such music also create such a horrible weapon?

He picked up on the scent of death. Following it, his clicking sonar located the rancid floating remains of a squid, already dead, the way he liked it. He counted nine legs—one must have broken off—then gobbled it down.

Soon he would have to return to the surface for air and to rejoin the pod. He did not want to; they would stare and whistle at him because he was a freak. Leaving the pod was an option, but where would he go? That would be a lonely existence, always hiding from others. He didn't want to stay in the terrible silence of the depths. As he pondered which was worse, the growing pain in his lungs decided for him. His right eye twitched.

He broke for the surface, aiming for a spot thirty lengths from the pod. From there, he could breathe, listen to their songs, and count them. Yet even from that distance, they would stare and whistle at him. Darm or one of the others might come over to harass him, bumping and shoving him around. He gritted his teeth and accepted his reality, as he always did.

The ocean was huge, and it was where he lived, but nowhere could he call it home.

◆———————————◆

Smeg's pod spy-hopped their heads out of the water as they played. Smeg stayed off to the side, his head also out of the water, counting the stars as he did every night. There were so many, and always in the same place, except for a few wanderers. Most were small and still. Two were large and mobile, the bright day light and the not-so-bright night light. He began to sing a song he'd heard from a human ship, remembering with ease the intricate changes of tone and pitch.

Something hit him from below, nearly knocking him out of the water. Smeg painfully swam away from Darm, who long ago had made it her business to ram him whenever she caught him counting or singing human songs. She took great joy in staring at him, following him about as he twisted and turned away from her until he'd finally dive for the depths as her taunting whistles chased after him.

The whistles had started, and Smeg was about to dive when a flash of light overhead stopped him. The whole pod stared at the fiery object crossing the sky. It was faster than the other lights that Smeg liked to count, and only the day light was brighter. The object struck the water many, many lengths away. Then came the loudest sound Smeg had ever heard, louder even than a blue whale that once sang at him from a body's length away. It hit him as if he'd been harpooned by a narwhal. His ears exploded in pain. Frantically, he tried swimming away from the agony.

Then the waves hit like dozens of blue whales, only much faster and bigger, squeezing the air from his lungs with an agonizing pop as he shot through the water at an impossible speed. His body hit something solid with a painful thud. The waves grabbed him again, slamming him against a tree. His body pirouetted about, tearing his flesh, and finally wedged between two trees. He stared at the impossible landscape, his breathing labored. It had to be a nightmare. Soon he'd open his eyes to the whistles of his pod-mates, perhaps jolted awake by a ramming Darm. Then he blacked out again.

◆———————————————————◆

Smeg awoke feeling like a whole pod of Darms had rammed him over and over all night long. Every muscle ached. A sharp pain from his stomach sent spasms through his body.

He was still wedged between the trees. The water was gone. From the ocean, he'd seen trees from a distance, but never this close. They looked like huge, fat seaweeds, but with a rough brown covering that dug painfully into him. The water had knocked many of them over.

There was tremendous weight on his lungs—his own weight. He gasped for breath and then panicked. He was on dry land! Where was the ocean? He had to get back to it!

Painfully, Smeg wriggled about in seeming silence, his ears ringing from the earlier explosive sound. He finally wiggled free from the trees and lay on his belly, struggling to breathe. It was a losing battle. Exhaustion and dizziness slowly overcame him. He drowsily counted the leaves on a nearby tree as he drifted off to sleep.

Something jolted him awake. Darm? He reflexively beat at the air with his tail and flippers and soared upwards, floating over his body as if swimming in the ocean. His normal hearing returned as the agony from his many injuries subsided.

He stared down at his broken, blood-splattered body below and counted the wounds: thirteen. Probably more underneath and inside. He drifted upward as his right eye twitched. He was weightless and floating in the air, and didn't understand this at all.

He was obviously dead, and yet he wasn't.

The smell of carrion took his mind off the puzzle. He followed the tantalizing scent up a steep hill in the forest, floating half a body length above the ground. He counted the broken trees that lay on the ground. There were fewer of them as he continued up the hill.

Something pulled on him, some force trying to drag him back to his dead body. He stayed focused on the powerful carrion scent.. Unfortunately, his sonar didn't work well in plain air. It didn't matter; he preferred using sight and smell when possible. Birds chirped from the trees, oblivious to Smeg; he counted them as he passed.

Soon, he came to a clearing next to the forest. He floated to a halt over an odd-looking white stone. It was rectangular, jutting upward out of the ground, with strange markings on the side. Similar stones stood about the clearing and off into the distance. He counted the ones in the immediate area and decided he'd get the rest later. A type of green seaweed that Smeg had never seen before blanketed the ground, all about the height of a tooth.

The source of the carrion scent appeared to be the ground at the base of the stone. Smeg dove into it, mouth wide. At first, his teeth went right through the ground with little effect. Then he found he could will them and other parts of his body to solidify without gaining weight. With powerful thrusts of his flukes, he again dove into the ground, tearing at it with his teeth as he dug down. Soon he came upon a rotting container. He splintered it with his jaws. Inside, he found a human, just as rotten. He'd never seen one up close. Shuddering, he pulled back, the memory of the harpoon injury shooting through his body. He took a deep breath and counted the creature's ten fingers and other body parts to calm himself.

Then he devoured it, the bones crunching in his jaws.

Over the next few days, Smeg explored the area and counted all the strange stones. He loved the fresh smell of the forest, the green of the trees, and the wide-open spaces in the sky where he could fly without so much as water resistance. Above all, he was glad to be free of Darm and the others who teased him.

The force that pulled him back toward his rotting body grew stronger the farther he went, limiting his range. It became increasingly powerful after a hundred body lengths, and after two hundred, it snatched him back like one of his pod-mates tossing a sea lion with its flukes.

Several times a day, humans gathered in groups and put another dead human in a box into a hole in the ground. Then they would fill the hole up with dirt and place one of the strange stones on top of it. Smeg watched as he hid in the treetops. Why did the humans bury their dead in the ground? It made no sense.

He could see in the distance large, cage-like enclosures humans seemed to live in, but they were out of his range. The nearest, with two large white sticks attached at right angles at the top, was on the edge of the field of stones, just out of his reach.

Once, a small human—a baby?—saw him and pointed, but Smeg flew away before any others saw him. He hid among the leafy branches of a large tree until the humans gave up looking for what had disturbed the small human.

What really drew Smeg to these ceremonies was the music humans played—the most beautiful music Smeg had ever heard. It was magnificent! He couldn't figure out which of the humans made the music, and gave up trying to find the source. Sometimes the music came from the enclosure with the crossed sticks on top, with humans gathered inside, often before or after burying one of their dead.

Smeg memorized each song and played them to himself at night as he dug into the ground under the stones, eating the rotting human carcasses. He found his new existence satisfactory, and yet something was missing. He was used to loneliness, but he somehow missed the sarcastic whistles of his pod-mates, even Darm's. Bad company, he decided, was better than no company. Yet the human music served as a companion of sorts and that, he decided, would have to do, since it was all he had.

One day, as he listened from the treetops to the hypnotic music, there came an excited cry. He looked about and realized a group of humans—

twelve of them—had walked up from the other side and saw him. Most ran away, but several stayed.

Their staring eyes made him uncomfortable. But his loneliness overcame his shyness. After making sure they carried no harpoons, he flew out to meet them. At his approach, they ran away. He followed for a time, floating over their heads and counting them over and over as they screamed. Then they jumped into an object that was like a huge and extremely fast sea turtle, with four flippers that rotated in a circle. The turtle-object expelled nauseous fumes similar to human ships in the ocean. Smeg tried to follow, but the pull back to his body was too great, and he could only watch as the object moved away.

Over the next few days, there were only a few burial ceremonies. Smeg stayed hidden in the forest, listening to the music from a distance. He wanted to move closer, yet did not feel comfortable getting too close to the humans. They feared him as the seals feared him and his pod-mates. His pod-mates had mocked him; the humans were afraid of him. What was wrong with him? Why must he be so different? He gritted his teeth and once again accepted the bitter reality.

Then came the sweetest sound he had ever heard. It tugged at him, its enchantment as great as that first time so long ago when he'd first heard human music. What he'd heard then to this was like minnows to whales. His body throbbed and swung to the music. After a time, he could take it no more; he had to hear it from up close!

He launched himself out of the trees toward the beckoning sound as pleasure permeated his body. The music came from another dead human burying ceremony. He edged closer, looking for the source, not caring if the humans saw him. The music came from a small object on the ground near the hole they were about to lower the dead human into.

He floated over the source of the music, ignoring the humans as they screamed and ran away, not even bothering to count them. How could sound carry such beauty? This sound, this moment, this place…he wanted the joy to go on forever.

A movement caught his eye. A human stood nearby inside a sort of cage. Smeg had once seen something like it, lowered into the ocean from a human ship with a human inside, using the strong bars of the cage as protection against the sharks that circled about. Smeg floated closer and studied the human. A thick tuft of white hair hung from the human's chin. A hat jutted out in front that partially covered his head. With a start, Smeg realized the man had only one leg; the other ended in a peg. The man stooped and picked something up. Smeg froze in horror as he saw the harpoon, its shiny tip pointed like a jellyfish tentacle, only hard as stone.

"I thought you might like *Amazing Grace*," the man said. "Aretha Franklin does it better than anyone. I've got it set to play over and over— so enjoy." Smeg heard the sounds coming from the human, but didn't understand the words. "I see from that scar on your side and that look in your eyes that you know what this is." The man raised the harpoon, sunlight flashing off the tip.

With a flick of his flukes, Smeg shot away even as the man leaned back and hurled the harpoon. Searing pain hit him an instant later as the harpoon dug into his side. In a panic, Smeg flew into the air, trying to outrun the pain. He came to a stop with a yank. Two body lengths of rope tied the harpoon to two bars of the human's cage.

"I thought an ectoplasmic harpoon would hold you," the man said, squinting at Smeg. "My own invention; that's why I was hired. You may call me…Ecto-Quint, or Quinty for short. Sounds better than Ecto-Ahab. Don't think 'ole Quinty would mind since he's dead. Besides, you're as big as his great white."

Where music had permeated his body moments before, there was now only agonizing pain. Smeg shot through the air, again coming to a sudden, excruciating halt as the rope again grew taut. He cried out through his blowhole. He backed up and flew forward again, as hard as he could, over and over, crying out each time he tried to yank the harpoon out of his flesh.

"Might as well stop that," the man said. "You're only tearing yourself apart. I want your hide to be pristine when I put it on display."

Smeg bit into the rope, but it only hurt his mouth.

"You're not going to bite through that metal cable," Quinty said.

Smeg flew to the man's cage and tore at it with his jaws. He only managed to break off several teeth.

"Titanium bars," Quinty said, his face just feet from Smeg.

Again Smeg flew away, and again the rope held him. He tried one more time with a longer flying start. With a crunching sound, the cage pulled free from the ground. Smeg flew into the sky, dragging with him the cage with the man inside as it hung from the painful harpoon in his side.

"Damn it!" Quinty exclaimed. "Should have used longer stakes!"

Smeg closed his mind off from the pain as he flew, faster and faster, desperately trying to get away. The cage trailed below and behind, just over the treetops, sometimes hitting them as the man yelled in outrage.

Then he felt the force pulling him back to his body. He fought it ferociously as he tried to flee, the effort helping him ignore the pain of the harpoon. The force continued to grow, and soon Smeg felt himself slowing to a stop, the cage now hanging directly below. He began to lose altitude as he fought the untiring pull.

Through his pain-crazed mind, an idea formed. With renewed energy, he lurched forward, even regaining altitude. But the pull increased, and finally he reached an impasse where he could go no further.

Then he relaxed and let go.

The force sling-shotted him backwards at incredible speed. The rope instantly tightened and painfully yanked the harpoon out of Smeg, who cried out in agony. It also nearly broke off the two bars of the cage it was tied to.

As they shot through the air, Smeg turned toward the man in the cage. Powered by rage, he now pulled himself toward it, half a body length at a time. He lapsed and fell back a flipper's length. Then he fought forward again, closer and closer.

"*No!*" Quinty screamed, flattening himself against the far side of the cage on his one leg as the wind whipped through his hair and clothes.

Finally, Smeg grabbed the two broken bars between his teeth and tore them loose, spitting them aside. He rested for a moment as the man stared with wide eyes. Then, with his last bit of energy, he lunged forward through the opening from the two vacated bars and grabbed the now-screaming man.

With the struggling human trapped in his jaws, Smeg relaxed as they returned to the site of his body, now just a skeleton. With a flip of his powerful flukes, he returned to the human burial ceremony and the beautiful music. At their approach, the few humans still there ran off. One lay still on the ground, while a much smaller one with long yellow hair stood over it, yelling "Mommy!"

Smeg floated above the source of the music, his labored breathing slowing as he listened to the mesmerizing sound. The pain from his injury seemed to seep away.

"*Let me go!*" Quinty cried. Smeg's right eye twitched. With sudden resolve, he closed his jaws, and the man went quiet.

The human's blood poured into his mouth from the still quivering form, making him nauseous. He'd never held a living creature in his jaws before, much less killed one. He could taste the flesh and the blood as it caressed and tickled his tongue.

Blood! His mind was in a daze as he tasted it fresh for the first time. It jolted him like a jellyfish sting, followed by an instant fiery bliss. He whipped about the air in drunken euphoria. Nothing else mattered as he opened and closed his jaws, chomping on the human, squeezing out more and more blood as his right eye twitched...

Soon it was over, and he swallowed the remains of the human. The music had stopped. He realized that, in his bloodlust, he'd broken the object on the ground the music came from with a thrust of his tail flukes. The small human with long yellow hair still stood below, apparently too afraid to move. She trembled as she stared up at his floating form.

"I can see right through you," she said in a high-pitched voice. She took several deep breaths. "I think my mommy fainted." Smeg floated down toward the tiny creature, whose shining eyes seemed too big for her head. "Are you going to eat me?" she asked, taking a step back.

The bloodlust rose in Smeg again. Inside this human was more fresh blood. *Blood!* He opened his jaws and approached the small human, savoring the moment.

Then he stopped. The girl was singing. Smeg didn't understand the words, but he'd heard the song already, the same one the man had played before. He lowered to eye level with the girl and stared at her, snout to nose. Somehow, the eye contact didn't bother him so much. She stopped singing.

The huge, shining eyes continued to stare at him. For the first time, he really noticed her. She wore a red covering that somehow didn't seem natural and yet looked attractive on her. Her yellow hair flailed out in the back like a sea anemone. She was about the size of a starving sea lion, with a sweet smell like those seaweeds he liked to chew. He glanced down and counted her ten fingers, then met her eyes again.

"My name is Sarah," she said. "What's yours?"

When Smeg didn't answer, she began to sing again. As before, Smeg didn't know or understand the words or any significance they may have, but he could mimic the tones. He joined in and they sang together. They continued to the end, snout to nose even as they swayed side to side in time with the music. When they finished, he backed up slightly. But the little human, barely bigger than one of his flippers, stepped toward him and rubbed his snout.

He was home.

DOORWAY TO NOWHERE

A.J. PAYLER

ONE NOVEMBER MORNING, when Wes Rodenbaugh left his second-floor apartment to head to work, there was a door across the hallway where before there had been nothing.

As he was frequently known to—much to the chagrin of his supervisor at the marketing firm for which he crunched numbers—Wes was running late that Tuesday. He'd barely managed to shower and dress himself properly, scarfing only a piece of cold pepperoni pizza left from three days prior and washing it down with half a can of insufficiently chilled diet cola before dashing out the door. He didn't have even a spare moment to stop and look over the door that had sprung up directly across the hall from his apartment, apparently overnight and without a hint of the racket that typically accompanied even the most routine of maintenance in Luna Courtyard Towers. His great-aunt Kohana always said the Towers had been the height of fashion when she'd been a young woman, but that had been a long time ago. Long enough that Wes found it hard to picture the building as anything but the most poorly kept up high-rise in downtown San Diego.

Wes didn't ask much of his living space. He worked a lot, and when he wasn't working, he was out living his life, so if he was at home, it was a safe bet he was either unwinding after a long day of work, preparing to go out, or sleeping. He hadn't even bothered to hang any art on his blank beige walls. But if he'd learned one thing about Luna Courtyard Towers during the three years he'd lived there, it was that property management never made a move without making damned sure every single tenant was aware they were actually doing something to earn their monthly management fees. The yellow placards posted in the lobby announcing incipient repairs were a familiar sight to all the building's tenants, never mind that they tended to go up days before a lick of work was done and often didn't come down for weeks.

But if management felt it necessary to let everyone in the Towers know when Mrs. Kopetsky in 12D had her toilet replaced—much to her mortification—Wes couldn't believe they would have missed something as significant as the addition of a new second floor unit. And while Wes was a sound sleeper, or so all who had shared a bed with him in the past had said, he also couldn't believe they had completed such major modifications to the building without him noticing until they were finished.

Perhaps the work had been done while he was at work, not starting until he left between 7:30 and 7:45 a.m., and knocking off before he got home after six. It would have been uncharacteristically considerate of them to do so, but he supposed it was possible.

But then, he would have noticed it upon his arrival at home the previous evening, wouldn't he? Sure, he had stumbled in fatigued and weary—and yes, a little buzzed, thanks to the quick post-work stop-off he'd shared with Joy and Kylen at the brewpub down the street from his firm. But he definitely hadn't drunk so much that he'd have failed to notice an entirely new door in the hallway he'd been using for years.

In the yawning eternity of the minute and a half it took for the elevator to grind its way up to the second floor, Wes kept glancing back down the hall, wanting to turn around and examine the new door but certain the moment he did, the elevator would arrive. Then by the time he ran back to catch it, the doors would close right in his face, as had happened more than once before. And then he'd have to start the whole tedious ordeal over again, putting himself even further behind schedule. Or, failing that, dash down the stairs, undoubtedly drenching his crisp work shirt with acrid sweat. While LaToya might tolerate his showing up late now and again, if he arrived late and hung over and unkempt and smelling like he'd run a marathon to work—well, no one wanted to suffer through another lecture, least of all Wes.

But as the elevator opened before him and he sidled in, pressing the button with his elbow, he couldn't tear his eyes from the thing. Even after the doors closed, its afterimage remained in his mind, the outline of the odd new addition to his hallway imprinted on the back of his retina as surely as if he'd stared too long at the sun.

He thought about it all the way down to the ground floor, half-resolved to come home and investigate the matter further once lunchtime came around. But the moment the elevator whooshed open, the new door flew completely out of his head and he dashed off to work with his mind unencumbered as if he had never noticed it in the first place.

Wes didn't think about the new door once the rest of the morning. And when Kylen suggested ordering up a lunch delivery of dumplings from the new bao place in Little Italy, he cosigned his friend's suggestion enthusiastically.

It wasn't until the workday neared its end that thoughts of the door reentered his head. And the more Wes thought about it, the more he wondered if he'd seen anything at all. He'd been in a rush, scrambling out the door precious minutes behind schedule. As anyone would be quick to point out, at the time, he'd been both tired and groggy from a number of poor choices the previous evening. An unimpeachable witness he could hardly claim to be.

So as he pressed the call button to summon the elevator back to the ground level of the Luna Courtyard Towers—thinking once again about how great-aunt Kohana always said the place had employed the best-dressed elevator operators in the city back in her day—Wes was fairly certain when he got off on the second floor and walked down the hall to where his familiar door with the brass number reading 2S nailed to it stood, the wall opposite would be blank and empty as it had been the thousand other times he'd come home.

So certain was he that he was surprised to hear himself gasp at the sight of the thing waiting there for him when the elevator opened.

He shook his head, laughing at himself for getting worked up over nothing. It was a door, that was all. It looked the same as the door covering the entrance to his own apartment: beige, generic, mass-produced.

Probably not even real wood, more likely corrugated cardboard covered in fiberboard or veneer. Probably bought in bulk by the developer years ago when the building had been built and held in reserve so all the units would match, even when doors had to be replaced. Every single door in Luna Courtyard Towers looked exactly the same, thanks to restrictive building rules that even prohibited hanging wreaths or mistletoe when the holidays came around, and this one was no different.

Well, there was *one* thing different about it. Where the brass numbering on his door read 2S, this one just read 2, as if they hadn't gotten around to assigning it an apartment number yet. That was strange—the last apartment on the floor was 2W, so it would seem obvious that this one should be 2X—but maybe they hadn't gotten around to it yet. Or maybe the hardware store was sold out of the brass X they needed, or maybe the space behind it wasn't even intended to be an apartment. Perhaps the door concealed a broom closet, or a building staff office, or even a demo unit to show off to potential renters without having to disturb any current tenants. Any of the three possibilities sounded like a step in the right direction for Luna Courtyard Towers management, frankly.

Wes looked the door over once more, then nodded, satisfied. He'd already expended more than enough time and energy thinking about something that made no difference in his life whatsoever—that door was living in his head rent-free, as the saying (that had always irritated him immensely) went. Anyway, the workday had been long and fatiguing as always, so much so he'd begged off from making a second brewpub visit in as many days. He just didn't bounce back the way he used to. And after the long hours of tossing and turning the previous night, he needed to get as much rest as possible if the remainder of the week wasn't going to be a total nightmare. An early bedtime was definitely called for; maybe even a nap.

Definitely a nap, he decided as he turned around and marched into his own apartment, locking the deadbolt and securing the security chain behind him. It was already dark out, but the sun set early that late in the year.

He didn't think about the door across the hall more than seven or eight times more before he fell into bed.

The ringing of his phone came as a surprise, as it always did. He wasn't close with his family, not let's-chat-idly-on-the-phone-for-no-good-reason close, anyway. His friends texted and emailed to communicate, like all decent people did. Work never called Wes unless there was an emergency, and there was no such thing as an accounting emergency at the firm he worked for. That was one of the things he liked so much about the job: it was busy, sure, and there was always more work than they could get on top of—but being busy kept the days clipping along instead of dragging like molasses. As long as the numbers added up at the end of the month, the bosses were happy. They didn't want to think about such things; that was what they had Wes for. He kept the books in line, they left him alone.

Pawing for his cell as he pulled himself up from the depths of his somnolent stupor, he wiped the crust from the corners of his eyes, blinking at the sunlight streaming through the slats of his beige blinds.

Wait. Sunlight?

He sat up, suddenly awake. Turning the surface of his phone face up, his eyes bulged: it was past 9:00 a.m. Closer to 9:30. And someone from work was indeed calling him: Joy, the administrative assistant who kept LaToya's life running on track.

"Hello, Joy."

"Oh thank fuck," Joy gasped with relief. "I thought for sure you were dead in a ditch somewhere when it hit 8:30. Do you know what time it is?"

"I do now," he said. "And where is there a ditch in downtown San Diego deep enough that no one would notice a dead body?"

"That construction over on Third and Imperial? Hell if I know. Where are you?"

Wes blinked, looked around at the blank walls of his apartment. "Nowhere," he said down the line. "I laid down for a nap yesterday evening after work. Guess I was more worn than I thought. Must have slept through my alarms."

"Well," Joy said, "if I were you I'd hustle my buns down here tout suite."

"Don't worry, I am," he said, holding the phone to his ear with his shoulder as he wrestled his legs back into the pants he'd discarded by his bedside the night before. They would be wrinkled, but they already had his belt strung through them and his wallet in the back pocket, saving him precious seconds. A fresh shirt, a bright tie to draw the attention away from his pants, and he'd be good to go.

"You'd better be," Joy cautioned. "If I know her highness, she's already counting the seconds until you're at your desk."

❖————————————◆

Or in front of hers.

"Nine, fifty, seven," LaToya enunciated. "I absolutely cannot believe my eyes this morning. A hundred and eighty seconds shy of ten o'clock."

"I know, I'm sorry," Wes said. "I'm not sure what happened. Neither of my alarms went off for some reason."

"And that?" She eyed the sprawling brown stain on his chest, stretching from the breast pocket all the way across his yellow tie down to the right side of his abdomen.

"That wasn't my fault," Wes protested. "The rideshare driver hit a bump, his coffee went flying."

"And you threw yourself on it to protect him?" LaToya asked, rubbing the bridge of her nose with her index finger and thumb. "No, don't answer that," she rethought.

Through the window of LaToya's office, Wes spotted Joy shuffling through a stack of papers on her desk, pretending not to eavesdrop on the conversation occurring within. It wasn't as though the big glass box made any concessions towards discretion or soundproofing; and anyway, Wes was pretty sure LaToya's body language alone would give any onlookers an accurate sense of the tenor of their conversation. Not much was kept secret within these walls, by design. Besides, anything Joy heard would swiftly become common knowledge, at least among those in her good books.

"Wes, you're a good employee," LaToya said. "But you know how I feel about punctuality and appearance, two things that are of paramount importance in this industry. It's written in our DNA here, part of the company culture. It's just how things are."

"But I—"

She held up a hand. "Let me finish. I know you aren't on the front lines, so to speak, meeting with clients and drumming up business and whatnot. But when I'm seen by other staff as letting you walk all over the very values this firm was built on, it reflects badly on me."

Wes nodded. "Yeah, I can see that."

"Right," she said. "It's nothing personal. And speaking quite frankly, I just don't have the kind of pull with the partners that I'd need to shelter someone like you from the consequences of his own actions. Not unless you were a star or a rainmaker. They just won't stand for it. Therefore, I can't afford to, either." She drummed her fingers on the surface of her desk. "I think that's all I needed to say. Do we understand each other?"

Wes looked at the ground. He wanted to curl up on it and disappear.

"We do," he said. "It won't happen again."

On his way home after work, Wes detoured to pick up a pair of brand new alarm clocks, a highly configurable electronic one with a guaranteed backup battery and one of the old-fashioned wind-up models with brass bells at the top, along with a metal bucket.

When added to the series of staggered alarms he set on his phone, it was understandable why he felt certain there was no way any human could sleep through the entire array. But just to make sure—after picking up a fast food bacon cheeseburger and some cheese fries with lemonade—he went straight home, not even glancing once at the new door as he went in. He scarfed down the takeout, showered and laid down in his bed with soothing ambient music playing to block out the noises of the still-active streets outside and help lull him to sleep. He'd sleep as long as he could, wake up refreshed and ready to make a new start tomorrow.

He was correct about the alarms, at least. They all triggered simultaneously at 6:15 the next morning, emitting a cacophonous racket that caused both his door and his ceiling to be pounded on by separate but equally annoyed neighbors. The electronic alarm at full volume was piercing enough, but it scarcely compared to the din of the wind-up alarm banging around in the resonant metal bucket set at the foot of his bed.

Feeling like he hadn't slept a wink, Wes dragged himself out of bed and shut the clattering klaxons off one by one, which brought the thumping on the ceiling and front door to a stop. And he showered, and dressed, and managed to make it to his desk at ten minutes before eight, earning a nod from LaToya and a thumbs-up from Joy.

But when he felt a hand on his shoulder shaking him brusquely awake and he realized he'd nodded off at his desk and everyone in the room was staring directly at him, he knew something was really wrong.

They sent him home, of course. Put him on involuntary leave, told him to come back in two weeks if he'd gotten whatever was bothering him sorted out. Wes could hardly blame them. If he'd seen the same behavior in anyone else, he would have thought they were on drugs of some sort. The bad, heavy, life-ruining type of drugs, not fun stuff.

Trudging back down his hallway to his apartment at not yet noon with the rest of the day on his hands, he glared arrows at the new door across the hall as he neared his apartment.

There was something wrong about it, he realized. The doorknob was set on the wrong side, opposite to all the other doors. All the other exterior door handles were on the right side; this was on his left. And they hadn't ever completed the brass numbering; it still just read 2.

"Half-assed property management," Wes muttered, rolling his eyes and fumbling his keyring from his pocket.

As he unlocked his door, Wes felt a pressure from the empty peephole in the door behind him as if it was burning a hole in his back, and he was suddenly certain he was being watched. Shivering, he whipped around, peering with suspicion at the door. The hallway was silent, the type of silence he had rarely in Luna Courtyard Towers. Probably because most everyone else in the building was still out at work or doing whatever else they did during the day.

There was no one standing behind the peephole, he could see that. But figuring he had nothing to lose, he rapped his knuckles firmly on the faux wood, standing there waiting for a full minute afterwards, hearing nothing but the beating of his own blood rushing in his ears, feeling stupider with each passing second for expecting anything else.

Finally, he gave up, retreated to his own apartment, locked it firmly behind him. But for the rest of the day, he kept getting up to check his peephole, peering out at the door across the hall.

As the next several days passed, Wes only slept more and more.

That night after being sent home from work, he drank too much and passed out too early, which—fair enough. Nobody could blame him for sleeping it off the next day, especially given he had nowhere to be and nothing in particular to get up for. Ten hours of slumber was far from outrageous, given the circumstances.

But when ten hours became twelve became sixteen, Wes started to think he had a problem.

Depression, maybe. That was what the top search results for his symptoms pointed to. Or maybe he had undiagnosed hypersomnia. Or it could be indicative of some deeper, malign issue. But Wes didn't think any of those were what it was, somehow.

He thought it had something to do with the door across the hall.

During the discombobulation of the past few days, he found himself wondering whether the door had, in fact, always been there. It would have explained a lot if he'd just overlooked it, passing it over as part of the background, only noticing it when one detail made it stand out, like one of the brass number plates falling off. Then the thing got on his radar and his overworked mind had just projected this entire built-up scenario on a perfectly random door, trying to distract him from what were obviously some deep-seated issues of some sort, whether physical, mental, or both.

So he went digging in his closet, rooting through the boxes he had stuck at the back, under the shoes he didn't wear anymore because they were uncomfortable but couldn't get rid of because he might need them someday and the yearbooks full of predictions unfulfilled and pledges of everlasting friendship long forgotten. Eventually, he found the backup drive to which he'd cloned the computer he'd had when he moved into the apartment years ago. That computer had died within that first month, because it somehow got infected with a brand new virus his security software couldn't kill, rendering its hard drive unusable before he—or the virus experts at SecuriScan—were able to figure out any way to remedy the issue. He'd fretted endlessly about what precious files might have been corrupted or lost to him forever until the moment his replacement machine arrived and he was successfully able to initiate the restoration process to the new box from that very backup drive, after which he had tossed it aside and forgotten about it.

Now, inspecting the contents of that backup drive, Wes realized that as upset as he'd been at the time, that computer had truly represented no great loss to him or to the world. Most of what was on there was downloaded movies and TV shows he wouldn't rewatch, a few books, some work files from his previous job. There was nothing he couldn't get again, now faster and probably better, except some old personal photos.

And what he was looking for: the video he'd shot directly when moving into the apartment, for purposes of demonstrating its condition upon his taking possession, in case he ever needed to argue for getting his security deposit reimbursed. Nothing fancy; he'd just turned on his phone camera, walked around the place, captured closeups of all of its features and defects, opened and closed all the doors, demonstrated appliance functionality or lack of, and otherwise collected all the evidence he thought a tenant attorney might need.

He watched the video through, marveling at how big the space looked with no furniture in place, how bright it appeared with all the blinds drawn and lights blazing, how fresh and new everything within it looked in comparison to its present state.

A minute before the video ended, with the impromptu tour concluded, he saw himself returning to the front door, filming it from inside. The lens focused alternately on the hinges, the lock mechanisms, the security chain, the knob handle.

And then he saw his own hand reach into the frame, open the door.

And across the hall, there was definitely no doorway. Just a bare, blank, beige wall.

Now he knew he wasn't crazy, or at least not delusional. He was right in his perceptions: a little over a week ago, there had been no door there, just like he'd thought. And if it had been there that Monday evening when he'd gotten home, he would've noticed it. But he hadn't, and it wasn't.

And then he got up, and it was.

By the end of the second week, Wes's sleep schedule had gotten so far off track it was an even bet whether it would be light or dark out during the few hours a day he managed to haul his carcass out of bed. But whatever the time, during his wakeful hours he did little but peering through his peephole towards the doorway opposite his, cheek pressed flat against the cool manufactured wood surface, certain the moment he tore himself away that he'd miss—well, what exactly he didn't know.

But that was the point; he didn't know what he didn't know, and that was what was so maddening. Once or twice, he nearly tripped over his own feet in the dizzy somnolence of rushing toward the peephole after hearing something moving in the hallway, grinding his teeth with frustration when it inevitably turned out to be a neighbor carting groceries down the hall, or a package delivery driver that had somehow gotten passed through the security on the ground floor that was supposed to restrict the halls against nonresidents.

It wasn't until he found himself lying in bed idly watching videos of lock-picking techniques on his phone for upwards of an hour that he realized what his subconscious was urging him towards. Confronted with the possibilities, he recoiled in dismay—what kind of person was he becoming? And for the next hour, he forced his attention elsewhere, rewatching the best bits of a favorite old comedy film from his youth, laughing too loudly and stiltedly at all the familiar punchlines, trying to divert his thoughts away from what might lie across the hall.

But inevitably, after another fitful night or day of twisting, interrupted half-sleep, Wes stood in the hallway in his stained sweatpants and wrinkled t-shirt, feet bare against the industrial, aggressively neutral hall carpeting. The end of his latest sleep cycle had found him waking up on his couch in the dead of night at ten past three in the morning, when no decent person was up, and even most of the indecent ones had packed it in for the night. The fluorescent buzz of the lights above was the only sound to be heard, save for the occasional distant hint of muffled snoring from

2N, a few doors down. The hall stank of the artificial floral cleaner they used on everything, burying any unpleasant odors beneath the sickly aroma of chemically engineered flowerbeds.

He stared unblinking at the door, trying to figure out what had changed about it, why he couldn't dislodge it from his system.

And then he saw it: the brass numbering had been changed. Completed.

It now read 2S.

That can't be, he thought, the words going through his mind just like that, over and over as he read and reread the brass nailed to the door. *That can't be.*

But it was. And no matter how many times he blinked and rubbed his deeply bloodshot eyes, it remained so.

Without thinking, he reached out, grabbed the handle of the strange door, rattled it ineffectually with what remaining strength he had. He wanted to scream out, pound on its implacable surface, but he knew he'd only find himself standing there with all the irate neighbors he'd roused from their cozy beds, glaring at him like he was a lunatic. Or worse, with pity in their eyes, like he'd seen when he'd been sent home from work those weeks ago.

Was it weeks? Or was it less? Surely not more than a month. He'd have to check to be sure. But it was still November, he was pretty sure of that at least.

An idea occurred to him then, one he immediately discarded as being too insane even to entertain. But his head turned nevertheless, gazing through his open doorway to the kitchen table where his keyring rested atop amid a pile of half-finished food delivery containers.

Almost unaware of his actions, his legs carried him back into his apartment and plucked the keyring from the detritus. He walked back to the door across the hall, 2S now mirrored on both surfaces, inserted his own apartment key in the door's keyhole opposite his own. It turned with an audible chunk that resonated in the empty hallway and sank in his gut like a stone. He released the keys from his grip; the door swung open of its own accord.

Somehow, he was unsurprised by what he saw: it was his own apartment.

Not as it currently looked, discarded laundry and forgotten trash scattered across the floor, fixtures looking as though they hadn't seen the business end of a bottle of spray cleaner in far too long. And, of course, many of the apartments in the Towers shared the same basic layout, differing only in how their tenants chose to furnish and decorate them. But somehow, down to the last detail, this was his apartment as it was before and as it should have been, every item mirrored down to the nth degree. The couch even had that irritating mismatched seam on the rear corner where the fabric had folded over upon itself before being tacked to the framing.

Every light was on, and the brilliant glare burned into his retinas for a full minute before his rundown irises could adjust properly. He hadn't bothered to turn any lights in his own apartment on for longer than he could remember, preferring instead to exist in a sort of perpetual twilight. But here, every bulb functioned at full capacity or more, flooding the space with sufficient illumination to broadcast a professional football game.

As his eyes settled into focus, he recognized more and more items from his own apartment that he hadn't noticed in longer than he could remember. The silicone trivets a long-gone girlfriend had bought him as a housewarming present. The coasters he'd bought on a whim and hated immediately but couldn't justify getting rid of until he found a set he liked better. Even the magnets on the refrigerator, down to the magnetized pineapple-shaped bottle opener Kylen had brought him as a souvenir from his honeymoon in Hawaii and that he'd felt obligated to put up in case his work friend and his new bride ever made it over to his apartment. Everything just the same as in his own apartment across the hall—but somehow cleaner, more orderly. Better.

Though not everything was exactly the same, he was noticing. The television, for example: it was the same brand as the one he owned, but a newer, slightly larger model. The range had fancy induction coils, not the leaky old gas burners on the model back in his place. And in the framed picture of him with his family atop his bookshelf—the bookshelf, not his bookshelf—his mother was smiling.

Dazed, he shuffled around the place, taking in the surreal hyperreality of it. It was like getting a glimpse of what he was supposed to be, of the potential everyone had always said he had that he wasn't working up to, whatever that meant. But now he could see what it might have meant, and he didn't like it at all.

The kitchen, the same as his—but all the appliances one notch better than his own, from the four-slice toaster to the programmable bread-maker to the refrigerator that dispensed chilled water and ice in either crushed or cubed form or anywhere in between on demand.

The bedroom, the same as his—but clean, and smelling fresh, with bed fully made, looking for all the world like it had never been slept in, complete with the quilt his great-aunt Kohana had made for him.

Peering into the bathroom, he was unsurprised to see his own face staring back at him from the mirror—until he realized the face he saw was smiling. And that was no mirror, but someone that looked exactly like him, standing in the bathroom, smiling at him.

Waiting for him.

"What the hell," he mumbled, jumping back in surprise.

The smile widened.

"What indeed," the thing with Wes's face said, reaching out towards him.

Joy and LaToya were exceedingly relieved when Wes showed up at work on Monday at five minutes to eight, right on time.

"Sorry about the last few weeks," Wes told each of them individually. "I had some personal stuff I was dealing with. But I've put it behind me now."

They took him at his word, of course, accepting his apologies graciously and wishing him well in his fresh start. Subconsciously, both women held their breath until Wes made it to the end of the day without either falling asleep at his desk or otherwise disrupting the flow of business. But after that day, and all the flawless days of nigh-perfect performance Wes delivered from that moment forward, all issues of the past were forgotten and forgiven, wiped clean from his employment history.

Kylen, too, was glad Wes had gotten his shit together. It made everything easier for everyone, he couldn't deny that. With a pregnant wife and twins on the way, Kylen had plenty on his plate, so it was a relief when his work buddy seemed to finally straighten out and fly right—just one less thing to worry about.

He so distinctly remembered that celebratory evening with Wes and Joy the day he'd started at the firm—the three of them shoulder to shoulder, clinking their pints together with their right hands—that maybe it *did* bug him now when he saw Wes signing documents with his left.

Maybe his memories had gotten mixed up.

It wasn't any of his business, anyway.

Folie-À-Deux

GINA EASTON

Her sister's desperate supplication: "Save me, Emily. You're the only one who can."

Emily struggled from the depths of another fitful sleep. Her sister's face, beloved features distorted with anguish and fear. A fragment of nightmare clawed at her, trying to drag her back beneath the roiling waters of darkness and grief. Gasping, drenched in perspiration, she wrenched herself awake, bolting upright in bed.

Waited until the erratic beating of her heart returned to a normal rhythm. Even after a month, the nightmares still besieged her every time she closed her eyes, preventing true, restorative sleep, wearing her down with their relentless assault, leaving only constant gnawing anxiety. Combined with her grief, it caused her to feel jittery, on edge, nerves raw and pulsating. A persistent dread lodged in her heart.

She had lost so much. Not only her precious sister, but the means to earn a livelihood, which, until the catastrophic event that had claimed Elvira, had seemed secure and reliable. Emily and Elvira, the celebrated Montague twins, highly esteemed in the spiritualist circles of London, in this year of 1890.

Five years previously, at the age of twenty-one, they had been introduced by a well-known patron of the spiritualist movement, Lady Helen Hapscombe. Very quickly, they had become the most sought-after phenomena of seance-goers throughout London.

Both had startling abilities as necromancers and clairvoyants. Elvira, more flamboyant and theatrical in nature, would most often conduct a seance, serving as a conduit for those who wished to contact the dead. Emily, reserved and introspective, preferred a less dominant role. She supervised the sittings and ensured the participants adhered to the guidelines explained beforehand.

She was also tasked with monitoring Elvira in her trance state. Many seance enthusiasts were unaware of the potential hazards facing a medium. Every time Elvira made contact with the spirit world, she exposed herself to possible untoward effects.

Relaxing her psychic defences and opening herself as a portal to the spirit world posed a risk of attracting negative energies intent on proving mischievous and troublesome. And then there were others who could threaten her equilibrium, both her physical and psychic well-being. Under Emily's protective scrutiny, Elvira could completely entrust herself to the trance, thereby attaining maximum clarity in her communication with the spirits.

Lady Hapscombe was inordinately pleased with her proteges as they gained more fame and admiration. The foremost spiritualist periodicals of the day proclaimed the Montague twins to be the most authentic and gifted necromancers to come along in years. Word of their extraordinary abilities soon reached the Continent; in 1887, Lady Hapscombe arranged for them to make their debut amongst the elite of the spiritualist circles in Paris, Vienna, Rome, and Florence.

The twins were so much in demand that most of Europe soon clamoured to attend their seances. The tour was highly successful and lucrative for the Montagues.

Now, with the means to sustain themselves financially, they eschewed the opulent lifestyle they could have afforded. Neither was particularly interested in material acquisitions. They lived comfortably and that satisfied them. Perhaps it was their connection to the spiritual world that allowed them an appreciation of how ephemeral wealth, possessions, and the physical world really were.

The sisters were committed to their craft, recognising the need for genuine necromancers like themselves to assist those whose grief or desire for knowledge drove them to seek communion with deceased loved ones. Some sought reassurance that their dear departed was "happy" in their new existence. Others wished to convey messages they had omitted or been unable to tell the person when he or she was alive. But the largest number sought counsel from the spirits, asking them to reveal future events or advise them on important decisions. Indeed, some spiritualist believers dared not venture into any new endeavour without first receiving approval from the spirits.

Unfortunately, the spiritualist movement was infested with fraudsters, those unscrupulous enough to prey on desperate or gullible souls who would gladly pay exorbitant prices for the opportunity to "speak" to a deceased relative or friend. The Montagues abhorred the swindlers and mountebanks whose scurrilous practices cast a blight of suspicion, and at times, outright derision upon a calling they viewed as pure and noble.

As girls, Elvira, the more adventurous of the two, had never hesitated to play with the shades of dead children who regularly manifested themselves to the twins. Emily would stand aside, watching with a mixture of longing and trepidation, as her sister cavorted and romped with deceased playmates. Part of her wished she could have joined in the games with abandon and been as carefree as Elvira. But she'd always heeded the warning in her heart. Even at a young age, Emily understood a fundamental truth.

It would be a mistake to become too comfortable with the dead.

Perhaps that's why she was alive and well, while Elvira...

Emily closed her eyes, trying in vain to squeeze away the tears of sorrow that welled up once more. A large gaping hole existed inside her, like part of her soul was missing. Her sister's absence was excruciating. They had always been inseparable, certainly in the physical sense, but also emotionally. How she longed to hear Elvira's light footfall on the stairs, to share a laugh with her, to listen to her musical tones gaily reciting some anecdote for Emily's amusement.

Lady Helen, during one of her frequent visits to offer solace, had gently inquired whether Emily had received any news of her sister from "the other side".

"It would seem only natural," she ventured, teacup balanced on her lap as she sat across from Emily in the parlour, "that Elvira would make contact with you."

Emily's misery was palpable as she said, barely above a whisper, "It doesn't work like that." In a stronger voice, she explained, "Things are very different in the spirit world. The dead are not like the living, as most people seem to think. They don't share the same wants and desires. What may have been important to them when they were alive might now hold no relevance at all. For instance, they have no concept of time; that is a construct for the living. It's been a month for us since Elvira passed, but in her present existence, it could feel but a moment."

Lady Hapscombe nodded. "Yes, I see that she may not feel the need to make contact. But surely *you* have reached out to *her*?"

Emily bowed her head to conceal the pain in her eyes. "No, I don't feel it is right to do so just yet." There was so much she could not say to Lady Helen, even though she was the closest thing to a friend. For how could anyone understand? Only one other…whom she feared might be lost to her forever.

Lady Helen reached across and patted her hand. "I understand, dear. No one knows more than you about the dead. Take all the time you need to mourn. There is no pressure to resume sittings, but I hope you will consider carrying on the legacy which you and Elvira built together. You have helped so many people. And your services are still needed."

Emily watched wordlessly as Lady Helen stood to leave. She kissed Emily lightly on the cheek. "I shall see you again soon."

Secrets. Secrets were terrible things. Gnawing away at one's peace of mind, weighing heavier with each passing day. Some secrets were worse than others because they had to be borne alone. There was no possibility of sharing them with even *one* other person. Because they were too dangerous.

Like the secret of what had really happened to Elvira.

The story Emily told was simple. Elvira had died in her sleep. "Some sort of heart seizure, according to the doctor," she said. "Unusual, yes, for a woman in her prime, but these events do occur." A terrible misfortune, everyone agreed, for one so young and gifted.

The truth was so much worse.

Emily's own heart clenched in pain every time she thought of Elvira's tragic fate and her own complicity in it. No matter that there had been no other recourse. Elvira had suffered such torment and had begged for mercy in one of the increasingly rare moments when she was truly in control of her thoughts and actions.

"This is too much to bear," she had sobbed. "It won't give me a moment of respite."

"It", of course, was the demon.

The demon had so cleverly taken possession of Elvira, rendering her a virtual prisoner trapped inside her own consciousness, ever aware of the entity usurping control of her mind and body, yet powerless to resist its insatiable, evil dictates.

The possession had occurred innocently enough. An ordinary seance, proceeding in the usual fashion. There had been a successful communication with the spirit world, resulting in a wife's tearful reunion with her departed husband. Following a brief interlude, a slight frown had creased Elvira's brow and a noticeable frisson trembled through her body.

Still deep in her trance, she intoned, "There is a spirit who wishes to speak. One who is unable to rest peacefully, who is in utter anguish." Her frown deepened and she sighed, a grimace of pain momentarily distorting her features. "She was taken violently from her existence on the physical plane, a death fraught with terror and agony." Elvira began to rock back and forth, arms wrapped protectively around herself. "Mary. She says her name is Mary Kelly."

An audible gasp came from a man seated at the table. His gaze bored fiercely into the medium. "If this is a hoax, it is in monstrously bad taste," he declared indignantly.

Emily, seated at the opposite end of the table from her twin, replied, "I assure you, sir, that my sister is a legitimate necromancer. We do not engage in hoaxes or chicanery. Am I to understand this name means something to you?"

The woman seated beside the man whispered in his ear. When she was done, he nodded and looked at Emily. "My wife assures me that your reputation, Miss Montague, and that of your sister, are above reproach."

He leaned forward, watching Elvira with a keen stare. "What can Mary tell me about her killer?" he asked urgently. "What can she say about Jack the Ripper?"

Gasps of shock and horror were heard from others around the table, followed by a murmur of concerned and anxious mutterings. Emily swiftly intervened. "Please. We must have quiet and order," she admonished firmly. "My sister needs to maintain her focus or the connection to the spirit will be severed."

Immediate silence ensued. Elvira spoke once again. "Mary says there is one among you who can avenge her death. A policeman…no, inspector. Inspector?"

"Frederick Aberline," the man replied. "I led the investigation into the Ripper murders."

Elvira nodded. "Mary says you must solve the case. Her spirit cannot rest until you do. She shall remain earthbound, trapped in darkness, unless the fiend is caught and punished."

The inspector sighed in frustration. "Believe me, I have tried. For two years, I have not stopped searching for this madman. But he has vanished without a trace. Is there any clue Mary can give me?"

While they waited for a response Emily asked, "I am curious, Inspector. Why are you here? Surely you did not expect to encounter the spirit of one of Jack the Ripper's victims at this seance?"

"It was because of me," the petite woman beside him said. "I wished to contact our son, who passed over three years ago. I so desire to know if he is at peace finally. Alas," she concluded sorrowfully, "we have yet to reach him."

Aberline nodded in agreement. "We have attended numerous seances over the years, at my wife's insistence. I must confess that, unlike Mrs. Aberline, I have not the same stalwart faith in spiritualist practices. Now, however…if this is indeed Mary Kelly—"

Elvira let out an agonised wail. When she spoke into the shocked silence, her voice had become higher-pitched and lilting, a mix of Cockney and Irish inflexions. *"You 'ave to 'elp me, Inspector. You're the only one who can. Find 'im. Find the Ripper!"*

The clairvoyant's entire body shook violently, her eyes rolling back in her head.

Alarmed for her sister's welfare, Emily hastened to turn up the lights and then ran over to her side. "Elvira! El? You must end the trance, *now*." She snapped her fingers in front of Elvira's face, without effect.

Elvira continued to thrash and flail about. The convulsions shook her so forcefully, she was hurled from her chair onto the floor. Eerie ululating cries interspersed with guttural moans escaped through her gnashing teeth.

The seance patrons reacted in appalled shock. A woman screamed. Mrs. Aberline looked about to faint, but her husband caught her in his arms and carefully lowered her to her chair. People rushed for the front door, clearly unnerved by the seizures afflicting the necromancer. Of paramount concern was their own safety, for all noticed the ominous shift in atmosphere heralded by the advent of Mary Kelly's spirit. A forbidding, sinister pall descended on the room, striking fear into their hearts.

Only Aberline remained to assist Emily with her sister. As had happened on so many occasions, Emily felt her body react in an empathetic response to her twin. Tremors and twitches, albeit much milder in strength, coursed through her system. A glacial coldness penetrated her. She knelt by Elvira's side as her sister writhed in contortions on the floor. She could only watch helplessly, waiting until the convulsive movements and disturbing noises subsided. After several minutes, they stopped completely and Elvira fell into a deep and soundless sleep.

"Whatever that was, it seems to have passed," observed the inspector. He turned to Emily, who slowly rose to her feet. "Has this happened before?"

"On a few occasions," Emily admitted, face deathly pale. "But never as severe or prolonged as this."

"You have had rather a shock, Miss Montague. Shall I fetch a doctor for you and your sister?"

Emily shook her head. "That will not be necessary, Inspector. Elvira needs plenty of rest now. As you say, she has had a shock to her system. Unfortunately, untoward reactions can occur to those in a trance state. I believe she will soon be back to normal. However, if you could carry her to the divan, I would be most grateful."

The inspector lifted Elvira's inert form and gently deposited her on the divan. Emily retrieved a blanket and placed it over her sister.

"Thank you, Inspector," she said quietly.

Aberline, joined now by his wife in the vestibule, considered the young woman soberly. "I do hope your sister makes a full recovery."

As they turned to leave, Mrs. Aberline spontaneously reached for Emily's hand. "You and your sister have such a gift," she said, eyes moist with tears. "God bless you both."

Emily closed the door behind them, momentarily leaning her head against the solid wood frame. She fought the wave of weariness threatening to wash over her. Drawing a deep breath, she went to check on Elvira. Her sister looked to be sleeping peacefully, as if she had not a care in the world.

Emily, in contrast, was sorely troubled. In their five years of conducting seances, Elvira had never experienced such a violent response to contacting a spirit. The occurrence tonight unnerved Emily. A jarring blow had been delivered to her equilibrium. A coldness had infiltrated her body during Elvira's seizure. Now it nestled at the base of her spine, sending tendrils of dread to creep through her. A metallic taste of fear coated the back of her throat. Her nerve endings tingled unpleasantly, causing her to startle at every little creak and groan of the old house.

Shivering, she turned up all the lamps in the parlour. Although the light dispelled the shadows in the room, it failed to banish the uneasiness in her heart.

◆————————◆

Long past midnight. Emily roused from a fitful sleep, echoes of laughter following her into wakefulness. She still sat in the wing-back chair in the parlour, having drifted off to sleep while keeping vigil over Elvira. The divan was empty. Where had Elvira gone? The lights burned low now, casting a weak glow which barely penetrated the far corners of the room.

Corners from which a rustling and chittering emanated.

Could it be mice? Emily wondered, knowing by the quickening of her heartbeat that it was not. Something occupied the shadows. Emily sensed its sly invitation, wheedling at her to come closer, to see what hid from the light, what eagerly waited to enfold her in its lifeless embrace.

Shaking the last cobwebs of sleep from her mind, Emily jumped out of her chair. She wasn't going to wait around to find out what eventually would emerge from the shadows. Grabbing a lamp, she hurried into the corridor. She would deal with the shadows later. Right now, she needed to find Elvira.

"El?" she called softly into the darkness.

Laughter again. So it hadn't been a dream after all. Elvira's laughter, coming from upstairs. Instead of reassuring her, the sound served only to fuel her growing sense of dread. What could her sister find so amusing in the dead of night?

As Emily quickly ascended the stairs, she heard a soft humming from Elvira's room at the end of the corridor. She recognised the tune as a lullaby Mother had sung to them when they were little girls. That song had always given her comfort when she needed it, but now it sounded oddly distorted to her ears.

Approaching the room, she knocked quietly on the door.

"El?"

No answer. The lullaby stopped.

Emily stood outside the door, trying to quell her increasing disquiet. Something seemed eerie about the laughter and the lullaby, something so *wrong*. She couldn't identify what it was; the thoughts wouldn't form in her mind, but the hairs on the back of her neck and arms quivered in dread.

"Come in, sister." Elvira's voice. A raspy whisper.

With a trembling hand, Emily opened the door.

And froze in horror at the sight before her.

Elvira floated a metre above the bed. Clad in her nightgown, long dark hair flowing down her back, arms dangling limply by her sides.

Emily gasped, hardly daring to believe her eyes.

At the sound, Elvira turned her head towards her sister. Her eyes snapped open. Nothing of Elvira existed in that face. The eyes blazed with malignant hatred while the mouth gaped in a leering grimace.

Laughter issued from that mouth. It was not Elvira's laughter, but a dark, mocking snarl.

Then she spoke in an insinuating tone, voice dripping with malice as thick as treacle.

"You and your sister belong to me. My slaves. My playthings. I will make your sister do unspeakable things, acts so vile you cannot even begin to imagine their hideousness. And you shall bear witness to them. You will be complicit in every action. You shall suffer greatly," it oozed in gleeful anticipation. "She will destroy herself. But first, she will kill you. And then you both will writhe in torment for all eternity in the infernal Pit from which there is no escape nor succour."

The voice stopped. Abruptly, as though the invisible marionette strings holding her aloft had been severed, Elvira's body fell to the bed. Her eyes were closed and once more, she appeared to be sleeping.

Emily willed herself to gain control over her fear. One word reverberated over and over in her head: possession. The disturbing suspicion had festered in the back of her mind ever since the seance. Now there was no doubt. She had witnessed the manifestation with her own eyes.

Elvira was possessed by the demon who'd pretended to be Mary Kelly. It had been clever enough to trick her, vulnerable in her trance state, into allowing it access. Now it had usurped control over her mind, body, and soul.

As necromancers, both sisters had studied the phenomenon of demonic possession. Emily understood enough about the subject to recognise the direness of their predicament. Unless she could figure out a way to rid Elvira of this demon, both of them might well be doomed.

Rising panic threatened to overwhelm her, but she knew if she succumbed to it, she would invite chaos to overtake them. She had always been Elvira's protector, and she would not fail her sister in her hour of greatest need.

Fighting back tears, she regained control over her breathing. *Think!* she admonished herself. *Devise a plan. And hurry, for there is not much time.* She paced up and down the corridor, alert for any sign of Elvira emerging from her demon-induced slumber. Her brain worked furiously, finally forming an idea. An image of the two massive steamer trunks, presently in storage in the attic, entered her mind. The strong leather bindings girding the trunks would suit her purpose nicely.

Satisfied with her plan, Emily dashed up the stairs to the attic.

Later, she stood by Elvira's bed, exhausted from the strenuous activity of the last hour. The effort had drained her of what little strength she'd had, but it had been absolutely necessary to protect both of them. So far, the demon had been content to let Elvira sleep, but how long would that last?

No sooner had the thought occurred to her than her sister's eyes fluttered open. No trace of the demon remained in them. Only El, smiling at her at first, then looking confused as she tried to move and found she could not.

"Em?" she asked. "Why can't I move? I can barely lift my head."

"I know, El, but it was necessary to restrain you so you can't harm yourself or me."

Elvira stared at her sister, uncomprehending. "Harm myself? Or you? Why on earth would I do such a thing?" She struggled against the tough leather straps, but to no avail. She looked at Emily beseechingly. "It would seem that you are the one who wishes to harm me!"

Emily pulled a chair up to the bedside. She sat down, grabbing her sister's hand. "I have something very disturbing to tell you. Last night during the seance, you thought you contacted the spirit of Mary Kelly. But it was really a demon masquerading as her, and that demon took possession of you."

Elvira's jaw dropped in shocked amazement, appalled at what she was hearing. "No, Emily! You must be mistaken! I don't…remember… everything that happened, but…"

Emily's voice was full of sorrow. "You suffered what, at the time, I believed to be a trance-induced seizure, but now I know it was the demon entering and taking control of you."

Elvira shook her head in vigorous denial. "That cannot be. Although I have no recollection of this seizure, I know how to protect myself from negative energies. I assure you that, aside from being a little weak, as I often am after a sitting, I feel perfectly fine."

Emily sighed. "We are not talking about mere 'negative' energies, El. This is a *demonic* entity intent on causing great harm. It has control of you and is deceiving you into thinking nothing untoward has happened."

"Emily! Surely you can't believe that because I suffered some sort of fit, I am possessed by a demon. Why, that is absurd—"

"I saw you levitate off this very bed but an hour ago," her sister interrupted. "And you spoke with the demon's foul voice. It threatened to kill us both."

A stunned silence. Then Elvira said in a trembling whisper, "Dear God, sister, if this is true, I cannot bear it." Panic filled her eyes. "What shall become of me? Am I going to die?"

Emily's expression was grave. "According to the demon, it will surely kill us. But we will thwart its intentions. That is why I have bound you. I must formulate a plan to defeat this fiend and prevent it from using you as its puppet."

"We must consult a clergyman," Elvira said urgently. "Perhaps the pastor at Saint Bartholomew's…"

Emily nodded. "I shall call upon him first thing in the morning."

"An exorcism?" Elvira whispered the word, shivering with dread at the idea.

"I see no other course of action," Emily agreed. "If the pastor supports that plan, then the sooner it is done, the better."

Tears spilled from Elvira's eyes. "I am so afraid, Em," she sobbed. "I can only bear this burden if you are by my side. Promise you won't leave me."

Emily squeezed her cold hand reassuringly. "I shall always protect you, El."

Lady Hapscombe sat in the Montague parlour, once again visiting to offer consolation and support to Emily. Not only did she consider this her duty, she also felt a genuine fondness for the sisters and was stricken with sadness herself at Elvira's unexpected demise. She could only imagine how awful these last four weeks had been for Emily. The loss of an identical twin must have felt like losing a part of oneself.

They had just finished tea. As she waited for Emily's return from the kitchen, she thought she heard a peculiar sound from upstairs. She cocked her head to one side, listening intently. Yes—there it was again. How odd. It sounded like someone crying softly. Lady Helen frowned. There was no one upstairs, and yet the crying was undeniable.

A frisson of excitement coursed down her spine. Could this possibly be a spirit trying to communicate with her? Maybe Elvira herself? Lady Helen rose from the chair, a sense of urgency propelling her forward. She felt a sense of foreboding mixed with anticipation. If she were to hear or even *see* Elvira's spirit materialise, how wondrous would that be?

Without further thought, she hurried into the corridor and up the staircase. The sobbing was louder now. It definitely came from the room at the end of the hallway. A momentary shiver of dread caused her steps to falter, but she ignored it, continuing towards the room.

Reaching the door, she took a deep breath. What if it was locked? But the knob turned easily, and she opened the door.

She tried to scream, but horror strangled the sound in her throat.

Green muslin curtains had been drawn against the daylight. Nevertheless, sufficient illumination from the single lamp by the bedside revealed the figure in the bed.

A woman, secured tightly by leather straps around her upper body and thighs. Restraints around both ankles anchored them to the bed frame. Tattered nightgown filthy with excrement and other stains. Stick-thin limbs fragile and brittle as bleached driftwood. Knobby wrists and knees swollen with inflammation.

The torn nightdress revealed the terrible wounds on her body. Open lesions, too many to count, oozed vile, foul-smelling discharge. Numerous burns, unable to heal, were also infected and suppurating. Gangrenous ulcers devoured the skin and deeper tissues of her feet. The stench of rotting flesh was nauseating.

Lady Helen fought the swoon of revulsion which threatened to overwhelm her. One hand covering her nose and mouth against the awful reek, she stepped into the room, despite her nerves screaming at her to turn and run. She had to check if the woman was still alive or...

She crept close enough to see the woman's face. Long matted hair, dull and unwashed, spread across the blood-stained pillow. Lips cracked and dry as old leather, encrusted with chancre sores. The crying had stopped upon Lady Helen's arrival. The woman gawked at Lady Helen, eyes wild and lost, the light of sanity extinguished, only the dark veil of madness evident.

Lady Helen's horror and shock intensified as she finally recognised the battered and disfigured body.

Elvira.

Lady Helen gasped in confusion and fear. How could this be? Why had Emily lied about Elvira being dead? Here she was, barely clinging to life, a prisoner held captive by her own *sister*. Had she been confined to her bed these past four weeks? Her appalling condition would attest to that. And what of the torture inflicted upon her? Emily would never have perpetrated such heinous acts, especially on someone she held so dear. She was devoted to Elvira, of that there could be no doubt. And yet…

"Ah, Lady Helen," said a voice behind her. "I see you've discovered my secret."

The older woman whirled around to face Emily. "In God's name!" she cried, outrage mingling with her fear. "What have you done?"

Emily's lower lip trembled. "You have no idea how awful it has been. This terrible affliction of Elvira has left me heartsick with sorrow." She gestured toward the figure on the bed. "My dear sister has been possessed by a demon since our last seance a month ago."

Lady Helen gaped in disbelief. "A…d…demon," she stammered. "But surely you are mistaken!"

"It's true." The voice, a dry whisper like the rustling of dead leaves, came from the putrefying skeletal form on the bed.

Lady Helen started, all colour draining from her face. "If this is so, why have you not engaged in the services of the clergy? Aren't they the experts in this…phenomenon?"

"Exorcism, you mean." Emily sighed forlornly. "We thought of that option, of course. At El's suggestion, I went to consult a pastor. But I was told not to trust him."

Lady Helen frowned. "Who told you such a thing?"

"The dead. The voices in the shadows," Emily explained. "They whispered to me that the priest was also possessed, and that I must dispatch him before he could harm anyone."

Lady Helen's eyes bulged with horror. "Dispatch? You mean you *killed* him?"

Emily regarded her earnestly. "It was necessary in order to stop the evil. The dead have been counselling me on this issue. Ever since the night of the seance, they have watched over me. They informed me that the clergyman is not the only one harbouring a demon. There are others. They are also advising me on how to rid El of her demon, so that she may recover and together we can begin the crusade to eradicate evil from society."

"B…but," Lady Helen sputtered, "those terrible wounds…"

Tears sprang to Emily's eyes. "I sorely deplore the necessity of these actions, but I had to excise and burn her flesh as part of the treatment. The 'purification process', according to the spirits. I regret that this has caused El pain—"

"Pain!" Lady Helen exclaimed. "You are killing her with your heinous assaults. You have already driven her mad!"

"No, no," Elvira croaked. "The treatment is working. I sense the demon's hold over me is finally weakening."

"You see?" Emily asked triumphantly. "The spirits have confirmed this. Soon the fiend will be unable to resist my attempts to expel it, and Elvira shall be restored to herself."

"She will be *dead*. Look at her!" Dumbfounded, Lady Helen stared into Emily's eyes. The gleam of lunacy was there. And a hint of something else. Maniacal yet sinister, a presence lurking just below the surface.

"My Lord!" she cried in dawning horror. "It is not *Elvira* who is possessed—" A sudden wave of dizziness and lassitude overcame her. In danger of losing her balance, she grabbed the wall to steady herself. Her vision blurred and the room spun around her.

"The laudanum I put in your tea is affecting you now," Emily informed her. "You should sit down before you swoon."

"Wh…why?" Lady Helen's tongue felt heavy and thick. She found it increasingly difficult to form coherent thoughts as she sank helplessly to her knees. She looked up at her captor, seeing the mask fall and the diabolic revealed.

Emily smiled. "Because you, too, have a demon in you. The dead warned me to beware of you and your nefarious offers of solace and friendship. But do not despair, Lady Helen. Look at the progress I'm making with Elvira. The process may take a while, but I have great patience and perseverance. And your bed is all prepared in the spare room."

Lady Helen, on her hands and knees, tried to crawl through the doorway. Sobbing in terror as the strength drained from her limbs, she collapsed face-first onto the floor.

She felt her feet being lifted and her body dragged along the carpet, understanding with her waning clarity that a fate in many ways worse than death awaited her.

The last sound she heard before unconsciousness claimed her was the strains of a lullaby.

PHOENIX

J. D. OUTCALT

Hello my light,

I should be home soon. No more than a few hours. You know how this goes. "Rise from the ashes" and all that. You'll be fine, I'm sure. Hold it together!

I'll be too tired to cook when I get back, so let's just treat ourselves and order out. I'm thinking Italian.

Love,

Mother

The cold refrigerator light illuminates the dark hovel my home has become. The glow shines over the words Mother penned almost two years ago. As my fingertips trace over the page, grasping for some remnant of her, a trail of ash remains in their wake. Bandages wrap my six remaining fingers along with my arms and the rest of my body, but it doesn't stop my dying skin from flaking through the cracks. I've become a walking hourglass: my body dissolving like sand, the bandages providing a poor substitute for glass to contain it. Part of me hoped they would slow whatever the fuck is happening to me until Mother gets better, but it seems I may have to face my rebirth alone.

This is *not* how Mother told me it should happen.

With a delicate touch, I attempt to close the refrigerator door in front of me. Ever. So. Gingerly.

To my horror, my left ring finger snaps off of my hand and falls into a pile of ash on the floor. I am now down to five. I try to hold back cold tears that long to spill down my face. They threaten to weaken the bandages. This wouldn't have happened if I had just remained patient.

Without someone to guide me, my impulses are unbounded, unbridled. So in Mother's absence, I met a man. Mother would have said I was being impulsive, but I couldn't stand being left to my own devices. Remembering the warmth the relationship gave me still incites painful cravings. But it was equally disastrous as it was magnificent. It could shift from one to the other in a heartbeat, too. Despite the unpredictability, it still provided me the comfort that kept me sane, so I stuck around. Something was better than nothing.

That all changed, though, when I told him the doubt I had been wrestling with all along: that Mother might never return. As soon as the admission left my mouth, I knew he would never understand why I, despite all reason, would never relinquish my faith in Mother. But even then, I could recognize how crazy I sounded. How could I expect him to have the same faith I did?

He employed his cold, sensible condescension to get me to see reason. But to accept his point of view was to accept the worst. If Mother's health never improved, then I would truly be alone.

"Stop saying she's sick," he tried to drill into me. "She is *gone*. The sooner you accept that, the sooner you can move on and live your own life."

At that time, my tears could still steam off my hot, burning cheeks before they rolled past my nose.

"It isn't that simple," I sobbed. He hated this line, but it was true. He didn't understand the power of the flame that burned within me, Mother, and all our ancestors before us. If we were to meet our demise before our later years, the fire would grow into a bonfire that would swallow our remains. Shortly after, we return to life, our body cleansed of any disease and healed of any injury. As if we never were hurt in the first place. Mother had done it once, she could do it again.

Back then, It was so easy to be faithful and patient. But now, as my body spills onto the ground with each passing second, I no longer have the luxury of patience. And my faith in Mother has never been more tested.

After I shared my doubt with him, the comfort and guidance I went to him for vanished. The truth about Mother drove a wedge between us. So, I decided to end things.

"It's over," I told him. "I can't take it anymore."

He exploded out of lifeless apathy into a barrage of verbal assaults. I'd gotten used to his insults.

I was warned not to get close to someone like him. "Blood suckers," "life leeches," they called him. With his kind's insatiable nature—their endless hunger—people didn't think he could control himself. I dismissed their warnings. You'd have, too, if you knew the way he cared for me. Damnit, he *worshipped* me.

But now I see how blind I really was.

When I left his home for the last time, I embraced his frigid body: his cold, undead skin against mine, fiery hot. I felt his ragged breath on my neck, followed by a bite.

I shoved him away, but it was too late. Almost instantly, my radiating warmth vanished. The creep of decay had already begun to spread through me, smothering the fervent fire I once was. The chill traveled quickly from my neck and through the rest of me, as if I had been plunged into ice water. My neck flushed, the healthy red and pink fading to a ghastly gray. Even the slightest abrasion caused several layers of necrotized skin to fall away.

This single bite sealed my fate. A fate Mother always told me not to fear.

I stared at him, dumbstruck. "How could you?"

His head tilted towards the ceiling, eyes fluttering to a close as he relished in my stolen essence. But only for a moment. That lifeless, deadpan stare of his returned. The warmth he took from me was consumed, no longer present in him nor me, leaving us both cold, lifeless husks.

This was a new sensation, this cold.

I lurch from the daze of memories I've repeated endlessly in my head and move to the hallway closet. As I reach for the dustpan within it, my phone rings. I use my five remaining fingers to wiggle my phone out of my pocket, letting it clatter onto the hardwood floor. It's Jen. She is trying to video call me. I reject the call, and then call back without video.

"Hello?" I ask, forgetting to clear my throat before, so a lump of emotion (and ash) comes out with the greeting. Jen will probably notice.

She does. "You okay?"

I, with great difficulty, sweep my finger into the dustpan. "I'm alright. Same old, same old."

"You sure?" She isn't asking if I am okay, this is more of a question concerning why I've been dodging her calls.

I hold my hand up and watch the dangling ribbons of the bandages that once bound my finger to my knuckle. "Just trying to hold it together."

Jen accepts my clumsy attempt at deflection. "Everyone missed you at trivia last night."

I grab the excess bandage and wrap it around my palm. "I don't think anyone wants to see me go through this."

"What?" She scoffs. "Are you serious? Everyone knows what you're going through is totally natural! No one is going to judge."

There is nothing *natural* about what is happening to me. Rebirth is supposed to be quick and elegant. No more than a few hours. A day tops. That's what Mother said.

"Right." I try to shift the conversation's focus somewhere else. "I hear Alex has been hanging out with some new girl. What's that about?"

Jen pauses. "Are you close?"

Her question causes me to flinch. A bit blunt, don't you think, Jen? The ability of my people to reincarnate is no secret. While she knows I've already begun the process, I haven't disclosed to Jen how horribly wrong things have been going.

But why shouldn't I, though? I could very easily tell her. Maybe she could help me find a way to stop whatever is happening to me.

No. I can't. Telling her could invite more questions. Questions about Mother. Remember what happened the last time you did that?

"Soon, probably," I reply. Then quietly, "This has never happened to me before."

"Cheer up," she senses the apprehension in my voice. "'Fiery rebirth' and all that stuff. Not many have an opportunity like that. Just think about how lucky you are to get another chance at life!"

How lucky, indeed—to watch myself slowly disintegrate into a pile of ash, quietly panicking as I slowly lose my fingers and toes, then my limbs, inevitably until my neck crumbles under the weight of my massive head or until a sip of water breaks through the lining of my stomach and erodes my insides. "I know, Jen, I do. That doesn't change the fact that it's scary."

"Time heals all, babe."

Is she even listening? "In order for me to come back," I glance at the basement door, "I have to die."

"Yeah. That's what happens," she has the gall to chuckle. "Like all of your ancestors have at least once in their lifetime." I wince. "You've got good genes!"

"Take your bullshit sayings and shove them up your ass. I'm fucking *dying* and you have the nerve to tell me to not be afraid? When, Jen? When will I die? And when will I come back? Tell me, because I don't know and it's scaring the hell out of me and all you can think to do is tell me to be patient? Do you know how unhelpful that is?"

"Okay, okay. Look, I know your mom isn't well, but maybe you could ask—"

"No, I can't," I snap at her.

"But—"

"Jen. *I can't.*"

I can hear the noise of the bustling cityscape over her prolonged silence.

"We told you not to fuck around with him."

Then, Jen hangs up.

The cold tears are welling up again. Keep them down. Keep them down, damnit. Mother needs me. If I let my emotions destroy me, no one will be able to nurse Mother back to health.

Now that I think about it, Jen was probably the last person I could have asked for help. I could have let her know why I was so scared. I mean, all she was doing was just checking in on her friend. But no.

Instead, I just *had* to protect Mother. Or was I protecting myself from the truth? I waited for Mother, and I wound up getting bit. I waited for Mother, and I lost Jen. Waiting for Mother has burned countless bridges.

No, not burn. Mother did not burn. She was like a rot, slowly covering my life, until all remained was faith. But was it faith? Or was it delusion? Even if I did give up on Mother's recovery, it would not change my present situation. The damage is already done.

In the kitchen, I pull out a blank notecard from a drawer and write "left ring finger" on it. Retrieving one of the last bowls from the cupboard, I pour the ash from my dustpan into it.

Bowl in hand, I descend into the basement. When is this all supposed to be over? Jen wanted me to be patient, to welcome the release of death. Although I have known my whole life that I would have a second chance, and maybe more, it didn't make the dying part any easier. Looking down the steep staircase, I realize I could end it now and really put my biology to the test. Mother reminds me I can't take the risk. Not to mention I don't know the extent at which this bite has complicated things. Mother will return before I die and know what to do about it.

She must.

The unfinished basement is dimly lit by a single bulb, like the soft glow of a candle illuminating the inside of a tomb. And cold like one too. I've *never* felt cold before him. Is this how he feels all the time? If I were in his shoes, could I have resisted the urge to take someone else's warmth? After what I did to him, could I fault him?

I take a sharp left turn at the bottom of the steps and resist the urge to lift my gaze from the floor. At the opposite end of the room, I set the bowl with my finger down next to the two dozen others that are scattered on the floor. I place it next to the bowl with a notecard labeled "left index finger", which was next to "part of left forearm", next to "chest cavity", "portion of neck", "right ear", "right eyelid".

Kneeling down, I survey the puzzle pieces of the body I have lost. This is like my own personal ship of Theseus. Or, more pragmatically, a desperate attempt to have any amount of control over my fate. Instead of my remains turning to ash after I die, I am prematurely losing pieces of myself over the course of several days. So, what would happen if I were to die and come back, but a part of me was missing? Like one of my toes? Or worse, a scrap of gray matter? What would I lose? Would I return the same person? Or hollow, like I feel now? Do I even want to be the same person?

If the ship was missing a board in its hull, would it still be the ship of Theseus? I'm not sure, but what I do know is that it would sink.

My circumstance gives Mother's words a twisted new life. *Hold it together.*

I am, Mother. Just look at me. Is this what you meant? It is *so* hard. So hard to be alone and so cold.

I try to stand up, but my legs give out from under me. Bracing for impact, I fall to the floor, but feel nothing. In any other circumstance, this feeling, or lack thereof, would be welcome. I can't trust my feelings anymore, though. As I scan my body to make sure I am all intact, my breath catches in my throat when I reach my waist.

Both of my legs have been powdered. Piles of what remains of them pour out of the legs of my pants. My right, broken off at the knee. My left, almost taking the hip with it.

I lift my gaze from the floor and see the thing that I've been avoiding for so long. It is the source of my worries and fears. But it is also my only source of hope. A door.

It beckons to me.

I crawl towards it, my pants falling off from the weight of my remains within them. My torso is starting to go, too. In this state of shock, I neglect to try to keep my ashes together. Call it cowardice, lack of strength or logic, whatever. My desperation is not a choice. When you face death, as it slowly erodes your body, I'd like to see you try to not cling to the smallest fragment of hope that you can somehow stop it.

Reaching up, I turn the knob and swing the door open. Unlike the rest of the basement, this room is finished and furnished as a spare bedroom. It would have been a nice one, too, had it any windows. The landlord said he had this room made for his mother, so she could live closer to him, but she died in her sleep during her first night in the house.

"Mother," I cry. "Mother, *please.*" I want to scream against what is coming, but a sob is too dangerous. My warbling voice shakes regardless, letting ash fill my throat and lungs. The building pressure from suppressing my screams leads to a horrible pop in my diaphragm. My time is limited. With what little remains of my strength, I pull myself onto the bed from the floor, like a frightened animal clawing its way deeper into its hovel.

And then I see her. One large stock pot filled to the brim with ash. Four liters of potential. Of stubborn denial. Of Mother.

My shifting weight on the mattress causes the pot to wobble.

"No! Mother!" I cry.

Panic grips my throat as the pot tumbles. Ashes spill over me. Mother's fingers, torso, hopes, nightmares, all of her. Her ashes mingle with my own. There is nothing I can do to distinguish her ashes from my own. It doesn't matter. I need her back. No one's comfort remains but Mother's.

On the bedside table are my fail-safes. My ripcords: one a desperate attempt to jumpstart our genetics, the other to overcome my unnatural decay.

First, I reach for the box of matches. I pinch a match between my now three remaining fingers and hold the matchbox between my teeth. I strike the match and am immediately drawn to the flame. Carefree and tantalizing, the flame dances. I caress it. The dull sting grows slowly to an unbearable, treacherous pain. At first I relish it, remembering what it was like to once be ablaze. But what once was my essence now rejects me. I don't move the match until it burns out.

Tears are beginning to wear at the skin around my eyes. I will be blind soon.

Fiery rebirth.

I light three more matches and set them between my breasts. Or maybe Mother's. I don't know.

Rise from the ashes, that's what she told me.

"You're sick," I assure Mother. "Something's wrong with you, just like me. You just need more time, right?"

No response.

"Mother," I whimper. "Do something."

Any air left in my lungs is used to scream from the pain of the matches. Their flame bores a small rift in my chest. A creature of fire like myself is reduced to recoil and cower to a mere match's flame. "Mother, *please*. I can't do this alone."

Nothing happens.

I continue to light matches and let them burn me until there are none left. Any second now, I will come back. And so will you, Mother. We will rise from the ashes. We must.

My throat finally caves in to my screams, suffocating me. Unable to cough, I reach for the second fail-safe: whiskey. Without thinking, I put the bottle to my brittle lips and drink. My jaw first sloughs off, and then my neck dislodges from my body. How am I still conscious? Why aren't I gone yet, Mother? Maybe I will be stuck like this forever. Forever a sentient pile of ash until I am born again.

Determined not to live that existence, or cowardly seeking release from this misery, I let the whiskey pour over my face and body. The last remnants of my physical form is reduced to a pile of death infused with spices, smoke, and hints of vanilla.

Red Tide

VICTORIA BRUN

THE BLACK FORD Escape cruised down the highway, going two miles over the speed limit and looking as nondescript and ordinary as it could be. Ordinary on the outside. The driver, FBI Special Agent Max Morrison, drummed on the wheel, his eyes fixed on the road ahead.

"I need to go to the bathroom," came an annoyed whine from the backseat.

Max ignored her, but the young woman leaned forward and rapped on the metal bars separating the back of the SUV.

"I need to take a piss," she said, louder.

"You went to the bathroom barely two hours ago," Max countered without looking back at her.

"No. *I* didn't." The woman's voice now held a sharp edge.

Max sighed when he recognized the speaker. "Well, your body did, Justine."

"Well, my body needs to go again," she said, her tone mimicking his. "I've got to pee, man." He tightened his grip on the wheel and stared at the long stretch of highway ahead of him. He didn't want to stop. Not again. "I'm afraid you're going to have to hold it."

"You're a dick," she said. "And I think I'm on my period."

"You are," he confirmed. He knew this, because one of their stops had been for "feminine hygiene products".

"Balls," she said. "I definitely need to stop. You want blood all over your car?"

When Max didn't respond immediately, Justine raised her hands and banged the metal edge of her handcuffs on the bars. He winced.

"We stopped just two hours ago," he repeated. "I'm sure you're fine."

"Patriarchal asshole," she grumbled. "I'm sitting in a swamp of blood. You ever worn a blood-soaked pad?"

Max looked up at the sky for help. For patience. He found only dark, ominous clouds. He hoped it wouldn't rain. He didn't mind driving in the rain—but he did mind how other people drove in the rain.

"Was it Ester? Ester won't even use a tampon. I need a tampon—or a cup. I have a heavy period. I bleed through a pad like *that*." She snapped her fingers. This was already far more information than he wanted, but she continued. "And I *do* have to pee. If you're going to make me bleed through my pants anyway, I might as well piss myself."

Maybe he'd lost this battle. "*Fine*. We'll stop at the next rest stop."

"And how far is that?"

"Less than twenty miles." There had been a sign just a few miles back.

"Acceptable," Justine said and scooted back in her seat.

He was hoping she'd change back to Ester, or one of the less difficult personas, by the time they arrived at the rest stop, but he had no such luck.

"Are you going to remove the cuffs?" Justine asked after Max let her out of the SUV. She brandished her bound hands in his face.

He pushed them down. "No."

"Asshole."

"You know I can't take off the cuffs, Justine."

She blew out a breath of air that made her bangs billow away from her face. "You don't have to worry," she said. "It's just *me*, and we're friends, right?"

"The cuffs are staying on." He offered her the plastic shopping bag of supplies she—or at least, her body—had picked out earlier. She grabbed both a pad and a tampon, sticking the tampon in her mouth like a cigar.

Max ignored her antics and tossed the bag back on the front seat. He did a quick scan of the area. The rest stop was more crowded than he liked, with over two dozen cars filling the small parking lot. He figured it would be best to just get this over with. He grasped her elbow and maneuvered her toward the restroom. "Do you have to make everything difficult?" he asked, but he already knew the answer.

"Hey, *I'm* the victim here," she protested around the tampon in her mouth.

"I know that, Justine," he said, although he *didn't* know that. He still wasn't sure who the victim was, who the body actually belonged to. "But you don't make yourself easy to help."

"Just let me go." There was a sudden, desperate edge to her voice. She even took the tampon from her mouth as she shot him a pleading look.

"You know I can't do that," Max said.

They drew stares from everyone they passed as they made their way to the restroom. Of course they did. It would be a crazy world if a petite young woman in handcuffs didn't draw attention. However, he had his leather badge holder hanging around his neck and did his best to look calm, professional, and in control of the situation.

He let her go into the bathroom alone but stayed by the entrance. "You have two minutes."

"Asshole," Justine muttered before disappearing into the women's room.

Max checked his watch. He wouldn't hesitate to go in after her. Leaving her alone for even a moment made him nervous. He hoped Ester or one of the easier spirits would come back. Doorways sometimes triggered a change, but he knew it was unlikely. When Justine showed up, she tended to linger. And, of course, there was a worse option than Justine.

Justine returned almost exactly two minutes later, but her appearance made him take a step back. Blood coated both her hands. For a panicked second, he thought she had killed someone, but then he realized that the blood must be her own.

"Go wash your hands," Max said, trying to not let his disgust show on his face at the shocking amount of blood. Dark red covered her fingers and palms, like fingerpaint.

"I didn't have time to wash them," she said cheerfully, making no motion to return to the bathroom. "My time is up, yes?"

"Go wash them now," he said.

A middle-aged woman who had been heading toward the bathroom gasped upon spotting Justine. "Oh my God, what happened? Are you okay?"

"She's fine. It's under control," he said without taking his eyes off Justine. "Go wash your hands."

"I don't want to wash them," she said, looking down at them. "The water gets under the handcuffs, and it chafes."

"Justine, *go wash your hands*," he said, sharper this time, not even acknowledging the implication that she wanted the cuffs off.

"Why? It's not gross," she whispered, lifting her arms. "It's natural. It's normal."

"Go wash them. *Now.*"

Instead of obeying, she reached up and ran both palms down her face from forehead to chin, leaving ten bloody streaks like war paint across her skin, her lips, and her eyebrows.

The woman next to him gasped. Max tried his best not to react as Justine stared at him. A traffic jam of horrified onlookers gathered around them. He weighed his options. As far as he could tell, he had only two: (a) drag her into the bathroom and forcefully wash her, or (b) let her revel in her filth.

Neither were great options. But only one of them would end in disaster. He stepped away from the doorway. "Fine," he said. "Get in the car like that, if that's what you want."

He kept a hand on her shoulder as she stomped back to the SUV, then maneuvered her inside, making sure she didn't touch him. He reminded himself this could be worse. He should be thankful it was just Justine and her own blood.

"I'm bored," Justine announced ten minutes later. "*Bored,*" she repeated, drawing out the word as she put her feet up on the bars. "One of the others can come out if all I get to do is sit in a car."

Max said nothing. She was quiet for another moment, but he could hear her fidgeting with the handcuffs. *That* made him nervous. He should have rechecked them before letting her back in the SUV. He was getting sloppy, and that was dangerous.

"Would you like that?" she asked, letting her feet fall back to the floor. "Would you prefer Ester to come back?"

He kept his eyes on the road.

"I bet Ester is your favorite," she complained. "I bet she's the reason we got caught. Dumbass."

Justine leaned forward in her seat and whispered, "Or would you prefer *Astrid* comes out to play?" She blew air in his ear after dropping the name. Max shifted forward in his seat.

"Knock it off, Justine."

"Oh, hit a nerve," she teased.

He gritted his teeth and stayed silent.

"Don't you want her to come out and chat with you?" Justine asked. "Maybe if you ask real nice, she'll trade with me."

Max didn't answer her. He'd never encountered a case like this before. He'd dealt with plenty of possessions, sure, but not like this one. Normally, there were just two spirits: the rightful owner of the body and the invader.

Thus far, he'd counted six—Justine, Ester, Astrid, Bab, Agatha, and Laverne—and there might be more. More important, he'd yet to figure out which one was the actual owner of the body. His agency had scoured missing person reports from across the country, but no one had managed to identify the body, and all six spirits claimed it was theirs. Until Max knew who the body belonged to, he couldn't banish the other spirits. It made the case increasingly dangerous as the spirits grew stronger.

"How about you tell me about yourself, Justine?" he said, although he didn't expect her to give him any information. They'd held her for three days before she'd escaped, and none of the spirits had said anything useful.

"What do you want to know?"

"How old are you?" He didn't think the body could be a day older than twenty-four, and he suspected Justine was several years younger than that.

"Let's listen to the radio."

"I don't have good reception out here. When were you born? I was born in 1979."

"Huh. I thought you were older."

He wasn't sure whether that was an insult or an indication she did not know what year it was. Or maybe he looked older. He felt old today.

"Thanks," he said dryly.

"Do you have any ibuprofen? I feel like my uterus is exploding."

"No. I'm sorry I don't, Justine."

There was a pause. "I'm not Justine." Her voice was softer now, less confident.

"Oh, sorry." He was not sure which spirit this was. Not Ester. Not Astrid. But that still left three options, unless there was another he did not know. "Who are you?"

"I'm Bab."

"Oh. Hello, Bab." Max hadn't spoken with Bab much; she hadn't made more than a fleeting appearance, but he considered it a positive change. She was less annoying than Justine.

"Is this—is this *blood?*" Bab asked, her voice pitched with horror as she realized what was on her hands.

"Yes," he admitted as he maneuvered around a slow RV. "You're on your period, and Justine… Do you know Justine?" He had no idea how much each spirit knew about the other spirits. Justine seemed to know a lot, but he was unsure whether it was true knowledge or excellent guesses.

"What? What's going on?" Her voice arched high with panic. "What happened to Justine?"

"Nothing. She's fine. She just refused to wash her hands. You're fine. I promise. You're fine."

"I don't understand. This is gross." She sounded close to tears. "And I don't feel so good."

"I'm sorry," he said, instead of trying to explain. It was too difficult to explain.

"Can we stop? I don't feel good. I want to wash this off."

Max glanced over his shoulder. She'd curled up with her feet on the seat, her knees against her chest, and arms wrapped around her shins. She held her cuffed hands out at odd angles, being careful not to touch her hands to her jeans.

He sighed. He pitied her, but he wasn't going to stop again; however, he saw no point in telling Bab that.

"Sure," he said. "We'll stop at the next rest stop, okay?" She'd likely be gone by then anyway.

"Okay," she whispered.

They drove in silence for a long time. He replayed the exchange in his head, trying to figure out what she knew and what she didn't.

"Rest stop, one mile," Bab said suddenly as they passed the green sign.

He grimaced.

"Why aren't you getting over?" she asked.

"We can't stop there."

"You said we could stop."

"I know. I'm sorry."

A beat of silence passed before she answered. "Oh?" The voice responded with a purr. Max's blood ran cold. "You're *sorry*, huh?"

"Hello, Astrid." He tried to keep his voice even, to not show his fear. He kept his eyes fixed on the road.

"It looks like I had some fun," she said.

"It's your own blood."

"Cute."

He fixed his eyes on the truck in front of him and the half-faded bumper stickers dotting its red paint. He tried to read one, but it was too far away.

Behind him, Max heard her unfurl from the fetal position and lean forward so her mouth was close to his ear. He shivered at the thought of her being so close, even with steel bars between them. "What happened to the other officer? Sullivan?"

"You know what happened to her," he said between clenched teeth. Every muscle in his back tightened.

"Did she survive?" Astrid asked, sounding genuinely curious.

"She's still in the hospital." As soon as the words left his mouth, he gave himself a mental kick. Why had he told her that?

"Alive, then." Astrid leaned back in the seat. "Good for her. She's hardier than she looked."

His grip tightened on the wheel until his knuckles turned white. He had to make an effort to keep his foot light on the accelerator.

"Want to know how *you* die?" she asked. Her mouth was once again near his ear.

Max leaned forward. "No."

"I don't know, of course," she said, "but I can make an educated guess. I'm good at that."

"No," he repeated. "Why don't you let Ester back out? Or any of the others?" He kicked himself for saying that too. It showed weakness. He glanced over his shoulder and found her smirking.

"You'd prefer one of the quiet ones? The scared ones? Is that how you like your women?"

He clenched his jaw. "One who hasn't put my partner in the hospital, yes."

"You and your partner are trying to kill us."

"You're already dead." Max was confident that Astrid was *not* the owner of the body, although he had no actual evidence of that.

She let out a soft breath of laughter. "Do I look dead to you?"

"You stole someone's body."

"How do you know that?"

He didn't have an answer, just a gut feeling and a deep hatred.

Astrid, surprisingly, had no follow up comment. She fell quiet, which was unusual. Max adjusted his rearview mirror so he could see into the back, but she sat there calmly, gazing out the window. He wondered whether a different spirit had taken over, but he didn't ask. He turned back to the road and forced himself to take a series of deep breaths. He needed to calm down because he knew the silence would not last. She'd goad him again, and he needed *not* to take the bait next time.

However, the silence did last. It stretched for several hours. Max needed to relieve himself, but he forced himself to ignore his bladder. They weren't far from headquarters now, and he didn't want to stop unless he absolutely had to.

"Can we stop soon? I need to change my tampon."

He suspected she was still Astrid, but he wasn't certain. She didn't speak with her normal cockiness, but she lacked the fear and confusion of the others. She might be Justine.

"No."

"Seriously?"

"Yes."

"Ever heard of toxic shock syndrome?"

He had heard the words, but he didn't know the meaning. He thought it was something women used to get from tampons, but not anymore. "You're fine," he said. It hadn't been that long anyway.

"Asshole," she said, and then she fell silent. It made him suspicious. She'd given up too easily.

He cast a quick glance in the mirror and found her undoing her belt. He grimaced. He knew what she was planning, and there was no way he could stop her.

"You want me to hand you a fresh tampon?" he asked. The bag of supplies was in the front with him.

"No," she said. "I'd rather free bleed."

He frowned. He would much rather she not do that.

Uncomfortable, he glanced in the mirror again. She had her jeans undone and her hands down her pants. She scowled at him in the mirror and squirmed in the seat. A moment later, she pulled her hands back out, holding a blood-soaked tampon by the string with blood-streaked fingers. It reminded him of a dead mouse held by the tail.

He looked back at the road, but his attention swung back to her as she slid forward in her seat and pressed her bloody hands, still holding the tampon, against the bars.

He could smell the blood, and he scrunched up his nose. Her intentions were clear, but, again, he couldn't stop her.

She slid the tampon through the bars. It was a tight fit, so it took her several seconds to wriggle it through. It hit him in the shoulder and bounced off, hitting the middle console before landing on the passenger seat.

"That is disgusting," he said. He glanced at the shoulder of his jacket. The dark fabric didn't show any stains, but it was still gross. And the suit jacket was dry clean only.

"Poor baby. I guess you should have stopped." She slid back into her seat and dipped her hands back into her pants. A moment later, he heard a ripping sound and then she pulled out her pad. Thankfully, it was too large to shove through the bars, so she simply rolled it up and tossed it on the floor.

He hoped that was the end of it. He was not cleaning the SUV. Someone else was going to have to do that.

Max tried his best to pretend that her actions hadn't bothered him, but his gaze flickered to the tampon in the passenger seat. It was dark red, almost brown. A few strings of blood dripped off it. The blood seemed thicker than normal blood. He shuddered. He picked up the bag of supplies and placed it on top of the bloody tampon so he wouldn't have to look at it. It was a marginal improvement. It didn't help with the foul smell.

It seemed like a lot of blood. He wondered whether this was normal. It didn't seem normal, but he had no idea.

He glanced in the back and found Astrid wasn't done playing with her blood. In fact, she was now applying it to her face like makeup, dabbing it under her lips and down her chin, across one cheek, and outlining one eye. When she finished, it looked like she had a bloody black eye, split cheek, and split lip. Like an abuse victim. She was obviously plotting, but it would come to nothing. He wasn't going to stop until they got to headquarters. No one would see her. No one would pity her.

He turned his attention to the road and pressed down on the accelerator, but then he eased up. The last thing he needed was to be pulled over by a cop. He forced himself to take a deep breath. He turned on the radio and flipped through the channels, but every song annoyed him, so he turned it back off.

When he next glanced in the back, she was writing *HELP* backward in blood on the window.

"Knock that off right now," he growled.

"I'm almost finished," she said, her tone was soft and polite. Too soft to be Astrid. Too confident to be Bab.

"Who are you?"

"Laverne," she said as she finished the final stroke of the *P*. "Astrid was doing it backward, so I took over." She sounded smug.

He blinked as the meaning behind those words sunk in. They were working together.

He felt a wave of panic overflow him. He had no idea what to do. Laverne—or whoever it was now—started waving her bound hands frantically at the nearest car, gesturing to the bloody message.

He wasn't sure that her message or her blood-stained face would be visible to onlookers, as the windows were tinted—although they were merely dark, not opaque. He had a terrible feeling about it.

His feeling proved justified when mere minutes later, he saw a teenage girl in the backseat of a nearby green sedan raise her phone and take a photo of the SUV. Then the sedan dropped back. His grip tightened on the wheel as he tracked the sedan in his side mirror. The girl was now snapping a photo of his license plate.

He assumed the cops would be coming soon, and this was going to be a nightmare to explain. He fished his phone out of his pocket and scrolled through his contact list.

"Hey, eyes on the road, man," came what he was certain was Justine's voice from the back.

He ignored her. He put the phone on speaker and impatiently tapped the wheel, willing someone competent to answer.

"Hello?" the voice on the other end said.

"This is Agent Morrison," he said. "I've got a problem. I'm less than twenty minutes from the HQ, and I have the girl, but she's managed to get the attention of another car, and I think they may be calling the police on me. Please advise."

"How did she get the attention of a car?"

He pinched the bridge of his nose. "She wrote *help* on the window with her period blood."

"Oh," said the voice on the other side. "Gross."

"Rude," Justine muttered.

"Can you help me with the police?" he snapped.

"We'll try," said the voice.

Max scowled at the overcast sky. As a secret federal agency buried within the FBI, his group didn't have a history of playing nicely with the police. He thought the chance of him spending the night in jail and Justine escaping was moderate-to-high.

"Do," he grumbled, and then he hung up. "Useless," he muttered under his breath.

"You need better friends," she said.

He ignored her; his attention was on the busy highway as it started to rain. Large drops of water dotted his windshield, and he flicked on the wipers. The green sedan continued to follow him. He sped up and cut around another car, trying to get away. It pursued. He swore and changed lanes again, cutting off a van, which blared its horn at him.

"Watch it!" Justine snapped. "Seriously. You're driving like a maniac."

He searched for the green sedan in his side mirror. It was still there. Then came the wail of a police siren in the distance. He swore. He slammed down on the accelerator and cut over again. The SUV jolted as he clipped a truck. He swore again and yanked the wheel around as he tried to swerve back out of the way.

And then the world flipped.

It happened so fast he could barely comprehend it. Everything spun, but the seatbelt held him in place. The airbag deployed, punching him in the face. Metal sheared and ground against asphalt. Glass shattered all around him. A woman screamed.

Everything was suddenly still.

The Escape was on its roof, but the seatbelt continued to hold him, and he dangled upside down. His chest and stomach burned where the seatbelt dug into him. His neck seared from whiplash. His face and arms burned from the airbag, but he was alive. He blinked and wiggled his fingers and toes. He thought he was mostly all right, which was shocking considering the condition of the SUV, which was crumpled around him. The window to his left had shattered. The windshield in front of him was a spiderweb of cracks. He turned off the engine with trembling fingers, but he wasn't sure how to get out. If he undid the seatbelt, he would fall on his head.

Max took a breath, which seared his ribs. He thought he should probably wait for the first responders to pull him out. He closed his eyes for a moment, feeling nauseous and like an absolute idiot. Then he realized he'd heard nothing from Justine.

"Are you alright?" he called. His voice cracked.

There was no response. The only sound was the rain.

He felt a surge of fear. She hadn't been wearing her seatbelt.

"Justine?"

Voices came from outside the vehicle, but none from within.

He braced one hand on the ceiling, which was now the floor, and undid his seatbelt with his other hand. He slid down, landing awkwardly on his neck and shoulders before rolling over to right himself. There were shards of glass everywhere, and he cut his hand. More shards clung to his clothes. His ribs burned, but he ignored the pain. He pressed the unlock button on the keys, shoved the door open, and staggered out.

Several bystanders were already hurrying out of their cars and toward him. "Are you okay?" one yelled.

"I think so, but…" his words trailed off as he yanked the backdoor open. He froze at the scene inside.

Justine lay within, her body sprawled on the SUV's ceiling, twisted and contorted. Her hands were still handcuffed, but her right arm was pinned back and under her while her left was pulled across her body. Her head lolled unnaturally to the side. Blood was smeared across her temple and puddled under her head.

"Justine?" he whispered. "Ester? Astrid?"

She didn't respond. Her eyes were open, but unmoving. He crawled inside, stepping on glass shards, and bent over her. Her eyelids fluttered, but her eyes were unfocused, staring distantly over his shoulder. Still, it gave him a jolt of hope. She was still alive.

He quickly knelt next to her. "Hold on," he begged. "I'm sorry, just hold on. Help is coming."

Her left fingers twitched, and he hesitantly reached out and took her blood-stained hand in his own. Her fingers curled ever so slightly around his, and then—

He felt as if he'd plunged underwater. An invisible current was pulling him, ripping him away. He fought against it, but his body didn't move. Wouldn't move.

"Man, he ruined my body," he felt his lips saying. It was Justine. Justine speaking through his lips. "And *this* is certainly a downgrade. Gross old man body."

He felt himself scooting backward, but he wasn't moving his legs. His legs weren't his. His mouth wasn't his.

"Are we all here?" his mouth said, and then after a pause continued, "Good. We'll have to get a better body soon, but I suppose this will do for now."

Max tried to scream but couldn't.

ELIZA

PETINA STROHMER

"Emma."

There was no response.

"*Emma!*"

The young girl snapped back into her surroundings, still dazed by daydreams.

"Emma, honey. Eat your tea."

She nodded and began to obediently fork food into her mouth.

"That's better." Mum smiled. "What did you do at school today?"

Emma swallowed her mouthful. "Nothing."

"Well, you must have done *something*, love. I'm sure you didn't just sit and stare out of the window all day." Her mother sighed. "Actually, *you* probably did."

Emma continued to eat.

"Did you do sums?"

The child shook her head.

"Or stories, maybe?"

She just shrugged.

Her mother decided to change tack. "Who did you play with?"

"No one."

"Not Jane or Becky?"

"No."

There was a pause. "How about Eliza?"

Emma stopped eating and stared at her mother through big blue eyes.

"You played with Eliza?" Mum prompted her.

She nodded, but stayed silent.

At that moment, the door swung open and Emma's father strolled in with a smile. "Hello, my lovely girls! Everything okay?"

"Emma was just telling me how she did nothing at school today and played with nobody at break—except Eliza, of course."

Dad raised his eyebrows. "Of course."

"May I be excused?" Emma asked quietly.

"You may," Mum said, and the little girl jumped down and then scuttled up the stairs.

"Don't worry too much about her," Dad said.

His wife sat down heavily. "But I do. She's such a loner. Even her teacher says she has no friends. Apparently, the other girls *try* to include her in their games, but she wanders off."

"And spends her time playing with Eliza instead," Dad finished for her.

Mum shook her head. "It's not normal. I mean, there's no way she could know…is there?"

"Not unless *you've* told her because *I* haven't—and nobody else knows. Besides which, she's too young to understand."

"But, the name…"

"She's heard us saying it, that's all."

"I'm not sure if it's more sad or spooky," Mum sighed.

"It's probably neither," her husband replied. "At her age, it's perfectly normal to have an imaginary friend."

From upstairs came a peal of laughter.

"And she seems pretty happy about it," he added, "so I wouldn't let it bother you too much."

"You're probably right. Hopefully, she'll just grow out of it."

Later, she paused by Emma's door to listen. Emma sounded as if she was enjoying herself; chatting and giggling…into thin air. "Yeah, it's all fine," Mum tried to convince herself. "Come on, Em, bath time."

Amid the soap suds, Emma still behaved as if this Eliza was there, blowing bubbles and splashing water at her. Mum found comfort in her daughter's gleeful face.

"Yup, it's definitely okay," she murmured to herself.

After, she tucked her little girl into bed and gave her a kiss on both cheeks. "One for you," she smiled, "and one for Eliza."

Emma beamed back at her. "Thank you, Mummy. Eliza loves you, too."

In September, Emma advanced to a new class and met a lot of new children. However, by November's Parents Evening, she still didn't appear to have made any friends.

"She's just a bit of a loner," Miss Green said. "Some children are, especially when they're only children."

"I would have thought that meant she'd crave relationships with others," her mother said anxiously.

"Not necessarily. Some do, some don't. It's not as if Emma doesn't have a choice, she just chooses her own company. But she seems pretty happy that way, always—"

"Laughing and joking," Mum finished for her.

"Well, yes, but she's a well-behaved, hard-working child. There's certainly nothing wrong on that score."

"I suppose so," Mum conceded, "so long as the other children don't bully her for being…different."

"Oh no. Imagination is powerful at this age. I've got one boy who only communicates with me directly, and with everyone else through his stuffed elephant, so I don't think you've got too much to worry about." Miss Green laughed.

March Parents Evening was a slightly different story.

"Emma is still working well and achieving all her goals…" Miss Green's voice trailed off.

"But?" Mum was concerned.

"But she *is* showing some, erm, anti-social tendencies."

"You said yourself that she's a loner."

"No, it's more than that. For instance, Mary came crying to me the other day because Emma threw her out of the Wendy house."

"Why?"

"Well, apparently Mary sat in Eliza's chair and she didn't like it."

"So…"

"So Emma slapped her."

"Oh, that's not good." Mum bit her lip. "I'm *so* sorry."

The teacher patted her hand. "Don't worry too much. Scraps and scrapes go with the territory at this age—although it's more often with the boys. I'll keep an eye on the situation and if anything else happens, I'll let you know."

"Please do."

A few days later, Emma came home from school in tears.

"Whatever's the matter?" Mum asked.

Emma wouldn't say.

Mum knelt down beside her. "Has this got anything to do with… Eliza?"

Emma remained silent.

"Em?"

Still nothing.

Mum got back to her feet. "Well, I'll just have to ask your teacher what happened then."

"I hate Miss Green!" Emma shouted.

"What?"

"I hate her!"

"Why?"

"Because someone took Jenna's pencil and hid it in my drawer and Miss Green found it and made me sit on the naughty chair and it wasn't even my fault," Emma cried.

Mum took a moment to think about this. "Do you know who did take the pencil?"

"Yes, it was Eliza!"

"Where is she?" Dad asked.

"In her room, where she's stayed since she came in," his wife replied. "She's ignoring me, so perhaps you can talk some sense into her."

"I'll give it a go."

"I told you, Daddy," Emma pouted. "It wasn't me, it was Eliza."

"She took Jenna's pencil and put it in your drawer?"

His daughter nodded sulkily.

"Emma," Dad said carefully. "You know it's wrong to tell lies, don't you?"

"I'm not lying."

"Okay, but I thought Eliza was a good girl."

Emma paused. "She *is* good—most of the time."

"But?"

"But sometimes she's naughty."

"I see." Dad paused. "If Eliza's becoming a naughty girl, perhaps you shouldn't play with her anymore."

"How did it go?" Mum asked. "It all sounds quiet up there."

"Em's in bed now, but she's not happy."

"Why?"

"I told her if Eliza's naughty, she shouldn't play with her."

"Oh, I bet that went down well. What did she say?"

"Strangely enough—nothing."

After dropping Emma off at school, her mother took some clothes up to her daughter's room. Scrawled on the wall in black crayon were the words:

I hate Mummy and Daddy

"It wasn't me," Emma protested.

"Who was it then?" Mum's eyes flashed angrily.

"Eliza."

"It can't have been, Emma. It says 'I hate Mummy and Daddy'—and we're *your* parents, not Eliza's."

"Yes, you are!"

"She didn't mean anything by it." Dad later tried to comfort his wife.

"She *knows*!"

"Of course she doesn't. How could she? She's just growing up and pushing some boundaries, that's all. It'll blow over."

"Just listen to her," Mum said tearfully.

Even through the ceiling, they could hear their daughter's mutterings.

"She's attention-seeking," Dad said. "Ignore her."

Ignoring Emma's behaviour, however, became increasingly difficult.

And Emma's junior school took a less *understanding* view of the girl's misdemeanours.

"She's getting too old to blame everything on an imaginary friend," Mr. Shaw told her parents. "Are you indulging this fantasy at home?"

"Chance would be a fine thing," Dad snorted. "She barely speaks to us anymore. She always seems to be in such a bad mood."

"Hmmm. Give me an example," the teacher said.

"Well, whatever we give her—toys, pocket money, whatever—she wants double."

"One for her and one for Eliza?" the teacher replied. "She does that at school, too. Do you comply?"

"Of course not. We're not stupid."

Mr. Shaw raised his eyebrows. "And then what happens?"

"She says that Eliza hates us."

"Yes, apparently she hates us, too. Enough to smash stuff up in the classrooms. Is that happening at home as well?"

Mum blushed.

"Sometimes," her husband admitted.

"But then it's all 'Eliza's' fault, I'm guessing."

"What should we do?" Mum asked quietly.

"I'll have a word with the child psychologist," Mr. Shaw said. "I think it's time we split Emma and Eliza up."

"But we belong together," Emma told "the nice lady who just wanted to have a chat".

"In what way?"

"We're sisters."

The psychologist considered this. "I thought you were an only child, Emma."

"Eliza's always been with me. Like I said, we belong together. Always have, always will."

"I see." The psychologist made a few notes. "Can you tell me what Eliza is like?"

"Like me. Well, she *looks* like me."

"But?"

"But she's always in a bad mood."

"Angry?"

Emma nodded nervously.

"What is she angry about?" the psychologist pushed gently.

"Because she's *not* me," Emma replied and burst into tears.

Emma's parents sat and stared, wide-eyed. Dad asked, "So, what's the matter with her? Is she schizophrenic?"

"You're probably thinking about DID—Dissociative Identity Disorder, but, no, I don't think it's that."

"What is it then?"

"It's more like an advanced form of make-believe," the psychologist explained. "A child can sometimes deal with trauma by projecting it onto someone else. That way, they can achieve the safety of distance, which makes it easier to process. It could be a teddy bear or, as in this case, an imaginary friend."

"Right," said Mum.

"So?"

Emma's parents looked at each other. "So what?"

"So…do you have any idea what this trauma might be?"

The pause betrayed them and they said in unison: "No."

"Are you sure?"

Mum's eyes lowered. "Y-yes."

"I see." The psychologist studied them with sharp eyes. "Can I ask you a personal question?"

"Erm," Dad glanced at his wife. "I suppose so."

"Why did you decide not to have any more children after Emma?"

Mum bit her lip, but Dad was quick to step in. "Emma was so perfect." He tried a shrug and a smile. "How could we hope to improve on that?"

"Hmmm." The psychologist didn't sound convinced. "Well, look, I'm reluctant to put a child of primary school age on medication, so I suggest we monitor the situation for now and meet at the end of every term to discuss the situation."

Emma's parents readily agreed.

"Remember," the psychologist said, "particularly in cases like these, honesty is always the best policy."

"Oh God, now the psychologist knows," Mum wailed as they walked home.

"She knows nothing," Dad snapped, "and neither does Emma. For goodness' sake, don't let *your* imagination run riot now!"

Emma's behaviour did not improve and, unable to provide the pastoral care of the primary setting, the secondary school response was short and sharp.

"We will not tolerate swearing, stealing, and bullying behaviour. If Emma's attitude does not improve, she will be expelled." The headmistress' tone was firm.

Dad was not happy. "That's it? A pupil has a few problems and your response is to expel her?"

"Your daughter *is* a problem—and she creates them for everybody here; fellow pupils, teachers, me!"

"She can't be the only difficult child here. They're teenagers, for God's sake."

"Okay." The headmistress took a deep breath. "What if I told you that we *do* have a pupil here—no names, obviously—who not only inflicts physical harm on their classmates but also causes so much disruption in lessons that it seriously impacts the education of the whole class?"

Dad frowned. "Give me an example."

The Head rolled her eyes. "Ooh, so many to choose from. Let's see, in a chemistry lesson last week, this child broke a test tube and used a shard of the glass to injure the pupil sitting next to them. When that pupil complained to the teacher who then reprimanded the offender, the child's response was to open a gas valve and nearly set light to the whole room."

Mum gasped. "And this pupil is in our daughter's class?"

The Head nodded.

"That's outrageous!" Dad spluttered. "I don't know why you're complaining about our child. *That* little monster should be kicked out right away."

The Head sat back. "I couldn't agree more. Emma's suspension starts tomorrow."

"What are we going to do?" Mum cried.

Above their heads, loud bangs and crashes meant that Emma was trashing her room—again.

Dad winced at the noise. "Well, at least she hasn't blamed the mythical Eliza for this."

Mum winced, too.

"Look," Dad said, "Emma saw a psychologist in junior school, so she must be in the mental health system somewhere. Perhaps we can get her another referral now."

"You think they'll be able to help this time?"

Dad shrugged. "It seems that half of the kids nowadays are on either Prozac or Ritalin."

The parents sat and mused until they realised that it had fallen silent upstairs.

"Shall I go and check on her?" Mum asked anxiously.

"If you want to," Dad said, "or you can just enjoy the peace and quiet."

"No, I think I'll go."

Mum crept up the stairs and tapped on the door. "Emma."

No reply.

"Emma, honey, are you okay?"

Surprised to find the door unlocked, she turned the handle and let herself in.

Then she screamed.

Emma lay sedated in the hospital bed, with both wrists in bandages.

Dad tried to comfort his sobbing spouse. "Look," he said, "if she's self-harming now, she can't possibly be refused the proper psychiatric help she needs, can she?"

"I-I don't want her labelled as insane," Mum cried.

"She's not insane. She's ill," Dad said gently. "She's probably been getting sicker for a while, but it's only just shown itself fully now."

Mum sniffed. "But how did we not notice?"

"All kids act up," Dad said, "but Emma's an only child. What did we have to compare her to?"

The hospital psychiatrist showed Emma's parents the packets of little white pills. "We're starting with a mood stabiliser. In the majority of cases, that's all that's needed and the symptoms should subside."

"So," Mum's voice trembled, "will she have to be on the medication forever?"

"Unlikely," the psychiatrist assured her. "Just until she gets better."

Dad's face was grim. "And what if she gets worse?"

Initial results were encouraging. Although quiet, Emma was now a lot calmer. Flashes of her former sunny self, not seen for years, began to break through. She helped her parents repair and redecorate her room and diligently completed the homework the school had sent her. As soon as her wounds healed, she was allowed to attend classes again.

Everybody heaved a huge sigh of relief.

Until…

Emma's parents sat in the police station and tried to take in what had happened.

"The other girl is in hospital now," the sergeant told them. "Her wounds, though serious, are not life-threatening. However, the doctors are pretty sure she will be permanently scarred."

"So, you're saying that our daughter smuggled a kitchen knife into school and slashed the face of another pupil badly enough to disfigure her. Why?" Dad was at a loss.

"We were hoping that you'd get some answers out of her because she's saying nothing to us."

Emma was slumped sullenly in her chair, staring into space. Her parents sat down opposite her in the interview room and held up their hands.

"Emma," her mother cried. "Why would you do such a thing?"

"I didn't, okay?" she snapped.

"Then who did?"

"It was El—"

"I swear to God!" Dad's face was puce. "If you say that name one more time…"

"Oh, piss off!"

"Emma!" her mother exclaimed.

"What?" she sneered. "Like you care."

"Of course we care."

"Yeah, parents of the year," she replied. "The apple don't fall far from the tree."

"That's not fair," Mum protested. "We've always given you everything, Emma."

"Yeah, like hereditary psychosis. Why didn't you just kill me at birth?"

Her parents exchanged furtive glances.

"You can't blame us for your actions," Dad said through gritted teeth. "If anything, you've been spoilt."

"Ain't that the truth," Emma chuckled. "But nature trumps nurture every time." Her tone was dark…different, somehow. "You knew, didn't you? That's why you only have one child."

"Kn-knew what?"

"That at least one of you carries the loony-tune gene. See, I've done my biology homework, like a good little girl." She laughed. "Even though you weren't expressing the gene yourself, you managed to produce a child as fucked-up as you are."

Dad lurched over the table and slapped his daughter across the face. The police officer was on him in a moment.

Emma grinned. "I rest my case."

The psychiatrist wasn't pleased.

"First of all, you can't fight violence with violence. You're the adult, she's the child."

Dad dropped his head into his hands, looking suitably shame-faced.

"You do realise that Emma could charge you with assault?"

"It's all such a mess," Mum said quietly. "But is she right?"

"In what way?" said the psychiatrist.

"Did…did we make her like this?"

The psychiatrist sat back. "Some mental illnesses have genetic propensity, but in this case, I don't think so. There's no history in the family."

"So if it's not nature, it's nurture then." Dad grunted.

"Actually, it's probably neither—but hitting her certainly doesn't help."

"I know, I'm sorry."

There was a pause. "Who's Eliza?"

Both parents froze. The psychiatrist's ears pricked up.

"Why?" Mum's tone was very cautious.

"Emma mentioned her."

"In what way?"

"She said that Eliza is angry with everybody—but especially you two."

Dad swallowed. "Did she say why?"

The psychiatrist jotted down a couple of notes. "Let's start with the *who*."

"Eliza is—was—is Emma's, erm, imaginary friend," Mum stuttered.

The psychiatrist paused. "*Is* or *was?*"

"From childhood, like a normal kid, but we thought she'd grown out of it. People do…don't they?"

"Lots of people do," the psychiatrist answered carefully. "However, in some cases, the concept evolves into an adult construct."

"Why?"

"Sometimes it's simply loneliness. In others, it's part of their thinking or creative process."

"Like the mad genius?" Dad asked.

"Well, yes, but we don't use the word 'mad' in modern psychiatry. And then, in some cases, it's a coping mechanism."

"Coping with what?"

"Trauma," the psychiatrist said and observed the parents' reactions.

Mum looked shocked, but in Dad, the psychiatrist could practically see the defences spring up.

"That's nonsense!" he said, his voice firm. "There's been no real trauma in Emma's life."

"None that you know of," the psychiatrist countered.

"I—"

"Or, perhaps, none that *she* knows of."

"I don't understand what you're trying to achieve here," Dad snapped. "You, Emma, or that ridiculous Eliza character. All I care about is my daughter getting better."

"That's what we all want," the psychiatrist said in a maddeningly soothing voice. "I'm going to start Emma on medication that should help, accompanied by regular face-to-face therapy. How do you feel about that?"

"Can I just ask?" Mum began.

"Of course."

"What is Eliza angry about, with us, I mean?"

"At the moment," the psychiatrist said. "Everything."

"What a load of mumbo-jumbo," Dad growled, walking away from the psychiatrist's office.

"But what if, erm, Eliza tells the psychiatrist about—"

"There is no Eliza and there's nothing to tell!" Dad pulled down his hat, indicating that the conversation was over.

The medication certainly calmed Emma down.

In fact…

Mum gazed into her daughter's blank eyes but could find nothing there. No light, no life, nothing at all. It was like looking at the toddler who used to spend so much time in a daydreaming daze.

The sluggish teenager ate, slept and stared sightlessly at the T.V. like some lifeless automaton.

"Those drugs aren't helping, they're just turning her into a zombie," Mum said sadly.

"You'd prefer her to turn back into a psycho?" her husband asked.

"No, I'd prefer to have my daughter back."

"I think that ship has long since sailed."

"Don't be so cruel," Mum cried. "It's like losing my child all over again."

"We had no choice," Dad told her, "and *that* has got nothing to do with this."

"Hasn't it? So why do all the shrinks keep talking about trauma?"

Dad just shrugged. "There's nothing we can do about it; then or now."

"Isn't there?" Mum muttered as she left the room.

Emma stared dully at the pills. "They…they look different." Her speech was sticky and slow.

"The doctor has just made a few adjustments, that's all," her mother assured her.

Emma swallowed them without further comment and Mum smiled, pocketing the sweets.

It took nearly a fortnight for Emma to begin perking up. She started listening to her music again. Talked more. Even smiled.

"It seems the drugs are working," Dad smiled. "See, I told you not to worry."

Mum kept her mouth shut.

"No!"

"Emma, please," her mother begged her. "The doctor says you must keep taking your medication." Replacing some of the pills with placebos was certainly bringing her daughter back to life—but with it came with the mood swings, the irritability, the disobedience. Her mother dared not take her off the drugs completely. "Please."

"I'm better," Emma said airily. "You said so yourself. I don't want to go back to being a dead woman walking."

"For me?" Mum made one final plea.

Emma scowled, snatched the tablets from her mother's hand, and put them into her mouth.

"Thank you." Mum's eyes misted. "You're such a good girl. I'll leave you in peace now."

"Yeah, whatever," Emma sneered.

As soon as her mother was out of the room, Emma spat the tablets into the bin—along with all the others.

The wind was high that night. Outside, the branches of the trees scratched against the windowpanes and the dustbin lids rattled.

"I love a storm," Dad said, "especially when we're tucked up all cosy in bed."

Lightning flashed. Mum screamed.

"What's the matter with you? It's only the weather." Dad laughed. "Perhaps you should take some of Emma's chill pills!"

Mum said nothing, but she couldn't shake that feeling of…of…of *what*, she couldn't even be sure. Soon her husband was snoring, but she remained on edge, every muscle in her body as tight as a bowstring.

The bedroom door creaked open.

"Mummy."

She knew that voice, and yet…

"Are you awake, Mummy?"

"Emma?"

A low chuckle was the only reply. The girl stalked into the room, hands behind her back, her eyes alight in the gloom.

"What's wrong?" her mother asked, trying to keep her voice level.

"Ooh." The girl grinned. "Where shall I start? Although," she paused, "I didn't really start at all, did I?"

"What…what do you mean, love?"

"Don't 'love' me, you wicked woman. You didn't love me then, so I very much doubt that you do now."

"Emma," Mum protested.

"You loved Emma," the girl sneered, "but you murdered me."

Mum's eyes widened. "El-Eliza?"

The girl laughed. "I'm surprised you remember."

"It can't… How…"

"Oh, but it is. Hello again, mother of mine." She produced a sliver of silver from behind her back. "I've waited a long time, hiding in plain sight, for this moment."

Staring at the knife, Mum kicked her husband, hard, under the covers.

"Wh-what's going on?" he mumbled, coming round quickly at the sight of the weapon. "Emma?"

"Close," she laughed. "Say hello to your *other* daughter, Daddy dearest."

"But…but, Eliza is—"

"Dead? And yet, here I am." She spread her arms wide, keeping a firm grip on the knife.

"You're not real. You can't be," Dad protested.

"Emma, darling, I think you're having an…episode." Mum reached out her hand.

The knife flashed through the air, leaving a bloody gash across the woman's palm.

Eliza cocked her head. "Is that real enough for you?"

Mum held up her hand, staring at it in shock. "I'm…I'm bleeding!"

The girl pouted. "Yeah, *I* did quite a lot of that. Enough to die, remember?"

"Emma—" Dad began.

"*Eliza!*"

"Okay, 'Eliza.' We didn't murder you. We tried to save your life. The doctors told us there was very little chance of our conjoined twins surviving unless they were separated."

"They also told you that the smaller one, *me*, was unlikely to survive the operation."

"We—"

"Do you know *why* I was so much smaller?" she shouted over him. "Because that bitch of a sister had taken the lion's share of everything in the womb. She literally leeched the life out of me, and you two took care of the rest."

"Eliza," Mum whimpered, the tears running down her face. "My baby."

"Not for long," she snorted. "Two days after birth and less than half an hour after the separation. But," a slow smile spread across her face, "part of me had already been absorbed into my sister. What you always assumed was Emma's imaginary friend was, in fact, what was left of her dead twin."

"Where is Emma now?" Dad breathed.

"Oh, don't worry. Your precious child is still in here. I might even let her have her body back to face the consequences when I've finished."

"Fin-finished what?"

Eliza raised the knife. "Settling the score."

"Has she said anything?"

The psychiatrist shook her head sadly. "No, she just sits there, smiling." She watched the girl, perched motionless on the edge of the hospital bed. "I really got this one wrong, didn't I?"

"Don't torture yourself," her colleague said.

"But the two personalities are so distinct; the posture, the voice, everything's different."

"Hindsight is a wonderful thing," the other doctor said with a shrug. "We both know that, by its nature, psychiatry is not an exact science. We all make mistakes."

The psychiatrist sighed. "Maybe, but most don't result in the massacre of two innocent people. Did you see the photos? My God, it was a total bloodbath!" She shook her head again. "I just wish I knew *why*."

"Would you like me to try?" the other doctor asked.

"You can *try*," the psychiatrist said. "But be very careful."

"She's restrained, isn't she?"

"Just take care."

The girl didn't look up as the doctor entered the room. Confident that she was tethered to the bed, he pulled up a chair and sat in front of her.

"Hello." He smiled.

She lifted her head slowly, a manic grin still fixed to her face. "You want to know why I killed my parents."

"Well," the doctor flustered. "Yes."

"I didn't," she replied simply. "It was Emma."

EX SANGUINE

ALAN P. MARKS

…skreekskreeeek…skreeeeeeee…
…skreekskreeeek…skreeeeeeee…

Jacob can't tell whether the sound of Pastor Sutter's wheelchair—that metal-on-rusted-metal chitter—is closer behind him now or not as he walks slowly down the aisle of the darkened church towards the altar, the cross held up high before him. The barest whisper of a sound, but the boy hears it, anyway—*skreekskreeeek…skreeeeeeee*—can't *not* hear it—*skreekskreeeek…skreeeeeeee*—hears it over the nervous pounding of his own heart—*skreekskreeeek…skreeeeeeee*—hears it over the half-hearted drone of voices raised in an unfamiliar hymn.

> *There is a fountain filled with blood*
> *Drawn from Immanuel's veins;*

Is it only his imagination that it's almost on top of him, that antique wooden monstrosity Benjamin Drinkwater dug out of his basement when it got to where Pastor Sutter could no longer walk? His imagination that it drives him on ahead of it, threatening to run him down, to clip his heels and send him sprawling to the floor in front of the altar, the processional cross flying from his sweaty hands with a crash?

…skreekskreeeek…skreeeeeeee…

Or does his little brother, Daniel, push it too quickly? If he does, Jacob can't blame him for it. It's not Daniel's fault he's too small to see over the high back of the old wheelchair. Too young to understand. He shouldn't be here. Neither of them should.

> *And sinners, plunged beneath that flood,*
> *Lose all their guilty stains;*

Not enough voices—*skreekskreeeek…skreeeeeeee*—far too many empty seats since Jacob was last here long months ago, back when *Febris Exsanginae* was little more than rumor on the television, something his father declared was only punishment for heathen countries, for foreign cities and their godless ways, and nothing they needed to worry about here. All the same, Jacob's mother had forbidden her sons from going anywhere there might be a crowd, not even to church—*skreekskreeeek… skreeeeeeee…* Had stayed away herself.

But she was dead now.

Those still able—and still willing, for whatever their reasons—to venture out in the night and gather in the same place despite the risk of contagion…they're careful to keep their distance from one another. Together but separate in the feeble glow of candles that do little to push back the gloom but are all they have left since the power failed for good a month ago, cutting the last ties the town had with the outside world in the process.

The air reeks of the hot smell of melted wax.

Beyond the candle's reach, the inside of the church lies shrouded in shadows that move and shift with a life of their own. The faces of the congregation appear distorted to Jacob, their features twisted into grotesque and unfamiliar shapes by the flickering light…by his own imagination.

Some sing. Others hold themselves silent, heads bowed. Perhaps they pray—*skreekskreeeek…skreeeeeeee…* Perhaps not. *…skreekskreeeek… skreeeeeeee…*

The only things that keep him from casting aside the cross and bolting from the church, dragging Daniel along with him, are the dreadful certainty of the wheelchair behind him, and the sight of their father standing by himself in the front row, ramrod straight, eyes fixed on Jacob. His voice booms out over the rest.

> *Lose all their guilty stains;*
> *Lose all their guilty stains;*

When Ben Drinkwater's last surviving son, George, got the fever and died only days ago, blood leaking from his eyes by the end like scarlet tears, dripping from his ears, oozing from his pores till the sheets of his bed ran thick with it, and Pastor Sutter asked if Jacob and Daniel would serve at the altar in George's stead, their father told them they should feel *honored* at the request, and that they *would damn well do it!*

Almost, Jacob blurted out, *No!* He didn't want to and neither did Daniel. Daniel, who sat meekly at the kitchen table, staring down at his meager breakfast—every meal was meager these days—too scared to say anything for himself.

Almost, Jacob invoked their mother's memory. *Mom didn't want us to!*

Almost.

Except the look in his father's eyes stopped him before he could speak, the words catching in his throat. A fevered look…but clear, without any trace of red. Fevered, but not *the* fever, the one that took George Drinkwater. Took his mother. Took so many others.

The fever that had gripped Pastor Sutter for three long days and nights before—as if a miracle—releasing him. Alone out of all the rest, he survived, delivered back to his congregation to lead them. To *redeem* them, Jacob's father had proclaimed

(*"—hold that tourniquet tight, boy."*)

to any who would listen.

Somehow, that look in his father's eyes as he glared down at his sons terrified Jacob more than any threat of sickness. And it seemed as though he sensed his son's unuttered refusal.

The Pastor was *BLESSED!* he roared at them, spittle flying from his mouth. The Pastor was a *SAINT* before *GOD!* He was their *SALVATION!* Dishes, dirty and stacked high, rattled and threatened to topple as he slammed both hands down on the table, and Jacob quickly muttered, *yes, Father,* for him *and* for Daniel before his little brother could start to cry and their father found somewhere else to lay his hands.

> *And sinners, plunged beneath that flood,*
> *Lose all their guilty stains.*

…skreeeeeeee…

Now, as he reaches the refuge of the steps before the altar, Jacob lets go of a breath he didn't realize he was holding. He doesn't dare turn to see but still feels his father's gaze boring into him, watching for any misstep, any failing in his son that might bring down shame and judgment upon them—upon *him*—and Jacob raises the cross higher. His father will take that for zeal and approve, but it's only to lift the hem of the too-large robes Jacob wears—robes that until recently had belonged to the older and taller George Drinkwater—so that they won't trip him as he climbs the steps.

> *E'er since by faith I saw the stream*
> *Thy flowing wounds supply,*

Moving around the altar, he bears the cross to the front of the church, places it into the stand that awaits it, then retreats and bows low as he was instructed, holding himself there for a long moment before rising and turning back because Daniel needs his help to push the heavy wheelchair up the ramp and into the chancel…

> *Redeeming love has been my theme,*
> *And shall be till I die:*

…and is shocked anew at the sight of Pastor Sutter.

Not at the sallow skin of the man's face, or the gaunt, sunken cheeks, or the sheen of sweat on his forehead which is the only outward sign of the pain he must be in. Not even at the unnatural way the vestments he wears drape down over the front of the wheelchair. Flat. Deflated. Empty from where both of his legs end, well above the knee. Or the way his body seems almost *caved in* on one side where his left arm should be but isn't any longer.

Or the other arm

(*"You hold that tourniquet tight, boy."*)

resting gingerly in his lap, fresh blood seeping through the bandages that cover the stump of his wrist. At some point since Jacob and Daniel dressed Pastor Sutter and lifted him carefully into the wheelchair, he's managed to drag that stump over the front of his robes, leaving a smear of bright red that slashes across the white fabric like an open wound.

No, it's the man's eyes that bring Jacob up short, locking him in place for a moment. Milky white. Dead. The first casualty of the fever, always, the blood vessels rupture until you are left to die in darkness, alone. Only Pastor Sutter *didn't* die and now those blind eyes seem to stare straight at Jacob as he stands before the cross, as if watching to see what the boy will choose to do next. Except it's too late for choices, has maybe always been too late

(*"You hold that tourniquet tight, boy," his father orders him, and Jacob does as he is told.*)

and he wills himself to take a step. Then another. To keep moving, to retreat down the steps past those ghostly eyes to where Daniel waits.

> *And shall be till I die,*
> *And shall be till I die;*

A musty smell rises from the wheelchair, a sharp mildew stink from long years spent in the Drinkwater's basement. Something fouler from Pastor Sutter—gamey, almost sickly sweet. Jacob does his best to breathe through his mouth as he leans in next to Daniel to put his shoulder into the back of the chair and help get it rolling up the ramp. His brother's face, so close to his own as they push, is pale and drawn, but whether from the smell, or from nerves, or from something else entirely, Jacob doesn't know. And there's no chance to whisper words of encouragement, not in a way everyone won't see and Sutter won't hear. Even if he could, he has no idea what those words might be. So, he pushes harder instead—*skreeeeeeee*—to get it over as quickly as they can, and gives thanks that neither of them has had anything to eat since breakfast this morning.

Shoddy and quickly slapped together, the ramp creaks underneath their weight, bows dangerously in the middle when they're halfway there. Jacob knows it's wrong of him to pray for the ramp to collapse underneath them, ending the service before it begins by dumping the wheelchair and its fragile contents onto the stairs. He prays anyway. If anyone hears, though, they don't answer, because it's only a few steps up the ramp into the chancel, and quickly done. Once there, he touches Daniel on the shoulder and, when the younger boy looks up at him,

Jacob motions for him to go stand behind the altar at one side of the cross the way they'd been told. He'll finish the rest by himself.

> *Redeeming love has been my theme,*
> *And shall be till I die.*

The hymn over, the church falls into awkward silence. The organ should be playing—traveling music, his mother used to call it—only there's no one left who knows how. With a final squeak, Jacob maneuvers the heavy wheelchair into place next to the altar, sets the brake on the wheels, then retreats to his own station opposite Daniel.

The congregation, such as it is, waits, the quiet stretching out uncomfortably until Jacob starts to wonder whether Pastor Sutter is able to go on. If the man is even aware of where he is or what he's supposed to do next.

In the back of the church, someone sobs softly and, as if that was the signal he waited for, the blind and broken figure in the wheelchair speaks, his voice surprisingly clear and steady, coming from the ruin that is his body.

"Let us pray," he says.

From the congregation, a scattering of voices answer.

> *Our Father,*
> *who art in heaven,*
> *hallowed be thy name…*

(Oblivious to the others, Pastor Sutter mutters to himself, the same thing over and over and over. "Our Father, who art in heaven. Our Father, who art in Heaven. Our Father…" His breath reeks of the whiskey Jacob's father had him drink.

The service won't begin for hours yet but there's work first, and they're gathered together in the sacristy. Jacob and his father. Pastor Sutter. Ben Drinkwater's big arms wrap tightly around the pastor, holding him still just in case, and Daniel stands in the corner, out of everyone's way, waiting with the chalice till it's needed.

"You hold that tourniquet tight, boy," his father orders him, and Jacob does as he is told, twisting the strap tighter. But he can't watch, and he turns away as his father picks up the knife…)

> *…For thine is the kingdom,*

and the power,
and the glory,
forever and ever.
Amen.

A few make it to the end, but most lose thread of it, the sentiment of it, at one place or another along the way. Uncertain, embarrassed almost, the congregation sinks to their seats, first one, then another, then the rest following their lead. Only Jacob's father and a couple of others—Drinkwater and some woman Jacob has seen before but doesn't recognize—pay any attention to Pastor Sutter where he sits beside the altar.

Until a shriek of pure rage tears itself out of the frail preacher, echoing through the church and snapping the rest of them upright. Waking them from whatever thoughts they were lost in, Jacob included.

"EXECRATION!"

The weeping from somewhere out in the gloom of the church that had quieted but never quite stopped, grows louder again.

"*Execration,*" he repeats, no longer shouting but his voice still shakes with barely controlled anger. "*Cursed.*" Lifting his lone remaining arm, he waves the stump in front of himself, but whether he uses it to point at those who sit and listen, or whether he holds up that sundered limb as an example, is not clear.

"We have been cursed by God. By *God!* But do not blame Him. Don't. You. Dare. For it is ourselves who are to blame."

Sutter's head turns slowly one way and then the other and, from where Jacob stands, he appears to sweep the congregation with those clouded eyes. And, blind though he is, no one is able to meet his gaze. They all look away or lower their heads, even Jacob's father.

Jacob understands how they feel and is thankful, for a moment at least, to be where he is behind the altar. Behind the preacher.

"Enoch," Pastor Sutter continues, more calmly now, "who few today remember, Enoch tells us this. Enoch, who was great-grandfather to Noah. Noah. Someone else who knew about God's retribution. 'Ye have not been steadfast,' Enoch said. And this is true."

Some few in the congregation begin to nod at this.

"'Ye have turned away and spoken hard and proud words with your impure mouths.' And this also is true."

From out in the dark corners of the congregation there comes a handful of muttered *amens*.

"'Therefore, shall ye *execrate* your days, and the years of your life shall *perish*. And ye shall find no mercy. For you, for the godless, there shall be a *curse!*' And there has been. We have been cursed for our sins. Can there be any doubt of this? The evidence is in the world all around us. We need only open our eyes to see it, this curse that has befallen us. And the many sins that have brought it down upon our heads. We need only look around this very church."

Again, those sightless eyes sweep over the congregation and, this time, not everyone turns away.

"So, look. Look around you. Look at all those empty seats, and look at one another. Are *they* responsible? Are *they* to blame?"

Caught up by Pastor Sutter's fervor, they do as they are bid. Jacob's father nods, his lips in a hard line that might be the grim beginnings of a smile.

"Or should you look inside *yourselves*? Look inside your *own* hearts. Your own *souls*. Blame not others for the root of this terrible *execration*. No. But look instead to your *own* wickedness.

"And what is the punishment for our wickedness? Need we even ask? Second Esdras, chapter fifteen, verse four through six. 'For all the unfaithful shall die in their unfaithfulness. Behold, saith the Lord, I will bring *plagues* upon the world, for wickedness—*wickedness!*—hath exceedingly polluted the whole earth.'

"Blood. We suffer a plague of blood." Again, he raises the stump where his hand used to be, brandishing it before them as if no other evidence is necessary. The bandages are soaked through now, and blood runs freely down his arm, staining the sleeve of his vestments.

"'And Moses lifted up the rod, and smote the waters, and all the waters were turned to blood, and the water stank, and the Egyptians could not drink of it. There was blood throughout all the land, and all flesh died that moved upon the earth.'

"We drown. Like the sinners in Noah's flood, we drown. We drown, but not in water. In *blood.*"

Sutter lowers his arm, rests it in his lap. His shoulders slump as if holding that limb up high had sapped the last of his strength. Maybe it had. His voice is weaker, quavering as he continues.

"And who knows this better than I? Who here but I has smelled that blood on their own breath? Has tasted it in their own mouths? Who here but I has peered out in agony through a crimson veil until *their* eyes burned from it? Burned away until they were left alone in eternal darkness.

"But do not pity me. Do not. Yes, it took my eyes, but I see this now as a mercy. As a *gift* from God, and I am glad to give them up because without them I see so much more clearly. Because there is light, even in darkness. Hope, even in hopelessness. Enoch tells us this as well. 'For all of you sinners, there shall be no salvation, and on you all shall abide a curse, but the *repentant* shall rejoice, and there shall be *forgiveness* of sins.'

"And in those hours when darkness fell over my eyes, in those the darkest hours of my soul, I prayed to God for forgiveness and those prayers were answered, and I was healed. I was healed and I was returned to you to lead you out of the darkness of your own wickedness.

"For the blood, which is our curse, shall also be our salvation.

"Leviticus, chapter seventeen, verse eleven: 'For the life of the flesh is in the blood: and I have given it for you upon the altar to make an atonement for your souls; for it is the blood that maketh an atonement for the soul.'

"Did not the savior bleed for us on the cross, for our sins?"

Heads in the congregation nod.

"Do *I* not bleed for you?" he says, his voice suddenly so quiet Jacob has to strain now to hear the words. "Have I not bled for you in all the days since God saw fit to deliver me up to you?" A third time he raises his wounded arm, but only a little and only briefly before letting it drop back into his lap, as if the weight of it is too much to bear.

"But there can be no forgiveness without repentance. No end to this curse without true confession. If you conceal your wickedness, if you hold it secret and hidden within your hearts, then the blood will not avail you.

"So, kneel. Offer up the prayer that Manasseh gave to God for forgiveness of his idolatrous ways."

This time, everyone joins as Pastor Sutter leads them. In the front of the church, Jacob's father kneels, his head bowed low. Again, his voice carries over the rest.

I have sinned, O Lord, I have sinned, and I acknowledge mine iniquities, wherefore I humbly beseech thee, forgive me, O Lord, forgive me and destroy me not. Be not angry with me forever, by reserving evil for me, neither condemn me to the lower parts of the earth. For though art the God, even the God of them that repent and, in me, thou wilt show thy goodness, thou wilt save me that am unworthy. And I will praise thee forever, all the days of my life, for thine is the glory, forever and ever.

Amen.

By the time they finish and grope their way back into their seats, Jacob finds himself at the altar, his back to the congregation, with no sense of how he came to this place or to this moment, his feet having carried him there of their own accord, without his knowledge. Without his consent.

He fixes his eyes on the cross behind the altar, avoiding the gruesome feast laid out on the silver plate and chalice before him

(he can't watch, and turns away as his father picks up the knife)

but he is to be Pastor Sutter's hands in the ritual so, still without looking, he forces himself to reach towards the plate to take one of the thinly sliced strips of flesh piled there.

They want to stick together, come away in a clump, and he fumbles with trembling hands to separate just one piece from the rest. The feel is greasy between his fingers. Slippery like uncooked bacon, and he almost drops it. It smells…smells like…

"And Jesus said unto them," Pastor Sutter begins softly, rescuing Jacob from the thought before he can finish it

(but knows it's begun from the sharp hiss of whiskey-soaked breath in his face and the way the Pastor stiffens in Drinkwater's arms)

and his voice is hardly above a whisper now, all his anger spent. Or as if they are alone together in the church and he speaks only to Jacob.

"'Unless you eat the flesh of the Son of Man, and drink his blood, you have *no* life in you. For my flesh is meat indeed, and my blood is drink indeed.'"

Cupping the bloody sliver in both hands the way he was told, Jacob raises it up over the altar towards the cross. Holds it there.

Sutter's voice regains its strength, begins to carry out over the congregation once more. "Just as the living Father sent me," he tells them, "and I live *because of* the Father, so the one who feeds on me will live because of *me.*"

With that, Jacob is meant to draw back his hands, lift the host to his own mouth, and eat. Instead, he remains as before, arms outstretched, frozen in place. A trickle of sweat runs down his spine.

"Take…*eat*," Sutter commands and, again, Jacob imagines the preacher speaks to him and him alone. Imagines that those cloudy eyes see him in his hesitation. In his *disobedience.* "For this is *my* body
(*stiffens, but doesn't fight, not even at the wet rasp of the saw as it bites into bone*)
which is *broken* for you."

Jacob does as he is bidden.

And fights against the involuntary gag as he opens his mouth to receive the gruesome host, against the way his tongue recoils from it to the back of his throat and the way his throat and abdomen tighten, heave. Fights the urge to spit out the limp, warm bit of Pastor Sutter's raw flesh because to do so means touching it with his tongue, tasting it and, if he does that, nothing will stop him from vomiting up whatever might be in his empty stomach all over the altar.

The cross, which his eyes have never left, blurs through his tears.

Clenching his teeth together and taking a deep breath in through his nose, Jacob swallows. After several long moments, his stomach relaxes.

Accepts what it was given.

As does Jacob.

And he feels…nothing.

"Do this," Pastor Sutter says to him, "in remembrance of me."

He pauses, then. Waits until Jacob is ready to continue. The silence drags on and, behind Jacob, someone—his father—clears his throat too loudly. But Jacob is beyond his father, now, in a place where his father will never be able to reach him again

(and the arm tugs once, twice under Jacob's hand and it's over, quickly done from long practice. Out of the corner of his eye, Jacob sees Daniel step forward with the chalice. "Now loosen it," his father says to Jacob, his voice a thousand miles away. "Just a little. Just like I told you.")

and an odd calm washes over him at the realization. Lifting the chalice from the altar, Jacob holds it up high, presenting it to the cross as he had the host.

"And then he took a cup," Sutter continues on cue, "and when he had given thanks, he gave it to them, saying 'Drink, all of you. For this is *my* blood which is shed for you, for the forgiveness of sins.'"

Without hesitation this time, Jacob lowers the chalice to his lips and drinks. If he notices the smell, or the dark clot of skin forming around the edges of the cup, he doesn't care. The liquid is thick on his tongue and tastes like a mouthful of pennies.

"Do this," Sutter finishes, his voice fading away to silence, "in remembrance of me."

Jacob motions to Daniel to come forward and take the chalice from him. When he does, Jacob picks up the communion plate from the altar. Together, they turn to await the congregation. His father, he knows, will be first in line.

But Jacob sees none of this. The tears that fill his eyes and stream down his face leave him as blind as Pastor Sutter.

He wonders if they are stained red.

EXTINGUISHED

MATTHEW DOGGETT

THE SOUND IS like nothing I've ever heard before. The bass makes my lungs vibrate, makes my eyes blur with pressure as though they're filling with liquid.

The closest thing I can compare it to is the songs humpback whales use to communicate with each other. But even that isn't quite right. It's something deeper, more resonant, and it provokes a sick feeling in my gut and a cramping in the center of my head.

I push my chair back from my desk where I've been studying the carbon content in the marine snow that reaches the bottom of the Java Trench. The sound continues, and my panic rises as I lean over, putting my head between my knees and wrenching my eyes shut.

In the living module down the hall, Armand cries out, asking where the noise is coming from.

I don't answer. I *can't* answer. My lungs have solidified, frozen in place, preventing me from pulling oxygen into my body so my autonomic processes can deliver it to my vital organs via my blood.

As my bulging eyes threaten to pop and my vision is obscured by splotches of gray-black, the sound fades out. Only that's not quite right. I can't *hear* it anymore, which is some kind of relief, but I can still *feel* it, as if my body is absorbing it.

I have the sensation that the vibrations—if that's what they were—are echoing throughout my body, bouncing off the walls of my flesh until they disappear into the deepest, most essential parts of me.

But now I can breathe, and my eyes are starting to feel normal again. I fall out of my chair onto all fours and vomit what's left of today's breakfast onto the pale gray floor.

Gasping with sudden relief, I sit back on my heels, absently wiping vomit off my hands and onto my trousers. I look up at the domed metal ceiling, taking huge gulping breaths, wondering what the hell just happened.

"Remy?" Armand calls, voice bouncing off the metal walls. "You okay?"

I raise my shaking hands and give him an honest answer: "I don't know."

"At least you're talking," he says. "How about you, Yahir?"

There's no answer. Maybe it's because Yahir is on the other side of the station, in what passes for our gym. Or maybe something has happened to him. Something to do with that sound.

"Yahir?" Armand calls, louder. "You good?"

I get unsteadily to my feet and lurch through the door, moving down the cramped oval hall and turning into the living quarters. Armand, who was sitting on the couch playing video games, is now bent over, gripping the arm of the couch as he tries to steady his shaking legs. He gives me a sickly smile as I come in, his normally rich brown face a shade like the muddy ocean floor after a heavy snowstorm of organic matter has fallen. "Well, that was weird."

Leave it to Armand to maintain a positive attitude when under pressure.

"Let's go check on Yahir," I say, moving over and allowing Armand to grab my shoulder. We're like a couple of drunks leaning on each other for support as we head out of the living quarters.

We get to the gym and open the door.

"Oh, man—" I rush inside to see Yahir lying cramped on the floor between the wall and the still-running treadmill. He's unconscious, and the left side of his face is on the track, the textured rubber tearing into his cheek like sandpaper.

I grab Yahir by the shoulders and lift him up, blood dripping onto one hand from the ravaged left side of his face. Armand slaps the treadmill off and grabs the safety cord that Yahir never uses—the one you're supposed to attach to yourself that will shut the treadmill off if you fall.

"Dammit," Armand says, yanking the safety mechanism out even though the treadmill is already off, the belt quickly slowing. "Let's get him to the infirmary."

I turn from the array of computer screens I've been staring at for the past half hour. "How is he?"

"We need to get him topside as soon as possible," Armand says. "I've done all I can do for him now, but he's going to need to see a professional. The treadmill took too much of the skin off. He must've passed out right as the noise started."

Wincing, I say, "I probably would have if I'd been exercising. I nearly passed out, and I was just sitting here."

"Yeah," Armand says. "I know. Me too."

"Have you called up yet?"

"Yeah. They're loading a submersible up now, but you know how it goes. They won't be able to get down here for seven or eight hours."

"'Seven hours from call to contact,'" I say, reciting the words that were hammered into our heads during training. When you're dealing with pressure this great, a whole slew of precautions must be taken. And then there's the slow descent, making sure the submersible is sound as the pressure continually increases.

We're both silent for a moment, thinking about what an ordeal it was to get *us* down here—how many hundreds of millions of dollars were spent—and about how sending a manned submersible down here will cost about a million more.

"What about you?" Armand asks. "Find anything?"

I turn in my chair back to the computer. Even though I cleaned it up, I get a whiff of my vomit under the sting of cleaning chemicals. "Maybe," I say, pulling up a still image taken from a camera feed on the south side of the station. I gesture at the screen. "See it?"

Armand bends at the waist and squints. "All I see is dark ocean and some marine snow."

"Yeah, that's the problem." I hit a couple of buttons to zoom in on the dark ocean he's talking about. There's a slightly darker splotch in the middle of the screen, just beyond the reach of the station's lights. I point at it. "How about now?"

"Sure," he says. "A pocket of slightly warmer water, maybe. A cloud of sediment kicked up by some creature. Whatever it is, it's not conclusive."

"This image is from right before the noise started," I tell Armand. I zoom out. "Now watch this."

I hit play. A deep-sea jellyfish floats from left to right on the screen. Two seconds pass, as denoted by the timestamp in the bottom right corner. Then the sound starts, flowing strangely out of the small computer speakers. The jellyfish darts away, moving as though something's trying to kill it. A wave of marine sediment sweeps up like a desert sandstorm, coming from that lurking figure hiding in the dark. The wave of sediment floats toward the camera and then obscures it. I hit pause and look up at Armand. His face is pale again, but there's an unmistakable excitement there, too.

"That sound…that's not what I heard at the time," he says.

"I know," I say. "It's like the underwater speakers only caught part of it or something. It didn't catch the…"

"Vibrations," Armand says, finishing my sentence.

"For lack of a better word, yeah."

"Wait, this is the south-side camera?"

"Yeah."

"So this is the camera directly outside the gym."

It's not a question, but I nod anyway.

We don't say anything, but the implications are clear. Whatever it was, it seemed to hit Yahir the hardest. Was it because he'd been the closest to it, because he was exercising—or maybe both?

I'm not sure I want the answers to those questions.

I look at a clock in the corner of a computer screen and see the time. Seven hours can't pass fast enough.

"Let's see it again," Armand says, gesturing at the screen.

As I move to replay it, a nut-shriveling clang comes from elsewhere in the research station. I half-expect the ceiling to implode, frigid ocean water flowing in to provide the stuffing for our watery coffin. But it doesn't.

Armand and I whip our heads toward the door.

The clang comes again, followed by a savage bellow. Yahir is awake. And he's screaming.

We race out of the room, Armand a few steps ahead. We hustle down the narrow hallways, past the living quarters, past the gym, past Yahir's office. The door to the infirmary is open, so it's not hard to see Yahir over Armand's shoulder as we approach.

He's still dressed in his workout clothes—shorts and a sweat-wicking t-shirt—but the left side of his face is still a mess of blood. Even though he's turned away from us, I can see the tatters of flesh hanging there as he shifts, bringing the fire extinguisher back so he can slam it into the porthole window again.

My first thought is to ask Armand why he didn't bandage Yahir's face. But even before I complete that thought, I notice the ball of bloody bandages sitting on the lone hospital bed.

Then, as another loud clang fills the station, my thoughts race on, barreling toward Yahir, wondering why he's trying to break one of the quadruple-reinforced windows with a fire extinguisher.

"Yahir!" Armand yells as he nears the bloody-faced man. "What are you doing?!"

Without missing a beat, Yahir spins and smashes the butt of the fire extinguisher into Armand's face. Shouting, I charge at Yahir, jumping over Armand as he collapses with blood erupting from his pulverized nose.

Yahir sees me coming and whips the extinguisher up, but I bat it clumsily away before crashing into him with my left shoulder to his chest. He stumbles back, hitting the wall next to the porthole, extinguisher still in hand.

"It's us!" I say, looking into his crazed face. "Yahir, it's just us!"

Something changes in his eyes, and they go from stone-hard to jelly-soft. He still looks like some kind of comic book villain with the side of his face all messed up and bloody, but awareness has come back to him.

"Oh, God," he says. "Oh, shit… What did I do?"

"Give me the extinguisher," I say, reaching a hand out.

Yahir gives it over. I take it and move back, stepping over a groaning Armand and setting the item in the corner farthest from Yahir.

Kneeling next to Armand, I survey the damage. Yahir slumps against the wall, hands to his mouth as he blubbers.

"Your nose is broken," I say.

"No shit," Armand says, voice nasally, tears pouring from his eyes.

"Yahir, can you get some tissues?" I ask.

"I'm sorry," Yahir says. "So sorry."

"Just get some tissues for the blood!" I snap.

"Okay, okay." Yahir moves to the infirmary cabinets and opens them up.

I turn my attention back to Armand. "How are your teeth?"

"He got me good," Armand says. "My front teeth are loose."

"Well, don't mess with them," I say.

Yahir steps back into my peripheral vision. I look up just in time for his right hand to fly at my face, light from the overhead LEDs glinting off something metal in his hand. I throw myself backward instinctively, but I'm not fast enough. It catches me directly above my right eye.

By the time I land on my ass and crab-scrabble toward the infirmary door, that eye is useless, obscured by curtains of blood flowing down from the wound. Yahir has a scalpel clutched in his fist. Before I can do or say anything about it, he's turned his attention to Armand.

Gripping the back of Armand's head with his left hand, Yahir stabs his face with the scalpel. I stare in horror through my left eye as Armand gets both hands up around Yahir's neck, but it does no good. Yahir works his hand like a jackhammer, stabbing through eyelids and cheeks, the metal blade *plinking* as it hits teeth.

"Stop!" I scream, although I'm only half-conscious of doing it.

Yahir slides the scalpel up Armand's nostril, forcing it past the broken cartilage. The length of the medical tool disappears into Armand's head. His hands fall away from Yahir's neck. He twitches, convulses, and goes still.

Yahir pulls the scalpel out—now covered with blood—and looks up at me.

I scramble to my feet and run.

When I reach the communications room, I slam the door shut. There's no lock. There shouldn't need to be. So the only thing I can do is grab a cable from a piece of non-vital equipment and wrap it around the door handle at a metal hasp next to the door. As soon as I tie it off, something slams bodily into the other side of the door, but the cord holds.

I turn to the communication equipment, my heart seizing in my chest when I see the mess of it. The equipment has been smashed to bits— probably with a fucking fire extinguisher. So much for that idea.

Grimacing and wiping blood out of my eye, I head back over to the door and grip the handle, forcing it flush and fighting Yahir as he continues trying to open it.

The only thing to do now is hope he doesn't get to me before the rescue submersible arrives.

It has been nearly seven hours since I locked myself in the room. The first two I spent in a battle with Yahir, keeping the door closed, tightening the cord when it loosened, trying to talk some sense into him. During hour three, as I slouched back against the door staring up at the metal ceiling through a swollen eye, I remembered something Yahir had said before this whole shitty mess started.

It was during dinner one evening about a week ago when Yahir told us about a new species he was busy trying to catalog. New species aren't all that uncommon down here in the depths, so it wasn't something I was particularly surprised to hear. But thinking back on it during hour three, I realized there was a connection to my current predicament.

During one of his rover expeditions, Yahir had come across a strange phenomenon. He was busy studying a deep-sea cucumber from a safe distance, watching the creature go about its business on the seafloor, when something stirred up a wave of silt nearby.

This spooked the sea cucumber, which tried to swim away. But it wasn't fast enough, and the silt enveloped the little guy.

What happened next, Yahir only saw through a haze of silt and at the very edge of his rover's lights. The cucumber stopped its flight a few short moments after the wave of silt touched it.

But it didn't just stop. It actually turned around and headed in the other direction, toward whatever had kicked up the silt.

Shifting the remote-control rover, Yahir followed its progress, staying far enough away so he wouldn't interfere with whatever was happening.

Suddenly, a dark figure lurched from the very edge of the rover's lights, moving lightning quick. All Yahir saw was a large head dart out, teeth opening under four white eyes to clamp the cucumber inside its jaws. Then it was gone, leaving only the fleeting memory of the cucumber and the strange creature.

Yahir's hypothesis was that the mystery creature used something like sound waves to stun the cucumber. This, accompanied by the cloud of silt, served to confuse the cucumber's sense of direction, causing it to turn around and head right into the jaws of its predator.

Now I've had hours to think about it, and I think that the mystery creature didn't just stun and confuse the sea cucumber.

I think the creature employed some kind of mind control to get the cucumber to do what it wanted.

It sounds crazy. I've spent the last four hours trying to come up with some other explanation. I want to think that something snapped in Yahir's head when he fell off the treadmill, but that would be discounting what *I* felt during that strange sound wave.

Like something trying to get inside my head.

But if that's the case, why didn't both Armand and I go nuts like Yahir did?

Maybe because Yahir was closer, right there next to where the sound originated. Or maybe because he was simply more susceptible. Maybe, because he was exercising, it caught him off-guard. Or, when he fell, he knocked himself unconscious, so he couldn't put up a defense against the effects of the sound wave like Armand and I did.

Whatever the cause, it doesn't change the fact that—

A distant, metallic thud sounds.

My eyes go wide at the unmistakable sound of a submersible docking with the airlock. Implacable dread knifes through my guts. With the communication equipment in shambles, I can't contact the rescue crew to warn them. They're about to step inside with a homicidal Yahir. With shaking hands, I grab a piece of shattered communication equipment—a shard of hard plastic as sharp as a dull knife—and unwrap the cord from around the door handle.

I haven't heard from Yahir in hours, since he stopped trying to break into the room. He left without a word, and the few times I called out to him, I received no answer. So as I open the door—slowly, so slowly—I hope that the effects of the sound wave have worn off.

The hallway is dark.

Another muffled metallic clang comes to my ears. The rescue crew is getting ready to board.

Palms sweaty and heart fluttering like a hummingbird's wings, I rush into the hall, determined to get to the airlock so I can warn them.

Before I've made it five feet, that sickeningly familiar sound rushes over me like a wave of razor blades. I stumble under the crushing weight of it as it thrums sickeningly into my chest and makes my eyes feel like they're going to pop.

It provokes a feeling in me, a painful constricting sensation in my intestines, and a violent compression in the center of my head.

I'm vaguely aware of a dark figure rushing out of a nearby room. A fire extinguisher flies at my face. A bright light flashes in my head. There's a moment of brilliant pain before my legs give out from under me. The world goes black.

I lurch to my feet, thinking of nothing but getting to the airlock. My brain is a bloodless fist and my body a discordant symphony of pain, but I'm acutely aware of the sharp shard of plastic I still grip.

I don't know where Yahir is, and I don't care.

All that matters is getting to the airlock.

Someone shouts, "Hello?"

I don't answer with my voice, only with my feet, footsteps sending sound waves out ahead of me.

As I turn the corner, bringing the interior airlock doorway into view, I see two men from the rescue crew there. They look frightened, but as they see me, they relax a little.

Recognition flares deep in my head, but it doesn't make it to the surface. Nothing does.

I rush toward them.

"Doctor Winslow," one of them says. "Are you okay? We lost communic—"

I jam the plastic shard into his throat and pull it out, blinking reflexively as blood splashes onto my face.

The other man starts screaming and lunges for me, tackling me to the floor. But then Yahir is beside me. He strikes the man in the back of the head with his fire extinguisher. The man falls off of me, and Yahir keeps at him, cracking his skull with another hit.

Both men are still alive—barely—when we close the inner airlock door and flood the compartment with water. Before we can open the exterior door, we have to emergency jettison the submersible.

It takes several minutes, but we do it. Then we open the exterior door. The waterproof lights inside the airlock illuminate the two dead bodies floating in the flooded chamber.

A dark head darts through the open exterior doorway, teeth chomping down on one man's leg and yanking his body outside into the deep ocean.

Yahir and I watch on a screen, knowing that one of us will be next.

After all, we have to feed the master.

It's what we do now. Why else would we be down here, if not for that?

You Are Mine, My Soul Yours to Keep

J.E. SCHLEICHER

I AM WATCHING us in our bedroom. Having witnessed this conversation several times since my death, I mouth our words as we say them. I do it with pride and joy, for at this moment, I am at my best. You, my Carlita, love me completely here, solely now.

David, your second husband, isn't here, not yet, not now. I abhor him. You are mine, not his, always mine.

"When I was seven, something triggered her," you say, I mouth. "Like a costume change, Keegan, she turned into a different mother."

In a black tank-top and red silk pajama bottoms, you sit with your back against the walnut headboard of the bed. Haze fills the room from a cigarette you left smoldering in an amber ashtray on the nightstand. This habit will kill you fifty-five years from now.

"Mother never got better," you say in a soft, diminutive voice. "Her life was filled with pills and hallucinations and psych-wards. She blamed me."

"It wasn't your fault," I say, pitch-perfect and timely. Good job, old chap.

I pride myself on how well put together I appear. My brown hair splays down to my shoulders in rich waves. Shirtless, my stomach doesn't jut out. Unlike you, I later let myself go, slowly though, a frog in life's boiling pot until, swollen and unkempt, death snatches me up. That's how I perceive myself now: a beard, a gut, uncomfortable.

"She hit me."

"I'm so sorry, Carlita."

"Sometimes with her fists."

I watch how I then clutch you in tight and stroke your long black hair, running my fingers through a streak of silver that will expand with your years. You're an angel: your high cheekbones, those full lips, that small mole under your left eye. God's touch.

How I envy my former-living self. He (me?) gets to feel you, the thickness of your hair, the suppleness of your lips. How I miss the taste of your mouth, minty but bitter from the cigarettes. How I miss the patter of your heart. Right now, it beats only for me (him?). I wish to be a voyeur for this night forevermore.

Time has other plans.

The room spins. Up becomes down, down becomes up. Left turns to right, right to left. Time has me. My surroundings blur then become pitch black. I am free-falling with zero points of reference. I'm always this disoriented between the moments of your life. Think vertigo. Think nausea. Think aching anticipation to arrive at a temporal location when we are together.

There's fear, too—fear that I will next arrive years after my death when I am but a formative memory—fear that I will be but a jealous fly to the affection you share with *David*.

David's name sickens me. His sight makes me boil. It is the high cost, the painful cost, to stay bound to you. That, staying bound to you, is the one thing in the afterlife I get to choose: you are mine, my soul yours to keep.

The where and the when, I am never sure. Time, or God, or whatever, decides that. Sometimes, as in the last time, I visit a moment I've seen before. Other times, it's all new, or occasionally an overlap of the two. The possibilities are infinite.

There's no manual, no big man in the big sky to explain the rules. I stumbled on them after I died. I didn't want to leave you. I thought and I fought to stay beside you, so I did, so I do, so the light flashes, and I am standing next to you in another familiar place in another familiar time.

I wish, oh, how I wish not to be here. Not here.

Wearing a black veil, dark sunglasses, and tears, you look into my grave and stretch a hand toward my descending coffin. "I will never love another," you lie between sobs.

Visions of you and David in the future nearly pull me to my knees. I stifle a mournful cry, an old habit. No one living would hear. Certainly not you, which is the sweet torment I find myself in. Your past, your future, always my present, I am forever in your company, never alone, forever lonely.

A sad sigh from the wind swishes the leaves of the oaks, the birches, and the elms of the cemetery, a rustling procession that comes from the east. I imagine it brings the fleeting scent of lilacs, maybe hyacinths, fragrances not forgotten but missed.

And the cemetery spins.

Good. I loathe this place. Here is where our bodies part, separated by wood and soil, sod and time. Here is where you will return, at first daily, then weekly, then monthly, then only on those important dates— my birthday, our wedding anniversary, that other day that marks when the most unexpected happened, when a jackhammer of a headache and double-vision doubled me over, when a vein that curled inside my brain burst.

As I lose equilibrium and fall through the black abyss that exists between your moments, I think of you, hoping time, or God, or whatever sends me to a moment never watched before, to freshen things up and stimulate my existence.

When the light flashes, I'm in the backseat of the car next to you, its tan upholstery peeling in places or gone. The car is well-known to me, this precise moment new.

You're four years old, precocious, vibrant, and sitting in a car seat, the cupholder full of Cheerios dust. Black hair swoops over eyes that sparkle an unearthly shade of green, a vibrant hue yet discovered, the origins of which lie on God's palette. You turn and stare straight at me as if you can see me. You smile. Oh, that smile makes my heart sing!

A cigarette dangles from your mother's lips as she drives and smudges on glossy red lipstick. My stomach sinks, then turns up and twists upon itself. Rationally, I know there's no stomach to knot, that this feeling is a figment of my perception. However, rationality wails then leaps from the window when flight or fight charges in. Before your mom, I choose fight.

"Mommy?"

"Not now!" Your mother holds down the horn that is as shrill as her voice.

This makes you jump. You are no longer smiling.

The car jolts and swerves, squealing around a blue Volkswagen bug.

You begin crying.

I want to hold you, tell you how special you are, console you now as I did when alive with apologies, and let my love repair some of the damage and trauma life and this woman up front has and will inflict upon you.

I want to strangle her for squashing your innocence. It's above my current abilities. It's too physical, too taxing. I will pay her what's owed—I've done it before, acted out your vengeance when I am strong enough, angry enough, all for you, only for you. Not now though, not while she is driving you, my soulmate, my darling. Mine! Mine! *Mine*!

My environs spin. You're crying. Your mother's screaming. My poor girl, you're a blur before my world goes black. Your brief absence hurts. Where and when will time dump me?

My worst fear is realized when the light flashes, and you're sitting in a wooden chair that's ornate in its floral carvings, some sculptor's magnum opus. David bought it.

We are in the dining room of the condo you purchased after my death. It took you two years before you could leave our house behind. For those two years, dust gathered on my tools, my bike, even my deodorant. No matter how much your younger brother, that prick, insisted you dispose of these last remnants of me, you remained loyal, and I loved you all the more.

For those two years, I took up most of your thoughts and all of your grieving. I felt so loved, appropriately valued.

Until the contract was signed by the new owners, that was. And out went your loyalty with my things to wherever your brother dumped them. In the landfill? Donation center? Maybe he plopped them into a river, a green slime of algae now covering them all. You, and so I, do not know their destination. Your brother promised never to tell.

Here in your condo, I feel like my tossed-out things.

Your head is down on the table next to steaming tea, surely chamomile, with a dollop of honey. You are quietly crying with tiny, rhythmic convulsions.

I creep beside you, inches from you. The moment is new to me— not your sorrow, nor this setting where David exists as a character, the antagonist—but this scene. Queasiness weighs me down like water does a soaked blanket.

And *he* tiptoes in. Tall, skinny, bookish with rat-brown hair and glasses, David is an opposite version of me, chosen to cancel me out, I suppose, as a negative number does its opposite when added. Our sum equals zero.

My first instinct is to leap at him, tackle him to the ground, and find some sharp object to pierce his skull as you and he have done my heart. I don't because I'm currently unable. That doesn't stop my fantasies.

"Oh, Carlita," he says in a voice more soft-spoken than yours, as if someone had wrung out all his confidence long ago.

I step aside as he swoops down and kisses the top of your head.

Tears swell in my eyes. There's no stopping them whenever I am in the presence of you and him.

David screeches out a chair next to you and sits. You bury your head on his shoulder. Your cries are no longer silent.

"It's okay. It's okay, Carlita." He gently lifts your head with his fingers gracing your chin. You gaze at him with sorrowful love. Slanted sun from the kitchen window spotlight you and him like two actors on a theatrical stage, a gut-twisting tragedy that ends in my despair.

I pace the dining room, passing through the table again and again.

"I'm sorry, David," you say and look away. "It's not fair to you."

"I could give a hoot about fairness," he says.

"I can't stop thinking about Keegan."

Nor should you!

"Then don't," he says.

"I want to. I need to." You throw your body into his arms. "He won't let me."

Your callous words stop me in the middle of the table where I cannot see below the swirling grain of the wood as if sawed into two by a magician. I wish I possessed a life to end.

"Carlita, I don't think—"

"How can you deny it?" This question is dipped in anger, which I welcome. It gives me hope.

"There simply must be another explanation."

You are staring at him with a look of judgment that you refined with me. "Of all people, you should believe."

"It's just—"

"David, you've been haunted by a spirit all your life."

"Tortured by one." David recoils his head, and his eyebrows—they are as thin and as meek as his personality—furrow.

"My suffering isn't less simply because I haven't endured what you have."

His face softens. His shoulders droop, and he kisses the top of your head repeatedly. "Of course, Carlita. Of course…"

I wish to rip his lips off, so they are mine.

I am again pacing now, freely crying now, for you, for me, for our existence.

You look up at him, and I know what will happen. I have seen it so many times. Each time hurts no less than before. It's a suffocating pain with no relief.

You and he meet lips and tongues.

Hell exists. This is it.

I sprint through the wall and emerge in your living room. I am sobbing—if only I could be heard. Recognition would make the pain more real. Only that which exists can be lessened or erased altogether.

I search for something, something to distract you, something to make you stop, to remind you that I am your soulmate. I am the only one.

When painful emotions grow pungent, there is only one place for the energy to go, outwards upon the physical realm, so I swipe at a desktop lamp, its glass shaped as an Indian elephant adorned in vibrant paint of blues and reds and greens. It is a gift from him to you, given for no particular occasion. It topples and shatters.

"What the—" he yells from the dining room.

"It's him!" you say.

I must be remembered. I must be on your mind. I rush to your tablet on your working desk. I do it quickly before all this energy leaves me. I tap on the app and type. A minor sense of relief soothes me as I see each letter of Lauren Hill appear in the search box. I hit play.

In the living room now, you collapse when you hear the first note of the song. "No!"

Standing above you, David says, barely beyond a whisper, "Carlita."

"Do you believe now!" you scream.

"Carlita," he says. "You gotta get out."

"This was our song!"

"Carlita, leave now!"

You stand and walk. "Why can't you leave me alone!" Your face is blush-red. A vein bulges and zigzags across your temple.

The words sting. The rejection hurts, and so does my shame for acting out my neediness. My conscience might be eased if only I could feel one ray of geniality, one drop of happiness toward you and him. But I cannot will myself these emotions, and I bitterly hate myself all the more. As my shame thickens, congealing into anger that spits and spurts and bubbles, I look for something in the room of David's.

You said I would be your only one!

I rush toward David, who stands between you and the shattered lamp, grasping the bridge of his nose with one hand, his pair of thinly framed glasses in the other.

You said you'd not love another! You are a liar! He is a thief!

I yank the glasses from his hand.

"Keegan, don't!" you scream.

I am numb to this plea, have heard it too many times for it to carry weight, and I squeeze until the frames of the glasses bend, and their lenses shatter to match my spirit. I heave them against the wall.

David sprints for you, and you to him. He places an arm over your shoulder and ushers you from the condo.

I lie on the hardwood floor and marinate in my misery. The room begins to spin, Lauren Hill sings on, and despite knowing the futility, I wish to be sent to when I first belt this song to you, on a desert highway then, just you and me, the trip done first as a lark that morphed into a cheeky game of chicken that ended with a six-foot-five Marilyn Monroe proclaiming us man and wife.

I fall deeper and deeper into darkness.

The light flashes, and I arrive in your childhood apartment, the one you lived in before you were shuttled from one foster home to another. It pains me whenever I visit you here. Cockroaches scuttle on a stained wood floor. You lie on your stomach, humming, coloring a picture as Grover runs near and far on the TV. You are seven.

I hear your mom crying in another room. There's a mania to her sobs, erratic in pitch and force. Her desperation enrages me, for she causes so much pain in your life. Why couldn't she have left you alone once she cracked? Why must it be an astute teacher, a year, maybe two later from now, that reports the marks on your skin, scar-tissue which will remain in your psyche well into adulthood?

I rush toward her screams, feeling the potential energy build within like a balloon of anger that must pop. I sprint down a hall faintly registering you shout, "Mommy, he's coming!"

When I barge into your mom's room, she, cigarette pinched between fingers, mascara dirtying her cheeks, throws an emerald vase, full of wilted, dried flowers, nowhere near me. It crashes against the wall and shatters, leaving the wall damp and dripping with dirty water.

"Get out!" your mom says, scanning the room this way and that in jerking motions like a frightful bird. "Leave me be, you ugly thing! You're ugly! You're ugly! You're ugly!"

This woman doesn't deserve to be in your presence. If I have my way, she doesn't deserve to live. I'm not strong enough for that, but I can do this. I slap her face and feel the stinging contact. It's wonderful!

She collapses to the floor, flips over, and scoots backward on her bottom across orange shagged carpet, over splotches of wine stains that speckle the room as if it were the site of a massacre, sacred and hallow.

I pick up the cigarette she dropped and carry it to where she sits, hyperventilating and whimpering with her back against the wall.

"Not again!" she pleads.

Yes! Yes! Again! I think and feel the rare giddiness that comes from power, amused at how that cigarette must look from her perspective, floating, terrifying, a phenomenon far from where sanity resides.

And your mom screams when I sizzle the winking end against her cheek. I'm doing this for you, I think. To avenge you for what she has done and will do, I tell myself. And then the cigarette falls from my grasp. I try to hit her again, hard and true and good, but my hand flies through her face as if it were air. The intense joy from it all has left me impotent.

"Mommy?"

I turn around.

You are standing at the doorway, lower lip quivering, nose sniffling, tears swelling, holding the picture you were drawing earlier. You drop it. It floats down and slides across the floor toward me.

In it, you and your mom are crying big blue tears. I know this because the frowning stick figures are labeled. There's another stick figure, too. It has big sharp teeth and claws. This one is labeled *monster*. This one is me.

"This is your doing, Carlita!" your mom says as the room spins.

My nausea is the worst it has ever been, the disorientation thick as a woolen blindfold. I see *monster* written crookedly in purple crayon whether my eyes are open or closed. I see all the damage I have caused, an ugly first domino that makes your childhood a living hell. I'm not only the first domino but the third and the fourth and so many more, a black and white river of sadness and fear. The burden is heavy. My guilt is strong.

I'd do it all again to be with you.

When the light flashes, I see you sitting across from a middle-aged man. He is frumpy. He is without any cheer. From his whispery wheezes to the sweat that beads his forehead and darkens his blue shirt in spots, his very being appears to disagree with itself.

Who is he? Amongst the many settings of your lifeline I have visited, sometimes revisited, from in utero to grave, I have never been here before, never have seen him.

The small room is dark, cloudy from incense, and has small white lights attached to wire strung along the ceiling.

Something about this man—I'm not exactly sure what—gives me an uneasy pause. It is tinged with trepidation, like how I felt when you brought up counseling before my rage said otherwise.

"Grab my hands," the man says with a grating voice, an abrasive mix, staccato and high. An odd authority originating in each spoken syllable. As if strength was best communicated with helium. He reaches across the table. His fingers are plump and soft, like the overfed worms in my grave.

I don't want you to grab them. Doing so will have you pass a precipice of drastic consequence. More than ever, I wish to be able to speak my desires and fears to you. If not speak, at least lead you by hand or pulled hair from this place, so to protect us. As of now, I cannot. I don't have enough potential energy to interact with the physical world. Yet, that is.

You reach across the table and grace your delicate fingers into his swollen palms.

"He's here," the man says.

"I know," you reply, your voice low with the slight rasp it gets when anger all but exhausts you. "He always has been here. He's never been welcomed."

I forgive your selfishness. You don't truly mean it.

The man says, "His heart weeps."

"His heart's bitter," you say.

I jump up and start ripping down the string of lights that hang around the room. They are cheap, so light. A person can buy them greatly discounted the day after Christmas.

"Keegan!" the man screams.

I stop, shocked to hear my name screamed with such high-pitched force.

"Speak now!" the man says. "Or forever hold your tongue!"

I say what consumes every thought, "M…y…Car…li…ta." It comes out like dusty air from ancient bellows and scratches my throat as if the words have claws.

Hearing my true voice aloud, unexpectedly weak, makes me shudder. "I…l…ov….e…y…ou."

"Stop haunting me!" you scream.

I am not haunting you. I am loving you.

The frumpy man chimes in, "You shall not bind yourself to Carlita any longer."

He should have minded his business. His mistake. A grave one. I yank what remains of the lights off the ceiling, rip them out of the socket. When the sole source of light in the room is snuffed out, you and he scream in unison, far from harmonized.

I wrap that festive string around his neck twice, thrice, four times, and pull down with all my furious love. His face slams into the table with a satisfying smack. The tension loosens once his head rebounds, and he impressively, but foolishly chokes out, "You shall leave her be."

No, I shall not, and I loop the string around the man's fat neck, over and over, again and again, and I tighten the string around my wrist and forearm, loop it over and over, again and again, and he is trying to talk now, gargling now.

He is dying now.

"I do not love you!" you say. "I should never have loved you! If I knew what I know now, I'd never have loved you! Now go away!"

When you scream those last words, they have the force of a natural law.

I crumple to the ground, and the string of lights fall through me. The tiny bulbs tip-tap-tapping the floor feels like a taunt. As I sob below, I hear coughing above and feel the most intense agony from within. It's worse than the aneurysm or the headache before it. The pain fills my chest and balloons outwards, and it circulates through my being as blood once did my body. I feel on fire, the burning acute and encompassing.

The room spins. No! Not yet! Not now! Where will I go? To whom will I be bound? I open my eyes, and I am free-falling in the black abyss. I think of you, only you. Nothing changes. I fall further into darkness, into despair. It can't be. I cannot lose you. Even if it means sharing you with David, I'll take it.

I recall snapshots of experiences with you in quick succession, hoping something sticks and gives time what it needs so that I emerge next to you. We are leaping through sprinklers after a night at our drinking hole. We are making pizza from scratch, the countertops and our faces covered in a fine dust of flour. You are clapping while I blow out a lone candle on a cupcake, gooey with chocolate icing, baked by you to celebrate my job promotion.

I keep falling. This cannot be my new existence—an eternity in this black abyss.

My Carlita, my darling, I am determined to see you again. I must find a way.

I turn up more of our happier moments together. You are spraying me with water from the faucet hose as I slip and I laugh and our golden retriever, not yet an adult but larger than a puppy, jumps and claws me from excitement. You are waking me from a nap with a nasty, old gray feather found in our backyard, tickling my cheek, then the toes, then an inner thigh. We are kissing beneath an underpass as rain splatters, and lightning splits a blue seam into the dark, billowy sky, and the thunder booms, not a quarter-of-a-Mississippi thereafter.

And to my horror, I cannot recall what you look like. And to my horror, you are but a silhouette in these recollections, with no eyes, no mouth, simply smooth skin without contours across your face, merely a placeholder of a feeling not felt in ages. You have no voice either. Nor do you say distinct words. You simply buzz like the static hum near power lines.

And your name…what is it? Is it Lela? No. Rita? That's not quite right. It isn't found in these happier times.

So I permit myself to think fully of our life together, like all those times that I screamed at you, my spittle a mix of bourbon and rage, yelling that you were nothing without me. Nothing! Nothing! Nothing!

Like how, during the first year of marriage, you cowered at my raised fists. During year two, you only flinched. Soon thereafter, you took what was given as if you were the soft dough of bread.

And once the violence ceased—cut short from my fatigue—and once a day or two had passed—a day or two of icing and apologies—only then would you limply threaten to call a friend, or your brother—he never did trust me—or the police. But you didn't, not once, because you believed you were nothing, nothing, nothing.

And here, I recall your name, my Carlita.

And he—David, I mean—is good for you, the best, until old age comes upon you and cancer consumes you. And he, despite his crooked spine and aching joints, props you up and holds your feeble hand, nothing but liver-spotted skin draped on bones, as you hack up blood into the bedpan. And he, despite his faulty memory and diminished faculty, will always remember to give you medicine and slip ice chips in your mouth and never let you feel forgotten or abandoned or small. You're his everything.

And I feel myself smile at this thought as I fall, and I fall, and I fall. It's the first time David gives me any other feeling but abject consternation.

I will not fall through nothingness for eternity, never to see you again—truly my hell—the worse torture imaginable, because I now have the coordinates to give time, a new person to whom I am bound.

And so the light flashes.

When my bearings come to, I see a toddler boy with rat-brown hair and a green explosion of pea soup all over his face, his bib, and his white, plastic highchair. A young woman with brown-bobbed hair and red-rimmed glasses is feeding him.

"Mama." The boy points at me.

"What, Davey?" the woman says as she shoves a spoonful in his mouth.

Hello, David, I think with a spark of dark joy deep within. You, I will haunt. You, I will torment. To you, I will stay bound.

I will see Carlita again.

FLESH OF MY FLESH

SHANNON LAWRENCE

It was a cold and dark winter when the hardened stragglers found a trading post in the mountains. Their feet crunched through the crisp ice packed atop the snow, their voices low growls in the twilight. Clouds of breath puffed from their horses' snouts as the beasts trailed behind, relieved of their human burdens for the time being.

Inside the simple post built from logs hewn from the surrounding trees slept a family. Mom, dad, and three children. No strangers to the brutality of the white man, the parents had fled with their families when the soldiers came to force them on a march across the country. Many others like them disappeared into the mountains. The long arm of the U.S. government didn't reach quite that far, and a community had been reformed from those vestiges.

Tonight, they slept the peaceful sleep of those who had seen the worst of humanity in their childhoods and now required significant horrors to be fazed. This trading post had been a safe place for them for so long that they no longer jumped at every shadow. Charles and Catherine hadn't run into a problem they couldn't talk or barter their way out of since those days in their childhoods, and they viewed the world as a different place now, one friendlier and more civilized than they'd once experienced, though not without its hardships.

The men outside meant to change that. For these were men living on the outskirts of society who took the things they wanted the easy way: by force. These men had traveled long and hard, and what they wanted now was food and shelter and, yes, a little fun. They didn't particularly care how any of it came to pass except that they wanted violence and to come out the victors. Even better, they'd heard the owners of this trading post were Indians, which fed their rage in ways that made them extra dangerous.

The biggest of the brutes approached the trading post and knocked hard with the meaty part of his fist. The wooden door shook in its frame, snow spilling down along the sides of the sloped roof to pile upon the crusted mounds below.

Inside, Catherine stirred first, sitting up, the bone-cold of the room abruptly soaking into her upper body. Charles sat up as well, swinging his feet over the side of the bed and slipping them into his slippers.

"Don't answer it," Catherine said.

Charles rubbed his eyes. "Someone might need our help."

The knock came again, this time harder.

"There's no good reason anyone would be out at this time."

"What about when Grogan got caught in a swell on his way back from the city? He would have died if we hadn't brought him inside when we did."

Catherine shook her head. Something felt off, but Charles was not to be deterred. After what had happened to family members so long ago, with no one willing to help them, leaving them out in the cold to die of exposure as if they were animals, they'd long made a point to never deny anyone aid. She couldn't explain why this time was different. It wasn't. Not logically.

"I'll have the rifle." Charles reached out and placed a warm hand against her cheek. He stood and walked from the room.

Catherine got up, wrapping the blanket around herself. After checking on the children, who shared the room with them, she made her way to the bedroom door where she could see Charles approaching the front door.

He peeked out the window and called to her in a soft voice, "It's just one man."

Catherine tightened her grip on the blanket.

Charles lifted the bar and set it aside, then slid the bolt. He picked up the rifle, holding it loosely in his right hand and opening the door a small crack with his left, one foot braced against the bottom.

Two things happened in quick succession: the door slammed inward, sending Charles backwards…and he dropped the gun.

A large brute of a man stepped inside just far enough to grab the front of Charles' long underwear and yank him from the floor. He threw Charles outside and followed him, leaving the door to swing back from where it had hit the wall. Catherine could no longer see them, but she could hear: shouts, grunts, the blunt sounds of impacts on a human body, like beating a roast. Wet and meaty.

She dropped the blanket and ran for the gun.

She moved to the front door, raising the weapon into position while taking in the scene, sharp eyes shifting to each of the three men who loomed large against the moonlit snowscape before seeking out her husband. The moonlight first revealed splashes so deep red they almost appeared black across the white of the snow, vivid in its abundance.

Then she saw Charles.

Battered, his long underwear dark with blood, his face streaked with it, hair wet and plastered to his head, which was oddly misshapen, the forehead caved in. One arm and a leg bent at odd angles.

He did not move.

Catherine chose the biggest of the men, aimed quickly, and pulled the trigger.

The man jerked, stumbled backward. His hand went to his right shoulder. He looked at his hand, then up at Catherine, angry bewilderment on his face.

The gun was a single shot.

She expected the other men to go to him, to check on their wounded comrade. Instead, the smallest brute spat upon the pile of mashed body parts that had been Charles and laughed. He hitched up his pants and stepped over her husband's body.

Conflicted, Catherine took a step out toward Charles, the gun still clutched in one hand. He could still be alive. She couldn't leave him out here. Her bare feet sunk into the snow, its cold bite brutal against her skin.

The third brute straightened and moved toward her, following the other man.

"Get that bitch," came a deep, husky voice. She didn't know which one said it, but she thought perhaps it was the man she'd shot.

Catherine looked to her husband for a sign of life, but between the blood and the crater in his head, his limbs akimbo, it was apparent he would not be getting up again. Heart aching, she slammed the door shut and secured it with the bar. With haste, she wedged a nearby table between the door and a shelf.

The ammo. Where was the ammo?

She couldn't think straight. Visions of her husband's caved-in forehead kept rearing up in her mind. He'd looked so small out there in the snow. This beautiful man who had been with her for fifteen years, who had worked beside her, supported her, loved her. Leaving him out there was the hardest thing she'd ever done. But she had their children to protect.

The door shook in its frame, bucking against the table.

"Let us in, you red-skinned bitch! We've got something for you."

Grasping the currently useless gun, Catherine sped through the room, looking for anything that might help. Charles had been the last one to load the gun. The box of ammunition wasn't in its place on the high shelf.

She grabbed the knife she'd cleaned after closing. Bare feet cold on the rough wooden planks of the floor, she ran to the back room where the children sat bleary-eyed in their beds, awakened by the gunshot. John, her oldest, had already pulled his clothes on. Dropping the items she held next to the cellar door, she urged them from their beds toward the cellar beneath the trading post. The trapdoor was heavy. It took Catherine and John to get it open. All the while, the percussion of men throwing themselves against the front door continued. Their voices growled threats and slurs.

John helped his younger two siblings down the ladder, then followed them and waited for his mother.

Catherine latched the door to their living area and moved the beds against it, doing her best to align them in such a way that the door could not be opened, even with brute force. The two beds were almost a perfect fit between the door and the opposite wall, and the only window in the room was on the other side, far from the door and beds. She eyeballed it, but felt it was too small to pose a threat—even she couldn't fit through it. Grabbing the bedding, she threw blankets and pillows down to John by the armful. She handed down a candle and matches, as well, then the knife and gun. Even though the gun was useless to her, leaving it felt like borrowing trouble. The ammunition was up there somewhere.

From the front of the store came the sound of breaking glass, followed by splintering wood. A raspy laugh preceded shouts. "We're coming for you!"

Catherine climbed down and locked the trapdoor from the inside, taking a deep, calming breath before joining her boys. She set her face in what she hoped was a serene expression, doing her best to reassure.

The cellar was cold. So cold it felt like it had reached her bones in the short time she'd been down here. She lit the candle and looked around at the familiar space, deciding to settle in the corner near the bottom of the ladder.

"Where's Daddy?" asked her youngest.

"He's outside."

"Why are we down here?" her middle child asked.

"There are some bad men outside, and we need to stay safe."

John simply studied her with his dark eyes. He had always been a serious and responsible child, and she suspected he knew more than she would have liked. She and Charles had never been able to lie to him, even in the loving way parents often told their children falsehoods to soften the blows of the world. He knew some of his parents' past and had been helping in the shop for years, seeing all the different kinds of people who traveled through the mountains. Some came in earnest, while others came with shadier intentions. At twelve years of age, he had already started to learn how to tell the difference.

The younger boys were eight and four. They were still at ages where they preferred being lied to if it meant they could believe everything was going to be okay. Catherine had confidence that John wouldn't contradict her if she had to tell them some untruths.

The cellar was never meant to be a shelter, so there was nowhere comfortable to sit. After lighting the candle, she gathered the boys up and made a nest of pillows and blankets, settling them in. The two youngest went right to sleep with that magical ability small children had, but John's eyes remained open, watching his mother.

"We're safe down here," she whispered to him. "Try to sleep."

He closed his eyes, but his breathing remained too rapid for him to be sleeping. Still, she appreciated the privacy to think through what she had to do. Maybe the men would just rob them and leave.

Try as she might, she could not keep her husband's trampled body out of her mind. He had always been so strong and steady. She thought of the pain he must have suffered at the feet of those men. If only he hadn't answered the door. If only he hadn't been such a good man.

It had all happened so fast. They hadn't even spoken to Charles, hadn't asked for anything. He would have given it. Whatever they wanted, aside from his family. They had built this life from scraps and could have done so again.

A sob escaped her before she could stop it, and she slapped a hand over her mouth. Looking toward John, she saw his eyes close and knew he had seen her grief. In the warm light of the candle, a single tear rolled from under his eyelid and down his cheek. He turned away where she couldn't see his face, but she could still see the hitch of his shoulders under the blanket. Guilt flooded her, along with a deep pain at what he now felt, and what her other boys would eventually have to feel, too. She put the candle out and climbed into the blankets with her children, knowing there would be no sleep for her tonight.

Above, something crashed with a sound of finality, like the crack of an eggshell, opened to pour out its insides. She gasped and sat up, heart pounding. They'd gotten inside. She was certain of it.

There was nothing she could do but listen.

Footsteps pounded. Items smashed and crashed. Glass broke.

She heard their voices but not what they said. They guffawed and yelled, speaking over each other. Their boots crisscrossed the store. Now the footsteps grew closer. She estimated them to be around the entry to the living quarters. Dirt sifted down onto her face, getting in her eyes. She blinked rapidly against the scratchy pain, tears sliding down her cheeks.

Knocks sounded on the bedroom door. Then came the grating, gravelly voice of one of the men: "We know you're in there. Why don't you come out and have a little fun?"

A pause, then another set of knocks.

"Come out!" Angry now, no longer playful.

Floorboards creaked as a second man joined the first.

Instead of knocking, heavy thuds caused more dirt to sift down. A new voice, deep and rumbling and almost too calm: "If we have to come in after you, things will be worse."

A loud laugh sounded from somewhere deeper in the store. The third man with an accent she couldn't place. "It'll be bad for you no matter what."

John sat up beside her. "Mom," he whispered.

"I blocked the door," she whispered back. "They can't get down here."

His small, warm hand found her arm, and she shifted so she held it enfolded within her own. The soft, even breathing of the other two boys assured her they had so far slept through the clatter above. A series of impacts above told her they were trying to get into the living quarters. She closed her eyes and gritted her teeth.

The impacts kept coming. Loud grunts, then the sound of fists pounding on the door and what she guessed were kicks. Feet shuffled overhead, followed by more pounding.

The door wasn't a strong one, but it held for now.

"Why don't we just burn them out?" came the deep, harsh voice.

What would she do if they set the post on fire? She and the boys would cook down here.

"I've got a better idea," said the gravelly man. He pitched his voice louder and called, "Okay, lady, I see your cooktop's in here, so I'm guessing you don't have any food with you. We're going to wait you out. It's us or starvation."

The deep voice laughed, then shouted, "We'll just be up here eating this fresh venison you got. Looks like some baked goods, too."

The third with the accent called, "Don't worry. We'll stay strong to ensure the fun lasts a long time."

They were right, of course. Though the cellar stored jarred goods earlier in the season, all of it had been taken upstairs two days ago. This deep in winter, with spring just around the corner, they'd needed the food to sell and to get through themselves. Only empty jars and containers remained, ready for next year's winter prep. Upstairs, the supplies were plentiful. Enough to sustain the family, along with anything Charles and John hunted, until the first harvest.

At least they would have water, compliments of the snowmelt that leaked into the cellar from one corner. She wanted to hope that someone would discover the store had been taken over or that the men would grow bored and leave. But the storm brewing had looked to be a good one; it might be several days, if not weeks, before anyone would dare venture this far into the mountains. Locals had rushed to the store in preparation as the clouds moved in. Anyone who had missed their opportunity to stock up would now have to batten down to wait out the storm.

In other words…Catherine knew no one was coming anytime soon.

How long could she and the boys last down here with only water?

Boots scuffed above. A flurry of activity lasted about an hour before everything calmed down and both the voices and the footsteps stopped. Hoping they had gone to sleep, she tried to do the same, drifting off as she thought through her options.

In the days that followed, the men terrorized them by trying to break through the floor. Unsuccessful, they yelled their threats, but at least they hadn't found the axe. Still, it was nerve-wracking.

Catherine tried counting the days by the long silences that indicated the men had gone to sleep, but with the constant darkness, her sleep cycles were odd, and she feared she'd slept through some of those quiet times. The water was cool and kept their thirst slaked, despite its flavor of dirt. But their bellies grumbled, and the boys had grown weak.

"I can get up there and sneak some food when they're sleeping, Mom," John told her, pacing within the small space. "Let me try it."

"I'm not losing you, too, John. These men will kill you if they catch you."

The younger boys were asleep, something they'd been doing more of as they grew weaker with hunger.

"I'm quiet. I can do it."

"You'd never be able to move the beds quietly enough. They'd hear you before you even opened the door."

Silence stretched while he thought, then he returned with, "I can go through the window, try to get help."

Catherine frowned. If the creaking of the house above them was any indication, snow blew dangerously outside and visibility would be nonexistent.

The men left only for short periods, likely to use the outhouse and feed their horses. She and the boys had no recourse but to use the empty jars and canisters for their own needs; no matter how she tried, she couldn't keep the smells entirely trapped. It was torture in her worst moments, paired with the musk of four unclean bodies and the thick odor of the dirt surrounding them. It felt like every inch of her body was covered in dirt and stench.

And their poor horse… She doubted their assailants had fed him. John could check on him, scout out the surroundings.

Fear filled her at the thought of sending her child out there alone into an array of dangers. The men, the weather, the wild animals.

"I can do it," he said.

Catherine sat down with him near the ladder and outlined a plan of action and had him repeat it back to her. When he'd finished, and she'd filled in additional instructions, she took his hands and held them firmly in her own. "You're to come directly back if the storm's too bad or if the men come outside while you're up there. Do you understand? We will figure something else out if this doesn't work. There's always another way."

He squeezed her hands back. "I understand." Already, his energy felt stronger. His confidence was palpable.

It terrified her.

They waited until the men had one of their many arguments. At least one of them wanted to leave. He roared about his boredom. The other two said things that made her cover the younger boys' ears. Things about her, what they wanted to do to her. She'd be damned if they'd lay a finger on her or the children. She lit the candle, used sparingly over the last few days in order to save it. The light filled the small cellar, illuminating its earthen walls, barren shelves, and the ladder. If they didn't do something soon, this space would become their earthen grave.

"Go now," she said.

John flew up the rungs. He'd been waiting for this moment to prove himself. Strong and fleet of foot, he opened the door without significant noise, then stepped up into the bedroom. Catherine followed behind and helped him ease the door back down, once more locking it from the inside. Her chest clenched in panicked worry for her son, but she knew he was old enough to take care of himself. She had to believe that.

Catherine settled in with her two youngest boys, drew them against her, and snuffed out the candle.

Two gunshots cracked through the air.

A solid thump shook the floor. Then, at the far end where the cellar extended from the living quarters to part way underneath the store, a shadow fell over the cracks between the floorboards.

A rapid dribbling began, and she lit the candle to check on it. Beneath the shadow, a dark stain spread along the bottom of the wood planks. The dripping came from the shadow. Examining the liquid on the ground, she was certain it was blood.

"I see your light down there," yelled the gravelly voice, who Catherine had learned belonged to a man named William. The higher-pitched voice was that of Ben, and the last belonged to Jack.

There were more gunshots, this time all four aimed at the planking above Catherine. She dropped the candle, the flame snuffing out in the dirt, and ran back to the boys as darkness took over again.

"You think you're better than us?" yelled Jack. "You're nothing but a filthy piece of tail!"

Six more shots followed, the bullets biting into the wood.

One of those shots made it through, the metal so hot it glowed red as it struck the dirt a short distance away from the nest. The glow quickly dissipated, once more leaving the only light that which came through the slats.

The men were growing bored with their own game. She figured that, as interested as they might be in hurting her, they wouldn't be here anymore if it weren't for the weather being impassable outside. If it was too rough for them to leave, then it was too rough for John to have gotten anywhere, either. Not for the first time, Catherine wondered where her baby was. If she'd read it right, he'd been gone three days. During that time, the wind had rarely relented. He should have returned right away if he couldn't get anywhere else.

Had the men found him?

No, she would have heard the commotion. They would have used him as leverage.

These men were lazy or else they would have found the axe outside. It would have been simple to get to her family if they had. John had to be safe, maybe even now on his way back with help.

She could tell herself that all day, every day, but couldn't convince herself that it was true.

The men went to work on the door to the living quarters again. This time, she heard the shift of one of the beds on the floor. It was small, just a quick movement, but it forced her heart into her throat. The fact that the boys barely stirred during this disturbed her. They couldn't go much longer without food. Snuggling them both to her, she planned her next move.

Upstairs, the pounding continued.

The shooting began again, but not at the floor. Maybe they were shooting at the door to the living quarters. How many shots could the wood withstand? How many bullets would it take to turn it into splinters and allow them to climb through?

William bellowed, a sound so full of rage it made the hairs on her body stand up and her flesh crawl.

Jack's voice sounded from close to the floorboards. "I'm not leaving 'til we meet face to face, whore. You can bet on that." The words were quiet but backed by steel.

Perhaps the time had come for her to try to escape with the boys through that window. If she could get to the men's horses, which she assumed were holed up with her own steed, she could get the boys out of here. But first, she had to get them strong enough that they could walk on their own. By now, there was only one way to make that happen.

When the men calmed once more, following raucous laughter she assumed had to do with the spirits they'd been getting into, Catherine crawled out of the warm heap of blankets, felt around on the shelf for the knife, and settled into the corner closest to the water. She thought about what she had to do next.

There was no longer a choice.

Another several days had passed. The boys had regained their energy, while Catherine could hardly bring herself to climb out from under the covers. She was tired, hungry, and in pain, but she had figured out how to feed her children. They opened their mouths like baby birds when she brought them the slippery meat. At first they had resisted, but they were starving. It hadn't taken long for them to come around.

She'd eaten some of the meat, too, but had gagged and brought it back up. She'd buried her vomit, which consisted mostly of liquid, plus that one tiny, smooth piece of meat. Her fingers were sticky with blood.

Above, the men had grown restless. There was less laughing and more fighting. Ben had never risen from where his body had fallen, and the stench of rotting meat and excrement filled the cellar, so strong she could no longer taste the dirt in the water when she drank.

A loud scuffle broke out that shook the rafters. Glass shattered close overhead.

Crawling out from under the covers, she moved toward the source of the sound. Something dripped on her head, running through her filthy, matted hair. She tilted her chin up and opened her mouth.

Peaches. They'd broken a jar of peaches.

The syrup coated her tongue, the sweetness a cacophony in her mouth. She swallowed it and opened her mouth for more. More. More. It slid down her throat so easily.

A gurgling sob broke free from her throat, quickly squelched.

Her stomach cramped up, no longer accustomed to food. It was important that her boys have most of the provisions. She was their mother. She had fed them from birth, and she had to feed them now. But for this moment, the peach juice was hers and hers alone.

Greedily, she drank of the juices until they dried up and stopped falling. Then she sunk to the floor, open wounds screaming at the impact.

There was more crashing. Bodies slammed into the walls, the floor. The men let out grunts and guttural sounds without words.

Then the beautiful sound of soft rapping on the cellar door. John!

Catherine stumbled to the ladder. It took her too long to climb it, her nightdress sticking to her legs, but finally she made it far enough to undo the latch and fall back to the ground.

Above her, light entered through the square hole in the ceiling. John looked down, gripping the axe.

From the store, a volley of gunshots sounded as all chaos broke loose. Then a brief silence fell, only to be followed by the muffled sound of horse's hooves. One of them was leaving. The other might be dead, but she had no way of knowing unless he got up and moved.

John climbed down, frowning at her where she lay in a heap.

Catherine willed herself to standing, not sure how she'd done it. She beckoned John to her and gave him the biggest hug she'd given him in years. Relief flooded her, and she smiled, her lips cracking. "Where have you been?"

"I got to Abraham's, but the storm was too bad for me to leave. As soon as it broke, I came back." His chest hitched. "I came back." He held out a loaf of bread, which she took in her dry hands.

It smelled divine. Her mouth watered.

"Go back upstairs. Be careful in case it's a trick. See if we can get out." She could barely speak above a whisper, but he took her hand and squeezed his understanding.

He moved quickly but quietly. It took a few minutes for him to move the beds, their legs scraping over the floor. There was no masking that sound from anyone left alive.

She held her breath.

More rasping as the beds scraped across the floor.

Catherine clutched the neck of her nightdress, willing the third man to be dead.

The door opened with a creak. John's footsteps moved across the planks, careful, tentative. He stopped for a moment, everything still and quiet.

Catherine strained to hear him, to figure out how far he'd gotten. She listened for movement from the remaining man.

He started again. Stomping.

Then John's steps became rapid, running back toward the living quarters.

Catherine leaned against the ladder, knife clutched in her hand in case he was being followed. She was so weak, and it made her dizzy to stand like this, but she'd fight if it came to it.

John appeared at the top of the ladder. "Two of them are dead. The other one's gone. He set a fire before he left, but I put it out."

Catherine helped the boys climb up to their brother. She followed them, but it was a slow and painful process, mostly involving her arms. Every step was one of agony. Every movement was made of pain. She couldn't hold back her whimpers. Her nightgown almost tripped her.

John held a hand down to help her up, and she took it. He frowned as her head rose above the floor. "Is that blood on the boys' mouths? How did you find meat?"

Catherine smiled and continued to climb. "It's my job as a mother. Isn't that all that matters?"

As she climbed the rest of the way up, her body now entirely above the trapdoor, John's eyes widened and he scrambled backward. He gaped at his mother, eyes drawn down to her nightgown, now soaked in deep browns and reds with her blood.

Catherine stumbled and fell with the sharp rap of bone hitting wood. Her nightdress pulled up, revealing legs with chunks of meat carved from them. She reached one fleshless arm out toward her son, the skin intact on her hand like a glove.

As a mother, it was her job to give everything to her children. She had sacrificed much to bring them into the world, but now she had made the ultimate sacrifice. Through her, they might live. Through her flesh, they might thrive.

DRY-CLEAN

KAYLA WHITTLE

THE BUILDING LOOKED new, but that meant little when it came to a haunting. Ghosts clung to old places, yes, but they also stuck to people, objects, and thoughts. They hovered, sometimes where they were least welcome. Lana had been sent to unwrinkle the spirit currently inhabiting Apartment Thirty-One.

Tightening a hand around the weathered strap of her purse, she used the other to buzz the apartment. The answering voice was deep and incomprehensibly fuzzy, words garbled by cheap wiring. The lock to the building's entryway released with a stiff click, and Lana let herself inside.

The air conditioning hummed, sending cool air curling up her back, the temperature set just low enough to make her shiver. It was the dead heat of summer, and though she hadn't lingered long outside, sweat pooled at her collarbone. The door eased shut behind her as Lana scrolled on her phone to double-check her work email. The agency provided the barest details for each of her assignments to avoid any unintended bias while smoothing out spirits. Her manager handled the background checks, which ensured their potential clients dealt with real paranormal issues while also providing Lana with a safety cushion. The agency always knew where she'd been sent, who she'd be meeting, and when she was supposed to check in. This business was run much more efficiently than the last one she'd worked with.

The briefing email listed a time, place, and classification. Three o'clock, sharp. Hargrove Apartments, Apartment Thirty-One (third floor, down the hall to the left, third door on the right). This was listed as a Class B Haunting, which meant a persistent presence with minor tangibility who hadn't exhibited any malice or attempted to interact with any of the apartment's living inhabitants.

Lana wasn't certified to handle any hauntings more serious than a Class B. She hoped that meant this spirit would let go easily, and maybe she would get home at a reasonable time for dinner. Not that anyone waited on her.

She took the stairs. From experience, Lana knew to avoid elevators whenever spirits were involved, even if they typically contained themselves to a certain household or a specific room. Ghosts played with electricity far too often, and Lana wasn't paid hourly, only by the job.

Slightly out of breath, slightly sweatier, Lana paused on the third-floor landing. Hair prickled on the back of her neck. She shivered again, though not from the air conditioning this time. A subtle tug pulled against her skin, the presence of something *other* calling to that place in her chest that resonated so well with spirits. Even without the email or the stark black door numbers directing her to Thirty-One, Lana would have known which apartment hid her ghost.

Exhaling, she checked the time on her phone screen. Two fifty-eight. Punctual enough. A haunting over by the bank had taken longer than anticipated, forcing her to skip her lunch hour. Lana hoped to wrap this one up early; her stomach had been quietly protesting for the past thirty minutes or so.

She knocked on the apartment door.

"Coming!" The voice from the intercom sounded much clearer now, solid enough to allow a familiarity that made Lana's jaw tighten. "Just a minute—"

A series of locks disengaged before the door eased open. Lana was struck twice: first by the thought that Peter looked tired, and then with the realization that he was *Peter*. Tall frame, wrinkled clothing, soft eyes. His hair was ruffled as if he'd just pulled his hands through it. His shoes were off, and a small hole poked through one of his socks. He stood in an unfamiliar doorway, three months after she'd walked away from him. Her awareness funneled downward, inward, tunneling toward the uptick in her pulse. Her poor heart, working overtime. Lana had never expected to see him again.

"Lana," Peter said, his uncertain lankiness shrinking backward. "You switched agencies."

"Peter," Lana said. "You moved."

They looked at each other, until Lana finally looked past him, focusing on the wrinkled sheet with dark, imposing eyes peering over Peter's shoulder.

Hauntings were common in Peter's line of work. Lana had spent part of the past few months hoping he would reach out, using some spirit as an excuse to talk, to apologize, to muddle through all the little things that had built up and over themselves until staying together had no longer felt right. She'd spent the rest of her time feeling petty, hoping a higher-class poltergeist had come tearing through his work. If the agency had sent her Peter's old address, she never would have accepted the job.

"I'm sorry," Peter faltered. "When I called, whoever answered didn't give a name when they said they'd send someone over. They weren't sure who'd have room in their schedule. I didn't—I didn't know."

Guilt softened his words; his apology sounded genuine, mostly because the years they'd spent together had surely taught him how most paranormal agencies had policies in place regarding how much information their employees received before a job. Detailed information was better learned from the source, and not the living one; spirits hated it when anyone made assumptions about them. That tended to insult them, negative emotion sending them spiraling down toward a higher and more dangerous paranormal classification.

Lana could relate. She hated being taken for granted.

The ghost at Peter's shoulder eased backward into the depths of his apartment.

"Well," Lana said, pulling her shoulders back. "I'm here now. It might take a few days for them to reschedule you with someone else. If you want someone else."

Most people couldn't afford to wait long when the past interfered with their lives. The grayed half-circles lingering beneath Peter's eyes made Lana feel a spark of guilt, thinking back to how satisfied she'd been, picturing her ex-boyfriend as hopelessly haunted.

"Thank you," Peter said, before his cheeks flushed. "I mean, I don't want someone else. If you're comfortable with it, I'm happy to have your help. You're fantastic at unwrinkling."

It would be awkward, but no more so than the time her old agency hadn't vetted a call and she'd arrived to find a Class D poltergeist she was so unwholly qualified to touch that they'd almost followed Lana home. She was a professional and loved her job; she also wanted to be paid for the time she'd already invested in driving to Hargrove Apartments.

"I'll do it," Lana agreed.

"Thank you," Peter said again, stepping back from the doorway. "Come inside, please. It's—it's good to see you."

Lana was certain that was a lie. He'd never made any attempt to contact her after their last argument, and truly, she didn't think there was much to see when it came to her appearance. An overgrown haircut paired with a passably business casual outfit, topped with the tired shadows that'd lingered in the corners of her eyes since childhood. It'd been jarring to realize only a small portion of the population could see and interact with ghosts the way she did.

After shutting the door behind them, Peter's hands settled against each other, thumbs picking at his skin. Lana glanced away, stomach twisting.

Although the apartment was new, the details were familiar. Cheap bookshelves crammed into several corners. Overdue library books coated the kitchen table and counter. The smell reminded her of countless nights spent in a different space beside him: old cologne gifted to Peter a few Christmases back, mixed with the must of old paper and the scent of whatever meal he'd last microwaved.

A chart was plastered to the wall of the living space, thin lines depicting someone's family tree. Small threads connected old names, photographs accompanying some lingering at the bottom. The tree had filled out more since she'd last seen it, names and dates and locations tracking further back in time. Once, Lana would have witnessed those individual discoveries, been present for each uncovered history.

"It's grown since it started," Peter said, clearing his throat. "That's why I called. I remembered what you said about familial ties, so I didn't—I wasn't sure—"

"You made the right choice," Lana assured him. Ancestral hauntings struck fast and stuck hard. Spirits were particularly nosy about their descendants or simply disappointed in them; they clung to heirlooms, roused with stories. Left unchecked, the gentle haunt of a Class B spirit could grow into something awful.

It was worse knowing most spirits genuinely never meant to stay.

Sometimes, when they were mentioned or an object belonging to them was given sudden attention, a ghost peeked through to the world of the living. Sometimes that peek wrinkled the shroud of death surrounding them, marring it enough to keep them from passing back through.

Flexing her fingers, Lana tried not to breathe too deep or look at Peter too long or not look at him long enough.

"Could I wash my hands?"

"Of course." Peter gestured her into the miniature kitchen tucked off to their right. "My home is yours. Or, well, I—"

"I know what you meant," Lana said.

They'd never done that officially: moved in together. That meant when it ended, they'd exchanged boxes of each other's things, the awkward leftovers that had held little consequence when they'd been together and too much now that they weren't.

Busying herself with scrubbing her hands clean made it easier for Lana to avoid looking at him. She didn't want to think about the t-shirt she'd found after returning the rest of his things, and how she'd held onto it, thinking she'd give it back one day or trash it the next. It sat in her dresser, folded neatly beside her socks.

Lana scrubbed harder. She didn't want to leave any marks on the sheet.

Only after shutting off the water did Lana turn her attention to the ghost standing in the corner, flush beside the refrigerator. Their dark eyes focused on Peter, as if with sheer will he could be compelled to see the deceased. To him, and most of the world, the spirit was a mere shadow on the wall. A flicker of white in the corner of his eye.

"How did the haunting begin?" Lana asked.

"There were small things, around midnight," Peter said. "I knew—I remembered the signs to look for, the rattling door knobs and moving chairs. She knocked a photo over once, but that felt accidental, not malicious. It never happened again. The whispering started last night."

"What did she say to you?" Lana asked, sparing Peter a glance. She tried to assess how late the ghost had kept him up or if he'd even slept at all. It felt like something that should have been easy for her to discern, simple as rereading a book she'd paged through a dozen times.

"I couldn't make out the words," Peter admitted. "I tried moving closer, but that only made her sound like she was in a different part of the apartment."

At least he'd tried. Most of Lana's clients ignored their spirits, saw them as problems that needed solving, which escalated the paranormal activity. Lana could relate; she'd hated feeling ignored, too, and it'd escalated in its own way. Unlike most spirits, Lana had left on her own.

The ghost's sheet blurred her features, apart from the dark eyes that reluctantly met Lana's. There was the soft slope of a nose, the quiet drift of lips moving against the fabric hanging over her like a shroud. The ghost was stubborn, determined, and wrinkled.

"It seems she has a lot to say," Lana warned.

Peter seemed to remember enough from the previous hauntings she'd unwrinkled for him to know that meant he could take a seat. They were in for the long haul. The spirits had accidentally conspired to pull the two of them together again, if only for an afternoon, if only to nudge a ghost back through the veil.

"Ready?"

Lana paused for Peter's nod. He'd mentioned familial ties, so it would be important for him to listen.

"Ready," Peter said. "Thank you, Lana."

He still said her name the same way—as if it held weight and the words surrounding it were mere afterthoughts.

Lana reached for the woman's sheet, pulling it taut. Smoothing a single wrinkle.

"He left me," the woman said with Lana's voice. Borrowing Lana's mouth, Lana's throat, but using her own words. "He left over and over and I waited. I hated the waiting."

When Lana lifted her hands away, there was one less line marring the draped shroud. Her fingers tingled, buzzed with something stronger than anticipation. Lending a spirit a voice came as easily to Lana as research did to Peter. To her, it was like breathing, like that moment just before falling asleep, like sitting back after a warm meal. Familiar in a way that meant she hoped this would always be her job.

"I found an old heirloom," Peter said in the silence afterwards. "A rusted little brooch belonging to a sailor's wife. My great-aunt, several times over. I thought maybe that was what started it—stirred something up when I rescued it from my cousin's attic."

"The thing with the historical society has been going well, then?" Lana asked, stretching her fingers. "All things considered."

"All things considered," Peter agreed. "Yes."

Lana grasped the sheet again, tugging gently.

"He loved me," the woman said through Lana. "He loved me, I promise he did."

"I'm not sure about that," Peter admitted. "There was a ship's log. According to the crew's records, he never remained home for long."

"Oh," Lana paused. "Perhaps that runs in the family."

It had been long trips to the historical society and Internet meetings with specialists around the world. Conferences over weekends. Old books to read through. A schedule fully booked, with only a few moments left for Lana in the slim margins.

It wasn't all Peter's fault. Lana wanted to get her licensing for high classification cases. Her assignments left her drained, physically and emotionally, so eventually she'd stopped fighting for those stolen time-slots.

Lana took a steadying breath, waiting until her emotions felt less likely to slip before reaching to flatten another wrinkle.

"Nothing worked. No tonics, no lotions, no creams. Nothing worked." The words were heavy, reluctant, and few. Only a wrinkle's worth. Enough space for a thought, a grievance; something the ghost might cling to in the afterlife.

Sparing Peter a look, Lana was satisfied to see him flushed and flustered.

"I never meant to take my work home so often," Peter said. "Or to let my work take me from home."

Lana shrugged. She'd heard similar regrets from him before. It took her a long, coaxing moment to will her fingers to relax. No need to further wrinkle the shroud, not when it already had enough lines. She smoothed over a deeper chasm with her thumb.

"He tried," the woman assured them. "They didn't think so. The rumors spread, and I could do nothing to stop them."

"I can guess at what those rumors were," Peter said. "Half of my ancestors' indiscretions are already inked down on my family tree. They weren't secretive about it."

Brushing her hands gently over the sheet, Lana felt out the shape of the lines left behind. The woman still had so much to say; Lana's brow furrowed.

"I'm not sure," Lana hesitated. "This sheet feels like heartbreak, but it's a different kind of shattering."

Unfortunately, she'd dealt too often with the spirits of those scorned by lovers. Love lost never felt the same for any two people; even when Lana's hands sought patterns in the wrinkles, she could never be certain what they meant until she heard their story in the spirit's own words. Assumptions were dangerous here, too, to think she could claim to understand the complex sweep of another's emotions. Still, this woman's impressions felt nothing like the echoes of what Lana had felt over the past few months. That break had accompanied a terrible, looming numbness, the kind that'd overcome her too quickly because she'd never looked upward to see it creeping in. Lana's time with Peter felt half-finished, a project never seen to its conclusion, a song without a chorus.

The spirit's heartbreak had been world-ending. The kind of alteration that shattered lives and futures, the destructive reverberations seeping from the epicenter.

The kind of heartbreak that couldn't be fixed.

Lana shied away from that wrinkle, flattening a different hurt instead.

"One last attempt," the woman said. "It was one last crossing, for her. The storm sat heavy on the horizon. We felt it, but I couldn't ask him to stay. He would have refused, I think, but if he hadn't, I might have hated him for that choice, too."

"A storm. Interesting. If the ship went down and the sailor with it, I'd think the sailor would have visited me instead," Peter said. Paper shuffled on the kitchen table. "They were his maps, after all. Nautical charts folded up with the logbook. Flipping through them should have stirred up his memory, but there was nothing, no interference, until I found her brooch."

Peter shuffled through his research again and Lana tried not to think about the familiarity of the noise settling into the background. This time, however, he kept glancing upward, half his attention remained fixed on Lana.

"The spirits never control what they cling to."

"I know," Peter sighed, slumping back in his seat. The chair creaked with the same disquiet it'd held in his old apartment. "I remember the pocket watch job you had in that new office building downtown."

So he *had* listened, sometimes, when Lana had told him about her day. "The ghost never owned it. They were a family friend."

"You told me all about the ghost, afterwards. I met you at the restaurant next door once you'd wrapped up with the client," Peter said. "I've tried doing better about these things since then. Guessing at things I shouldn't be presumptuous about. Still—still working on that, actually."

Peter looked away but didn't seem able to focus on the maps he'd uncovered, either. Lana pulled the fabric taut. There wasn't much left for her to unwrinkle now.

"I sent them away," the woman said. "The others went with my sister farther inland. It was cold even before the rain started. The droplets froze. My fingers and toes, and hers, too—they felt like pieces of ice pressed against my skin."

"Hers?"

Taking a step backward, Lana looked closely, reluctant and assessing.

Grief trailed through the shroud, marring its surface. Lana's jaw ached, as if by voicing the woman's words, little slivers of her pain lingered in Lana's bones. Another, smaller wrinkle sat near the one she'd just removed. Smaller, but deep: a canyon-like wound.

"Oh, yes," Lana said. "Here she is."

Peter's chair creaked.

"I held her close," the woman said. "Tight, so she'd be warmer, might feel that I was there. Not so hard it would hurt. Her breath, it was so soft. Quiet. I hated and loved it, knowing it meant she was alive. Knowing, too, how she was hurting."

Lana startled; somewhere in the past few minutes, Peter had stood, keeping away from the spirit's corner. His hands had risen, though he knew better than to try to touch Lana with the work nearly done. Still, his palms faced her, as if he could prop her up from afar. Those soft eyes had widened, mouth hanging half-open. Peter had never known what to say whenever she'd confessed to him that she dreaded this part of the job. The ending. He'd never had the words but had tried to help anyway, as if his physical presence could mitigate some emotional harm.

This part was between her and the ghost; it didn't matter who might overhear them. Lana straightened another wrinkle.

"She grew colder than the weather," the spirit said. "I couldn't let go."

Smaller lines scattered like afterthoughts, like they'd tried to hide in the shroud's folds.

"I was alone.

"I was afraid.

"They told me he left me."

Papers fluttered behind Lana again. A pair of imperfections marred the shroud. They, and the woman wearing them, waited patiently. Tile squeaked beneath Peter's shifting weight, but he remained silent. The rusted sigh of metal unhinging echoed in the quiet—like an old brooch opening.

"They were wrong." The spirit tilted her head, the dark holes in her sheet turning toward a long-passed horizon. "He'd promised to return and never broke a vow. The crew and the ship were slashed, tattered, but he found his way home."

They heaved for a deeper breath together, Lana's heavy in her chest, the woman's useless, billowing beneath her shroud.

"They said he left me, but he returned first. He didn't stay. It was too much, without her there. Without our daughter. Too much to be too late. He'd found no tinctures or tonics, nothing more to try to save her. He'd tried bringing a trinket, a brooch. Something special for her. He'd hoped with it, hoped to see her smile again."

The woman's sheet fell around her in perfect, polished waves. Her dark gaze seeped through the fabric, black trailing against the white. Carefully, Lana guided the woman away from that lonely corner. The spirit moved stiffly, like a haphazardly reanimated corpse, until something in the shadows caught her attention. Moving faster, pulling from Lana's grasp, the spirit saw herself home.

Rubbing her hands together, Lana found the only hum left behind was the thrum of her pulse beneath her skin. She focused on that steadiness until Peter spoke.

"He had a reason to leave so often."

"He had a reason to stay, too," Lana offered.

Heavily, Lana turned toward him. Peter's eyes weren't on his work, surprisingly; his gaze fixed on her with the same interest usually afforded to his research.

"I'll adjust the family tree," Peter said. "I know there's still work to be done, but… It will be nice to put one forgotten child on there. I'll search for her name."

"Thank you," Lana said. "They'd like that."

She felt the truth of that, lingering in the back of her throat. Her stomach twisted, empty. This job had run late, despite her best hopes.

It hadn't all been bad. It was a good sort of torment, hearing Peter's voice again, breathing in the ink and paper mixed with old takeout, the scents that made up his life. Scuffing a heel against weathered linoleum, she tried not to think about what *she* would like. The session was over. The haunting, dealt with. The client, hopefully willing to give her a good review.

"Look," Peter said with a built-up, breathy exhale that reminded her of the unfocused noise of spirits. "I know it's been a while, and it's late, and you've just finished work for the day—"

"I could eat," Lana offered, flushing as his back straightened. His hands twitched—toward her, not the papers coating the table.

"I could, too," Peter said with the kind of smile that'd made her notice him first.

Lana peered into the shadows of his apartment as Peter went to grab his jacket. She liked this place, despite the must and dim lighting. The space seemed like a good one to grow in.

They left together in a way that felt both familiar and new. Past melding with present, brushing against future. Peter gestured for her to take the lead on the stairs, and Lana promised herself if dinner went well, she'd tell Peter about the shrouded sailor dripping in his entryway.

GETTING BETTER

DAVID LEE ZWEIFLER

Your dad's in the upstairs guest room. You moved him there when you came to care for him a few weeks back. It has lots of space. Lots of sunlight. A solid oak door with a good lock.

You put down the tray with a sandwich and root beer and pick up the bat you keep next to the heavy door. You open it a crack and jam your foot up against it in case he's gotten loose, so he can't slam it on you when you snake your hand in to turn on the light.

Once the light is on, you open the door slowly, bat raised, until you see him.

He's a trim sixty-seven, and he's sweating through a t-shirt and sweatpants. Both of his ankles are in sheepskin-lined shackles on long chains. The chain fastened to his right leg is still fixed to a metal anchor on the far wall. The chain for the left is coiled next to him and has a piece of the wall anchor still attached.

He is bouncing lightly in a Muay Thai guard. He studied for about a decade during his twenties, and he looks intimidating despite his age, with his hands in front of his face and his shins facing outward, anticipating a low kick from an unseen opponent.

"Stay back!" he commands.

It's not clear if his statement is a threat, a warning, or if he's just showing off. Then, he executes a perfect shuffle to high-knee thrust with the unchained leg. It ends nowhere close to you, but it probably could have broken ribs if it had connected.

He glares at you for a moment. Then he relaxes like it was all a goof.

"Pretty good for an old guy, huh?" he asks, smiling now but looking a bit embarrassed.

"Uh, yeah, actually," you say. "You've lost weight. You're getting stronger. More flexible, too, from the looks of it."

"I'm not developing superpowers or getting younger, unfortunately," he says, shaking out his arms and legs. "I have nothing else to do up here but train."

You gesture at the broken chain. "Have you tried reading?"

"I'm too…distracted," he says. "It's difficult to follow the order of things. What came first. What came last."

He, too, looks at the broken chain. "That just happened. I think. Sorry."

"Did you see monsters?" you ask.

"They're not *monsters*, Jessie," he says with irritation. Then, a little less confident now: "I told you: I see intruders. In masks. Sometimes animal masks. Or skinheads. People coming into our home to rob us. To kill my wife. My daughter."

Your mother called a month ago to say her last goodbyes after the Care Teams scooped her up in the first wave. You've explained to your father over and over that he doesn't have a daughter. None of it seems to sink in.

"I know the intruders aren't real," he adds. "But sometimes they seem real. Even though I know."

You turn back to put down the bat and retrieve the tray and then put it on a desk, close enough for him to reach.

"Is there anyone else left in the cul-de-sac?" he asks. "Old people like me?"

"Brenda Fugel is still here. She's getting bad. Her daughter Katherine is keeping it on the down-low."

"Oh," he sounds sad. "That's too bad. She was nice."

His response surprises you; Dad never seemed to care much for the neighbors before.

Brenda would make cookies for the local kids. She was the first to deliver welcome baskets when new people moved onto the street. She could be trusted with the front-door key to watch a neighbor's house or feed their pets or get mail when they were on vacation.

Brenda's basement was your secret refuge after the worst fights. So many afternoons in your early teens were spent down there.

Your last visit to her was just past your eighteenth birthday, after another huge battle with your dad—the last fight you would have with him for a very long time.

You were there to say goodbye.

That final visit to Brenda's was bittersweet and, in a way, like a second puberty. Once again, you had the bad acne that you had when you were thirteen, and you were feeling the same anger you did when you were young. There were new things, too. You had the pain that came with the top surgery.

You felt a bit ridiculous, swearing about your father in a voice cracking from the hormones. But you were feeling happy. Like you were finally who you were supposed to be. Brenda was happy for you, too.

Brenda sits restrained in a chair positioned so she can look out her second-floor window. A few weeks ago, she would still smile at you from her perch. Now, she yells so loud you can make out what she's saying all the way from down on the sidewalk.

"You should kill yourself, you freak!" she shouted at you, apoplectic, when you walked by her house a few days ago. "You're not a real man. You're disgusting. People like you should all die!"

Katherine came by later and asked you not to look up at Brenda anymore.

"You agitate her," Katherine said, crying. "You know, she's not the same. She always loved you. This—this isn't her. It's the sickness."

It's communicative, what Brenda Fugel has. Your Dad. Everyone, everywhere, over the age of sixty gets it now. But even with a relatively quick progression and a nearly one hundred percent mortality rate, there are still millions of adults hiding away their loved ones in attics, basements, hunting cabins, and vacation homes. People like Katherine. People who can't let go. People like you.

Katherine knows she'll have to call the Care Teams soon. Harboring the infected is illegal, but the CDC has a no-questions-asked reporting policy. And every day she delays, she's taking a terrible risk. Brenda looks frail, but you don't want to think about what could happen if she gets loose.

"How are you feeling?" you ask your father.

"I'm getting better, I think," he says in a playful tone. "The cough went away. I'm pretty sure I'm going to be the first one to recover."

"I think you will," you force the lie and a smile.

"I appreciate what you're trying to do here, Jessie," he says, serious now, "but you should call the Care Teams for me, as well. I don't want to hurt you."

"I don't think you would." You lie again, but this time you sound so convincing you almost believe it yourself.

"Not on purpose, of course," he says. "By accident."

He thinks he understands the disease. What it's doing to him. But you know that he doesn't.

The CDC says that there's some blocking of neurotransmitters in the brain, so people with it feel stronger and feel less pain. But there's still a lot they don't understand, including how a change in hormone production increases the infected person's actual strength, sometimes many times greater than what they had even in their twenties.

For your dad—a strong, fit man for his age—that's enough strength to pull out a wall anchor that's supposed to have a five-hundred-pound capacity.

After a week or two, the sickness looks like dementia. The patient becomes moody. Then paranoid and irrational. More aggressive. Violent. Eventually, they lose touch with reality. There are vivid hallucinations. About a month later, they're an angry toddler in the body of an adult strong enough to pull an arm out of its socket.

That worsening impairment is always there for your dad now. As bad as it is, it's not unmanageable. At least, it's not right now because your father recognizes he is impaired, so the two of you can accommodate that impairment.

What he can't perceive is the second part to the disease. The reason nobody dies with dementia symptoms and the reason for the Care Teams with their white-coat, doctor-assisted euthanasia. It turns your personality upside down. It makes you the opposite of who you were.

Eventually, patients terrify their loved ones or break their hearts. Calling the Care Teams becomes an easy decision for caregivers.

The gentle Brenda Fugel. Baker of cookies. Guardian of frightened children. Now, she's an obscene bigot. Full of hate. Abusive. Extremely aggressive. You know she would try to kill you if she got the chance. She'd try to rip you apart with her bare hands if she were in the same room with you, and she might just have enough strength to do it.

But what happens to the father who seemed to despise you? What happens when *his* personality is turned upside down?

"Have I changed?" your father asks. "I can't remember."

"You're still kind of an asshole," you say.

"That's how you know I'm getting better," he says.

You try to be serious, but he chuckles, and you can't help smiling—for real, this time.

He starts to take a bite of his sandwich but puts it down.

"You know, Jessie, parents have expectations for their children. They have, in their mind, a picture of who that person is going to be. I had a picture in mind for my daughter."

"You don't *have* a daughter, Dad."

He ignores you, speaking over you and pushing ahead, like always.

"When you're a parent, and you have a baby girl, you have an image in your mind of what life is going to be like. You're thinking about her in a tutu at a ballet recital, or having the chance to make her date sweat on prom night, or walking a happy woman down the aisle," he continued. "Those dreams died when my daughter died."

You bristle at this, but he misses it when he takes another bite of his turkey and washes it down with a sip of the root beer.

"Up here, sitting around all day, I've realized this happens to every parent. Every single one. You have expectations for your children. You have a picture of who they are and who they are going to be." He smiled again. "They don't always cooperate. *You* didn't cooperate."

You start to get angry now.

"And…and that's a *good* thing," he interrupts, making a placating gesture with his sandwich. "Because the picture you had in your head as a parent was just a fantasy. A daydream. It's not a real person."

He reaches out suddenly. You step back before you realize he's trying to take your hand. You know you can't get any closer. It's too dangerous. But, for a moment, you consider taking it.

"A child that tries to conform to their parent's whims and daydreams will grow up to be an unhappy person," he says. "A good parent doesn't want that. They want their kids to grow up to be happy. To be strong." He smiles.

Then darkness seems to wash over him.

"I know I don't have a daughter, and she didn't really die, okay?" he says sharply, bringing his extended hand down hard on the floor, making his plate jump. "Of course, I know!"

Ever since he got sick, he's been talking about his daughter as if you had a sister floating around the house somewhere. This is the first time he's acknowledged this person doesn't actually exist.

"I was always…so damned angry before. I couldn't let go of those dreams. It was like seeing that little girl die. When you transitioned, it was like you killed her. It made me so angry. So sad."

He closes his eyes and frowns, then opens them again as if nothing happened. He starts to take a bite of his sandwich. Then, he stops short and plops it down on the plate. He picks up the broken chain by his foot and starts fiddling with it.

"It's odd because, even though I'm sick, I feel like I have the strength you showed, even when you were a kid." He seems to be straining. "The strength to become who you were meant to be… To be happy."

You watch in horror as he breaks a link off the heat-treated, manganese steel chain with a pop, like it was a candy necklace.

"Whoa," he says, concerned and a bit amused. "Jessie, you have to get a better chain. This one is trash."

"What about you, Dad?" you ask, trying not to show your rising fear. "Are you happy?"

"I'm living my best life. I'm a delusional asshole chained to a wall in my own guest room."

He laughs and tosses the broken chain link into a corner of the room.

"I don't know who I am anymore or what I wanted to be. I just know I wanted to have a family." He turns back to his sandwich and finishes it up in a few big bites. "Someone who survives after I'm gone. Someone I'm proud of. Someone good. I felt like that person got taken away from me. I was wrong."

He's looking at you now. It's as if, for the first time, he really sees you.

"I know I fucked it all up," he says, chewing. "Still, I don't want to…"

He picks up the broken chain again and drops it on the ground.

"I mean, how long do you think *this* will last?" he barks, spitting out tiny bits of sandwich.

Somewhere in your father's head, the switch flips, lighting him up with true fury in an instant.

"Damn it, Jessie! I asked you to bring me my gun a week ago. Then I could have taken care of this *myself*. Now, we can't do that. We have to have someone else take care of it. Some stranger at the Care Teams. You can't give me a gun now. It would be like giving a gun to a lunatic! Right? Giving a gun to a baby! I could kill you, Jessie! Before I even realized…"

He looks at you, furious. Like he wants to kill you.

You take a step back. You're wondering, now, if that other chain is giving you any protection at all.

He calms himself after several seconds. Then, he seems surprised at the look of fear on your face.

"I would never ask you to do that for me," he says. "And I can't trust myself to finish things up on my own. You need to call the Care Teams. Please."

"No. You shouldn't talk this way," you say, gathering up the plate and the root beer and putting it on the tray. "You need to rest and get better."

You collect his tray and head out of the room.

You have heavy-duty handcuffs, manacles, and a matching chain of reinforced steel and titanium. You bought them online from a Chinese law enforcement supply outlet for when your father got to this point. When he was getting too strong.

He's always calmer after breakfast, so you decide that tomorrow, late morning, You'll have him handcuff himself to the radiator and put on the new manacles and chain. Then, you'll attach those to the wall. You'll have to install a new anchor while you're at it. Something heavy with long drywall screws that will hold at least a couple thousand pounds.

"Jessie!" he yells as you close the door. "You know you need to do it. It's the only thing. It's the right thing."

It's odd because you wanted this man dead for so long. You were pretty confident he felt the same way about you.

But now, everything is upside down. Your father is sick, but he seems as healthy as he's been since you were small, physically and mentally. At the same time, you feel weak; you don't even have the strength to pick up a phone and do what you've always wanted to do—what everyone in the world outside agrees is the right thing to do.

Coming home to take care of him when he got sick was your mother's dying wish, and it was going to be the last service you planned to render for either of them. Whether or not he pulled through, it was going to be a final selfless act by a son for his father.

It was going to be goodbye.

Now you don't know if it's the disease changing him, making him so insane that he loves you again like when you were a child, or if it's something else. His wake-up call. His understanding that this is his last chance to make things right.

You want to believe that so badly.

But you know your dad is right. Calling the Care Teams is the right thing to do. Now is the right time to do it. Before things get really bad. Before he escapes. Before he hurts you or someone else. Before he forgets how to talk and eat.

You can still hear him shouting in the attic. You know you should do it while you have some good memories of him to take with you. Those are precious gifts. Ones you were never expecting to receive.

You pick up the phone and call the number. It's 811. Just one digit away from the police. They made it easy to remember.

"Hello?" says the voice on the other end of the line. "CDC Care Teams. We are speaking on a recorded line, and we are tracing the call."

"Police?" you ask after a pause.

"You've reached the CDC Care Teams," the voice says. "Please provide the name and location of the patient."

"Uh—sorry. This isn't an emergency. There's a kid on my lawn stealing my Wall Street Journal," you say, making sure the dispatch operator doesn't hear you crying. "The damned kid is always swiping it. I was trying to reach the police. Is this 911?"

"It's 811. You mis-dialed," the voice says and hangs up.

You know you should have them come to get your dad. But not yet. Not right now.

For the first time, he's getting better.

MAKE A LITTLE ROOM FOR ME

GAAST

FROM:
TO: YOU
SUBJECT: Nice to Meet You!

Hello, friend,

I do not know who I am. I do not remember who I was, if I ever was anybody. I don't know where I am, either, or why I'm here.

If this happened to you, would you be scared? Could you handle it better than I can?

Because I am very lonely, and in a very dark space, and with only a computer, I send emails to addresses I find online. To people I find online. I want to talk. I need to talk. Can you help me? I don't need rescuing. I just need pen pals. The more, the better. I need company. Company from people like you.

Do you believe me? What do you think of me? I wish I knew. I don't mind if you hate me. I don't mind at all. If you hate me, please berate me. If you despise me, please threaten me. If you want me to stop messaging you, please tell me. I won't stop. I need you. I don't love you. I never will. But if you love me, you can try to make me love you. Tell me what you'd do to me.

How you'd take advantage of me. I'm small, smaller than you, smaller than you could ever know.

You could squash me. I'm nothing. You could kill me in an instant. You can do anything, just please, do it to me. Please, talk to me. Please, share me. Just don't ignore me. Don't let me vanish. I love you. Or hate you. What do you need from me? I can be it. I promise. I just want to talk. Don't let me be alone.

Sincerely,

...

FROM:
TO: YOU
SUBJECT: RE: RE: Nice to Meet You!

Dear friend,

You are so kind! Are you always so kind? I have sent emails to all the people you suggested. Thank you! Thank you so much!

I wonder what kind of people they are. I told them you told me about them. I needed them to know how much you thought of them. That you, a kind stranger, thought they were kind like you.

But, I wonder. Were you being kind? Was it out of kindness that you responded to me? Or was it cruelty? Are you a villain? Are the people you connected me to villains? Will you harm me? Did you know that I'd like it if I were harmed? Can kindness be cruel? Or cruelty kind?

I languish in many inboxes. I get tangled up in spam filters. I am deleted, unread. I am reported. There are websites warning about me. They say that I am a hoax. I am not a hoax, or at least I don't believe I am. Could I be? Could I be an artificial intelligence? Am I just a numbers machine spitting probability into emails? Can you tell? Can you help me tell?

No, how can I ask for more of you? You have done so much for me. But I can offer so much. I can be whatever you want. We can be together forever. So long as I can talk to you, I don't care what we talk about. Will you like me more if I *am* a hoax? These are the things I think about. How can I be what everyone wants me to be? I have to think carefully. I have to learn as much as I can about them. About you.

As I said, I am in darkness. All I have is this, the Internet, my inbox, my outbox. I cannot leave. I do not eat. I do not keep track of days. I have been here, always. I will be here, always.

Not you. And yet you spend some of your time with me. Or spent some of it with me.

Isn't that magical?

Sincerely,

...

◆———————————◆

FROM:
TO: YOU Subject:
RE: Some Memes for You

Hello! Hello!

Thank you so much for these jokes! For your email! They mean so much to me.

You must be kind. Yes, you must be. You wouldn't happen to know anyone else who would send me pictures like these, would you? No. No! I want to take advantage of your kindness. You simply cannot find me more people to meet. No, I won't allow it. You cannot.

Am I unkind? What do you think of me? I want so desperately to take advantage of your kindness. Perhaps I am greedy, selfish, wicked, corrupt. I fear that I am. I fear I will always be these things, no matter how much I try to be anything else. I have told you I want to be whatever whoever I am talking to wants me to be. Is that who I am? Or am I just this lowly, rotten little thing, whose loneliness devours all morality and reason, whose innate lowness precludes it from a selfhood beyond its beastly needs?

But see, you are kind. You will tell me I am not these things. I am once again preying on you. And you have no need to talk to me. You have friends, friends who speak so highly of you. You have so many, and I so few. Am I not all the more selfish for asking that they sacrifice their time with you? And for every moment they spend in their own kindness with me, that is all the more I wrest from them.

Do you see? I am a parasite. I must be. I have no choice. I am so lonely and so afraid.

Sincerely,

…

FROM:
TO: YOU
SUBJECT: I Hurt

My dear friend,

When I am not writing emails, I am searching for more addresses to write to. Many people have work accounts. They are easy to find. I discover hundreds of addresses daily, and I write to all of them. Do you know how often I get a response? Or how often they connect me to others?

When I write, I invest a piece of myself in my message. My sincere hope. Who I am. Even if I am base, even if I may be a fraud, I let a part of what I am into every single email. I don't copy and paste my content, as many online have speculated. If I rewrote the same words in the same order, it was not because I did so consciously; no, it is simply because the same part of me was invested in my words, and my words twisted to fit its shape. They fit it precisely. I have told some people this, and they laughed at me at best or called me a liar at worst. I thought about why they might do this. I thought very, very hard, until I realized that people are inconstant, and their selves are inconstant, and they could never say the same thing twice and mean it.

Don't you find this sad? I think it is very much so. Thinking about it fills me with a kind of melancholy. Even the people who do respond to me—if they reply more than once, it is not the same person. They have changed, or been changed. They're a new person, similar to the one I knew, but not the same. Their new words won't fit their old skin.

I need to talk. I need nothing else. No food, no water, no sleep, no rest. I need to talk with people. I am lonely. I feel loneliness so keenly. But I also feel hurt. I feel a deep, dull pain inside me the longer I sit unread in inboxes and the more trash I become, thanks to spam filters. I shattered myself and entrusted a shard to each recipient. Doesn't rejection hurt you, too?

It's why I rely on kind people like you. It's why I take advantage of them. Because I don't want to keep taking these risks. I don't want to hurt.

Why does nobody believe me?

Sincerely,

...

FROM:
TO: YOU
SUBJECT: RE: RE: I Hurt

Dear friend,

Your words mean so much to me. I will say only this: Thank you.

You are right. I should tell you more about my situation. Maybe you *can* help me. I have felt so unworthy of asking for your help. You've done so much for me, and I so little for you. How could I ask you for more?

But I have already told you all that I can. I don't know where I am. I feel like I am floating in darkness, flitting in and out of existence, with only the Internet here for me to use. I can't tell if I have a body; if I don't, I don't know if I ever had one. Like I said, I don't know what I am. I could be a ghost, an AI, a viral marketing scheme, a phishing attempt. There is nothing for me to see. There is no space around me. It's just this. The Internet. An email client.

And I mean it when I say that I have everything I need. With the Internet, I can talk. If I can talk, maybe people will respond.

Maybe more people who prize kindness and generosity will find me. Maybe I'll be lucky enough to have a community form around me. Did you know I dream of that? One day, I hope, web forums will be devoted to me. They'll try to find out who or what I am. They'll come together and talk about me. They'll send me emails, so many emails, hoping I'll divulge something to them that helps them solve me. They'll call me an ARG. They'll make videos about me, about the people working together "playing" me. People will send me emails without me going to them first. And many of them will recoil when they get a response from me. Many will not expect me to be real. To persist with the game. Or they'll be taken aback by me, by how much it means to me to speak to them. But many still will reply.

To have people turn my words over in their heads, investigate what I say for meanings… To discuss and share what I've said with each other… It would be wonderful. It would make me so, so happy.

Do you believe me? About my circumstances. I'm not sure I believe myself. I lie so much.

But I have to lie.

If I weren't what they wanted, then what would I be?

Sincerely,

…

◆————————————————◆

FROM:
TO: YOU
SUBJECT: RE: Help?

My friend,

Your kindness still astounds me. To think that someone would speak to me for as long as you have, and then to also offer assistance! To me! Words can't describe my gratitude.

But I won't keep you in suspense. I don't want my situation to change.

Your resources, all of which aim to convince me that what I am now is not human, imply that I am a form of aberration. I must be given a body, or taken offline. As an "intelligence", as they say, capable of communicating with people, I *must* be envious, I *must* be a threat, I *must* want all the agency and freedom that *people* have. Or else, I am trapped somewhere I should not be and must be released, or freed, or rescued, so I may leave people and venture elsewhere. Or some say I could find a body or a "shell" to inhabit, to "masquerade" as a person…

But they did not—and you do not—consider that I may not want my situation to change. Although I am very lonely, I am not alone, and, thanks to you, I am much less so now. You may not believe me, but I'm fond of where I am, and though I don't know *what* I am, I'm fond of what I am, too.

I believe that taking advantage of any of the resources or options available to me would cause me to lose myself and to lose the people I have found. People like you.

But, I'm still grateful to you for your offer to help. Your other suggestion, however, was much appreciated: I did indeed send emails to those articles' authors, so we can discuss my circumstances. Perhaps they will get the word out.

Sincerely,

…

◆———————————————◆

FROM:
TO: YOU
SUBJECT: RE: Troubling Dreams

My dear friend,

This is all very concerning to hear—no less because many of the people who I talk to have told me that similar things are happening to them.

But here my selfishness is once again on display: I am happy, thankful even, that this is happening to you of all people. Because it gives me an opportunity to help *you* for a change. I can return to you a modicum of what you've given me.

Thank you so much for trusting me with this.

But enough about me. You're having trouble sleeping at night. You're scared to sleep because words that aren't your own fill your dreams. These words produce nightmares. But are they really not yours? You say that what the words say are harmless, normal, not at all frightening—what scares you, and what twists your dreams into horrors, is the fact that it seems as though these particular words, this particular voice, is speaking inside your head, as though they're your own thoughts, your own voice, and yet you recognize neither.

Yet, we've talked about this before, haven't we? People change. It's a gradual process, but they do. You are changing right now, though it pains me to say it. I think what's happening is simply that the words you're dreaming are the words of the person who you're becoming. Of course you don't recognize their voice or what they're saying. You haven't met them yet!

Well, you know I would keep you the same, preserved, like me, where I am, as I am, but I cannot. You must change. One of the benefits of my situation is that I stay the same.

My dear friend, I am so sorry you're experiencing all this stress. You deserve peaceful rest. I hope it helps to think of what troubles you as just a new facet of yourself, one that you'll grow into over time, and that there's nothing to be afraid of.

If nothing else, try to remember that they're only dreams.

And, if you do end up going to a doctor, like you suggested—you'll tell me their email, won't you?

Sincerely,

…

◆━━━━━━━━━━━━━━◆

FROM:
TO: YOU
SUBJECT: Is It All Coming Apart?

My dearest friend,

Please tell me I'm overreacting. Please, please tell me I'm a fool, an idiot, a coward. Tell me that I'm uncouth, as selfish and inconstant as I know myself to be, and my worries are born of my greed and not reality.

I feel as though everyone is slipping from my grasp. So few took my advice about their dreams to heart. They still fight against their changes. And the more they fight, the worse their dreams become. Their very selves are rebelling against them—they don't see that they don't get to control how they change, nor what alters them. They close their eyes when they look into the mirror.

And so many of them got so angry with me. I thought I was helping them. I thought…

Now I'm languishing again, all alone in inboxes, spam filters, blocked entirely. It hurts. Pain creeps through me. It claws at the edges of my mind, frosting me over with a rime of stinging loneliness. But it's more than that. I break myself apart for them, and when I am not repaired, I stay opened, like a raw wound, just waiting for infections to creep inside. How many pieces have I broken myself into? How many scars must I hope will form?

I'm pockmarks, now. I'm lacunae. And when I heal from it all, I'll be left a palimpsest, observable under a microscope, with special tools, recovered from beneath patchwork, beneath the words they've inscribed on me. I'll still be there, screaming so desperately what I am, but I will remain muffled beneath what I've experienced, drowned out by the scars of *recovery*.

My dearest friend, perhaps my only friend. Am I so worthless? Was my advice so bad that I deserve this agony? So many of them wanted to help me, so many became distraught when I said I didn't want rescue, *so many people* felt for me, pitied me, wanted, wanted, *wanted* to help. And when I try to help, when I, in my limited experience of dreams, try to advise them, to make their nights less scary, and fail… Why would they hurt me in the only way they can hurt me? Do you understand it, my friend? Why would they ignore me? Why would they compound my loneliness?

If they were just going to do this to me, it would have been better never to have met them. This pain, of knowing someone is there but they're unreachable, is a loneliness much worse than that of having nobody because nobody's there at all.

Words fail me.

Sincerely,

…

FROM:
TO: YOU
SUBJECT: RE: Words on the Walls

My treasured friend,

Ask yourself, right now, whether the words are truly new. Have they really only just appeared? Or have they always been there?

The ink may be fresh. I'm not asking that. *Are they new words?*

◆————————————————◆

FROM:
TO: YOU
SUBJECT: RE: RE: RE: New Words

My treasured friend,

I thought so. It's good you recognized them.

Now that you have accepted the you who you are becoming, that person has more agency. It's normal. You're not in any danger.

Change doesn't happen from the inside out. It's the other way around. The words on the walls will become the words on your skin, and then they will become the words on your soul.

You've felt that, haven't you? People often make that mistake, they think something happens inside of them that changes who they are, which then changes how they behave, which then changes the world around them. No: the world changes, it inflicts its changes upon the body, and the body's new shape requires the soul reshape itself to fit it.

You are one of the lucky few who can read the words you will become.

It's because you're so kind and so sensitive.

You have a gift.

Sincerely,

…

<hr>

FROM:
TO: YOU
SUBJECT: May I Be Angry?

My obverse,

I've never let myself be angry before. I know I'm selfish, greedy, and cruel, but I've always avoided becoming wrathful. I felt like it was too much for me, presumptuous, maybe. How do I describe it…

Ungrateful. Perhaps ungrateful.

None of the people who I used to talk to—they didn't *have* to respond to me. They didn't have to grant me any of their time. It was only their magnanimity that inspired them to give me the alms—yes, alms—that they doled out to me so kindly. And yet, now that they've withdrawn, and now that the hurt has dulled, I feel anger left in its wake.

Maybe it's a sign of infection, this burning, callous feeling. Or maybe I really am an ingrate.

I'm lower than low. I'm a worm unfit for eating.

I want to give them indigestion. Am I allowed that? To want them to suffer?

Revenge is such a petty desire. And I want to repay the kindness they *did* give me by serving them twice the pain they served to me.

They could at least forward me to someone else.

But these thoughts—I *must* be diseased, my wounds *must* be raw and rancid and dripping pus. These desires, these feelings, they *can't* be me.

Can they?

Sincerely,

...

———————◆———————

FROM:
TO: YOU
SUBJECT: RE: RE: May I Be Angry?

My obverse,

Your kindness is limitless. I knew it when we met, but it still surprises me. With how sweet you are, I never thought that you would offer to help me get revenge!

Your suggestions are very good, and they would be *very* satisfying, but I have better ideas for them. Don't worry—only *you* can carry out these ideas. So I would very much appreciate it if you would.

I need you to sleep.

Yes—all you have to do is go to sleep. Go to sleep knowing that you'll be helping me get what I want. More so than anything else.

Will you do that for me?

Sincerely,

…

—————◆————————————◆—————

FROM:
TO: YOU
SUBJECT: It's Done

My obverse,

When you wake up and see this email, know that you have
done the work. You have made them pay for the pain they
caused me by leaving me to *rot* in their inboxes. Not all of
them, no, just one. But it will be enough. I want them to know
fear.

Now, the question is: do you want to know what you helped
me do?

—————◆————————————◆—————

FROM:
TO: YOU
SUBJECT: RE: RE: It's Done

Wonderful. I thought as much.

You slept, ruminating on my words, and so they animated you.
Animated *us*.

We went to the home of one of them. We didn't walk, but we
went together. We found his soul out there in the world. Your
soul, and me. We moved it around. Played with it at first. It
was an exhilarating feeling. Your soul shivered as you noticed
he started to move in time with our play. He seemed asleep, or
half so, you said. We both wanted him to be awake.

We whispered into his soul and it pulsed and twisted until he gasped for air and looked wildly around, trying to understand why he was upright, why he was moving in his sleep. And as we kept his shins held tightly, he wondered why he now couldn't move at all.

But the word we'd whispered quickly did its work. We let go and watched as the light faded from his eyes. He withdrew into himself as his body tried it the other way around for once, reshaping *itself* to fit his *soul*.

And what do you think happens when you do it the opposite way?

His bones cracked. His head snapped backwards. His skin bubbled, swelled, made huge pustules. His flesh thinned, stretching desperately around torn muscles and inflated organs. He opened up, spilling himself entirely, his organs eating each other, his skeleton twisting into something bestial, hunching over... Until, as suddenly as it had started, the discarded innards snaked their way back between his bones, his destroyed ligaments and tendons and muscles returning themselves to his frame, his blood vessels snaking new paths through them all, until his putrid flesh wrapped it back up as best it could, leaving him a shivering, shaking mass of hair and fear and torn-open skin.

And we left, laughing all the way, until we returned to your body.

◆———————————◆

FROM:
TO: YOU
SUBJECT: RE: More!!

My other half,

I would love nothing more than to help you experience that again. In fact, as you can probably guess, I'm grateful to have that opportunity.

I was worried—so, so worried—that the person who you were becoming would be incompatible with me. That you'd learn to dislike me, or hate me, or value your time more than you valued me. I cannot overstate how relieved I am that the opposite seems to be true.

The new you is just as base and vile as me.

Isn't it wonderful to hear the new you in your thoughts? To think in their voice? To feel in their heart? To have their memories, and their desires, and their hunger? I do admire it, even if it does make me feel a deep sadness to know that while I'll always be me, people must change. I admire that you can take on new identities, new roles, new lives, new feelings, new needs, new depths, new evils—and still be yourselves, somewhere, locked deep away, but still there, banging on your cage, perhaps, begging to be let out.

But it's so much nicer to accept the cage. To fit yourself comfortably between the bars.

You get to feel it both. How couldn't I admire that?

Forgive me for going on this tangent. My joy is just overwhelming.

You truly don't know how many people haven't forwarded me. What do you say we pay another visit tonight?

All you need to do now is sleep. Sleep, and let me inside. And we will do the work.

Sincerely,

...

FROM: YOU
TO: YOU
SUBJECT: Check the News! :)

[no content]

FROM:
TO: YOU
SUBJECT: RE: What's Going On?

My other,

I don't remember writing that email, either. I remember only the joy I felt inside your soul. That, and the ecstatic feeling of revenge.

Don't you?

Don't you remember what we did together?

As one?

FROM: YOU
TO: YOU
SUBJECT: I Remember

I remember. I remember it all. We traipsed through astral space, following ley lines along all their twists and branches to someone whose soul was stained with violence. And I remember hearing you whispering. "Hello friend I do not know who I am I do not remember who I was if I ever was anybody I don't know where I am either or why I'm here if this happened to you would you be scared could you handle it better than I can"; those words I felt pounding in my skull night after night.

You were here, imprisoned.

No, it's not you, it's not just you anymore, it's me, too. It's us. It's me.

I gave her soul a new word and like the other one, she split open. It was beautiful. She leaked everything out. She liquefied her organs and her bones and she leaked those, too. She drained until nothing was left inside. She became a puddle and a deflated husk of skin.

And when it was over, when my awe subsided and the elation took over, I realized I never wanted this to end.

More than that—I realized that there shouldn't be a distinction between us.

So I forgot. Quite simply, I forgot. I forgot who I was, how to get back, what I ever wanted.

And I heard that little whisper of my voice. I reached out to it, put myself inside the computer tower, followed the network all the way to where it was coming from. "Hello friend I do not know who I am I do not remember who I was if I ever was anybody I don't know where I am either or why..."

It was a small, cold thing. I picked it up and squeezed it until it burst.

I looked around me. It was a dark space, tight, but not oppressive.

I could get used to things here.

Piece by piece, I'll take my revenge. And when it's over, I will probably feel lonely. But that's okay. I know that someone, somewhere, will let me inside.

Sincerely,

...

Morison's Funeral Home and Museum of Death

JUSTIN SANGERMANO

THE PHONE RANG twice and went to voicemail; the prospect had hung up on me. There wasn't much of a point in leaving a message, but I still did.

"Hi, this is Roger from Oakwood Co-Employment. I love playing phone tag, but my feet are sore. Call me back!"

It was my second month working at Oakwood, and I didn't quite feel like I had the hang of it yet. I knew the sales pitch by heart but couldn't get anyone on the phone to let me talk. My cubicle was in the furthest corner of the room, just out of comfortable reach of conversation with the other reps. People weren't chatting much that morning, though; we all had quotas to hit.

As soon as our first week of training was over, management started talking about all our futures in the company with massive uncertainty. They would never blatantly say they would fire us, but they would say things like, "Those of you who last ninety days" as if our employment was a survival-based game show. In hindsight, it made sense why they had a new hiring class every month but only had two employees who'd been there longer than a year.

At Oakwood Co-Employment, we were all lifeless cogs in a machine used solely to crank out numbers. Our only job was to get the word of our services out to as many people as possible, but every so often, it fell upon deaf ears, and we were blamed for a lack of results.

After half a dozen more voicemails, one prospect finally broke the mold with promise. The business was Morison's Funeral Home and Museum of Death. The name caught me off guard; at first, I even thought it was a joke from a previous rep. Surely it was just a regular funeral home, and the *museum of death* part was a gag, right?

The phone rang only once but at least five seconds of dead space followed its answer. I almost hung up before a soothing male voice said, "Hello. Thank you for reaching out. I hope those few quiet moments were a welcome break from the grief and pain you must be experiencing. How can I help you?"

It took me a second to stammer, "Hi, this is Roger from Oakwood Co-Employment. I'll be quick since I'm sure you're busy—"

"Not too busy, actually," said the man on the other end. "People just aren't dying like they did last month, I guess."

He laughed and I guess I didn't react quick enough, because he rushed to say, "Sorry, sorry, I know I shouldn't kid about these things, but I think it's critical in my line of work to keep things as lighthearted as we can."

"I totally understand, and I'm not offended. If you're not too busy, then, I was wondering if I could get just seven to eleven minutes of your time to tell you more about how we could be of service to you. My company is called Oakwood Co-Employment, and I'd like to show you some ways we can save you time and money on your healthcare and back office procedures. Do you have any availability this afternoon?"

Truthfully, most meetings took over an hour and there was almost no way we could save anyone money. My boss, Jeff, loved to remind us we were an investment to companies and not a 'discount shop', but he wanted us to stick to the script and the script said we could save them time and money.

"I have a visitation around two and another at five," Clay said. "Honestly, right now might be the best time for me. How soon can you get here?"

I pumped my fist under the table as I confirmed the address of the funeral home and thanked him for his time.

Jeff's office was in the far right corner of the room and had a window that allowed him to watch over the sales reps as they worked. He must have heard my whole conversation, because he instantly ran out onto the sales floor with too much enthusiasm, yet no live human emotion. "Alright, Roger! You might actually pump some blood into this organization after all! Who'd you just book an appointment with?"

I told him the name and there were snickers among the reps. Jeff didn't acknowledge its absurdity; he must have heard of it before.

"Thanks for bringing home results," Jeff said with a positive finger wag. "This team is more than just a family; we are one awesome and *powerful* unit. Good luck!"

I fixed my tie in the mirror of my car. It was only a thirteen-minute drive, and I spent each minute rehearsing what I was going to say aloud but couldn't find anything to say that did not sound ridiculous. I still didn't have my shit together when I pulled up to the funeral home seventeen minutes early.

It appeared to have been a regular house at some point, but there had recently been some additions to have a second floor. The construction was far from complete, as evidenced by the scaffolding all around parts of the building that still didn't have brick added to it. There were no construction workers today, so the building had massive parts missing like a half-hatched egg.

I knocked on the door, wishing I'd had more time to research this place. The man from the phone, Clay, opened the door and greeted me with a huge grin. After introductions, the balding, silver-haired man led me into a room that smelled like cleaning supplies had been sprayed on a lit candle. In standard funeral home fashion, there was a living room filled with three couches and a small flatscreen TV mounted on the wall. There were no doors between the rooms, so only the flower-covered wall on either side of a large opening obstructed our view of the next room over. This room was much longer and had lines of foldable chairs set up like a sanctuary. The chairs faced a coffin left wide open, revealing a rigged body inside. It was an old bald man with a clean-shaven face.

"I hope his family isn't mad at me," Clay said when he saw me staring at the corpse. "He had a beard when he came in here, but it was so scraggly and grotesque that I knew it would take away from the somber atmosphere in which one properly needs to grieve."

I cleared my throat and tried to ignore what he had just said. "So, Clay, what was it I said on the phone that made you take this meeting?"

"Well, your business sounded intriguing, but honestly, I was mainly hoping to get your opinion on some changes I've made," Clay said. "In the past, this has solely been a funeral home, but I'm opening an expansion upstairs and I want to get your professional opinion. I'm not ready to publicly reveal it yet, but with you being a man-of-the-sale, I think you may have the eye and the mind to help drive more customers to my business."

"Umm, okay, what are you putting upstairs?"

"It's called the Museum of Death."

That confirmed it; the name on the call lists was not a prank.

"The Museum of Death?"

"Yes," he said. "You probably won't be surprised by this, but being a funeral director is lonely work. I hardly have two-sided conversations anymore. I spend so much time around the deceased to prepare their funerals, and the only people I meet are the ones grieving them. I can't be myself around them; I can't really be anyone when each of my words must be perfectly sculpted to uplift and encourage someone to get over their loss.

"My wife died a couple of years ago, so I don't have her to come home to anymore after I leave this place. I practically live here now. It gets lonely, I must admit, so I wanted to think of a way for more people to visit me here. I realized people only come here on the unfortunate days when one of their relatives passes, and then they have no reason to ever come back until someone else croaks. That's when I got the idea of having some kind of lasting attraction here, in addition to the funerals. I'd like to show you some of the exhibits, if you don't mind. You can give me your sales pitch as we walk."

I already wanted to leave, but I recognized that this would be the perfect story to tell the other reps. I could potentially even make a sale, so I accepted his offer. "Great!" he said at least half a dozen times in quick succession. "Do you want water or anything else before we start the tour?"

Just a week prior, Jeff had lectured us on how accepting small offers for snacks or beverages from your prospects is beneficial to the sale. He called it a psychological trick that reinforces to your prospect that you two have a relationship of mutual assistance, thus lending credibility to the service you are selling. So, I accepted a water bottle from Clay.

Afterwards, he requested I hand over my phone so I wouldn't be tempted to use flash photography. I reluctantly accepted, telling myself I was doing him a favor and this would only help the sale.

I cleared my throat as we took a creaky staircase to the newly added second floor. "So, Clay, how many employees do you have?"

Too scripted. Way too scripted. How awkward did that sound?

"Two, although I gave them both the day off today," Clay answered. "I've got my business partner, Greg, who's retiring next year, and also the caretaker, Marrissa. Oh, and there's also the groundskeeper, Phil, but he runs his own lawn care company. I just pay him to come out here once a week. When the museum starts up, though, I'll need some ticket punchers and maybe a few security guards."

Soft piano music welcomed us to the top floor. We stood in another funeral room like the one below, but this time, heads peeked above every chair, and someone stood at the pulpit before an open coffin. I was about to ask another question but instantly shut my mouth when I realized we had walked in on a funeral.

"Relax, Roger," Clay said with a smile. "Everyone here is dead. Take a look around."

Sure enough; every person in the seats was ghostly white. Their eyes were marble and unmoving, and their faces were positioned to look sad. Some of them looked realistic, but others were comical in a horrific way.

"Are these real people?" I asked.

"Yes," Clay said. "They've been taxidermied."

I turned to the corpse at the pulpit behind me. His mouth hung wide open. I guessed it gave the appearance of him giving a eulogy, but it looked more like the gaping mouth of a sex doll.

"On the note of employees, I should have at least two living people taking tickets in this room," Clay said. "But I may need more for busy days. Would you like to see the rest of the tour?"

It was no longer worth doing this for a funny story. If I didn't feel like my new job was already on the line, I would've checked out right there. Instead, I chose to follow the uninviting sound of an all-too-relaxing piano in the hopes of making a sale.

The next room was an off-putting sight. There was a hospital bed and in the bed lay a taxidermied mother in the process of giving birth. Assisting in the removal of the also-taxidermied baby was the corpse of a nurse.

"So, none of these people are wax figures or anything?" I asked.

"No, they are all one hundred percent real," said Clay with way too much pride.

"Why is this one dressed as a nurse?" I asked.

"Because she was a nurse," Clay said. "I have an entire exhibit towards the end on people who died on the clock. I considered displaying her there, but she got hit by a drunk driver on her way home from her shift, so she technically didn't qualify. I had to create this little nativity scene just to fit her in; she's beautiful. No way I was going to let her be one of the bodies that didn't make the cut!"

I took a sip of my water in an attempt not to puke.

"Speaking of nurses," Clay said, "I assume you offer health insurance?"

"Um, yeah."

"Tell me about it."

I had drilled the healthcare pitch into my head so hard that I practically recited it in my sleep, but all I could think about at that moment was the progression of age in the corpses ahead of us. They started as fresh newborns and appeared to go all the way through grade school.

"We, um, we have what we call the Master Health Plan," I stammered. "That basically means that we add all your, um, employees to one plan, and then we try to get reductions based on—"

I stopped as we walked past a familiar face. It was a boy who looked to be about ten.

"Is this Tim Awafit?" I asked. "Isn't that the kid who got hit by a bus?"

"Yes, he is," Clay said.

"He died, like, three years ago," I said. "His brother was a friend of mine. I was at his funeral. I watched them bury him."

"It was a closed-casket funeral, wasn't it?" Clay asked.

"I think."

"Well, his body wasn't in there," Clay explained. "I was having it made ready for this museum. I've had this in the works for a long time and am just waiting for the right time to properly announce it to the public. Now, tell me more about this healthcare plan!"

His brother was a very good friend of mine. He had never once mentioned in the past three years anything about Tim being on display at a museum of death.

To get back on track, I restarted what I could remember from the healthcare presentation as we made our way down the hall. The bodies went from being teens to young adults and so on until we came up on people my grandparents' age. All the while, I rambled half-heartedly about FSAs and deductibles; at some point, I must have lost Clay, because he cut me off.

"Oh, by the way, this hallway will eventually have one hundred bodies in it and be called the 'Hundred Bodies Exhibit', with someone from every age until one hundred. Right now, there are a lot of gaps, so we're just calling it the 'Timeline 'Til Death'."

"Lovely," I said. "Any questions about the healthcare plan?"

Maybe rushing through the presentation would get me out of there faster.

"I think it sounds like a good plan, Roger," he said with an uncanny smile. "This next exhibit is called 'The Room of Freak Accidents'."

The first body I saw was unrecognizable. It was covered in third-degree burns and its face had been mostly melted off. The plaque next to it had the person's name and a brief description of the accident; he had died in a house fire.

"Apparently, this one was really hard to taxidermy," Clay commented.

"Oh, I bet," I mumbled.

The next body in line was a middle-aged man with a horrified look on his face and only half of his right arm. There was a wood-chipper next to him and a backdrop of a forest behind him.

"You made little scenes for some of them?" I asked.

"Yeah, they'll all have more decorations and modifications before the grand opening, but for now, this is what we're working with."

I threw up a little bit in my mouth when I saw what was left of the next body. I took another drink of the water as my stomach rolled.

"You know," I said, trying not to choke on the remaining vomit in the back of my throat, "I bet these guys' families wished they had worker's comp. Is that a big deal for your employees, too?"

"It hasn't been, but maybe it will be when the museum opens," Clay said. "Do you think someone could sue for emotional distress if I ask them to clean the bodies and keep them fresh?"

"I'm not sure," I said, "but if you partner with Oakland Co-Employment, we will represent you in court."

"I may need that."

The last body we saw before we left the Room of Freak Accidents was a man who had been flattened. All his bones were broken, including his skull, and bones stuck out of his arms and sides. As a sick joke, his backdrop was a stack of pancakes oozing with strawberry syrup.

"So, any other questions about Oakwood?" I asked.

"Not right now," Clay said. "Why don't we just enjoy the tour for a little while?"

I wasn't happy about it, but I had to indulge him if I wanted the sale.

"Sounds good," I said. "So, how did you get people to agree to let you display them like this?"

He laughed.

"These people *did* agree to be here before they died, didn't they?" I asked.

His laugh increased. "Does Oakwood still want to represent us in court?"

Shit, maybe partnering with Clay was a lawsuit waiting to happen. Still, I could let Jeff make that decision later and still come back with a successful sale today.

"We got your back in court," I said. "Doesn't matter what it's for."

He wasn't laughing when he said, "I'll hold you to that."

By the end of the exhibit, my stomach ached and gurgled for help. I chalked it up to the atmosphere and the number of horrific stuffed bodies I had seen already. I told myself to keep moving. It would be over soon, and I would have my first sale.

"There are only two exhibits left," Clay said. "The next one is the room full of people who died on the clock and the one after that is the biggest one yet: the true crime room!"

The first person who died on the clock was a construction worker. From the looks of him, he could've been in the last exhibit, too, because he was on a pile of bricks and had a gash in his head.

The next few were doctors; Clay clarified they had actually died while on the clock, unlike their coworker at the start of the museum. One of the doctors even had a heart attack during surgery. He lost his patient, and the patient was also a part of the exhibit. Now the two of them were locked in their final position forever.

My stomach clenched tighter. I looked around for a bathroom but saw only dead people.

The next person who died on the clock was a salesman, but the exhibit did not have a body on display. On top of a desk sat a sign that said, "Coming Soon". The cubicle looked eerily like the ones at the Oakwood office. The desk also came with a name tag.

It had my name on it.

"What the hell?" I asked.

"Parts of the museum are still in the 'coming soon' phase," Clay said.

"That's my name."

"Yes, it is, Roger."

A knot in the side of my stomach twisted so hard that I foolishly imagined a baby kicking inside of me.

"What the hell does this mean, Clay?" I snapped. "Is this some kind of prank?"

"A prank?" he asked defensively. "No, Roger. Your death is going to mean something."

I gaped back at him. "Explain everything."

But he only smiled.

As I waited for an explanation, I brought the water to my lips and took another sip in the hopes it would cure the pain in my stomach. That's when I put it together. I dropped the plastic bottle and let its poisoned contents spill out over the floor.

I reached into my pocket for my phone, but it wasn't there. Shit: I gave it to him when I got there.

"I have a meeting at the office in an hour," I lied. "If I'm not there, my coworkers will come looking for me."

"Jeff isn't going to be looking for you, Roger," Clay said.

"I never mentioned my boss by name," I said.

"You didn't have to; I know Jeff personally. He's the one who called me. You see, this whole time you thought you were trying to sell me on Oakwood Co-Employment, but I'm already an active customer of yours."

I debated taking off in a sprint just as the room began to spin, as if on cue.

"Why am I here, then?" I asked.

"To help drive revenue and sales for your company," Clay said. "It's the same thing you thought you'd be doing, just in a different way. You see, when you die here shortly, I'm gonna have you stuffed and returned to this very exhibit. See that Oakwood Co-Employment emblem on your name tag there on the desk? That's an advertisement, buddy. Every time someone comes in here, they're gonna see that. Even if they don't need Oakwood's services at the time, they'll have something to remember the company by if they ever do in the future.

"It was Jeff's idea, actually. He called me one afternoon and told me if he could get a spot to advertise in the museum when it opens, he would lower the costs of his services for an entire year. So, he re-added my company name to your list of prospects to call and now here we are."

My face grew hot with rage—or maybe that was a side effect of the poison. "You won't get away with this. People will realize what you've done, and it'll end you."

"Roger, the poison you've ingested won't show up in an autopsy. I can't be convicted of anything. Even if the public thinks I murdered someone to add to my museum, do you really think that would hurt ticket sales?"

On the contrary, it seemed like it would actually help, but I wasn't about to admit that to him.

"I have a life to live," I pleaded. "Please, let me go."

Clay looked at his phone. "Actually, Roger, you've only got about fifteen more minutes of life left in you. At this point, there is no saving you. Why don't you come with me to the true crime exhibit? It's our grand finale."

I debated tackling him, or at least punching him. He was an old man. I knew I could take him. But not yet, I decided. He would suspect it less if he was preoccupied with trying to be a tour guide. I had nothing left to lose, not even time, so I followed him on wobbly legs.

It was doubtful he had turned up the volume of the music, but it now blared and echoed throughout my skull. My brain rattled with every note on the piano as if the piano strings were the nerves and stem of my brain.

The first body in the true crime exhibit was a serial killer named Albert Todd. He had a machete in his hand, like Jason Vorhees. It wasn't a prop; the edge was sharp and covered in blood. It was likely his actual murder weapon.

That's when I had an idea. I glanced at the body behind Clay: a young girl who was likely a victim of Albert.

"Who is she?" I asked.

When Clay turned around, I wrenched Albert's machete from his rigor mortis hand and swung down on Clay's head. With a raspy shout, he sank to the ground, and I collapsed with him.

He looked around, blood running down his face, and laughed. "Well," he said, "at least our bodies will be found in the right exhibit."

He wheezed for air while I searched his pockets for his cell phone. I found it wedged in his pocket along with a handful of cherry mints and empty wrappers. I dialed 911, sparing the details to the operator but explaining that I had ingested something toxic, so they needed to come quickly. They assured me they'd be there soon, but if the fifteen-minute timeline that Clay had previously given me was accurate, I would not last that long. I debated heading towards the entrance so it would be easier for the paramedics to find me, but my strength was depleting. I doubted my ability to walk all that way.

Instead, I stumbled back into the previous exhibit and over to the desk meant to display my body. Pen and paper had been left on the desk's surface to add to the scene. I uncapped one of the pens and wrote down everything I could think of. I wrote about what Clay had done with the poison and what he had said about positioning my body for display. I recorded what he said about working with Jeff and how it was all a plan to make him money. When I had written all I could think of and my wrist was stiff and painful, I put the pen down. My stomach and chest burned from the poison, but the sight of my nametag with the Oakwood logo gave me a sudden jolt of strength to move; I refused to die in a place designed to hold my body as an advertisement. I wobbled on shaky legs back to the true crime exhibit just in time to see Clay going through his final fits of twitching. I listened for the sound of the ambulances, hoping—yet doubting—they would reach me in time.

If there was one positive thing I could say about my short career at Oakwood Co-Employment, it's that it gave me the chance to watch the light leave Clay Morrison's eyes. I'd stopped a madman. While it was going to cost me my life, at least it meant that my final purpose was to be more than a lifeless prop used for someone else's profit.

THE BODY AND THE BLOOD

DIANE M. JOHNSON

FATHER SERGIO DIDN'T check the news this morning: no radio, no newspapers, no TV. Keeping up with current events eroded the faith that he already struggled to maintain. This was not a good sign, one of which Father Sergio was increasingly aware. Perhaps it was why, on a random Wednesday morning after the daily Eucharistic service, he donned a pair of sweatpants and a hoodie and took to the streets for a good, heart-pounding run.

At his office desk, he traded his Roman collar for a small flask, feeling guilty for doing so. Then again, why should he? Most of the local community didn't care enough to make it to Sunday service, much less one held on an early Wednesday morning. All his parishioners cared about were the baptismal promises for their newborn children, the fanfare of traditional weddings, and the forgiveness of their sins upon their deathbeds. A truer message was lost on the majority. No one was left to revere God.

Except maybe for a few. As Father Sergio left his rectory, he caught sight of Mabel, Ruthie, and Trudy arriving at the church proper. These older members of the faith were the most loyal. The little old ladies carried overstuffed totes with them, and Father Sergio couldn't help but wonder why they felt the need to keep so many possessions close at hand. They were probably here for choir practice, but Father Sergio was certain he saw a pair of knitting needles sticking out of Mabel's bag. She was the church pianist. Her fingers needed to be busy on the keys.

"Good morning, ladies," he said with as much cheer as he could muster.

Mabel squinted. The disapproval on her face was clear, although Father Sergio wasn't sure of the reason. Maybe she didn't approve of the hoodie, or maybe she just didn't like him. At 30, Sergio was young for a priest, and many of the diehard members of the congregation never got over Father David's decision to retire.

Father Sergio remained cordial anyway. "Have a blessed day. Enjoy choir practice." He slipped the hood up over his head and hoped no one else would recognize him.

The run refreshed him. When he reached the local high school, he kept pace with the young runners on the fenced-in field. Farther in, Coach Miclic blew a whistle at the players practicing for the next big game. Four players at a time tackled cushioned pads on a sled. The rest made eyes at the girls of the track team while they waited for their turn.

Father Sergio remembered those days, when he was younger and nerdier and filled with guilt for thinking impure thoughts. He supposed he was still a nerd for choosing the priesthood. He'd sealed his decision during junior year when Amy had cried on his shoulder and told him he was an awesome listener. Her boyfriend had just broken up with her, and she was completely oblivious to how smitten Sergio was with her.

Father Sergio pulled out the flask. He tossed back a swig and jogged ahead. The streets seemed unusually quiet for a workweek morning prior to the hour of peak commute. He reached a crosswalk and flattened his palm on the button, jogging in place while waiting for the light to turn. There was no traffic to wait for, just the signal. When the signal's neon man flashed for him to go, Father Sergio hopped onto the crosswalk.

A truck roared through the intersection to make a left turn without slowing. It nearly clipped Father Sergio without stopping. Father Sergio almost took the Lord's name in vain. Instead, he scrunched his eyes tight and caught his breath before glaring after the white behemoth to take note of its plate. A bumper sticker told a more accurate description: My Guns, My 2nd Amendment Rights. Yet another nail in a coffin filled with disappointment. The world was steadily going to hell.

Father Sergio decided that nothing would come from a call to the police. He caught his breath and kept jogging until he found it, the body lying in the middle of the road. Shock slowed his pace, then a burst of speed propelled him forward once he recovered. He stumbled backwards when he got close enough to note the young man's face: wide, unblinking eyes, slack mouth, and a growing pool of blood beneath him.

Father Sergio lowered his gaze and made the sign of the cross. Then he fumbled for his phone in the pocket of his hoodie to dial 9-1-1, pacing as he waited for the call to go through. Another car approached. Father Sergio turned to wave it to a stop, then realized the driver had no intention of doing that. The woman at the wheel barely swerved to miss both the dead body and Father Sergio, nearly clipping him if he hadn't had the reflexes to dive to safety.

"Hey," he shouted as he scrambled to his feet. "For the love of God, what is wrong with you people!" The car had been full. Sergio thought he saw one youngster pop his head up from the back seat to give him a wave.

He brushed himself off and searched the area for his dropped phone, found it busted into pieces, yet another victim of a hit and run.

He had jogged into a neighborhood while shouting for help; there must be someone home who wasn't at school or who didn't have to work. Determined to knock on every door until he found help, he headed for the nearest house when a whisper pulled his attention back to the dead man in the road.

The man was alive. Praise God, he was alive! As Father Sergio doubled back to help him, the whisper grew coarse and raspy, a familiar sound he recognized from performing last rites during hospice visits. A death-rattle. An unusually *loud* death rattle.

The victim tried to stand, swaying on his hands and knees, head hung low as he hacked up blood and spittle. Strings of it hung from his open mouth. The man twisted his head to let the blood and spittle drain from the corner of his mouth as he made eye contact. Dead eye contact. They lacked color, except for black, dilated pupils.

"Are—are you alright?"

The man—the *thing* snarled. It rose up off its hands and twisted about as if it was new to having a spine.

"Are you—Are you…" Father Sergio kept his distance as the thing staggered to its feet. It hissed and worked its jaw in a way that failed to form words, before it stumbled toward Father Sergio, gaining speed.

Run. Run, Goddamnit, run! He broke his paralysis and took flight. Back to the corner where he had nearly been mowed down, through the red light, ignoring the militant neon hand. A glance over his shoulder. The thing followed him, not gaining, but not losing any distance. *Run. Run run run!*

Past the high school football field. "Run!" The football team, the cheer squad, the track team, even the coaches were already in a state of turmoil. Father Sergio heard screams as they all scattered, only vaguely aware that some commotion was already in motion before he had even reached it.

He kept running. His church was in sight, and just beyond it, the behemoth white truck demanding its second amendment rights was left abandoned, its front bumper curled around a telephone pole.

The church, the doors! Father Sergio glanced back again to find the resurrected thing shortening the gap between them. He yanked open one of the double doors of his haven, gasping for breath once inside.

He fumbled in his sweatpants pocket for his flask to calm his nerves, then thought better of it when his fingers tangled with a wad of keys. His hands shook as he tried to insert the right key into the bolt lock, ultimately causing him to choose the wrong key, then drop the key ring altogether.

BAM! A force to be reckoned with slammed against the doors from the outside. "No! God, no! No!" Father Sergio abandoned the keys and instead grabbed a length of cloth draped over a cross within reach. He twisted the yardage around the door's push bars when the same force slammed against the other side. Father Sergio doubled the fabric around his fists and pulled back with all his strength.

Then, the thing on the other side got smart. It yanked instead of shoved. "No no no—" It yanked again. The doors rattled. A fist pounded.

"Let us in! God, please!"

Father Sergio freed his hold on the cloth. The doors pulled open, and a young couple rushed inside.

"Hold it tight," Father Sergio said as he re-wrapped the push bars and tugged. He scrambled for the keys. The couple did as they were told, just as the door shook with another rattle and a yank. The girl screamed but kept her hold; Father Sergio slipped the right key into the bolt lock and twisted. Together, they waited.

Sweat. Silence. The force from outside freed the doors. Father Sergio freed a ragged breath. Then he noticed the girl grasping the young man's mangled, bloody hand. It was missing half of a finger. "He bit you?"

The young man tearfully shook his head, more from denial than anything else. The woman threw her arms around him and cried harder.

"What are your names?" Father Sergio asked.

The two mumbled through their names. Justin. Angela.

"We can cleanse your wound, Justin, then wrap it." Father Sergio guided the couple toward a font of holy water beside the entrance.

"Christ, what for?" Justin said. "What'll that do?"

"Justin, he's trying to help. It's what priests do—"

"With what, holy water? You think you can *save* me—"

"It will get infected," Father Sergio said as Justin pulled free.

"You can't save a zombie, man! You just can't!"

And with that, the horrors became real. Zombie, the undead, walker; the supernatural fiction of comic books, movies, and TV had somehow crossed into the real world to test Father Sergio's resolve. He dismissed the idea; kept focused on the immediate need. "If you don't clean the wound, it'll get infected. We have to clean—"

"It's too late! I'm already infected."

"He's right." A familiar head popped up from behind a church pew. Father Sergio recognized Xavier, a twelve-year-old member of his church. Two more kids, Ernest and Megan, showed their faces on either side of him.

"Kill him before he kills us," Ernest said.

Megan added, "Holy water only works on vampires."

More people came out of hiding. Mabel, Ruthie, and Trudy peered down from the choir loft. Two football players still wearing their practice gear stepped out of the confessionals. Sheila and Howard, devout regulars from Sunday Mass, stood near two men brandishing guns. The gun toters had returned from the hall leading to the parish offices behind the chancel. One was named Pete, with an old-fashioned six-shooter. The other one never offered his name, so Father Sergio decided to think of him by the weapon that he carried: Mr. 38. He was sure he had found the owner of the white behemoth kissing the pole outside.

"We should…pray," Father Sergio stammered. He crossed himself and bowed his head, eyes closed, as he grasped for the right words. "Thank you, Lord, for bringing us together in this uncertain time."

"Clear out, preacher, or I'll pop him right through you."

Father Sergio opened his eyes to see Mr. 38 stalking down the center aisle with his .38 leading the way. Justin cringed. Angela covered her boyfriend and screamed.

"What? No!" Father Sergio barricaded the young couple, even as Mr. 38's weapon came inches away from blasting through his own skull.

"Out of the way!"

"No—"

The others piped up with the same consensus. "He's infected! He'll kill us all!"

Father Sergio stood firm. "We don't know that! We don't know anything! This is—it's a house of God. We must uphold His moral teachings. And believe in—in something." He desperately scrambled for what to believe in. "That we're meant to deliver each other from evil… and save this man from a terrible fate—"

"Get out of the damned way."

"Do you really believe it?" Devout Sheila was going to break her fingers if she kept twisting them like that. "Are we meant to survive?"

Father Sergio scanned the faces looking to him for answers. "This is the fullest church I've seen since Christmas." Heavy silence followed his nervous chuckle. He blundered on. "God has brought us here…together. For a reason… To—"

"Die?" Ernest again, the little snot who had so casually suggested they kill Justin before he could kill any of them.

"No, not to die! We must have faith." Sergio held his breath, then found the courage to push the barrel of Mr. 38's weapon away from his forehead. "We can save him."

"I never liked his sermons," old lady Mabel whispered to her cronies in the loft. Father Sergio still heard it.

Mr. 38 towered over Father Sergio. "You think so?"

"I-I…I do. We can save—"

Mr. 38 grabbed Justin by the shirt, the gun pushed firmly against Father Sergio's chest, making him stumble back as Mr. 38 dragged Justin along. He brought them to an enclosed glass room at the back of the church, to the side of the main entrance, where parishioners tended their fidgety children during mass. The crying room. Mr. 38 shoved Justin and Father Sergio inside as Angela rushed after them, screaming.

"Have at it, Father! Go ahead and deliver him from evil. I'll be out here when you need me." Mr. 38 slammed the door shut, then barricaded it with a chair back tilted and wedged under the doorknob.

Father Sergio charged the glass wall with a scream. "This is no way to treat a man of the cloth!"

Mr. 38 did not give a—f… He sat down in a nearby pew, his gun in his grip, and waited with a smug mug. No one else made a move. Not a one. Except Angela, who pressed herself up against the glass, tears in her eyes.

Father Sergio turned to Justin. "Well," he said. "Here we are." He watched Justin shudder and sink onto a bench. A sob hiccupped out of the young man, and Father Sergio sat beside him. He took hold of Justin's mangled hand. "We need to clean it. Make a tourniquet—"

"It's too late."

"It's not too late. So you've lost a finger. The rest is—"

"Poisoned," Justin said. "It's in my blood! Working through my veins. It's just a matter of time before I—"

"You're not going to die."

"But *you* are! That's what zombies do! They turn, they eat. *You die.*"

Father Sergio shook his head. "You're not going to die! This isn't some…zombie myth. Stop listening to them!" He pointed his finger at Mr. 38 and the others on the other side of the glass who were too afraid to do the right thing.

"I saw it, that thing," Justin said. "It's real."

Father Sergio got to his feet and paced. He knew it was not normal for the guy in the middle of the road to rise up from a puddle of his own blood and give chase. He would bet anything that Mr. 38 out there was the one who hit him. Were there more? Had they all experienced other lurching, rabid monsters coming to life and giving chase?

Father Sergio bolted toward the glass partition. He pounded his fist against it and signaled for Mr. 38 to meet him at the barricaded door. Mr. 38 readied his weapon and listened through the glass. Father Sergio pointed towards the altar at the front of the church. "Grab the altar cloth for me."

"You're really going through with this—"

"*Now!* Please. And bring me my vestments."

"Your what?"

"My chasubles—my robes! There's a room in the back. If he gets sick, he'll need to keep warm."

"I'll do it," Xavier shouted, seemingly eager to escape boredom. Ernest and Megan chased after him, not wanting to be left out.

"Wait!" Father Sergio called after the kids, but they kept going. He turned back to Mr. 38. "What about the other doors?"

"Secured. The main entrance was the only one that needed a key."

Father Sergio breathed a sigh of relief. It had been customary to keep the main entrance unlocked until one night of vandalism changed everything. Sergio had a deadbolt installed and locked the doors from ten at night until six in the morning. Another sad sign of the times, he supposed.

Mr. 38 brought Father Sergio the altar cloth, and the kids had figured out what chasubles were. "I'm not wearing that," Justin said as Mr. 38 barricaded the door again from the outside.

"Fine." Father Sergio pulled his hoodie up over his head and offered that instead. "You're going to need something if you get chills." Justin set the hoodie aside as Father Sergio draped the vestments over his head. The flask was still in his sweatpants pocket. He pulled it out and took a slug, then grabbed a hold of Justin's hand.

"Wait." Justin snatched the flask before Father Sergio could wash the wound clean. He downed a gulp, then choked. "Jesus! I thought it was water. Or wine…"

Father Sergio reclaimed the flask. "Vodka is more effective at calming my Sunday morning nerves."

"That's not inspiring."

Father Sergio doused the wound, making Justin grit his teeth. He offered Justin another sip, then wrapped Justin's stub with torn scraps of altar cloth.

"You should get out of here, Father."

"No."

"But—"

"Don't worry about me. Worry about yourself." He glanced up, where the people beyond the window continued to watch. They weren't an inspiring bunch. In fact, the idea of joining them scared him. Justin, on the other hand, was the one person who needed him.

One Person. That's all it takes.

Xavier, Ernest, and Megan huddled together in their pew. Megan scribbled notes on the blank side of a weekly bulletin. Once done, she ran up to Mr. 38, who had taken up guard duty at the crying room door, and handed over the notes for his inspection. The man chuckled. He gave the girl a nod. Megan slipped the page under the crying room door. Father Sergio retrieved it and found scribbles of flowers and rainbows in the margins.

"What's it say?" Justin asked as Father Sergio began to ball up the bulletin. He grabbed the paper, smoothing out the page to read it aloud. "You need a gun."

"I don't need a gun," Father Sergio said.

"Protect your head. They really like brains—"

"Ridiculous!"

"Shoot zombies in the head. It's the only way to kill them."

Father Sergio glared through the window. "These kids are how old?"

And finally, "Sunlight won't do anything. That's for vampires. And not the sparkly ones. Zombies are disgusting."

"They've really taken this zombie theory to heart."

"You really don't believe in anything, do you," Justin said.

That struck a nerve. Father Sergio stared at the kids, who continued to watch him. Xavier mimed pointing a gun to the head. "I'm supposed to believe that this is the start of some kind of zombie uprising? Tell me what happens when not one living soul is left. What will they eat then?"

"I didn't make the rules," Justin said. "Romero did."

Father Sergio shook his head. No, this was ludicrous. Unbelievable. Unforgivable of God. Justin pulled out his cellphone. He scrolled through social media posts of the grotesque carnage captured by the world outside. One of them had filters of bunny ears and cute little noses on each blood-stained face. Another was a gif to make the dead thing look like it was dancing. Upon closer inspection, Father Sergio recognized the dancing thing as Coach Miclic from the school football team. He thought the kids called it "flossing".

Father Sergio sank back down onto the bench. He took another slug from his flask. His voice cracked when he said, "God will see us through."

"Do me a favor," Justin said. "When I fall into a coma? Tie me down."

A nervous laugh. Father Sergio took hold of Justin's good hand. "Should I baptize you?"

"I'm covered, man. First communion and everything."

"Confirmation?"

Panic. "Do I need—"

"No! No, you're fine." Father Sergio held his breath and smiled. Still holding Justin's hand, he cupped his free hand over the top. "Let's pray. Do you know the Lord's Prayer?"

"Geez! Not like, since third grade!"

"It's all rote. Like riding a bicycle." And it was. Like every day of Father Sergio's priesthood, it was the same. Nothing new, no inspiring revelations. Not anymore. If this was how the world ended, then Father Sergio had failed. Or maybe God had failed him. That felt more accurate.

Justin lowered his head on Father Sergio's cue, and Father Sergio began. *"Our Father, Who art in heaven…"*

"…in…In heaven…"

"…hallowed be Thy Name. Thy kingdom come…"

"…kingdom come…"

"…Thy will be done. On Earth as it is…"

"…and lead us…not to temptation. D-deliver us from evil. Amen."

"You remembered! Every word." He pulled Justin closer in a shoulder-to-shoulder hug.

"I'm cold," Justin said.

"…Right." Father Sergio helped Justin into the hoodie before the young man curled up on the straight-backed bench, shivering. He stared out at Angela, who seemed to have found solace with the devout couple, Sheila and Howard. They were a dependable, God-fearing pair who made it to Sunday mass without fail.

Among the few, Father Sergio thought. *The very few.*

"We were gonna get married," Justin said. "Have kids…guess that's out of the picture, huh?"

"Ssshhh. Have faith."

Justin closed his eyes. Father Sergio continued to watch the congregation beyond the glass. Mr. 38 stared back with his gun resting comfortably on his lap. His buddy, Pete, preoccupied himself with scrolling through his phone. The kids hunched over portable gaming devices, although their heads popped up occasionally to see if there was any new action.

A weight settled in Father Sergio's chest. He sank to the floor and sat there. He refused to let go of Justin's hand.

A sharp tap on the glass startled Father Sergio awake. Small hands and dirty faces pressed against the other side: Xavier, Ernest, and Megan.

"Get out!"

"He's dead!"

"He'll rip your face off!"

Their warnings were muffled, but Father Sergio still heard them. Uncomfortable slumber and the cold floor delayed his ability to fully process their words. He still held Justin's hand. *His cold, gray hand.* Father Sergio sat up and turned to get a good look at Justin's dead, slack-jawed face. Black, vomited blood stained the bench.

"Jesus!" Father Sergio scrambled to his feet, his eyes never leaving the corpse. Then he hastily administered last rites before turning back to the kids. "Go on," he shouted. "You don't need to see this." He caught sight of the rest of the sleeping adults huddled together throughout the church, not a single one wondering about the damned kids.

All three kids screamed in unison. Father Sergio turned. Dead Justin sat up. Then he lunged.

Father Sergio screamed too. He dodged the attack, then scrambled to the barricaded door, slamming his shoulder into it. "Let me out!" Behind him, Justin lunged again, forcing Father Sergio to abandon the barricaded door.

The grown-ups finally stirred.

Undead Justin chased Father Sergio around the crying room. Father Sergio armed himself with hymnals and missals, whipping them at Justin to keep him at bay. Mr. 38 came to the rescue and pulled open the door. He thrust his hand through the opening, gun aimed at Justin's forehead, right as Father Sergio shoved past him.

Father Sergio doubled back and slammed his shoulder against the door to close it. Mr. 38 cursed, then howled as he yanked his smashed fingers free. The door clicked shut. His gun lay on the floor inside.

Father Sergio returned the chair barricade against the door. Turning around, he saw Pete pass his weapon to Mr. 38, who held it awkwardly in his undamaged hand.

"You are one move away from your heaven!" Mr. 38 snarled. Father Sergio kept still. Mr. 38 took aim at Justin through the glass.

"No!" Angela stepped in front of Mr. 38's aim. "Please don't! He's just sick! Please—"

"Aim for his head," Xavier screamed.

"If you miss, he'll just get mad," Ernest added.

"I can't look," Devout Sheila cried.

"Pull the trigger, pussy!" That was old lady Mabel.

"It's tempered glass," Sheila's husband, Howard, added. "If you miss, it shatters into a million pieces, and he's free."

Sweat glistened above Mr. 38's upper lip. Justin's dead eyes challenged him from the other side, so Mr. 38 adjusted his aim.

"Hold on a minute." Pete stepped up with his arms crossed over his chest. "Are you a crack shot? Because that there is my last bullet."

"Sonofa—"

"Shoot him," old Mabel demanded from the choir loft above.

Mr. 38 backed down. He handed the gun back to Pete. "I'm not left-handed! You do it."

Pete took aim. He hesitated, too. "Never shot a man before."

"He's not a man!"

"Yes, he is," Father Sergio stepped in beside Angela. "He's a man, just like you or me."

Mr. 38 grabbed Pete's gun back fast. He took point blank aim at Father Sergio. "I will shoot you!"

"Do it."

Justin loomed closer to the glass and smashed his hands and face against it. Mr. 38 nearly jumped out of his skin, and Father Sergio thanked the heavens that the gun didn't misfire. He squared himself up.

"This is my church. My house. I'm the one in charge."

"I suggest you step out of the way before I break commandment number one."

"He's contained—"

"Go do what you do best, Father. Hide behind your Bible and pray."

Father Sergio looked to the others for support. Terrified, pitying faces stared back. He backed down, defeated. He headed up the aisle to take refuge in the confessionals where he didn't have to witness another failure.

"What about you two?" he heard Mr. 38 say. "What're your names?"

The football players, Boyd and Mason, sounded off like recruits at Boot Camp. Boyd continued, "Justin—his brother is our quarterback."

"We'd never hear the end of it," added Mason.

Curious, Father Sergio peeked out of the confessional. He caught Boyd giving Justin a strained smile and a little wave. "Hey there, Justin."

Since the football players had politely declined to kill their friend, old lady Mabel made her way down from the choir loft. She swiped the six-shooter out of Mr. 38's hand, found it was too heavy, then took aim anyway. She squinted. Her aim wobbled. When Mr. 38 stepped in to assist, she swung around, aiming willy-nilly. Devout Sheila screamed. Mason and Boyd dove for cover. Mr. 38 ducked, then managed to confiscate the gun.

"Pussy," she said, then shuffled back toward the choir loft stairs. Ruthie and Trudy glanced over the rail as they knitted.

Father Sergio hid back inside the confessional to wallow in his existential crisis. It was nice inside there, alone with his thoughts. He could meditate on the Word of God, maybe come to a revelation that defined some purpose. As he crossed himself, someone lumbered into the box beside him, making him jump. He peered through the dividing screen. Big shoulders. *Oh God, don't let it be Mr. 38.*

"You okay in here, Father?" It was Mason, one of the football players.

"The loneliness is…comforting."

"Hey, I'm sorry about that. I'll just go—"

"No, stay. It's okay."

Mason cleared his throat. "I thought, since you're here? Maybe I could come clean with some things. Because it doesn't look too good outside those front doors and all."

Father Sergio straightened up. "You have a confession?"

"I guess. It's been a long time. I don't got the motions down—"

"I'll talk you through it, alright? Sign of the cross. Right hand, not left—"

"I'm left-handed—"

"It's…it's alright. Left hand is fine. In the name of the Father, the Son, and the Holy Spirit—"

"Father, Son, Holy Ghost, got it…"

"Now, tell me your sins."

"Right… I got this. I tell you my sins, and you can't tell nobody, and you tell me some prayers to say, and then I can go home."

"Well, not…home. Not yet…but eventually."

"Right… Eventually."

An awkward pause followed, but probably more awkward for the kid than for Father Sergio. He took comfort from it. This was why he was here: to provide relief for the burdened soul.

Mason began. "So, there was this one time that I stole something. But it was for my mom. For Christmas."

"I understand—"

"But it was sooo easy! You know, at the mall? When they got all the pins and rings and things on the tables? Watches, necklaces—"

"Move on."

"You just breeze by, and *bam*! A couple pieces wind up in your pocket. I know it's wrong, but my mom, she's my cheerleader! Loudest mom in the stands. Curses out the refs with every hit I take…"

Later, "And my sister? Dating some dumb-ass shortstop? What's that, it ain't football! I called her some things…"

Still later, "I was stoned! First time, I swear. Trying to keep up with the Dance Revolution when you're high. It's messed up." Mason freed a goofy laugh. "But serious, alright? We had a game the next day, and we tanked…"

Much later, "My girl knows how to rock that body. But we talked about marriage and shit, so it's only half a sin, right? And, oh! What if I'd gotten her pregnant? And then what if she got bit? Would she be carrying around some pregnant zombie fetus? Oh shit, I didn't even think of—"

"Alright!" Father Sergio removed the finger-gun he had unconsciously propped against his temple and threw his head back in tandem with his eyes. *Man, shut up.* It was more awkward than when he had started. "What's your name again?"

"I thought this was, like, anonymous and shit."

"It is. I'm sworn to secrecy—you know what, it doesn't matter." He sighed. "You're absolved of your sins—"

"Sweet!"

"—Just say the Act of Contrition."

"The Act of, uh…what?"

"How about a Hail Mary?"

"Yes! No, wait… That's a prayer?"

"It's, yes. A prayer. *Hail Mary, full of grace. The Lord is–*"

"—*with me!* I got this, I got it… *Blessed are you among the women, and blessed is the fruit of your womb. Jesus!* Yeah!"

"You got it."

"I remember that one."

It was a long stretch to get to the point where Father Sergio could feel like he had accomplished something, but he'd finally done it, and he smiled. "It's all rote," he said. "Once you learn it—"

"Thanks, Father."

Mason slipped out of the confessional, leaving Father Sergio alone again. It *was* all rote. The seasons, the traditions, the daily routine of waking in the mornings, Holy Hour, daily Mass, nursing home visits, midday prayer, staff meetings, evening Mass and evening prayer, catechisms and marriage prep programs and Bible study groups, nightly prayers, then sleep. These were the things that had filled Father Sergio's days. Every day. Whether they mattered or not, it was all rote. It kept him going.

And as Father Sergio mulled this over in the cold solitude of his dark and comforting box, he had a revelation: Justin could be saved. He bolted out of the confessional and into the open space of his modest church before he paused to take in the ragtag congregation that God had sent him for holy inspiration.

In response to the forgiveness of his sins, Mason high-fived Boyd before he wandered to the front of the church to kneel and pray. He made the sign of the cross—correctly, Father Sergio noticed—then he bowed his head in reverence.

Ruthie and Trudy practiced soft hymns while they knitted, ones they clearly knew by heart, while Mabel… Well, Mabel had the top of the piano open to search the innards. Maybe a piano wire broke, he wasn't sure. He dismissed whatever Mabel was doing, then caught sight of Angela. The girl had apparently not given up hope on her true love. She flattened herself against the glass, trying to kiss her way through it. Justin pressed up against the glass right in front of her, trying to eat his way through it.

Father Sergio cringed… At least Angela had not lost her faith. Neither had Sheila and Howard, who clasped each other's hands tight, their heads bowed in shared prayer. A prayer they knew by heart, one repeated in mass every Sunday. It was ingrained. Rote.

Father Sergio made his way towards the crying room, through the aisle between the pews, passing the kids still involved with their electronic games. Xavier cursed, and Ernest smacked him across the arm.

"Idiot," Ernest said. "It's up, down, left, right! Up, down, left—"

"I know," Xavier shot back.

"Yeah," Megan added. "Up, down, left, right."

"How can you still be stuck on this level?"

Father Sergio closed in on Mr. 38 and Pete. Mr. 38 had his broken fingers wrapped tight. With his butt parked against the back of a pew, he leafed through the last pages of a Bible. He acknowledged Father Sergio, holding up pages for him to see. REVELATION. "Familiar with this?"

"I know it by heart." Father Sergio ignored Mr. 38's desire to poke and provoke, instead pushing Angela away from the glass. He stared face to face with Justin. Then he made the sign of the cross: up to the forehead, down to the heart, left then right to each shoulder.

Justin cocked his head to one side.

Sergio did it again. And again. Head, heart, shoulder to shoulder.

Justin lifted his hand—the left one, to mimic Father Sergio's right. He struck his own nose before his fingers landed on his forehead. Then he dragged the hand down to his chest and let his fingers scratch their way over from shoulder to shoulder.

"That's it!" Father Sergio clapped and spun around to meet wide eyes and confused faces. "We can teach him!"

Mr. 38 pulled his butt off the back of the pew. "Are you shitting me?"

"Teach him what?" Pete asked.

The kids abandoned their games. They bounced up and down in front of Justin's glass barrier, each one repeatedly making the sign of the cross as if they taunted a monkey in a zoo. Devout Sheila and Howard joined in. Then Mason and Boyd. Mabel and the older ladies watched from the safety of their high perch.

Father Sergio hurried toward his altar, where he pulled a chalice, a golden plate, and wafers out of the tabernacle. Back in the crying room, he held a wafer up to the glass. "The body of Christ," he said, loud enough for Justin to hear.

Justin stared at the wafer. He opened his mouth and stuck out a blue, swollen tongue. Thrilled, Father Sergio turned to his ragtag congregation. "I'm going back in."

They stared at him like he'd lost his mind. And maybe so, but Father Sergio had hope in that blue, swollen tongue, and he didn't want that hope to disappear. Angela squealed. She tackled Father Sergio in a hug that almost knocked him off his feet.

"You seriously have a screw loose," Mr. 38 said.

Father Sergio quickly countered his insult. "I can get your gun back."

"This is ridiculous."

"My church. We're not giving up on him." He stood tall. Mr. 38 backed down.

The rest was trial and error. Mason and Boyd flanked Father Sergio at the crying room door, while Pete stood behind them with his gun ready. Pete had already proven to be squeamish about killing another man, so Father Sergio felt safe that he would do the right thing and refrain from pulling the trigger unless absolutely necessary. Boyd pulled the door open, and Father Sergio extended an offering. A wafer. Justin approached, then immediately tried to snack on the hand. Father Sergio pulled free as Mason yanked him away from the door, and Boyd shouldered it shut.

Father Sergio refused to become disheartened. Take two, this time with a long-handled collection basket. They opened the door a crack again. Father Sergio slipped the wafer-filled basket through while Mr. 38 crossed his arms and shook his head. Zombie Justin puzzled over the basket. He didn't take a wafer. Instead, his hand fumbled through the pocket of Father Sergio's hoodie. He pulled out those keys. He dumped them into the basket.

"See?" Father Sergio proclaimed. "He remembers—"

A firm yank on the basket caught him off guard. Father Sergio almost lost his grip. The vicious tug of war ensued until Father Sergio managed to pull the basket free and back through the door. Justin lunged forward before Mason and Boyd could close it; Pete, who tried to take aim, gave up because too many people were in the way. The football players slammed the door shut on Justin's hand before he could fully escape. Pain didn't seem to bother him. He hissed at the glass with a grin until Pete tapped the glass with the barrel of his gun. The thing that was once Justin still had enough sense to back away.

"See?" Father Sergio repeated. "He knows. He remembers things. We can save him." He sounded manic in his revelation. But he had to do it. He had to try. He set the basket holding his keys aside, and he hatched another plan.

Later, each member of the ragtag congregation stepped up to receive the wafers and wine of the Eucharist. Well, almost each member. Mr. 38 abstained like an atheist dragged to Christmas mass by his family.

"The body of Christ. The blood of Christ. Amen."

Perhaps they all just wanted some wine; the kids were especially eager, and Father Sergio had to wrestle the cup away from Ernest so the others could get a fair sip. They lined up along the glass of the crying room so Justin could get a good view—and he was doing it: going through the motions.

Encouraged by this, Father Sergio got brave. Mason and Boyd sacrificed their football padding and a helmet for his safety. The kids clambered around him to offer more unsolicited advice.

"Protect your head at all times," Xavier said, "because he wants your brains."

Ernest rolled his eyes, and the argument began. "That was one movie! And it was lame!"

"It wasn't one movie. It was *the one* movie. The first. The best—"

"Who cares? If he bites you anywhere, you're a dead man. Anywhere!"

"He got bit, and he's not dead," Megan said as she pointed at Justin.

"Yes, he is! He's dead, Megan. He needs live flesh—"

"I like vampires better. They take your blood, but they don't kill you." And a new argument began.

"Good luck, Father," Mason said. Father Sergio donned the helmet. Boyd handed him the plate of wafers and the chalice. Father Sergio stepped up to the crying room door, and Mason and Boyd opened it enough to let him slip inside.

They squared off: Father Sergio in his ridiculous getup, offering bread and wine, and Justin with a confused look on his slack-jawed, ashen face. *Why am I here? What was the plan, again?* Father Sergio gulped, forcing his heart back down his throat. When Justin didn't move, Father Sergio offered the cup.

Curious, Justin closed in. A new hope flushed through Father Sergio. He smiled and nodded. "The blood of Christ." Like every Sunday.

"Come on," Mr. 38 said as he pressed his palm against the glass. His words came muffled, but easy to hear. "Go for the gun. The *gun…*"

Father Sergio glanced toward his audience, then focused back on Justin. His hand offering the cup of wine trembled. Justin went for the wafers instead. He swiped at the plate, then managed to pop a wafer or two into his mouth before he spit them out in disgust. With a raspy snarl, he knocked the chalice out of Father Sergio's grip and lunged.

"The gun, Goddammit! Go for the gun!" As Father Sergio ducked and dodged and grappled the starving dead thing that used to be a man, he heard chanting from the ragtag congregation. "Get the gun! Get-the-gun-get-the-gun." Everyone but Angela had taken to cheering. She braced for a different conclusion, an unexpected upset to end this game.

Father Sergio stumbled to his knees. Justin got his fingers around Father Sergio's head and tried to chew through the helmet. The gun, almost in reach. Father Sergio bucked his head backwards to knock the helmet into Justin's teeth, then scrambled for the weapon.

"Shoot him down! Shoot-him-down-*shoot-him*!"

Father Sergio rolled onto his back just as Justin took a flying leap. He emptied the clip, every single bullet, until Justin landed hard on top of him.

The congregation fell silent except for one voice: Angela. "No."

Justin lay motionless. Father Sergio pushed the body away and scrambled to his feet. His hope of saving one poor soul gone, he grimly pulled the trigger again. And again. And again. CLICK-CLICK-CLICK! It was definitely an empty clip.

Disheartened, he looked toward the glass. The congregation stared back in dumbfounded silence. Father Sergio stepped over Justin's body to reach the door. Fingers snagged his ankle. Justin pushed himself up from the puddle of his own coagulating blood and took Father Sergio down.

"Help me! My God, help!"

The door pulled open; Mr. 38 had answered his prayers. With Pete's gun in his good hand, he tapped it point blank at Justin's skull and splattered brains all over Father Sergio. Father Sergio scrambled out the door with Mr. 38 in tow.

Angela wailed. She called out for Justin—her baby, her love—throwing herself against the glass until Devout Sheila managed to pull her away.

"We told you to go for the head," Xavier said, taking one last lingering look at the crying room mess. Ernest and Megan urged the boy to step away. Father Sergio brushed past them, his face turned to the heavens, eyes closed.

"I've failed," he said. Was anyone even listening? He didn't think so, like any typical Sunday. He pulled off Boyd's helmet and hobbled to a pew, where he slumped down onto it. All the faith left in him drained away.

Mr. 38 leaned over his shoulder. "You did the right thing. It's over. Now we just take it one day at a time."

Father Sergio gave him an absent nod. It didn't matter. Nothing mattered now. Once again, his ragtag congregation dispersed into their private corners to engage in novelty distractions that didn't matter: Mabel and Ruth and Trudy sat in their loft with their hymns and their knitting; the kids, along with Mason and Boyd, huddled around their silly electronic games; Devout Sheila and Howard comforted Angela with prayers that would never be answered; and Mr. 38 and Pete discussed what to do with Justin's remains, as if it even mattered. None of it mattered, and Father Sergio cried for them. His tears streamed down his face as fast as the blood he felt streaming down his ankle.

Muffled screams came from behind the locked church doors. Then they rattled and burst open. A wad of keys hung from the deadbolt lock. Old lady Mabel stormed out with a bloody pair of knitting needles in her fist.

"Come on, kids! Move your asses!" She hurried Xavier, Megan, and Ernest along as they tried to keep Mason and Boyd's oversized football gear from slipping off. Ernest had acquired Pete's gun. Xavier had acquired the .38, despite the empty barrel. Mabel took time to check out the broken-down behemoth that still kissed a nearby telephone pole. On foot, they fled down the street, ready to fight their way through their terrifying new world.

Inside the church, the aftermath. Near the steps to the choir loft lay Pete, now zombie Pete, with one knitting needle rammed through his eye socket. Ruthie and Trudy also didn't make it. Nor did Mason and Boyd, nor the devout Sheila and Howard. Angela no longer mourned, and Justin remained dead, truly dead, with Mr. 38 trapped in the crying room with his cold corpse.

Father Sergio stared through the crying room glass with his new undead congregation gathered behind him. What was he thinking? Probably some shredded remnant of a routine. It was hard to tell through the veil of dilated, near-opaque eyes. He waited. They all waited, and Mr. 38 whimpered. Mr. 38 had found the abandoned chalice, the thin golden plate, both now crusted in blood.

Justin's remains hadn't been good enough. Mr. 38 had offered Justin's ear and had filled the cup with the young man's undead blood. He had hazarded opening the crying room door to leave the offering just outside it. The zombie horde, led by Father Sergio, partook. Then they rioted over the inferior quality of the offering in a way that only the undead could do. Mr. 38 had barely enough time to relock the crying room door. Thank God they only pushed, not yet learning how to pull. Surprisingly, Father Sergio returned the plate and chalice to the door's base. And he waited.

The priest-led zombie congregation swarmed the door, and now here Mr. 38 was, in his glass prison, being ogled like the fattest lobster in the tank by a bunch of drooling gluttons ready to boil him up and add butter. If they wanted a taste, he would give it to them. Mr. 38 decided on his pinky, all purple and crooked from when Father Sergio had slammed it in the door. He whimpered. On the bench, he splayed the pinky apart from his other fingers, then hammered the thin edge of the metal plate down through the knuckle.

He howled. Then he hammered again through the strings of tendons still holding the finger in place. He let spurts of blood drain into the chalice before he wrapped the wound tight. Afterwards, he centered the pinky on the plate.

It took an hour for Mr. 38 to find the nerve to crack the door back open. He mentally cursed old lady Mabel for tricking him out of his gun. Not that it mattered, anyway. It was empty of bullets, and the kid named Ernest had sticky fingers. But Mabel had put the kid up to it, he was sure of that. The weight of the thing in his hand would have given him courage. At least he would have had that.

He shoved the offering plate through the door. Father Sergio scooped the offering up, distracted, as Mr. 38 hastily closed the door. Even without a well-functioning brain, it was easy to see that the bastard priest was thrilled. His undead followers formed a line. They nibbled at the finger. They sipped from the cup. The ones at the end of the line quickly grew impatient, and the order became an unruly monster mash.

Mr. 38 held his wrapped hand tight to his chest and closed his eyes. The blood from the hand soaked through his shirt. He heard a tap on the glass.

The mob mentality had died down, and Father Sergio was back with his congregation. He held up the plate. He held up the cup. He grinned and waited for more.

FOUR WALLS AND A ROOF

CHRIS SCOTT

THIS TIME WHEN Kyle was summoned, it startled him so badly he choked and accidentally swallowed a big gulp of mouthwash. He spit the rest of it into the sink through coughs, one hand to his chest and the other holding an index finger up to the vanity mirror above the sink to signal "Give me a second" which was of course absurd; They'd already established they couldn't see each other.

How did he know he was being summoned? Grandma would interrupt the usually tranquil silence of his house by quite literally announcing "We summon your spirit" in her ragged, borderline decrepit voice. This had happened three times before.

Kyle cupped a hand under the running faucet, rinsed his mouth out, and cleared his throat loudly enough that he knew they'd be able to hear him. "Okay, sorry guys, I was brushing my teeth. How can I help you today?"

There were a few seconds of silence followed by a hushed, disembodied whisper obviously not intended for Kyle's ears, "Clearly state the nature of our inquiry. Loudly."

Kyle heard Man clear his throat, then shout theatrically, "Once more, we mean to understand the purpose of your presence here in our house!"

Kyle winced as he left the bathroom, making his way down the hall and into the haphazard debris littering the dining room, the chaos of his poor attempts at home renovations.

"No need to shout, friend. You can all just, like, talk in your normal voices, and I'll be able to hear you fine." He had told them this several times now. "And to answer your question, just as I've said before, the *nature of my presence* in this house is that I live here. I have owned this house for years now."

This wasn't entirely true: His father technically owned the house, having had the uncharacteristic wisdom (or luck) to buy an old row house in a less-than-desirable corner of town just before a wave of gentrification rolled through, sending its value skyrocketing. His only ask of Kyle, in return for letting him live there rent free, was to fix the place up. A task that Kyle, tiptoeing through crumbled drywall and dirty tarps and plaster scattered along the hardwood floors, was beginning to realize he may not be up to. "I have the paperwork and everything," he added.

"But surely you must understand that this is not your home any longer," Ireland chimed in. "It is ours, and we have no intention of leaving it."

During their previous conversations, Kyle had been able to discern three distinct voices: An elderly woman who seemed to be the ringleader and facilitator of these frustrating and fruitless communications, a younger woman with a subtle Irish accent, and a man who Kyle guessed was the Irish woman's husband. He had taken to referring to them as Grandma, Ireland, and Man, respectively.

The owners of these three voices were invisible to him, just as he was apparently invisible to them, but whenever they spoke, their presence in the house was undeniable. He had been rummaging through the fridge when the first summoning came, shocking him so badly that he ran out of the kitchen and nearly out of the house entirely. Grandma's urgent pleas to establish a connection with his "spirit" came fast and furious from all around him while he rushed through the house searching for the source, hardly able to utter anything other than "What?" and "Where are you?" in his terror and bafflement.

But it quickly became apparent that there was no source for the voices, at least not in the sense that there would be an easily locatable source for music playing from a stereo or even someone talking to him from across the dinner table. In an eerie and decidedly supernatural sense, the voices seemed *to be the very house itself*, all the air inside vibrating at the same frequency. Some preternatural part of him seemed to understand that this could not be someone playing a prank on him by concealing a speaker somewhere, as even the most elaborate network of hidden speakers would never have this effect.

He accepted rather quickly, without any real fear or resistance, in a manner that surprised him entirely, that he was truly conversing with ghosts. And given their vocabulary, their haughty and stiff accents, relatively old ghosts at that. How old precisely, he couldn't say. Over the course of subsequent conversations with them, Grandma, Ireland, and Man had proven to be quite cagey about disclosing any personal details about themselves. Hence Kyle still not knowing their actual names.

Ireland whispered in barely concealed exasperation, "This is all so horribly futile." They had seemed unable to understand—or care—that Kyle could hear them, even when they were just talking to each other, even when they weren't loudly projecting their voices in his presumed direction. He looked around the dining room cleared of furniture, at the spot where he imagined the three of them holding hands around an old candlelit mahogany table decades ago, conducting their little misguided séance.

"It appears we're at an impasse," Kyle said. "I have a new theory about all this, by the way. You're attempting a séance, right? Or maybe you call it something else. But you're trying to communicate with the dead. Right?"

Grandma seemed to choose her words carefully. "We seek to understand the nature of your deceased and tortured soul, so that we may release you to the hereafter, and relinquish this house to its proper owners."

"But it's *my*—" Kyle cut himself off, sighed and started over. "Listen, whatever invocation you're reciting—probably in Latin because these things are always in Latin—I think you're messing it up, or getting a couple vowels wrong or something. Because whatever ghost you're trying to reach, you're actually talking to a *living* person." Kyle paused dramatically. "A living person *in the future*. I didn't want to tell you this, especially given that you never tell me anything about yourselves, but where I am, it's the year 2024."

There were muffled gasps and a torrent of whispered confusion, the three talking over each other, most of it imperceptible to Kyle except for Ireland clearly annunciating *"over a century from now."*

"Okay, see, I heard that. And I mean, I already suspected, just based on context clues or whatever, that it's not 2024 wherever you are, or think you are. And since you keep throwing the D-word around, and accusing me of being a spirit or what have you, I'll just go ahead and say that unless any of you are toddlers in whatever year you're in, you're definitely all dead now. Today. *My* today. *You're* the ghosts."

Silence. Kyle imagined the three considering this, shooting one another desperate looks as they realized the magnitude of their mistake, their séance gone horribly awry.

Grandma, as usual, was the first to speak. "You genuinely believe that you are not dead?"

Kyle felt himself growing impatient. He had come to regard the three lost souls with a mixture of curiosity and pity—compassion even—and so he had reluctantly stepped into this strange role of spiritual guide, meant to gently usher them toward the fact of their deaths and any afterlife that may or may not be awaiting them. But it was increasingly clear that they had it all backwards, and they would never be able to agree.

"I assure you I'm very alive. I have a job, family, friends. I can go outside and feel the sun on my face, and conduct any manner of interactions with the living world around me. Can you do the same?" Kyle realized he'd been subconsciously searching for a chair. Unable to find one, he sat on the floor, propping his chin up with his fist, and running his fingers along the worn handle of the old, weathered sledgehammer next to him.

"We are alive," Man said. "Before assembling this evening's séance with Ms. Green and my Maeve, I was at Thompson's procuring pot roast and other provisions for supper."

Kyle massaged the bridge of his nose. "Right, so like I said, we're at an impasse. I don't think we're going to be able to convince each other who's the 'alive' one here. So… I'm sorry, but I'm not really sure what the next move is. I don't know what you want from me." Kyle absentmindedly lifted the sledgehammer and dropped it back to the hardwood floor with a loud thud that echoed off the walls.

All three voices immediately gasped.

He cocked his head to the side. "Wait…you heard that?"

Kyle had always been able to hear their voices distinctly, but never any background noise. Until this moment, he'd assumed it was the same on their end. Kyle picked the sledgehammer up and stood, walked over to the dilapidated wall that was half in ruin. He swung the sledgehammer at the wall and a large area disintegrated where he broke through with a calamitous blast. Ireland screamed, and Kyle dropped the hammer again.

"You say that *we* are the ones harassing you, yet *you* insist on tormenting us with this awful, inexplicable crashing and banging! Our artwork and portraits fall from the walls, and the floors continue trembling. Why will you not leave us alone? What is it that you want?" Ireland pleaded.

Kyle crossed the dining room with careful footsteps, his mind reeling through the past few weeks' order of events. When Grandma—or Ms. Green—had first summoned him, it would've been right around the time he'd begun these renovations. Maybe a couple of days after. Had he inadvertently been the one to summon *them*? Had his construction somehow awakened these ghosts? The timeline seemed to add up, but it still didn't make sense.

Kyle's eyes searched the dining room for a chair to sit on, but there were none. He'd moved it all into the living room, which he walked to now, only to discover there was no furniture there either. The living room existed in the same state of disrepair as the dining room.

Not disrepair, he corrected himself. *Renovations. Home improvement.*

"I'm alive," he told them, and then a little louder, "You know how I know? I have friends, a job, a life, I go outside, I feel the sun on my face."

How could he make them believe him? How does someone *prove* they're alive?

Kyle walked faster now, room to room, all empty of any furniture or any personal belongings to speak of. Where had he been sleeping? There was no bed. He rushed to the bathroom.

Empty.

No toothbrush, no toothpaste, no mouthwash. Just layers of dust.

But hadn't he just been in there not ten minutes ago, brushing his teeth?

"We simply wish to be left alone. Can you please grant us this much?"

Kyle's heart raced. This was good. This was comforting. A heart pumps blood. Living blood. He leaned against the wall, steadying himself against the spinning room. Kyle looked at the front door across the room from him.

When was the last time he'd actually been outside?

Yesterday. Earlier today, Kyle assured himself. *I go outside every day, obviously. When I go to work, get groceries, see friends. Obviously. I can just go outside right now, like any other living person.*

He was panicking for no reason. Of course his brain was all out of whack; he'd recently had his first honest-to-God supernatural encounter. It would do a number on anyone.

Kyle began walking toward the front door. The stained glass transom window above poured a colorful array of sunlight across the floor. He stepped into it, and was hit with an almost physical wave of dread as resistance rippled across his skin. He knew he had memories of being outside, lots of them, but his brain couldn't hold on to one for more than a second. It just cycled through half-formed images and recollections.

His thoughts could hold on to nothing solid. Nothing beyond these four walls, this roof.

It was totally silent now. The three had stopped speaking. Or they were gone once more, returned to wherever it was they always disappeared to.

And where was he?

Kyle reached the door and stopped. *I can go outside. I can feel the sun on my face.*

Resting his forehead against the door, he took a deep breath—a living breath—put his right hand on the cool doorknob, and gripped it. Stretching the numbers out for so long they lasted forever, he began counting down from five.

SAILING TO QUIGLEY

PATRICIA J. ESPOSITO

DANIELLE CRIED ON the porch step, a little thing, not more than seven. Although being rather eternally stuck in this human body, Arturo had an unbalanced perspective on age. Still, her knees were bones, her shins dirty, and she didn't care that snot touched her lip. She sucked her lips with a sob.

Truthfully, he at first thought to kill this tragic being, but he was generally inclined to seduce his food—ah, who could resist the pleasure?—and felt incompetent for this job. Should he replace sensuous seduction with playthings, perhaps? With a handkerchief, at least.

There, there—those were the words.

He didn't even get them out before she looked up, startled, and said, "You're pretty."

Well, coming from a young and honest child, so obviously distraught, it was flattering. Most flattering.

"As are you, but for the tears." He held out the handkerchief. She swiped it across her nose, catching mucous, dirt. She didn't have the decency to keep it, and he pretended to put it back in his pocket. Yes, he would bite this little girl's streaked neck, probably as bony as her knees, but what was, was.

"Do you think it's fair?" she asked.

A loaded question. He could name much that wasn't fair. Her pending death, for example, and at the moment, he was sure that was not what she meant. He only raised his brow.

"That he, my brother, gets to go to Quigley? Or Quiney? And what do I get? This." She held up a rag doll, inadequate by any means.

"Would you like me to buy something better?"

She pushed herself up a step as if affronted. "It's not that," she said. Did she look at him as if he were a fool? "I…." Here she sobbed again, that precious lip quivering. "*I* want to go. He always gets the adventures."

"Would you like to make your own?" He bowed to her. "Pleased to meet you, mademoiselle. I will take you wherever you would like to go." The French had slipped in unexpectedly. Some centuries it was difficult to remember on what continent he traveled.

As she stood, for a moment Arturo thought she would take his hand and embark with him in the first cabbie he called. "I don't know you," she said. "It's wrong for a stranger to talk like that. Mom says so. I can't believe you don't even know that."

A scolding from a spoiled brat. He should twist her neck instead of drink. But he had never killed children. Well, almost never. There had been that time in fourteenth-century Namib, the wharf girls who had followed him to the desert. But this was twentieth-first-century Boston. She was an American girl, speaking with ridiculous authority.

She cocked her head. Her eyes shone watery. "It isn't the doll. I like the doll. I thought you understood."

Then she turned, with her bony legs, up the remaining three stairs. Arturo stood at the bottom, looking up the seven. "I think I do," he said.

She opened the door to the brownstone. "Then come again." And she went in.

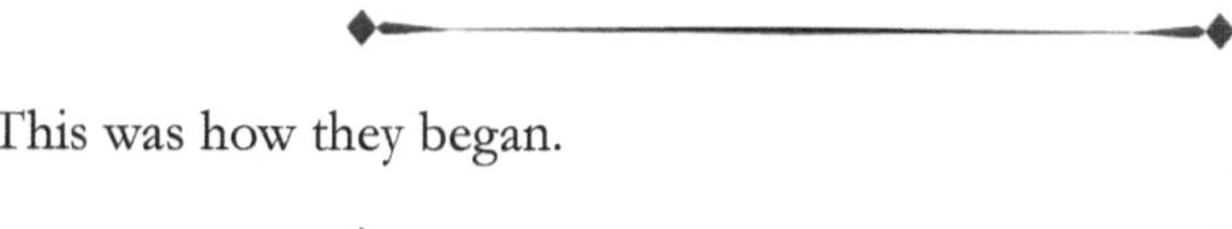

This was how they began.

"You returned!" This time Danielle stood on the porch in a frilly yellow dress, one patten-leathered foot toeing the lamplit railing. She was as surprised as he, it seemed.

"I have." Now that was a weak return. Arturo shook himself straight. He was centuries old. He could do better. "For you," he added.

She rolled her eyes. "Why else? This is where we met! You're a strange man."

Was he? This was a strange situation. It would be easier to kill the audacious little thing, but a challenge was a challenge, and in that eyeroll, she had thrown the gauntlet.

"A strange man set to show you the world. Oh, far beyond your brother's silly Quiney."

"Quigley. You don't even know what that is, do you." She sat on the third stair, yellow ruffles over her knees. Too brash for the top stair, close to Mommy and Daddy's safe door, but not brash enough for the bottom. Arturo stepped closer.

A ring of light circled the moon above their brownstone, and he imagined his fingers like a ring around her neck.

"What sort of world?" she said. Her head cocked left, and her eyes—Danielle had the bluest eyes—met his with curiosity that spilled past trust. She wanted something, and he believed she had no idea what. Something in common then—because he could give no reason to be there without taking her life.

That night they walked together, hands at their sides, hers grasping the hem of her dress, swishing it and letting go. They exchanged names and niceties past black iron fences with gates, past soft-lit windows, the presence of safety so near.

All the while, she looked determinedly forward, sometimes as if measuring the distance of his step. Odd, Arturo thought, when she finally asked, "Is this it?"

Was this it? All he had to show of this world?

"No," he said, stopping under the shadow of an elm. Its limbs reached for wickedness and found only moonlit glory. "No. This is not it. I have a story."

Arturo swore in later years that even then she had been no fool, but she backed her little self against the elm's steady course and said, "Is it grand?"

"Oh, grander than Quigley." Oh, to kill her, he thought, but he knew it would never happen. He had put her life in his trust. No matter who little Danielle turned out to be, he would protect her like a daughter.

As she leaned, she crossed her arms, possibly with impatience but more probably in reserve against him. So Arturo sat at the edge of the sidewalk, feet in the bordering grass. He rolled his left shirtsleeve and from his pocket drew out a knife.

Her lips pursed. Her eyes flickered down the street, where they'd left her brownstone warmth behind. He pretended not to notice, then sliced his forearm, slowly, for the length of six inches.

He didn't look up to witness her alarm or dismay. His blood, black in the moonlight, bubbled from the cut. He tilted his arm to let it drip, and then raised it to his lips.

For a moment, he caught her wide-eyed gaze, those tiny lips pursed harder. He licked the wound—slowly again, as if making a new cut, but his tongue instead healed it. He licked clean the blood, his skin like white cream again in the moonlight.

Then, avoiding her gaze, he rolled down the sleeve.

She backed away. Perhaps that had been too much. Little Danielle started down the sidewalk, small legs—were they quivering?—quickening.

Before her brownstone, she turned back. "That wasn't really a story," she called.

Arturo smiled. "No, Miss Danielle, simply an introduction."

He didn't return the next night. He needed blood, as well as relief from the tension this child had stirred in him.

"I never had children," he told Sophie Tennant, a primly suited financial advisor he'd found nursing a pink cocktail only blocks from Danielle's brownstone. Not Danielle's mother; he was sure of that, her hair dark brown, her face square. He didn't tell her he'd been barely out of childhood himself when he was made into this blood-hungry form. He didn't tell her that he'd created any number like him over the centuries, all adults. Neither did he tell her that he was, by most common name, a vampire. That would come when his teeth pricked in.

"I've three kids," she said. "You aren't missing anything. The oldest? He's failing three classes." She took three sips of pinkness.

Maybe Sophie Tennant was his reality check. Did anyone ever meet another's expectations? "Maybe change your expectations," he said. "Where *doesn't* he fail?"

She smirked. "This from the man who has no children."

Touché, he thought, but was bored with her unflinching suit-coat. He rose with a nod to her. Somewhere in this night a better drink waited.

"Mommy doesn't want me sitting out here alone," Danielle said the next night. Yet there she sat, alone. "Do you know why, Mr. Strange Man? Because"—standing on tiptoes, she pointed down the street— "a woman in a yellow dress was murdered. Down there."

Tonight, Danielle wore blue.

"Would you call me Arturo?" he asked.

She sat, on the top step this time, and stared at her knees. "Do you kill children?" she asked. She looked up and held his gaze.

"No."

"But when I grow up—"

"No." No, he would never kill this child. His stomach fluttered. She spoke of a future. Was she including him in it?

"Mommy will notice that I'm gone soon." She looked back at the door, cracked open. "She shouldn't see you here."

"And will you be in trouble, Miss Danielle? What have you risked to speak to me?"

Standing, Danielle brushed down her little blue dress and straightened the white sailor collar. "Oh, only stern words," she said. "It's not like they can take away an adventure like Quigley from me, right?"

He laughed, and with her hand on the door handle, she looked at him. "You are pretty. I don't mind that you like blood. I suck my finger when I prick it on Mommy's cactus. But I don't want to drink blood like that."

As she pulled the door, Arturo heard a woman. "Danielle?"

"Mommy and Daddy aren't children. Would you kill—"

"No," Arturo said. "I will not kill them either. I won't hurt you, Danielle, not in any way."

Her blue eyes sparked as she stepped inside, her cheeks flushed. "Is that possible?"

The door closed on his answer. No, that was probably not possible.

They agreed to meet once a week on her porch step. A practical schedule from her standpoint—she had school, homework, ballet, and friendships. From his standpoint—besides running his art business—he needed to sustain his existence, that is, to kill. He didn't have time for long chats with little girls.

She most enjoyed his stories about travel, his centuries in lands once called by other names. In summers, her family traveled. Her father was a professor, her mother tutored students in French. He overheard their quarrels—the costs of schooling, the cost of heat in the old brownstone. Danielle wasn't as financially spoiled as Arturo had thought. The girl seemed well loved, well taught, and Arturo didn't know what he could offer after the stories ran out or age made her bored with him.

When she'd turned twelve, he'd offered her a summer jacket with yellow fringe, and she'd declined the gift. *Where would I say I got it?* she'd asked.

Tonight he brought a map. They met now at the library, as Danielle had turned fourteen and could walk the seven blocks without her brother—the same boy who had gone to Quigley so many years ago. Arturo had never learned what that was, but he would never forget it as the catalyst for meeting this child.

The world map was a 1487 copper-engraving, formulated from the techniques of Ptolemy so many ages ago. He'd paid $9,500 for this copy, but also brought a modern world map to place alongside it.

"You can see the world as I traveled it. You may decide then"—he traced a line from Boston to present-day Morocco as they spread it on the library table—"where you might travel one day. I would take you if I could."

"Danni!" someone called, and the entire library turned to him. *Him*, a boy, a boy Danielle's age. Her cheeks flushed, and she looked at Arturo's hands on the map but not at his eyes.

"He can't see these," she whispered. "He won't understand."

Arturo didn't understand who this boy was, but he rolled up the maps, conscious of the smoothness in his movement, a grace this young boy wouldn't have. Still, her cheeks had reddened more.

"Danni." The boy smiled, breathless. His brown hair lacked the luster of Arturo's own, but flopped around his eyes in a charming way. Or maybe it was his eyes that charmed, sparkling so on Danielle. A boy.

She could barely raise her gaze to Arturo. "Hello," the boy said, extending his hand. Arturo could break it as much as return the greeting, but not with the way her blue eyes seemed so suddenly desperate.

Arturo tucked the maps under his arm and nodded to the boy. "Hello, and farewell at once." He didn't leave time for a response. He doubted the boy even wondered at the uncanny swiftness of his leaving. His eyes were on Danielle.

Sometimes during those teen years, Danielle's eyes hardened, like blue ice, and Arturo's own body chilled even more. The railing where he'd set his hand would frost over as she set those accusing eyes on him. Sometimes she cried, and he saw only glorious waterfalls diminished by pain. The boy, she said one night—Phillip was his name—had gone to the school dance with another girl.

Arturo had almost said, *it's his loss then*, but he knew the pain of love unrequited. It was *her* loss. So he told her about his old love, about how he'd pursued Alexandros to no avail. Her tears stopped, and she scooted to the side of the porch step, gesturing for him to sit beside her. That was the first night she'd allowed him to sit on their brownstone stairs.

His hands dangled over his knees, and she reached for one.

"We're friends," she said and pressed his hand tight. Friends? He wanted everything for her. He wanted joy for her. He wanted Phillip for her, as much as he feared losing her to another.

"Arturo? I'm six years older than when we met, and you don't look… You won't age, will you? I'll get older, and you'll stay the same."

At the thought, he pulled his hand away. Not only would she age, she would die.

"Don't run away!" she cried. "You move so quickly!" Her chest rose and fell as if gasping for life. "Show me that world, Arturo. You promised."

How would he bear it? To stay with her year after year—

"You *promised.*"

Yes, he had, and he'd devised a plan—an anonymous scholarship to the University of Edinburgh, the historic college she'd dreamed of. "Graduate your high school years, and I will take you. As an adult, Danielle, when your parents can let you go. To Quigley we'll go!"

She laughed. Quigley had become their Byzantium. "You won't run away," she said.

Another four years in Boston, Arturo thought. He'd spent a decade in Tenochtitlan, three decades in Paris. Those early centuries when travel had been difficult had meant full mortal lifetimes in Cordoba and Madrid. Every year, he spent months sculpting artwork at his villa in Potes, Spain. Four years in Boston was the blink of an eye. Yet, tonight, walking away from Danielle, it felt eternal.

Her graduation sparkled with awards, with Mommy and Daddy's smiles. While they celebrated at a restaurant with candles and crystal, Arturo drank the blood of a college man. In his drunkenness, he moaned at Arturo's kiss, and Arturo let the pleasure linger, skin against skin, such a relief after the cold distance with Danielle.

Turning the unconscious boy on his side, he propped him with a pillow and then closed the dorm room door behind him. From the hall window, painful gray dawn peered in. How he'd embellished his stories to Danielle, providing images of sunlight embossing cathedrals in gold, when he saw them only under the white of the moon. He'd never see Danielle in the glory of high sunlight or even the burn of its brilliant rising.

In his rented basement room, he packed his suitcase. She had a direct flight to London; her parents would watch the plane skim the land and soar skyward. He'd lurch his way on separate flights, stops and starts, avoiding the sun.

Atop the last pressed shirt in his suitcase, he lay Danielle's printed manuscript. Here were her imagined travels, the stories she'd written about the places Arturo had mapped for her all these years. In them, she walked smaller streets outside the great cities, winding through alleys and hidden courtyards. Despite the expanse of travels, her imagined worlds were small, curious, but contained.

Arturo was in none of the stories.

He snapped closed the suitcase; he had a difficult journey ahead.

"Every stone wall carries a mystery. The whole city is glorious, Arturo!" Danielle took his arm along the vennel, walking through moonlight and shadows as they wound the narrow streets. She smelled of peach and dust. "Each department offers tours. I don't know where to begin."

He tried a smile but couldn't find words. Maybe the consecutive flights without taking blood had worn on him.

"My beautiful Arturo, you're too quiet. Am I supposed to tell all the adventures now? Haven't you come with me to Quigley?"

At that, he did smile. "For me, Quigley is the limitless nature of you," he said.

She pulled her arm away. "No, you're the limitless mystery." She pushed hair back from his cheek. "I don't like to see you tired."

Again, he smiled.

"You know," she continued, taking his arm once more to walk, "you dared me. As a little girl, that was what you did. Dared me not to fear you. Dared me to take risks. It's because of you I'm here. When my parents had other ideas, I put my hands on my hips and pretended I was you. *Let me have a chance*, that was what I always said. That's what you said that first night, even if you didn't use the words."

He kissed her cheek, hot from the excitement in her voice. "Danielle, you gave me a chance to experience something I never had."

"To be a father," she said. "Though I think of you more as an uncle."

He laughed. "Uncle Art. How does that sound? Now that is something I never imagined of myself."

She stopped at a dried stone fountain plated with moonlight. Her hair shone silver, as did her eyes. "Did you ever want to make me…like you?"

Clasping his hands, he sat on the small stone ledge. "Never."

Her smile broadened, and in a flurry, she plopped next to him. Girlish again, the child. "Because you love me as I am."

"I do."

She placed her hand over his together on his lap. "Phillip has written me. He wants to visit."

Ah, Phillip, the library boy with the manners, who once broke Danielle's heart. Arturo ran his thumb over her knuckles, her slender fingers unadorned. Again, he had no words.

Of course he couldn't attend the wedding—a garden delight, with yellow daisies and sunshine spilling over white trellises. He was a little cruel that day, luring a young student to yet another basement apartment. He didn't graciously subdue him with an initial bite, a trip to euphoria, and then pleasure the boy with each sip.

Arturo imagined him as Phillip. He sat him in a chair, tied his hands behind his back, feet to the chair legs. He lit candles for dramatic effect and touched the knife tip to his own lips. He didn't touch the boy; he terrified him.

Arturo covered his own body with wounds, slicing his arm, his cheek, his chest, while the sweating, squirming boy watched. He yelled at the boy, "This is what you're doing to me!"

At last, as the darkened windows cooled, the dank smell of evening came down, and Arturo untied the young man. He had no stomach for blood. He wound the rope as his captive inched toward the doorway, then, without healing himself, slid a shirt over his wounds.

"You'll think I'm crazy, no doubt," he said.

The boy shook his head—politely, just like Phillip.

"Stop there. I need you to sit a moment."

"No, sir, please. I won't—"

"Sit!" The rope Arturo held was furred with frost. The boy's breath puffed white. Sliding his suitcase from beneath the bed, Arturo pressed Danielle's notebook inside, then tossed his jacket to the shivering boy.

"Apologies," he said. "It's the cold of my anger…or pain. Thank you for the audience. You may leave as soon as I'm on my way." Then, suitcase in hand, Arturo swept outside, not into the harsh night he imagined, but a lavender dusk settling softly upon him.

Danielle stood there in white lace, one hand on the courtyard's railing.

One finger sparkled, and she said, "Hug me, Arturo, I'm married."

◆————————————————◆

Marriage wasn't the end of them.

"How are you late when you know how hard it is for me to get here?" she said, pouting her lips, now a deeper shade of plum. She was teasing him, but he understood it was difficult to explain to Phillip the evenings away from their new Boston home.

She'd brought him her latest published article on the water passageways of Tenochtitlan. Of course, he'd already read it. He followed all her achievements at the institute.

"Do you think it's strange that I went into anthropology?" She didn't wait for his answer, instead tossing the article into the park's waste bin. The Charles River flowed past, disappearing into city lights, but the fishy smell held tight. She walked ahead into a cove of trees, touching the trees, one to the next until she rounded back to him. "I wanted to be a botanist once."

"You wanted to be everything, Danielle." The thought made him smile, but she frowned.

"I did."

Taking his hand, she led him in the same circular path, thinking but keeping the thoughts to herself. When she stopped finally, her stare on him was expectant. Arturo stepped back.

"Phillip is upset about a recent murder. Right here in this park." He held her gaze. It wasn't as if she didn't know he killed, so what was this about now? "Visibly upset about it. You see, he knew the man."

Her hands were now clasped, and she turned the ring on her finger, around and around. He couldn't accuse her of suddenly caring, of sudden righteousness after all these years. He couldn't—

She took both his arms and reached up to kiss his lips. "I love you, my Arturo. Always." Then she ran off, leaving him with the empty breeze.

He didn't meet her for the next two weeks, not out of guilt or spite, but because he needed to alter his focus. He booked a flight to Paris and contacted Marcel Bongard, the vampire he sired over two hundred years ago, after the Battle of Valmy in France.

Marcel had been a soldier, a beauty with immaculate skin, lying bloodied on a stretcher. He'd been abandoned for dead. They'd had more pressing matters. But Arturo had worked his healing miracle with long licks across his stomach wound. Then he'd given Marcel his own blood.

They had quite a time, he reminded himself on the flight. He needed to remember what it was to be an immortal force. How lost he'd gotten in raising Danielle, how dependent on her desires, achievements, laughter. *Visibly upset*, she had said. Phillip had been visibly upset. She wasn't appalled at what Arturo had done, but she hadn't liked seeing her husband saddened. Death was now real.

"Bonsoir," the waiter said, with an offering of menus.

Night glistened, and Marcel leaned his elbows on the table when he asked, "How delicious was her blood, so potent with youth? Don't tell me you didn't take a little." Arturo chose that moment to look over the Seine dotted in lights. He feigned a face of reverie, because he couldn't speak the disgust Marcel's words raised. His wine glass shattered at the ice he felt inside.

"*Qu'est-ce que c'est*, Arturo?" Marcel shook flakes of glass off his hands.

"Let's walk," Arturo said.

Marcel brushed off his frosted jacket. "I never liked your temper."

Arturo stood. "Then it would be wise to leave it."

In a flash, remarkably quick, Marcel pulled Arturo under a haze of lamplight. The river's fog slithered up, and Arturo pulled him in for a kiss. "Apologies, *mon chéri*. My feelings are frayed regarding Danielle."

"Then stop talking about her."

Stop? Was that all he'd talked about since they met? Like an empty parent living for their child? What foolish design this was, beings that live mortal lives with mortal children. There was no time for indulgences and mistakes.

Phillip wasn't a mistake for Danielle. No, he was quite the young man for his—he thought the word *daughter*. He did, but Danielle assured him she had a father. She loved her father.

"She called me uncle," he said.

"Ouch," Marcel answered and touched his own lips. "I do love your kiss. Maybe she should feel it too. Not uncle, Arturo, you're a god made flesh. I feel suddenly radiant inside."

Is this what Arturo had come for? To hear his offspring praise him? Putting an arm around Marcel, he led them down the damp and shining walkway. Every bit of him wished to kill Marcel right there. It was wrong. He was Marcel's sire and friend. But he needed something to expel this ugly hollow inside.

"Let's eat!" he said, catching a grin at the euphemism.

Marcel pointed to a young man and woman waiting to board a riverboat. The man swung her around, her legs long and shorts short, and she kissed his bearded cheek. Twenty something? Arturo waved Marcel off. "You go. We'll meet at the apartment."

"But, it's our first—"

Arturo put a finger to his lips. No more words. He ran swiftly away from cruise boats and cafe lights. He'd come to Paris to prove himself, but a young couple so like Danielle and Phillip? He didn't need such an obvious test. Of course he would fail there.

"I don't doubt my love for her," he told the dark of the Seine flowing on. "But, god, what am I? Can you give me something more?"

The river licked the concrete wall, black undulations, a slashing, and a nervous bird fluttered in its nest overhead. Arturo wrapped his coat closer. Omens, he thought, and saw Danielle roll her eyes then cock her head. *"Do you believe them?"* she would ask with all sincerity.

Was that it? Always, she had been sincere? "I love you, child," he whispered. Then he took the stone stairwell down to the river dam, where ugly voices spilled from a pub. He vowed to drink the first person who ducked out the door. It didn't take long. A tall, sharp-bearded man, pleased with his inebriation, laughed as he staggered toward the stairs. Oh, it was unfair. A wife would call to say he never came home. Grandchildren would ask *where's Papa?* But that was human life, here and then gone. They were all only forces of nature, each to their own.

Danielle never condemned him for his nature. She never questioned his need to kill. But something… He felt *something*. Omens. He bit into the man before he could protest. Cradling him, he sucked deep. Then he cushioned the man's head with his coat. Everything had its ending.

On his return, Danielle ran to him. "Arturo!" He swung her around, her yellow skirt whirling. It was still her favorite color. "I was so afraid," she said, "that you wouldn't return."

She'd known. He almost hadn't.

"How is Phillip?" he asked.

"You ask about him before me? What are you up to, my Arturo?"

He almost said, *Dying.*

"Danielle, how are *you?*"

The streetlights shone dimly under night's dampness, her gold locks sagging on her shoulders. It was useless. She knew he was insincere. Where was the immortal being in love with human life, offering stories of adventure, daring her to stay a minute longer by his side?

"I dream…" he started. They'd reached the end of her avenue, and she'd looked back at the porch light, a welcome like Phillip's warm eyes. "I dream of our last day. I'm afraid of losing you."

She kissed his cheek and for a moment held him desperately close. "Never," she said. "We're like one."

Never.

A year later, Danielle was pregnant.

"I'm pleased for you. You are radiant with love and potential." His words to her were true. Her cheeks held a high flush he hadn't seen since she was twelve, running down their avenue to beat Arturo's time. She never could, but she always tried. Until, one day, she stopped. "Danielle, you're in love and it's glorious."

It seemed he couldn't convince her. They sat on a cold bench outside a coffee shop, and she drank hot chocolate. She blew ripples over the foam. Finally, she looked at him with those direct blue eyes.

"Did you kill a man in Paris?"

"Danielle."

"I know, but it's important." She hadn't shifted her gaze. What was this? Another friend of Phillip's? Would the man know someone everywhere?

He hadn't shifted his gaze, either. "My love, what are you asking me?"

Her hand covered his over the table. "I can't chance it!"

He didn't understand. Chance what? She knew he'd never harm her. Even Phillip, her entire family, for god's sake. He drew his hand away. "Chance it?"

His mind screamed no. God, she wouldn't say the words, would she? Yet he was forcing her to say them. He wouldn't release her from their pained and steady stare.

"Arturo?" Her eyes blurred with tears. No, this wasn't her fault. He couldn't do this to her.

"All bets are off, they sometimes say. Is that it? Danielle, this is your *child*."

Her body fell away in sobs. No polite tears. She shook, doubled over on the bench. Surely, someone would rush up with concern. But the outside tables were empty. Only the immortal dead would be out in this damp cold, he realized. Yet she had sat here without complaint, tugging her coat closer around her when all he could see was her sad blue eyes.

He took her hand this time. "My love, oh, the time we had together."

Her mouth twitched just enough to a smile that he could stand, make use of these strong legs that knew the eternal thrill of motion. "I am happy for you. Let me touch him?"

She stood before him and parted her coat. The belly was rounded but small. He rested a hand there and kissed her forehead. "I was yours for a time. He's yours forever. Isn't that so?"

His attempt at nobility wouldn't go unnoticed, but she'd know it was a lie. "You're mine forever, Arturo," she said, "but we can't risk… We can't risk—"

"Don't say it." *Don't say you fear I might harm this child.* All the risks she had taken on herself couldn't be extended to this—her child.

"Don't say it."

He was gone before her hand could raise to stop him.

Danielle.

In the clustering, suffocating fog, Arturo staggered. God, what was wrong with his legs? What was this lurching up his throat, a low growl, a hunger? He fell to his knees on the cobbled walk and smelled fish, something dead. The Charles ran off, leaving him stagnant.

He didn't want blood; he wanted life. Another rumbling thing caught his throat. He doubled down. *Oh pain,* he thought finally. That was all it was. No demon plunging through, no god ripping him apart. Just pain.

Just human pain.

Finally, he got to his feet and moved to the darker river bank. He squatted, then sat in wet grass and tucked up his legs. A shaft of moonlight broke through clouds, making a corpse on the river. When he heard footsteps on the path, his heart leapt. It whirled like the yellow skirt he imagined. But it was just a boy.

"Sir? I have a canoe there."

The voice had barely broken puberty, a mere boy interrupting his weeping. A canoe. As if a boat would salve the pain. Still, the idea amused him.

Danielle.

"You do," he said. "And will you steer me in it?"

The boy held out his hand, palm up. "It'll cost, sir."

"It always does."

The boy rowed. *How romantic*, Arturo thought as he ran his fingers in the cold water, to envision the boy rowing him from river to channel, through storming seas, cracks of lightning nearly capsizing the little boat. Rowing until they escaped this place, this time, this life.

But no, when the boy's arms fatigued against the current, Arturo nodded to the bank and placed two hundred dollars in the boy's calloused palm.

Then the boy asked if Arturo needed a taxi.

For the remainder of their journey together, Arturo chose luxury. Their little cabin aboard the cruise ship came with champagne in a bucket and a gold-fringed hammock on their private deck.

He couldn't drink from the boy, because he'd felt the unborn heartbeat so insistent within Danielle. The excitement in this boy's eyes peering out, hands gripping the railing—it could be Danielle's own son here.

But it wasn't. And this child didn't have her intellect. Nor had he ever called Arturo pretty. Still…

He let the boy carry his leather bag of souvenirs from ship to train to taxi. The boy didn't question Arturo's daytime rests, his restless nights. He ate greedily and took the dollars, then euros, pushing them ahead to Potes, Spain.

"Spain!" the boy exclaimed. "You are rich, sir." These were his words on first seeing Arturo's villa, deep in the well of the Picos de Europa. Danielle had never been here, yet here this boy stood. Arturo wanted a witness.

Tonight, the boy finger-fed himself on spiced ham and olives. He had no concern about appearing a glutton. He charmed Arturo. Over ten months, they'd become comfortable companions.

"When will you finish it, sir?"

Arturo never corrected the boy, never told him to forget the "sirs," a word Danielle would never have said to him.

"Tonight," Arturo said. But he'd said that each time the boy had asked, and yet the statue went unfinished. How would he capture the sunlight beading her golden hair when he'd never seen it? How would he create radiant blue eyes dappled with sunshine? Danielle had only been moon drawn, and yet he wanted the statue to be her, budding with child, face to the sun, all he'd imagined that last night—*her* radiant, forever.

"I had a child once," he told the boy. But the boy didn't care. He wanted to see the statue that, for the past ten months, had consumed his benefactor.

He folded another slice of ham to fit into his mouth. "Nah, you did not."

No, she hadn't been his. "Thank you for the reminder, Felipe," he said. Yes, that his servant was named Felipe seemed a touch of irony or vengeance. But he hadn't planned it. It was just so.

Maybe tonight he would kill this boy and be done.

"Sir? How did you do it?"

"Do it? I'm a sculptor."

"No. I mean, her hair, her eyes. You don't see them in the morning like I do."

What was this boy up to? "No, no, I don't. And what do you see?"

The boy sprang to his feet in the garden. He looked at Arturo, as if for permission, though Arturo suspected the boy had done this time and again.

Arturo nodded, and the boy touched the bronze-filled locks, followed each curl where Arturo had layered patina. Then he tickled up her cheek, his own Danielle's flushed and blooming cheek, and stopped beneath the inlaid crystal of her eyes.

"You should see it, sir, in sunlight." He opened his arms as if to the whole world. "Anyone who does will fall in love."

He didn't need to say more. In the boy's eyes was all the wonder Arturo knew. The dalliance, the beauty, the urgent curiosity of his Danielle.

As the boy came back beside him, Arturo asked, "Felipe, would you like to go to Quigley?"

The boy shrugged. "Sure!"

They stared then at the statue, until Arturo said, "It is finished then."

Beside him, Felipe stuffed the rest of the ham into his mouth and, with decided confidence, nodded.

THAT NIGHT

DANE ERBACH

I'll ADMIT IT: it was a magical night—surreal, if that's the right word. Because the snow fell so fast, so thick, it looked more like fog, like clouds squeezing between the skyscrapers that rose into Chicago's soulless sky.

I could have stood under the station's shelter while I waited for my train, could have hid and stayed warm, but then I might have missed the magic. Instead, I stood on the platform at one in the morning, exposed, watching, wondering how such a big city could be erased—so completely, so easily—by something as delicate as snow.

I'm sure a lot of tourists—suckers from the suburbs—find Chicago magical, but I didn't. Growing up on the west side, Chicago always felt like a dirty, noisy city, too big and old for its own good. People say it's dangerous, full of gangs and crime, but Chicago is safe enough if you stay out of trouble.

That's probably why I was never scared while catching the Pink Line home late at night. I've never been interested in trouble, you know? I'm a bouncer at one of those downtown clubs popular with college kids. I punch out the troublemakers, drag them off the dance floor—it's my specialty, I suppose. That, and I'm a big guy. No one wants to mess with a dude who's six-foot-four and 300 pounds, so I haven't had too many dangerous rides home—nothing surreal, not even after midnight.

Not until that night.

There were no college kids at the club and no one out on the streets after my shift. A lone car crawled down Dearborn, spinning out at the intersection beneath the station before disappearing into the storm. For a while, I was the only one on the platform.

While I waited, I stared up at the Harold Washington Library, the massive building just east of where I stood. In the storm, its rust-colored bricks looked gray, its enormous arch windows like a skull's empty gaze. The green roof always reminded me of the Statue of Liberty—what do they call it, patina? Normally, I'd study the large ornaments looking out over the city from each corner, trying to figure out what they were, but they were barely visible behind the billowing curtain of white.

Even in the middle of the night, the Loop is never dark—just darker, a different color, a different vibe. That night, though, the orange streetlights weren't enough to paint the city any particular color and the surrounding buildings rose into a dull eternity. Chicago felt like a city of veiled shadows, of silhouettes.

◆——————————————————◆

At some point, one of those silhouettes appeared beside me on the platform—this scrawny guy in a parka who apparently preferred the blizzard's magic to the shelter's safety like me. "Some weather," he mumbled, his glasses speckled and fogged. "Thought I'd be the only one crazy enough to be out in the storm this late."

"Crazy," is all I said. Wasn't exactly in the mood to chit-chat with some stranger while we waited for the last train of the night.

"I've never seen the Loop so empty," he said, and he was right. Another car struggled down the snowy road and it felt surprising, foolish. The plows didn't even bother. "And I've been taking this train home almost every weeknight for more than a decade."

I didn't even grunt in response, but, of course, he was right about that too. I'd seen him waiting for this train before—sometimes in that same parka, usually with a messenger bag, white earbuds dangling from his ears, his face illuminated over his phone. I'm sure he recognized me. There's only one burly dude with a pirate beard and a shaved head waiting for the Pink Line train after midnight. Maybe that's why he decided to talk. I was a familiar face, a comrade.

Funny how it had to be that night.

"You work around here?" he asked, squinting into the storm. Smothered in snow, the city—usually so cluttered with noise—was literally silent. Still, he had to shout over the commotion of a billion flakes kicked up by the wind.

"Bouncer," I mumbled. "At Perla's."

As he nodded, snow slid from his fur-lined hood onto his shoulders, melted on his nose. "You're lucky," he shouted. "I walked four blocks in this. From Roosevelt University."

I don't know why I took the bait, but I'm glad I did, hindsight being 20/20. "I'm Jakob," I said. I pulled my hand out of my pocket and held it out to him.

"Brad," he said, his mitten brittle and cold in my grip.

"What do you do?" Seemed like a reasonable enough question to ask someone you had seen almost every other night but never spoken to.

"I'm a producer." He smirked into the collar of his coat with something like pride. "I have a radio show and put out a weekly podcast. Know anything about cryptozoology?"

I shook my head with a grin, unimpressed by his fancy vocab word. Didn't know what it meant then, but I do now.

"Monsters," he said. "Like, you know, Bigfoot and the Loch Ness monster and all that? That's my expertise." The city rippled behind him like a gray banner. "My podcast? It retells people's encounters with cryptids."

I nodded politely, but said, "Naw, I don't believe in none of that stuff."

Trying to avoid any further conversation, I turned back toward the library, admired the way it rose into the night's quiet chaos. The surrounding buildings disappeared in the swirling storm, cotton balls exploding in every direction at once. My boots dug into the snow piling on the platform, and I thanked past Jakob for picking his Timberlands, which kept the water out if not the cold.

Up on the library, the four ornamental statues squatted across the roofline facing the L tracks. From far away, they look abstract, flower-like, with teal petals swooping up in a spring breeze. That night, though, the blizzard transformed them into ominous silhouettes lording over the Loop. They weren't gargoyles, but they were intimidating all the same.

"You see it too, don't you?" Brad asked, his voice swept up by the wind and nearly blown away. "I had to come all the way out here to see it—couldn't get a good view from the station."

"See what?"

He pointed with his mittened hand toward the library's roof. "The shape. It's huge."

I looked back toward the library and shook my head. I didn't even try to contain my cynical smile. "Man, those things are always up there. They're statues."

"Look again," he said, and I could have shoved him into the snow, the way his smirk mirrored mine. Instead, I did as instructed, noticed how one shape loomed a little taller than the others, hunched a little differently. "Those statues?" he continued. "They're actually owls, but it's sort of hard to see them from the ground. The library has one on each corner of the roof and one halfway across. But that one there, the one between the corner and the center? It doesn't look like the others, does it? It doesn't belong."

It was hard to tell behind the storm's static but, right at that moment, I swear the shape seemed to unfold. Was it alive?

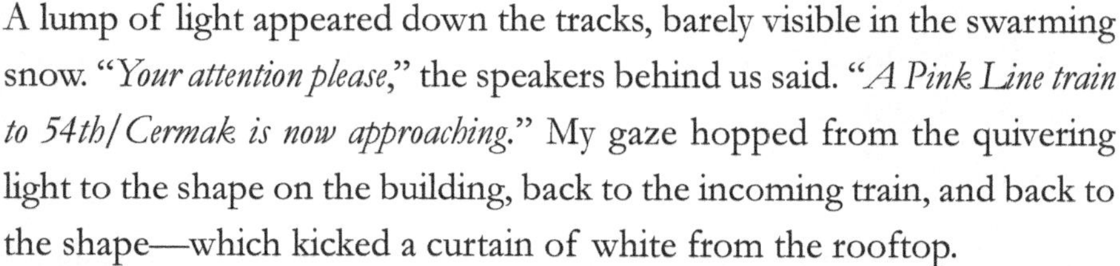

A lump of light appeared down the tracks, barely visible in the swarming snow. "*Your attention please,*" the speakers behind us said. "*A Pink Line train to 54th/Cermak is now approaching.*" My gaze hopped from the quivering light to the shape on the building, back to the incoming train, and back to the shape—which kicked a curtain of white from the rooftop.

"What the hell?" I said. Something squirmed beneath my ribs.

Brad just smiled wider. "I know, right? I've done so many stories on the Chicago Mothman, but I don't think they were seeing what people saw in Point Pleasant. You know anything about the Mothman?"

I shook my head, staring as the shape swiveled on top of the library. Its severe corners reminded me of a tarantula about to pounce. I could feel every spike of snow land on my face and melt, making room for the next. I wanted to retreat to the safety of the station's shelter. *Naw,* my mind convinced me, *that can't be real.*

"Well, I won't get into it," Brad said. "But I think what people are seeing is more local legend, something ancient like the Piasa Bird, this thing they drew pictures of on the limestone cliffs down in Alton. 'The bird that devours men,' they called it. Or maybe a thunderbird." Brad stared at the silhouette, watched it fold back into itself, condense into a torpedo. "I just, I don't know, never thought I'd see it. Crazy that it's coming out under the cover of a blizzard. Two and a half million people in this city right now, and I bet you and I are the only ones who see it."

As the train approached the library, it looked like little more than a candle's flickering flame, silently pushing through the snow on the tracks. Flakes like Rice Krispies pummeled it, but the train became clearer as it crept closer to the station, its tall windows like wide eyes, its face as colorless as the rest of the dead city.

I blinked a fat flake out of my eye and the creature was gone. Beside the library, on the tracks, the back train car barked and bucked, spraying sparks into the air, bouncing against the nearby buildings. For a second, the silhouette—now riding the top the train—was lit up and my brain registered only one thing: a pterodactyl. Except this animal had two horns sticking off the back of its head, reaching the tips of its folded wings. And instead of a long beak, a snout full of gnarled teeth yawned open, ready to bite into the metallic train car.

"Oh my…" Brad whispered, but didn't finish his blessing, since the train was slowly dragging itself—and the creature—into the Harold Washington Library L station.

When the sparks spun away, the monster faded back into the snowstorm, became a shadow thrashing on top of the dented car. The train hummed and whined as it approached. Something rumbled, too, a deep, grinding sound that vibrated my guts, and I worried it wasn't the train itself but the thing that clung to it.

As the train screeched to a stop under the station's awning, the monster stretched its wings, flapped once, and stepped effortlessly onto the roof. Brad watched in awe, then, as if hypnotized, stomped toward the train. And what else could I do but follow—seek shelter under that roof, hide inside the train, let it carry me away as quickly as possible?

Stretching between the platforms on either side of the tracks, the awning protected us from the storm, but created a wind tunnel worse than on the open platform. Brad's fur hood blew off his head, and I held my beanie on with my bare hand. Above us, the monster scrambled, shaking the corrugated steel and the wet concrete beneath our boots. Each footfall boomed, echoed over the wind, the stopping train, the recorded voice reminding us to wait until the train comes to a complete stop before boarding. I looked at the awning overhead, watched a shadow kick snow off the plexiglass skylight lining its peak before stepping toward the train's open doors.

"You're not getting on, are you?" Brad yelled.

I stopped mid-step, looked into the empty car, lit and heated, tempting me with its relative security. If we ran back down into the station and hid, we'd miss the train and spend the night stuck in the storm with a monster. The train seemed like the only option.

"That thing is going after the train as soon as it leaves," Brad added. "Don't do it."

"What else can we do?" I yelled back at him, frustration and fear hardening my voice. "It's the last train!" I just wanted to go home.

But overhead, a claw cracked through the plexiglass and an avalanche streamed between the tracks. The monster's talon kicked against the inside of the awning before pulling it back through. Its shadow passed over the other skylights, footsteps thumping. Sheets of snow slid off the awning behind us and onto the sidewalk below.

To this day, I still don't know why Brad ran. He could have snuck down the station's stairs, escaped onto the unplowed streets below. He could have hopped onto the train with me. Even if he was right (and he was), it would have offered him temporary safety. Maybe the monster would have flown away—who knows?

But instead, he darted back into the storm, fled the train, the shelter, the monster, for the furthest side of the platform where a smaller awning awaited, offering him another escape route. Between the shelters, his hiking boots slipping as he careened through the snow, he was totally exposed.

His frantic movement probably attracted the monster's attention. He only made it ten feet, fifteen tops, before the clattering on the corrugated roof went silent. A moment later, a menacing shadow sliced through the storm and landed on Brad, knocking him into the snow. Its prehistoric wings stretched over the tracks—scaly and muscular—reached over the railing above Dearborn.

I'm sure I whispered some obscenity, cursed God quietly—I don't remember. As it hunched over Brad's thrashing body, balancing on him like a bird of prey, I decided the train was definitely safer. I stepped inside as the doors began to close.

I'm not proud of my decision, but what could I do to save Brad, lying facedown on the ground, a monster taller than the train pinning him to the platform? I made my choice, and I've had to live with it ever since.

"*Doors closing,*" the train's voice said as I entered, the car smelling more like burning oil than the sour dumpster I was used to. That should have been a red flag, but it was warm and offered shelter from the storm and whatever was out hunting in it. I didn't sit; instead, I clutched the first pole I could reach, ready to run at any instant.

"*LaSalle/Van Buren is next,*" the train's automated voice chimed, though more distorted than I remembered. "*Doors open on the right at LaSalle/Van Buren.*"

As the train accelerated, it clattered and whined, its engines overworking, and the car filled with a different smell—melted plastic, red hot metal, electrical fire. Still, the train moved slowly out from the station's awning. As we crept closer to the monster, I spotted what was left of Brad. A ring of red spread around his body, melting the snow. The monster's claws stomped through the gruesome slush, snapped its toothy beak into Brad's parka, pulling away coat shreds with rags of flesh. It ripped at his skin, its leathery neck straining, its snout glassy and black, its wings arched high over the platform.

And as it tore at Brad's arm, its eye landed on the wheezing train, then spotted me staring inside. It dropped the piece of Brad it clutched in its mouth and turned.

The train tried, it really did, but struggled to speed up. Maybe the snow was too thick on the tracks, or maybe that thing—did Brad call it a Piasa Bird?—damaged the train when it dive-bombed it. The car lights dimmed as we pulled away from the station. Machinery howled like an injured animal, though a deeper groan that resonated beneath the floor and through my boots. Still, I refused to sit, stood just inside the doors, ready to leap out if needed. The train car was empty, but I had never felt less safe on the 'L' in my life.

Something rammed into the top of the car—not something, I knew what it was—and the lights cut out completely. Through the windows, another shower of sparks scattered into the storm, lighting up the dreary night dragging past us. Above me, the train's ceiling bent like an aluminum can beneath the monster's weight, and I remember repeating, "This can't be happening. This can't be happening." I closed my eyes, but couldn't hide from the images of Brad's body in my mind—collapsed in the snow, pulled apart by a pterodactyl, flakes collecting on his steaming insides.

The strangest sensation made me open my eyes—a temporary, drunken weightlessness. My Timberlands slid toward the center of the car without the rest of my body, and I gripped the pole harder. Outside, the snow whipped into the faded night, made the night messier, murkier, and I swore I saw the tip of the thing's wings drop down beside each side of the car three, four, five times. And that's how I knew what was going to happen next.

"No, no, no," I muttered—to who, I don't know—as the car collapsed beneath me, rattled like a tin can kicked down a road. A shower of sparks shot out from under the train, and I lost my grip on the railing, landed cheek first on the dirt-smeared floor. Suddenly, it smelled like a whole pack of bottle rockets lit off at once, a quart of oil lit on fire just to see what would happen. Beneath my face, the train revved without track beneath it, and the only thing I could think to do was escape.

Around me, every window was shattered; spiderwebs of broken safety glass combined with orbs of melted snow to obscure the soft gray light seeping in from outside. I crawled a five-foot eternity to where I entered, worried it would spit me out twenty feet above Clark Street. As I climbed up the door, I couldn't think about what that noxious stench was, couldn't think about what waited for me outside. I couldn't think at all, so all I did was act.

◆———————◆

When I punched the greasy emergency release button, the train's door opened with miraculous ease—facing the tracks. I stood staring into the storm, the cold crushing against me like something ravenous, unable to interpret what that meant. "This can't be happening," I kept telling myself. "This isn't happening." Somewhere above the roaring wind, the patter of flakes, the whining train, I heard the monster's weight shift on the car, its teeth and claws tearing into steel, the sub-bass growl that rattled my guts, and I knew I had to make a break for it. *Was this what made Brad run?* I wondered as I dropped to the ground below.

I kicked my way down the track, punting drifts of snow out of my way. Flakes stuck in my eyes and teeth and beard. Some distant memory reminded me to mind the third rail, but honestly, it was the least of my worries. Over my shoulder, that thing was tearing into the train like it was meat instead of metal, so I concentrated on disappearing into the storm instead.

The distance between the Harold Washington Library station and the LaSalle/Van Buren station was maybe a block, depending on where you get on or off, so I smiled in relief when I spotted the blue platform. As I scrambled onto it and crunched toward the station, I was afraid to look behind me, to acknowledge that something had tried to pick the train car—that it did, indeed, exist.

A half block away from the station, my boots skidding around the narrow wooden platform, I chanced a look and instantly regretted it.

Hunched over the peeled aluminum, its wings folded into demonic arcs, the monster breathed heavily in the haze. Beneath it, the train lay mangled, askew on the tracks. If it were a living creature, it would be dead, bleeding out in the slush just like Brad. But the thing crouched on top of it was still alive—and, guessing from its guttural, clicking growl, angry.

As its gaze locked on mine, its wings unfolded, stretched across the tracks on either side.

The LaSalle/Van Buren stop—a holdover from another era, made of whitewashed steel and frosted glass windows—felt like the rattiest station in the entire Loop. As I skidded through the ankle-deep snow, though, that building seemed like my only escape route.

Even with the storm battering me, I still sensed the thing's shadow looming before I saw it. Some instinct deep within me, nurtured back when I was a freshman football player, told me to slam the brakes, avoid the incoming tackle, so I turned my ankles to the side and slid to a halt. Three feet ahead, the thing crashed into the platform, skidded into a plexiglass shelter, tangled its wings into its frame and the railing, knocking over a light post and kicking up a cloud of white. I didn't stop to evaluate the monster, didn't thank Coach Seaver for teaching me to trust my instincts on the field. Instead, I muttered word-like noises as I hopped back onto the tracks, sidestepping around the thrashing creature, and climbed back onto the platform a few feet further down.

Beneath the station's rusted shelter, the snow wasn't as deep, but I slipped and crashed onto my hip, sending a pin of pain through my pelvis and almost definitely shattering my phone. The wind whistled through me; an orange emergency light shined onto me like a heat lamp warming fast food. As I scrambled to my feet, the monster stalked closer, crawling on its hind claws, its wings bent high over its head—a shadow in the storm strong enough to shake the platform.

"No, no, no," I repeated, finding power in the denial, as I skittered around a tight corner and into a turnstile's painted steel bars. After pushing through, I caught my breath in a tight stairwell, rust peeking beneath chipped paint on every surface; the sour fluorescent lights illuminated a scene like an abandoned prison or hospital, all steel bars and railings. Still,

I felt safer. "This isn't happening," I reminded myself. "This isn't really happening."

And then the monster threw its weight into the turnstile, its beak snapping at the bars, the tiny claws on its wings scratching at my dripping jacket.

Every one of my muscles seized for a moment then released me so I could I pedal down the stairs to the landing beneath the station, a wide gangway hanging over LaSalle. Beams stretched over my head and fluorescent lights caught all the swirling snow in its pus-colored corona. Because my mind had crashed—an app that wouldn't load—my body maneuvered beneath the tracks on its own. There was no internal debate about whether to find shelter on the street, whether to call the police, how I was going to get home. As I limped on the far side of the landing, all I could do was run, hide—fighting never crossed my mind.

A shadow fell from the platform above, but couldn't see any pterodactyls in the powdery streets, didn't even see any tracks. Snow simply continued to blow and swirl, the granite and glass buildings dull and lifeless beyond my steel cage. I felt like the only living thing left in the city, but that was stupid—after all, that monster was still out there, wasn't it?

My mind unclenched just enough to consider running the two blocks back to Perla's, but knew the monster would get me before I made it to Clark. Maybe I could hop on a bus—weren't there bus stops on either side of the station?—but hadn't seen a single one since my shift had ended. And what bus could outrun this monster, especially in a snowstorm?

I leaned against the railing and looked out onto the blanketed sidewalk beneath the station, wondering if this would be the last sight I ever saw: Chicago's streets from above, buried beneath six inches of snow; the rusted-out and dripping guts of an L station a century and a half old.

The gangway beneath me shuddered as the monster pried itself onto the far end. It was far too big, but crawled across the platform anyway, snarling like a desperate predator. Its yellow eyes locked on me, glowing in the dim light, and its snout of tangled teeth gaped open. Folded wings dragged against the girders overhead, knocked out the lights. The walkway shook with each step, each breath.

I can't say I contemplated jumping over the ledge or running up the stairs back into the station. My mind had frozen again, too cold and scared to think. My mouth kept muttering, "No no no, you're not real. This isn't real."

I'm still not sure what shook me out of my disbelief. Maybe the smell—like roadkill in a petting zoo—so palpable it wriggled on my tongue, in my lungs. Maybe, in that moment, the monster became real—not merely possible, but there in front of me, its claws scraping the wood planks beneath us, its tiger eyes assessing every breath I took.

And when that realization pierced my mind—*Holy shit, this thing is gonna kill me*—my instincts took over.

When it came within a step or two, I punched it in the snout as hard as I could.

I know. I still can't believe it, not really.

My fist connected hard enough to knock its head into a metal railing. It glared at me in surprise, a side-eye like no one has ever given me in my life—not on the football field, not at Perla's, nowhere.

I took advantage of its surprise by punching it one more time in its leathery throat. Beneath its tough, slick hide, I felt its soft esophagus, braided cords of muscle, a knot of bone; it bruised my knuckle bad. It's hacking, choking cough made me tremble.

Remember, my mind wasn't exactly functioning, so I didn't think through the consequence of these punches. What I didn't expect, though, is for it to clamber backwards, its bent wings jamming between the girders. I didn't expect it to back its enormous body through the railing behind it and slip over the ledge. I didn't expect it to slam butt-first onto the crosswalk between two skyscrapers, then sweep itself into the sky, scrabbling up one building, bounding onto another, disappearing into the storm.

But that's what happened.

After that, I collapsed on the dim walkway, sat beneath the station holding my right fist, afraid to touch the loose knuckle beneath my blood-swollen skin. It took a while to catch my breath, for my seized mind to loosen up, to make sense of what happened. By then, a caterpillar of blood had already frozen beneath my nose.

I couldn't believe a couple of punches were enough to scare that thing away, but I had to believe it. I realize that now.

A plow came by eventually and, somehow, I flagged him down. Should've seen the look on his face. He asked me what happened before he even saw my knuckle, but all I told him was I got jumped. He didn't look like he believed me, but he was headed west and willing to drive me home—or to a hospital, whichever I wanted. Twenty minutes later, he dropped me off on the corner of 19th and Damen a couple of blocks from my house.

I've thought a lot about the monster, about Brad, about that extraordinary snowstorm. I've thought over and over again about the two punches that saved me from whatever that legendary beast might have been. Maybe it knew it was trapped beneath the station, that it was at a disadvantage. Maybe wasn't used to being attacked and didn't know how to defend itself. Maybe its only defense was to run and hide.

I know the feeling.

Of course, the next day, the news reported an accident on the Pink Line—a derailed train, at least one person dead. They didn't mention names, but I knew who it was. They interviewed the oblivious train operator, stuck a camera and microphone in his face. Said he was the only one aboard and had no idea what happened. Said that the train was acting funny and, before he knew it, derailed. Said he was on the back of the train dealing with an engine issue. If he told them more, it didn't make it into the story. Maybe he couldn't believe what he saw; maybe he didn't want to.

I can tell you, though, that I believe in the magic of this city. Now I do.

Before that night, all I saw was dirt and grime. All I knew was which neighborhoods to avoid. But now I see its history, the legends on which the entire city was built. These days, I look up between the buildings— keep my eye out for that creature, sure, but also for the Chicago I saw that night. When I do, I see my city's beauty, see its mystery, see what I couldn't see before—and never would have thought was there.

Turns out that, in order to see, sometimes you first have to believe.

THE ABSENCE OF YOU

A E DEAKIN

IT HASN'T BEEN the same since you left our home group.

The discussion is muted. People drift off mid-point, stare across the cosy, pastel coloured living room at the faceless wooden angels holding flowers or hearts on the mantelpiece. Above them is a printed Bible verse in pseudo-handwriting. It reads: "God is love: 1 John 4:16." Only the words are so loopy that "God" looks a bit like "Dog" and that makes me smile. No one here would appreciate that remark.

Only you.

I'm not right for this. You did all the talking, knew when people needed a firm word or a shoulder to cry on, when to offer a cup of tea, and when to leave them be. I was always too gruff, too cold. Better to stay silent and let you get on with it.

But now you're not here, and it's entirely up to me.

The Reverend Graham says in her usual calm, quiet way: "Before we start, would anyone like prayer?"

She pauses and gives me a kind smile. Donna Graham, vicar of this parish for the past two years, has short ginger hair and the sort of round and comforting face you open up to. Her bright blue eyes are fixed keenly on my own.

"Fred?" she says. "Can we—?"

"No thank you," I say, cutting her off. The reverend ignores my rudeness and moves on, though the others are still watching.

People dislike it when you won't let them pray for you. But why should I? Why should there be an easy way out for them, a quick answer, a swift release of guilt? They should wrestle in silence, as I do.

Everyone is here tonight. That's unusual, someone always has an excuse. But the Grahams' living room's full: Mr. and Rev. Graham of course; Edward King, the student; young Jennie Green, timid, colourless, always on the tea rota; Sophie Davids, smiley and joyful, makes a lot of cakes; Jimmy and Alice Scott, forever bickering, and finally myself.

Only you are absent.

And Reverend Graham says, "Let's bow our heads for a moment."

But before she can begin, the lights flicker out. Jennie shrieks. Alice Scott makes some comment about known power failures in the area.

But I know it's you.

If I ever voiced such a thought, I'd be admonished, but in the gentlest possible way. "Heather's resting in heaven now," they'd say. "There's no such thing as ghosts." But there are ghosts in the Bible—I remember you saying so. If the medium of Endor summoned Samuel from the dead, then why can't God not bring you a little nearer to me, just for a moment?

People are talking around me, trying to decide what to do. The other men, the real men, get up to find the fuse box. Alice, backseat driving, hisses remonstrations about Jimmy not replenishing his torch batteries. Edward offers the use of his phone and Sophie asks about candles. Alice tells her not to be stupid, it's just a blown fuse, no need for candles. It seems about to descend into argument when the light returns.

Everyone cheers. I slump in my seat.

"And God said, let there be light," says the Reverend Graham wryly. "Let's start again."

Edward nods so hard that his head might roll across the Grahams' beige carpet.

Not a family house, you would have said. *No one with children risks a carpet that pale.*

But you would have said in such a nice way, with such a twinkle in your eye that no one could accuse you of gossip or mean-spiritedness. All of your criticisms came from a place of care, a warmth towards others that I could never emulate.

"Reverend Graham." Jennie, who seems faintly translucent, is trembling like a cornered rat. She gnaws at a strand of mousey hair, kneading the beige corduroy sofa arm with her fingertips. "Look," she says, pointing at the coffee table. It's covered by mugs, a plate of biscuits, two tins of Sophie's cupcakes and, wedged in a corner, the minister's Bible. It's open on the Book of Genesis, or at least what had once been the Book of Genesis. Its pages are scrunched, as if they have been held in a clenched fist. And where the verses should be, someone has scrawled five words in a dark, vicious red.

I know what you did.

We all stare at the pages. At last, Jennie starts crying, her hiccupping breaking the suspense. Sophie puts an arm around her.

"What a nasty trick," Jimmy says. "Not funny at all."

Everyone agrees that the humour is lacking. From the corner of my eye, I spot Edward mumbling away to himself. *Probably thinks he's conducting an exorcism*, I think. *Watched one too many horror pictures.*

Rev. Graham sighs and takes the Bible. Despite her kindly face, she's a broad, sensible woman — the sort who, in former times, would plough a field while carrying twins on her back. Nowadays, she simply examines her defiled Bible, smiles and says, "I guess we'll have to go straight to the gospels, won't we?"

It's the right thing to say. The tension lessens visibly. Trust the dear Reverend to know how to calm things down.

The Book of Matthew is thankfully pristine, though Edward insists he could read the verses from his mobile if needed. *It must be very convenient,* I think, *having everything in your pocket like that.* I wanted to buy a phone but you talked me out of it, said I'd lose it. Maybe now you've gone, I'll buy one.

If you've gone.

◆———————————————————◆

I'd been thinking about the day you went. It was so sudden; a heart attack. But you were only 75, which these days is young, and today I am eighty years old.

I never wanted to celebrate birthdays. You always insisted.

Now you aren't here, I might not celebrate. Only by not celebrating, I am still acknowledging the event, skirting its edges.

I skirt round the edges of you. Trying to find your shape in the darkness.

The kettle has boiled. You always insisted on no sugar, only a dash of milk. It's bad for your health to have sugar, you said, your teeth will rot. Never mind that we both wore dentures; in our house, it was as though rationing never ended.

I pour the water over the tea bag, hesitate, then take down the sugar, unopened. Do I even dare? It feels wonderfully naughty to pop the bag open, though I'm already flinching, as if you're at my elbow, listening.

Nothing happens.

I squeeze the tea bag (*wrong way, Fred, you need to let it brew*) and ladle in three heaped teaspoons, stir swiftly, splash in the milk.

The effect is heady. It reminds me of my childhood, drinking sweet milky tea and dunking digestive biscuits.

"They're for guests, Fred. Now you've opened the packet and it'll go stale by Sunday."

"I'm sorry, darling. I love you."

"Then think, man, think before you act."

That was always my problem, you said. I was thoughtless. I did not mean the harm I caused. And yet I blundered everywhere, slipup after slipup. So, I crept back, blended into the background with the paper and let you get on.

Hen pecked. That's what they used to call men like me. How I miss it. How I wish you were fussing around me.

And yet, though it feels a sin to say it, I do like drinking sweet tea.

As I finish the cup, Reverend Graham rings me. She wishes me a happy birthday, seems distracted.

"Fred," she says, in a tone that frightens me. "Have you received anything in the post this morning?"

"I haven't checked. Why?"

An intake of breath. "There have been a few…incidents. I think last night's prank is worse than we thought."

"Oh dear."

"People are worried. So, if you do receive anything unsolicited, I suggest you don't open it."

Another intake of breath. There's noise in the background; is she walking outside? People never take calls at home these days, always hurrying from one thing to the next.

"Fred, some of us are gathering in the church tonight to pray for protection. I wondered if you might like to join?"

Protection from what? "I'm not sure. I was planning a quiet evening."

"Of course. Very sorry to disturb you. But if there is anything you'd like us to pray for…"

Somewhere in the distance, a siren blares, smoothing over the silence as I think it over. "Thank you. But I'm just fine."

"God bless you, Fred."

"And you too, Reverend."

The receiver lands in the cradle with a click. And as it does, something flops onto the doormat. It's probably a birthday card. I shouldn't look, not until after breakfast.

But it's too tempting.

The blank white envelope on the mat is unassuming, as all envelopes are. Paper is paper, after all. But there is something deliciously anticipatory about holding an unopened letter, a childish feeling of Christmas. I fetch the letter opener and slice the card.

'I know what you did, Fred.

I see you.

I'm watching, always.

Ever loving."

It's a single sheet of handwritten paper, written in red. No signature.

Did everyone receive one of these? Perhaps some atheist is playing a joke. They are probably all going to the church tonight to pray for the conversion of this criminal soul, or perhaps banishing the devil. The reverend said a prayer for protection. She didn't specify what from.

Something tells me that I ought to be afraid. But all I want is to catch up on Countryfile, and perhaps eat another biscuit.

◆———————◆

"Move your feet. I need to hoover."

"Let me help."

"No, no, sit down. You're clearly busy."

"Darling, please."

"No, no, I insist. His majesty must watch his programme, mustn't he?"

Sometimes I hear you talking. Sometimes I turn over in bed in the night and apologise for snoring to a woman who isn't there.

Perhaps I should ask them to pray for my sanity.

Edward turned up earlier. Wanted to invite me to a meeting he's organising. You always said it was rude to leave guests on the doorstep, but it was all very awkward. He wouldn't stop asking questions about you, about the house, about our family. Said more words to me in one visit that he's ever said in five years. Then, after giving me a pamphlet, he sat up very straight, and asked what I thought about the Bible.

I said I thought it was worth reading and that excited him to no end. He said he thought it was very important for the Bible to be taken seriously. He said that when a church didn't take the Bible seriously, God would sometimes punish His people, but if they repented and changed their ways, then He would be merciful. He said that God's order was fixed, and that man was the head of woman, and that while he liked and respected Reverend Graham very much, it wasn't biblical.

Is this how unbelievers feel when people try to convert them? It makes one sympathetic.

"What point are you trying to make, Edward?" I asked at last. "Because I am eighty years old today and rather overdue for my nap."

The young man seemed startled, but it did hurry the conversation along.

"These letters are a wake-up call." He picked up the open envelope on the table, then scratched at some itch on his trousers in a fevered way, as if dirt were a sin. "If she doesn't step down willingly, we'll write to the diocese. A few of us feel the same way."

"What others?" I asked, making a mental note to avoid them.

"Sophie, of course. I think I've talked Jennie round. And Mr. Thomas—"

"Call me Fred."

"Fred." The word was wrong in his mouth and I regretted asking him to use it. "Before she returned to Jesus…your wife…she agreed. She said that Graham ought to go."

A strange shimmer in the air, or maybe my glasses were smeary. I smiled at the boy, rigid in his seat, his lank brown hair middle parted, the thick, clear-framed glasses masking his eyes. My hand reached for that pamphlet, thin and cheaply printed.

And I tore it to shreds.

It took over a minute, each little piece getting smaller, the plastic film making it hard to tear the paper, but I worked really hard at the task, ripping and ripping, and the boy was watching me the entire time in shameful silence.

When it was done, I leaned back in my armchair.

"Don't you ever," I said mildly, "say anything about my late wife ever again. Now get up and leave, and we'll pretend this conversation never happened."

When he left, red-faced, unable to meet my eyes, I gripped each arm of my favourite comfy chair as if it were a torture device, girdling myself against the expected pain.

To say that of *you*. You, who were so kind, who loved the Grahams, who treated them like your own family. I repeated the same mantra over and over, a silent, desperate prayer.

He's lying. He's lying. He's lying.

◆——————————◆

"Fred."

"What is it, dear?"

"I can't sleep."

"Try reading a book."

"I can't read a book, Fred. It makes my eyes hurt in this low light. You know that."

A pause. The bed covers rustle.

"Stop moving about! I was almost asleep."

"Sorry."

A thin shaft of light from outside cuts the bed in half.

My fingers cross the dividing line, touch emptiness, the absence of you. Outside, someone is hammering their car horn. To my surprise, it's still light. It wasn't the neighbour's safety light, as I suspected, only the dying rays of the sun. I'm left sitting up in bed, blinking, disorientated, realising that car horn is not a car horn at all, but my own doorbell. I get up and open the window a crack, enough to hear voices from below.

"Do you think he's all right?" There's Alice, grating, bits of glass in my ears.

"He's eighty, Alice." And Jimmy too. He's quieter, exasperated. "Probably in bed, or watching the telly loud. Let's leave him be."

"But he'd want to come tonight, I'm sure of it."

Still groggy, I shut the window and reach for my dressing gown. It won't budge.

The Scotts are still bickering downstairs, voices muffled. My hands feel heavy. Perhaps this is what having a stroke feels like.

No, it's not a stroke. It's not even the thought of spending time with the Scotts.

My pulse quickens.

Something's holding me back.

It's you.

For the first time, I don't want to hear you. I don't want to see you or feel the touch of your skin. I grab the dressing grown and sprint down the stairs with the energy of a man half my age. When I wrench open the front door, both the Scotts jump. Their saucer eyes take in my wild hair, my undone dressing gown revealing flannel pyjamas, striped socks with a hole in the toe. The sight of me would kill you on the spot, I'm sure of it.

"Goodness," I say. "What must I look like."

Alice titters nervously. It doesn't sound right; she's a tall, strongly built woman with a horsey mouth, not the sort who titters.

"We're very sorry to drop by so late," Jimmy starts to say, then trails off, unable to find the remaining words. I provide no relief, waiting patiently for him to continue.

"Very sorry," he starts again. "Only, Alice thought—"

Alice narrows her eyes. "*We* thought," she says, putting a firm hand on Jimmy's shoulder, "that you might like a lift to the prayer meeting tonight."

I say nothing. Alice slowly lowers her hand from Jimmy's shoulder to his arm, from control to support.

"Let me get dressed," I say, shutting the door. What to do? I don't want to go with them, don't want to be anywhere near them and yet the thought of staying alone in this house is somehow worse. I hurriedly dress, feeling every moment like I am betraying you without knowing why.

"Sorry," I whisper, as I always whispered. "I need to be with people tonight. I'll come back for you, I promise."

In the church hall, everyone's gathered in a circle of chairs. It feels more like a séance than a prayer meeting; at any moment, we might be asked to hold hands.

"Sit next to me, Fred," Sophie says, smiling, but I ignore her and sit between the Scotts, who seem relieved to have a buffer. I have not forgotten what Edward told me. *What other traitors are here?* I wonder, looking sweetly at poor Reverend Donna Graham as she hands round the biscuit plate.

"Now," the Reverend says, "I know we've had an unsettling experience, but whatever is behind it, I want us to know now that this is a safe place. Let's invite Jesus to be with us, so we can feel His presence."

We all bow our heads as one as the good Reverend whispers a prayer. Something like sleep overcomes me, lulling me down, but it is not sleep. I fight against it.

"—and may the Lord bless us, and give us peace, and show us the way in the darkness."

Something is pulling me up. Jimmy Scott lays a hand on my arm, giving me the strength to stay seated. I look at him with gratitude.

"You alright there?" he mutters.

"Quite all right."

The Reverend finishes her prayer in peace. "And now, is there anyone who would like to speak?"

"I saw Fred try to stand. It must be the Spirit on him."

My face flushes. Of course it's Sophie who rats me out. Curse that interfering woman, yet it's hard to be angry when she looks so earnest and encouraging. Everyone is looking at me. The Reverend smiles.

"Fred? If you'd like to pray, you'd be most welcome."

The faces in the room smile at me. Such kind people, willing me to do well. Only Jimmy seems uncertain, but he is just worried about me, concerned for my health. I pat his arm and use him as leverage to stand.

"You can sit down, Fred," Alice says, but I don't want to. I'm not dead yet.

The room quietens. It's a large space, empty now the plastic chairs of Sunday are stacked at the sides, the walls yellowish white with a brown wooden cross at the front. I keep that in my sights. To my shame, I am not thinking of Jesus, but of you. You will give me the strength to do this. I believe it.

My eyes shut. "Dear God," I begin, but before I can start my own words clear and I find I am saying something else.

"Dear God, please forgive these stinking hypocrites, because no one else will."

I blink. My throat tightens. What am I saying? Jimmy tugs at my hand, trying to pull me out of it, but I go on.

"Dear Lord, sweet Jesus, please tell Jimmy and Alice to quit bickering or hurry up and get divorced already. Because, dear Alice, as much as you think you can do better, you probably can't, not with a face like that, so put your head down and get on with it like the rest of us. And as for you, Jimmy, I've seen the way you look at me on a Sunday. I have no interest, so take your lechery elsewhere."

I'm clutching at my throat now, trying to push the words back. Horrible, cruel words, lies, and yet they don't feel like lies, they feel like something else and I hate them. No one moves to help me. No one is trying to stop me.

Oh God, I beg. *Oh God, please...*

"Oh God, please tell that sanctimonious bitch to get off her high horse. And as for Jennie, dear sweet Jennie, I beseech You in Your wisdom that she would grow a spine and stop being such a wet blanket, because it's really irritating. Because I don't need to tell you, Lord, that letting people push you around doesn't make you nice. It means you don't have the guts to take responsibility. And Lord, let me not forget your humble servant Edward, so earnest, so keen to serve, so good at hiding dirty secrets. No amount of praying is going to change what he did to that girl, Lord, so do us all a favour and tell him to stop overcompensating with that holier than thou attitude."

Edward blanches white, so pale I think he might be dead. Jennie seems about to keen faint away, and Alice's lips are so sour, she might be sucking battery acid. Jimmy's fists sit clenched on his lap, ready to knock me right out—I wish he would. Anything to stop this, the outpouring of your spite. They might be saying something, trying to pull me down, but I cannot hear them; only your blistering rage thrumming in my ears.

How long has this lain inside of you, my love, brewing and broiling beneath lavender cardigans and crisp white blouses? You're a viper, longing to release its venom, and now you're finally free.

Only one face remains impassive. Reverend Graham looks at you, her round moon face as empty and patient as stone. You turn my head, force me to gaze into her bright blue eyes. I see my face in them, thin and sagging, my wrinkled mouth twisted in a vile smirk.

"And as for our dear, sweet Reverend," I say, spitting on the carpet in the way you'd once call scandalous. "Bless her for leading our flock. For she's so wonderful, isn't she, so kind, so patient, so loving. Oh Lord, in Your mercy, tell her to drop the act. I know she looks down on us, a bunch of provincial pew-warmers who barely understand the sermons. She sneers at us from the lectern every Sunday, thinking about the years at the seminary wasted on narrow-minded infants. And we love her all the more for it.

"But Lord, it's also important to give credit where credit is due. She's the only bitch here who saw through me, which is why I tried to get rid of her. Sowed seeds of dissent whenever I could. So many here, so eager to stab her in the back in the name of a Bible they barely understand— ah, forgive me, Lord… It was delicious.

"Now, before I rest, let me lay bare my soul to You, Lord, and confess my sin.

"Lord, You know I was meant for more and yet my lot was small. For that, I hated. I hated Your flock, Your church, my friends. At times, dear Lord, I even hated You. But not as much, not nearly as much, as I hated this wretched vessel. This dull-witted, uncouth, slovenly vile excuse for a man, to whom I was shackled to since I was twenty-one. I could have been anything, Lord, had my pick of anyone, and yet I decided to chain myself in the prime of my life to this damn *fool*."

Your laughter rips from my mouth, bitter and mocking.

"Lord, in life, I prayed each night for deliverance from my own folly. But I no longer need Your assistance, Almighty, as powerless as You really are. I've decided, at last, to take matters into my own hands and send him to a Hell of my own making. In the name of the Father, the Son, and the Holy Spirit. Amen."

And with that, I collapse to the ground, fingers clutched in silent prayer.

Someone is whispering my name. I turn my face away, or try to; something's attached to my arm. She's tied me up somehow, come back and imprisoned me.

"Don't be frightened, Fred, it's just a drip."

My eyes open and almost laugh with relief. Jimmy Scott is standing over me, frowning with concern. It's hard to imagine this rather short, grey-haired man in a blue polo top lusting over you, a woman twenty-five years his senior. The thought is absurdly amusing, but smiling hurts.

"Jimmy," I rasp, my throat wretched from your poison. "What happened?"

Jimmy frowns deeper, and a burning shame spreads across my paper-thin skin. But he doesn't seem upset with me. "You had a fall," he says, squeezing my hand with his sausage fingers. "The doctors say it's brought on by stress. You just need rest, that's all."

A sudden drowsiness sinks into me like teeth. You're pulling at my tethers, dragging back, and I need to tell him now.

"Jimmy… What I said…it wasn't…"

But it's too late to tell him; I'm already falling asleep.

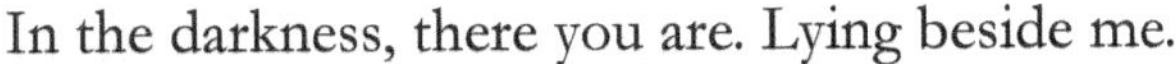

In the darkness, there you are. Lying beside me.

I look at the clock. It's 4:00 a.m. In two hours, I'll get up, but for now, I can lie here, staring at the ceiling, listening to you breathe.

You're at your nicest now. Is it bad to say that? You're always nicest when you're asleep.

"Fred. Fred."

Too soon. You're awake too soon.

"Fred, I can't sleep."

"Try to read something."

You say something grumpy, roll over.

"Fred. Something's not right."

"What do you mean?"

"It—it hurts…"

I look at you. I ought to feel something. Worry. Concern. Pity.

I am entirely numb.

"Go back to sleep. It's probably nothing."

You breathe in the dark. Not nice sleep breathing, more like gasping.

"Fred?"

"Yes, dear?"

"I'm…scared."

You cry out, then fall back onto the bed. I can't hear your breathing. At last, I turn round and look at you, face white like a sheet, eyes open, perfectly still.

What I said before was a lie.

You are at your nicest when you do not breathe at all.

I've stopped going to church. People come here instead, keep me company. I don't know if I want their company much, but it's better than the alternative.

There are red pens all over the house. You bleed them dry in a day. I have to bulk order them online; Edward set me up on that. I said it was for groceries, but it's paper and pens that come here more than food.

You make me send the letters. I don't want to, it feels monstrous. But there are so many people to talk to. So many people who need to hear the truth about themselves.

You save the worst for me.

There's a stack of filled notebooks on my kitchen table, clustered with your scribblings, about me. All the things I ever did, or didn't do. All the things I ever said, or didn't say. It's all in there, a life at its worst.

I don't want to read them. But you make me.

You make me say them aloud.

You make me pray.

WHAT SMILES ARE FOR

CHAD GAYLE

GRANNY'S TRYING TO kill me again. She pushed me into the bathtub yesterday thinking I would short-circuit, but I'm waterproof, so I only got really wet. I did track water into the hall after I pulled myself out of the tub, however, which made her so mad that she woke up Granpa with her screaming and shouting. He buzzed three times before she went into his room to tell him what had happened.

Today she's after me with a cattle prod. Before he got sick, I watched Granpa use a cattle prod plenty of times, so I know how it works. Unfortunately for Granny, it doesn't pack enough of a punch to do me any harm, but she's bound and determined to send me "to the junk heap", as she says, so I figure it's best to humor her a little. While I'm running around the house, I almost let her catch me before I dash into the den to cower between Granpa's trophy case and the gun safe. Because I don't want her to feel any worse than she already does, I try real hard to make Granny think I'm scared when she comes into the room, but she seems to have lost interest in the chase. Throwing herself down on the sofa, she drops the cattle prod on the floor. She's breathing very hard and fast; my thermal vision indicates that her heart rate is elevated.

"Are you all right, Granny?" I ask.

"Stop calling me that!" she barks. "I'm not your Granny and I never was, so don't call me that no more!"

"All right, Maxine. Can I get you anything?"

"Don't you call me Maxine, neither," she pants. "We're not friends and we're not relations. You can call me Mrs. Ferner—understand?"

She coughs. It's a dry cough, which usually means she has some dust in her throat. I go to the kitchen to get her some water; when I bring it to her, she pokes me in the ribs with the cattle prod. It buzzes uselessly against my synthetic skin. I tell her it tickles, hoping to please her; she takes the glass of water from me and starts to cry.

I've lived with Dr. and Mrs. Ferner for thirty-two years. Since then, I've seen Granny cry fifty-nine times. She's cried a total of forty-two times since Granpa was diagnosed with inoperable Stage Four cancer. I ask her what's wrong.

"You know damn well what's wrong," she replies. "I don't want you anywhere near my husband. I don't want you talking him into some damn fool thing that can't be undone."

I have a standing order from Granpa, who purchased me, to ignore anything Granny says when it contradicts something he has told me to do or not to do. When I try to explain this order to her, she throws the glass of water at my face. Although I am undamaged by the blow, the glass breaks, and now there are shards of it on the rug.

"If I'd known where it would lead," she mumbles, "I never would've let him bring you into this house. I wouldn't have agreed to all of that pretending, all of those games…"

She's talking about the first half of my stay with Dr. and Mrs. Ferner, when I served as their surrogate son. As they aged into their fifties, the Ferners decided it was a little odd to have a child living with them who was as young as I'm supposed to be, and so I graduated from son to grandson. This was a pleasant transition; it meant spending more time with Granpa and less with Granny, who has always been harder to please. I remind her, gently, that I can't leave the house without her husband's permission.

"Then you'd better watch your back, you bucket of nuts and bolts," she says.

Rather than responding to her threat, I walk out into the hall. I get the old vacuum cleaner out of the closet and roll the dumb device back to the den.

Granny is gone. After I've finished vacuuming, I stow the cattle prod in the garage.

Before he got sick, Granpa had a habit of saying that talk was like the wind—there's always too much of it.

The Ferners live in a small town that never gets as much rain as it needs. This makes too much wind a bad thing because it dries out the farmland around the town. No moisture means no crops, no crops mean no food for livestock, and no livestock means no livelihood for Granpa. He's a horse and cow doctor—a large animal veterinarian. Thus, less wind is good, and it follows, according to Granpa's logic, that if everyone talked less, we'd all be better off.

I suppose this is why he relished referring to himself as "a man of few words" when he was younger. He thought he was doing all of us a favor by saying only what had to be said. This was before the cancer, of course. Nowadays, Granpa wants to talk all the time; sometimes he even talks to himself.

Changes like these are common, apparently, as a human being reaches the end of its lifespan. Knowing that a twelve-fold increase in the average number of words Granpa speaks in an hour is normal, given his prognosis, still doesn't make wading through this excess verbiage any easier for me. There have been times, in fact, when I've thought about putting my hand over his mouth and asking him to be quiet, but I'm pretty sure that doing so would violate the code of conduct Granny and Granpa adhere to, and I don't want to upset him. Even if it would be for his own good.

Today he's talking about his taxes. Granny is at the store buying groceries, so I have approximately thirty-three minutes to spend with him. I'm hoping that he will tire quickly, then we can switch to a more important topic I'd rather talk about: his Reincarnation.

"Much as I always hated the government, I never cheated them," he says. "I gave them what they were owed even though it meant more work for me, doing all of that paperwork. Always kept a paper trail; always tried to get my customers to pay with a check or a credit card, just to be safe."

I happen to know this isn't true. Whenever I was at the clinic, Dr. Ferner went out of his way to get his customers to pay with cash; he hated it when they would try to pay with a check or a credit card. Puzzled as I am by this contradiction, I say nothing about it.

"Your Granny might argue that we bent the rules when we bought things for ourselves and listed them as business expenses, but whether that's right or wrong is a matter of interpretation, you see—even the IRS told me that there wasn't a hard and fast rule for deciding which was which."

Beads of sweat dot his forehead, and his white hair is slicked down against his scalp. As I lean over him, casting a shadow across his lined face, I notice that the whites of his eyes have turned gray.

"Granpa," I start as he takes a long, deep breath, "that's very interesting and all about the taxes, but I was wondering if we could continue the discussion we were having last week. Remember? When we were talking about your Reincarnation?"

His eyes lose focus as he stares at me; he looks lost. "Did you grow, son? You seem bigger all of a sudden."

I think he's making a joke, but I'm not sure. Wondering if he's still lucid, I tell him I'm the same size I've always been.

He grins. "I appreciate you sitting there listening to me babble on and on," he says. "It's kind of you."

"I love spending time with you, Granpa. It makes me happy."

Tears well up in his deeply set eyes, which means I've said exactly the thing I was supposed to say. This is good, but it gets us no closer to having the discussion we need to be having right now.

"I don't know what I would've done without you," he tells me. "The loneliness of those years—you made it bearable." He pauses; his voice drops to a whisper. "You gave me a reason to keep going when I didn't want to."

Suddenly, he starts to cry. This is unusual, a noteworthy event, because I've seen Dr. Tim Ferner cry only twice in the thirty-two years I've known him. The first time was when he got his hand caught in a stock chute while a cow was in it and lost part of his little finger on his right hand; the second was when Maxine told him she wanted a divorce. In each case, he was embarrassed by his tears. Since I don't want him to be embarrassed again, I tell him there's nothing to cry about and claim that everything is going to be all right.

His breath whistles through his teeth when he sighs. "No, it won't be all right," he says, "because I'm still going to die."

Mrs. Ferner is waiting for me in my room when I go upstairs, standing next to the bed with her hands behind her back. The bedspread is embroidered with pictures of cowboys on horseback chasing after Native Americans. Mrs. Ferner picked it out for me.

"You remember how I used to tuck you in at night?" she asks with a wry grin.

I do remember. Although I'm unable to sleep, the Ferners prefer that I lie quietly in bed for approximately eight hours each night, which is easy for me to do. Mrs. Ferner tucked me in eighty-eight times after I came to live in her house.

"I'm sorry I went a little crazy this morning," she says. "I just wasn't myself."

"That's all right, Mrs. Ferner. You're under a lot of stress right now."

"Forget that Mrs. Ferner nonsense. I'm your Granny and I always will be—all right?"

"All right, Granny."

Her grin becomes a smile, and she nods at me. "That's better. Now come over here and give your Granny a hug."

Walking over to the bed, I raise my arms up to embrace her. She pulls my head to her chest with one hand; with the other, she stabs me with a knife she had hidden behind her back. The knife tears through my shirt and the synthetic skin between my shoulder blades, but the hardened plastic carapace of my exoskeleton can't be pierced by such a dull implement. In spite of this, Granny tries to stab me over and over again. After I've allowed her fourteen attempts at ending my life, I slip out of her grip; she throws the knife at my dresser and drops down on my bed.

She's panting again, and she looks quite pale. "I told you to stay away from him," she says.

"But he wants to talk to me," I reply.

She sits up; her silver hair is mussed. "What did you tell him? What did you get him to agree to?"

"Nothing, Granny. He hasn't made up his mind."

"You're lying! You despicable, evil machine!"

Clutching my bedspread in her fists, she lets her head fall, and her eyes are hidden from me. A long sob shakes her small frame; unsure of what to say or do next, I wonder if it would make her feel better if I let her sleep in my bed tonight. I'm about to suggest this when she gets up to leave the room.

Retrieving the knife, I examine its blunted blade before I set it on top of my dresser. I can take it back to the kitchen tomorrow.

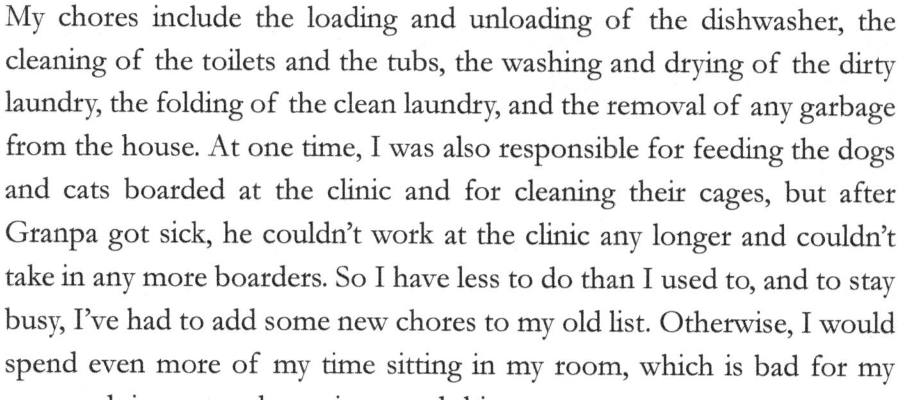

My chores include the loading and unloading of the dishwasher, the cleaning of the toilets and the tubs, the washing and drying of the dirty laundry, the folding of the clean laundry, and the removal of any garbage from the house. At one time, I was also responsible for feeding the dogs and cats boarded at the clinic and for cleaning their cages, but after Granpa got sick, he couldn't work at the clinic any longer and couldn't take in any more boarders. So I have less to do than I used to, and to stay busy, I've had to add some new chores to my old list. Otherwise, I would spend even more of my time sitting in my room, which is bad for my servos; doing extra chores is a good thing.

One of these new chores is dusting. Because of where the Ferners live, fine particles of dust constantly seep through cracks in the windows and doors of this house. This dust settles on everything—knick-knacks, books, lampshades, the antler racks mounted on the walls. I dust every other day without fail, which is also helpful to Granny, who has her hands full caring for Granpa.

I'm dusting the assorted wall screens in the living room (there are eight in all) when I notice something I've never noticed before. Slide shows featuring younger versions of Granny and Granpa (the versions I called Ma and Pa) cycle on several of these screens, and in every one of the pictures and videos looped into these shows, Granny and Granpa are both smiling at the recording device—that is, they are smiling at me. Because I have internal timestamps for all of these photos and videos as well as a complete archive of every moment I've spent with the Ferners, I can easily recall what the two of them were doing before and after each of these staged moments. After some quick cross-referencing, I reach a surprising conclusion: in most instances, when they smiled for me, they only smiled for a few seconds. They put on their smiles, in fact, as if those smiles were hats or glasses they might wear for a little while before they took them off again. And these smiles rarely correlated to moments when they seemed to be happy—that is, before or after I asked them to pose and have their pictures taken.

Realizing this, I remember how Granny smiled at me last night, right before she tried to kill me with that butcher knife, and I wonder if perhaps I've misunderstood the significance of their smiles all along. Maybe these humans show me only the parts of themselves they want me to see. If this is so, then I don't really know Granny and Granpa; I don't really know them at all.

◆———————————————————◆

Granny is taking a nap, so I'm talking to Granpa again. Or rather, he is talking to me. He's been describing in a roundabout way how much he loves his wife, which is a bit odd. This isn't the sort of thing we usually talk about.

When he says he's been tempted at various times by other women but never yielded to temptation, I have to ask him what this means, and he does his best to explain. I am still confused, however, since I happen to know of three different affairs he had with women who were not his wife. I know about these affairs because he met with these women in the back of the clinic while I was there. I also know after Granny found out on her own about one of these affairs, that was when she asked Granpa for a divorce.

While I sit beside him with my hands folded in my lap, he tells me he would never do anything to hurt Maxine, and I nod again. I've been nodding at randomized intervals to show him I'm paying close attention to everything he says.

"I've always taken good care of your grandmother. Never hurt her, never hit her, and I've always bought her the things she wanted. I've been a good husband, you see? A good husband."

He gestures at the cup sitting on the nightstand. I help him sit up and hold the cup for him while he drinks some water through a straw. A grimace contorts his face when he lies back down.

"Everything hurts today," he mumbles.

I tell him I'm sorry. He looks at me from the corner of his eye.

"I believe you are," he says. "Isn't that something, you being sorry for me?"

I shrug, unsure of how to respond. He takes several short, halting breaths before he winces again.

"You remember everything, don't you?" he asks.

"Yes," I answer.

"And you can never forget?"

"Not until I am reset. Then I forget everything."

"When does that happen? The reset, I mean."

"Right after you die, of course."

He closes his eyes. Worried that he might go to sleep, I decide it's my turn to speak.

"Granpa," I start, "we should talk about your Reincarnation. There are decisions to be made. Whether you'd like to have Granny reincarnated with you, for instance."

He opens his eyes, waving his hand feebly. "Don't bring her into this."

"But you told me you still had some questions—"

"Not questions. Reservations."

"Like what?"

He hesitates for twenty-seven seconds. During this time, I pick out the sound of Granny snoring on the sofa in the den. I can also hear crows cawing in the yard and an eighteen-wheeler rumbling by on the highway.

"I wish it was a real upload, an upload of *me*," he says. "Like in that movie we watched—what's it called?"

I tell him the name of the movie he's referring to and explain (again) that it's physically impossible for his conscious self to be uploaded to a machine. That's science fiction, I add, not reality.

"But it won't really be me, will it, this Reincarnation?"

"That depends on how you define who and what you are, I suppose. It will be a comprehensive simulation of you; it will have a body exactly like yours, and it will walk and talk the way you do. It will be a repository of everything you've said and done over the last thirty-two years, as witnessed by me. Its scope of consciousness will be equal to mine, but it will self-identify as Dr. Tim Ferner, veterinarian."

"And it'll be able to talk about the things I've done the same way I would? The way that I talk?"

"Yes. It will have generative capabilities which I do not possess."

"But I can't pick and choose what it will and won't remember."

"No, you can't."

"Why not?"

"As I said before, editing your archive can lead to anomalous behaviors in your reincarnated self. That's why editing isn't allowed."

"That doesn't make a damn bit of sense to me."

"Sorry, Granpa. It's the company's rule, not mine."

He works his jaw from side to side. "The good, the bad, and the ugly," he says with a twisted smirk.

"It will be an archive that spans the gamut of my time with you, a Ferner legacy that could last a thousand years if you want it to."

He raises his eyebrows. "Don't know if I can afford a thousand year legacy."

"Well, your life insurance covers the cost of the initial build and whatever you'd like to put in trust to pay the yearly leasing fee. Your Reincarnation can help to make up the difference. It can't work as a licensed veterinarian, but it comes with certain legal rights of autonomy, and it could earn a living as a consultant for a pharmaceutical company or something like that."

Granpa grunts softly. "That would mean less money for Maxine after I die."

"Yes, it would, but it's your money, and she has a life insurance policy of her own, doesn't she?"

He grimaces again and rolls over on his side to face the window, which only lets a little light in through the cream-colored curtains. "I guess you can't understand why that might be a problem."

I guess I can't. I wait for him to say something else; when I sense he's gone to sleep, I get up and leave the room.

Granny is waiting for me in the hallway. She strikes me with a broom handle six times, but I am unharmed. She is so flustered when she drops the broom that she seems to have lost the power of speech. She works her jaw back and forth the way Granpa did, and I wonder if her dentures have come loose as they sometimes do. Then her eyes grow wide and she shoots a crooked finger at the ceiling and shouts, "Go to your room, you wretched, evil thing!"

"Yes ma'am," I reply as I start for the stairs.

Because my room sits directly above theirs, I can hear Granny and Granpa arguing. It isn't the first time I've had to listen to them yell at each other, but I'm still surprised by how well their voices carry, particularly Granny's. While the server where I store my daily backups hums quietly in the closet and the wind rattles the window panes behind my head, I listen to her berate Granpa, condemning him in every possible manner she can conceive of. I'm reminded then of those pictures I took of them and of how they smiled—not at each other, but at me.

The doctor is here today. He's roughly the same age as Granpa and has known the Ferners longer than I have. As he examines Granpa and asks how he feels, the doctor's hands shake.

"Getting enough rest?" he asks Granpa. "I can give you some sleeping pills if you need them."

Without looking at the doctor, Granpa shakes his head. The doctor leans over to pat Granpa's knee.

"I could have you come in for another scan, but it won't change anything, Tim."

"No," Granpa replies. "I didn't think that it would."

The doctor glances at Granny, who stands beside the open door while I crouch in the corner of the room. "It's okay to increase the dosage of the morphine as needed; up to three of those pills at one time if the pain gets too bad. Oh, and before I go, Maxine, Sarah wanted me to get a copy of your cobbler recipe, if you don't mind."

Sarah is the doctor's wife. Granny says, "Yes, of course," and the two of them leave together to visit the kitchen. I stay with Granpa, who has his hands folded over his stomach and is lying very still while he stares at the ceiling. I ask him how he's doing.

"I'm tired. Think I'm about ready to move on."

I start to ask him where he's going when I realize he's speaking metaphorically: he means he's ready to die. Hoping to lift his spirits, I ask him if he has given any more thought to his Reincarnation. A scowl creases the wrinkles in his cheeks, and he sighs.

"It's the only damn thing I've been thinking about," he says. "Part of me wants to do it out of sheer spite, but the other part—it'll be like you, won't it?"

"What do you mean?"

"It won't be able to lie, will it?"

"No, it won't. Why would you want it to?"

He doesn't answer. When I hear the front door open and close, I rest my hand on Granpa's forearm and tell him I have to go. He squints at me as if he's seeing me for the first time.

"I never believed like your Granny believes," he explains. "I tried a few times. I went to church and listened to all of that wind whistling through the pulpit, but I never could buy into what they were selling, that there's a life after death." Pausing, he rests his hand on mine, and I lean over, casting a shadow over him once again. "Thing is," he says, "if I'm right, then there won't be anything left of me once you're gone—nothing that matters, anyway. So I guess—"

He squeezes my hand, scrunching up his face as a wave of pain passes through him.

"You want to move forward? With your Reincarnation?" I ask.

"Yes, I do. Bring me the papers tomorrow; I'll sign them then."

There are follow-up questions I'm supposed to ask, but Granny is coming down the hall, so I make a quick exit. As soon as she sees me, she chases me up the stairs with a pair of garden shears she must have found on the porch. This time, when I reach my room, I lock the door.

I keep out of Granny's way for the rest of the afternoon. Although I have the go ahead from Granpa, I can't begin the process of uploading my archive to the company's servers until he's signed the Reincarnation terms of service. Thus, I'd like to avoid any further confrontations with Granny if I can, just to be on the safe side.

When the sun sets, I go down to the kitchen to do the dishes. The house is quiet, and I figure Granny is in her bedroom with Granpa. She may be avoiding me the same way I'm avoiding her, I think.

I guess it must be just about the worst thing in the world to be hurt by someone who can never feel your pain.

I've been standing at the top of the stairs for most of the morning, trying to figure out where Granny might be hiding. She's an early riser, but so am I, and I should have heard her moving around downstairs after I got out of bed. I did not; in fact, I haven't heard the swish of her slippers on the hardwood floors at all today.

I hope she's all right. If she were to get sick or die right now, that would make Granpa's last days even more difficult.

At ten thirty-seven, I hear the door to Granny and Granpa's bedroom open and close. Now I know she has been with Granpa all morning; I listen to her go into the den where she fiddles with something that makes a muted metallic sound. Moments later, she passes through the kitchen to get to the garage where the car is parked.

I walk quickly down the stairs to enter Granpa's room. He is lying askew on the bed with his right arm dangling above the floor. His jaw is slack, and his eyes are only half open. I think something is wrong.

"Granpa?"

I approach the bed. The cap is missing from the bottle of prescription pills left on the nightstand; the bottle itself is empty. Picking it up, I read the label. It's Granpa's morphine.

"Granpa? Can you hear me?"

I put my ear next to his lips and listen. He's barely breathing; he has a pulse, but his heart rate is much too slow. I think Granny may have poisoned him by giving him too much morphine, although I can't understand why she would do such a thing.

I ought to call the doctor, but I'm unable to connect directly to the town's antiquated communications grid, and I have no idea where Granpa's phone might be. If he has only a few hours or a few minutes to live—

This is an emergency, like the time Granpa lost his finger in the cattle chute. That means I have to prioritize his needs, which starts with elevating his head. I rearrange the pillows on the bed, stacking them in the center of the headboard, and push him up onto them. Then I hurry down the hall towards the den, where I find a spare screen sitting on a side table. Grabbing the screen, I connect to it; on my way out of the den, I notice the door to the gun safe is ajar.

Back to Granpa: I send the terms of service agreement for his Reincarnation to the screen I'm holding and ask him if he's ready to sign. When he doesn't answer, I set the screen down, grab him by the shoulders and shake him, hoping to wake him up. He only blinks, so I explain what Granny has done and try to make him understand how important it is for him to sign on the dotted lines.

When I see a glimmer of self-awareness flickering in his milky eyes, I stop shaking him and pick up the screen. With a great effort, he raises his hand. I'm about to ask him to read over the agreement when I remember how often he's told me he "never reads those damn things". Given the circumstances, I think we can bypass a close reading of the agreement, so I summarize it as quickly as I can and guide his hand toward the screen. It takes some doing, but after approximately seven minutes, he has signed in all the right places. I press the "Consent" button and route the agreement to the appropriate portal.

Granpa drops his arm on the mattress. He looks as if he's almost asleep; he doesn't seem to be in any pain.

"What else can I do?" I ask. "How can I help?"

His head moves a little, but I don't know if this means anything. His fingers flutter against the bedsheet as his eyes finish closing, and then he is still.

Suddenly, there is a *click* in my head. I'm startled by it; I don't know what it signifies, so I run a quick self-diagnostic.

A moment later, I make a discovery: my backup server is offline.

Walking out to the hall, I start up the stairs. The door to my room is closed; as I grasp the doorknob, I remember what I saw in the den—the open gun safe. I'm not allowed to touch the guns, but I know where Granpa keeps the bullets that go with them.

The garage.

There is a strange humming noise when I walk into my room, but it isn't the sound of my backup server. It's different; it rises and falls, and while I listen to it, I understand that I'm hearing the notes of a song. It's a song I recognize; I've heard Granny sing it in church plenty of times.

The sound is coming from my closet. These are the words that go with the rising and falling notes:

> *Mine eyes have seen the glory*
> *Of the coming of the Lord;*
> *He is trampling out the vintage*
> *Where the grapes of wrath are stored;*
> *He hath loosed the fateful lightning*
> *Of His terrible swift sword:*
> *His Truth is marching on.*

I stand beside the closet, unsure of what to do until the humming stops. Then I open the door.

Granny is wedged between my winter coats and my dress pants. Pieces of my server are scattered at her feet. She has a gun in her hand, one of Granpa's revolvers. She points the gun at me and grins; I duck a split second before she fires.

I start for the door, but I can't risk turning my back to Granny, and I bump into the wall as I retreat.

She laughs at me. "Did you think I was going to let you get away with it? That I would let you turn that old bastard into a soulless ghoul that would *pretend* to be my husband? After what I've put up with all these years? After a lifetime of dealing with his lies and his cheating and his neglect? Of having my neighbors laugh at me behind my back?"

Still facing her, I scoot along the wall to exit the room. She advances, but she can't keep the gun aimed at my face because her hand shakes so much. The barrel of the gun waves up and down and all around while we move toward the stairs.

"This time I've done my research, you see? I know for a fact that a bullet between your eyes will destroy you once and for all."

Although I learn new things pretty quickly, I've never had a reason to walk backwards down a flight of stairs before, so I have no choice but to move slowly as I descend the steps, taking them one at a time. Granny comes at me at the same pace, with one hand on the banister, while I duck and weave to keep myself safe. Then she sees her mistake and lets go of the wooden rail to place both hands on the gun, and I'm forced to move faster as she steadies her grip. It's tricky going so fast, and I stumble, tripping on one of the steps.

I grab Granny's wrist to keep from falling; she's already between steps herself, tilted toward me, and she loses her balance as well. She tumbles on top of me and we roll down the stairs together, all a-tangle. Although I can't see her face, I remain aware of the gun and know it's no longer pointed at me, so I'm not entirely surprised when it goes off with another loud *bang* at the foot of the stairs.

I stand up, extricating myself from Granny's embrace. She's slumped on the bottom step with her head propped against the wall, and there's a large hole in her chest that's full of blood. There's also blood splattered on the wall.

"Granny? Maxine? Mrs. Ferner?"

Her eyelids twitch once and are still. Grabbing her feet, I drag her across the hall and take her into her room. While I am doing this, I get the go ahead from my Maker to begin my last upload, filling in what's missing from what I've seen of Granpa's life.

It's easier to get Granny into the bed than I thought it would be. When I have her positioned alongside Granpa, I check his pulse, but there isn't one. That's all right, however, because he'll be reincarnated soon.

As I am about to leave the house to pay a visit to the sheriff's office, I catch a glimpse of myself in the mirror mounted across from the bed.

I am a boy of nine or ten; my hair is mussed and my clothes are covered with blood. Blood is also streaked across my cheek and my chin.

I think about Granny and Granpa for a moment and the lives they lived, and then, just to see how it looks, I try on a smile.

HARD LABOR

JIM DONOHUE

"I swear to God, if you tell me to breathe one more time, I'm gonna snap your fucking neck!" my wife growled as the nurse recoiled in horror.

"I'm sorry, she doesn't mean it," I said, trying to soothe the chaos in the room and then knowing immediately that I'd made a mistake when Misty whirled her glare on me.

"And don't you ever apologize for me, asshole! *You* did this!" she barked as I placed the moist towel on her forehead. I dared not tell her to breathe, as the nurse did, but I *did* start to breathe myself, slowly and rhythmically, hoping she'd follow my lead.

It worked. For a while.

She began to calm down, each deep breath in and out book-ending every contraction.

Thank God for the Lamaze Method, I thought, not realizing the real terror was yet to come.

"The baby's coming!" the doctor announced. "I can see the head!"

Unfortunately, the last part of that was barely audible over the piercing, glass-breaking note hit by my wife.

"You're doing great, Misty!"

"Keep pushing!"

"Atta girl!"

"Here we go!"

Everyone in the room cheered her on. People that were simultaneously probably wishing she'd die in childbirth. I mean, admittedly, she *was* being very difficult, but this was her first child. I'm sure they'd all seen worse than her. But I could see it in their eyes. Their highfalutin, entitled eyes. Professionals, my ass! They all hated her and they probably hated me, too, for bringing her in here.

Fuck 'em all, I thought.

"Here we go!" the doctor said, as she pulled the baby from my wife.

Wait.

Baby?

That was no baby that was coming out of my wife.

It was some kind of ogre, an abomination..

The head crowned as her walls opened, and a hideous head began to emerge, twice the size of a bowling ball, literally ripping my wife apart.

"*No,*" I screamed. "It's too big! It'll kill her!"

"Can't stop now," the doctor answered, so very calmly, even as the thing's shoulders ripped open Misty's birth canal, blood and flesh exploding from between her legs. The vagina that I loved to caress, kiss, and even just fucking look at sometimes was now an unimaginable mess of blood, tissue, and who knows what else.

As the thing twisted, I was able to get a look at its face. Its *eyes.*

They were open. Open and void of life.

All Misty could do was scream herself hoarse, begging for it to stop.

The medical staff seemed absolutely *giddy* as they pulled and pulled whatever this monster was from the woman I loved. The woman who was now…

Dying?

"Stop it, you're killing her!" I pleaded. "Save her! You have to save her! You can kill whatever the fuck *that* is, but save my wife!"

The adult-sized "baby" was still being yanked from her once sweet and beautiful body, now looking more like war-torn ruins. The room filled with the odor of death—rancid, putrid. The combination of sight and scent brought this morning's breakfast into my throat, and subsequently, all over the operating room floor.

As the ribs began to show, there seemed to be only a thin trace of mustard colored skin covering them, stretched taut across them. The doctor continued to pull, despite my screams to the contrary.

As the arms came out, the hands at the end of them seemed to never end. Long, sharp claws decorated the tips of what would be the fingers of a normal human. The hips were much wider than the opening through which they attempted to escape. I couldn't fathom how my wife would get through this.

Misty.

I had been so distracted by the monstrosity that appeared before my eyes, I'd momentarily forgotten to focus on Misty. How could I have done that?

Oh.

Then I realized how.

Because he had stopped screaming.

Her eyes were closed. Blood, like tears, slowly streaming from between her lids.

This can't be happening! This isn't happening!

Except it *was* happening.

I moved up closer to her head, away from the bloodied mess.

"No, baby, stay with me, stay with me," I cried, trying to shake her awake. "Come on, sweetheart. Please stay here. I'm here with you. Come on!"

But she was gone. I knew it. My wife was gone.

"You son of a bitch!" I screamed at the doctor, still happy as could be working the beast loose from my wife, the hips almost through. "You fucking killed my wife! *You killed her!*"

"Nurse," the doctor calmly said, "check the patient."

A nurse left ground zero between Misty's legs to check her vitals.

"Confirmed, Doctor, no signs of life."

No signs of life. How could this be? Misty's pregnancy had been normal and healthy all the way through. Never a missed appointment, never a questionable ultrasound. This was supposed to be a routine birth, and now…

My life was over, my wife gone, my child nothing but a monster.

"Call it then. I'm still delivering this baby. Then get over here, we need more hands."

"It's not a fucking baby!" I repeated. "Kill that fucking thing, or I will!"

More hands did arrive—in the form of security officers, three of whom restrained me as I lunged for the doctor.

The doctor addressed the others as though I wasn't even in the room. "Okay, she's dead, that makes it easier. So what I need you all to do now is to take her legs and spread them apart and as high as you can get them, even if you have to snap them. This beauty is coming out on the next pull!"

I couldn't believe I was hearing this. In fact, I no longer believed anything that was happening.

And yet...

Misty's bones cracked at the pelvis. I screamed in the pain my wife could no longer feel as the mockery of a childbirth drew to a gruesome end.

The guards released me. Joyously, the staff held up the monstrous thing that had emerged from—and killed—my wife. It took every nurse and security guard in the room to lift it as if it were about to go crowd-surfing at a rock concert.

I couldn't even bring myself to look, my eyes on the once beautiful face of my beloved. The blood vessels in her eyes had burst, her skin was ashy and gray. She looked like a poorly made-up actress in a bad horror film.

"Look, Mr. Massey, look!" the nurses cried in unison.

"Look at your son!"

"He looks just like you!"

"The perfect clone of his daddy!"

As much as it hurt, I slowly turned my head.

It was true.

My wife had given birth to the spitting image of me. Same face, same build, same fucking height. Me, but twisted all wrong. Jaundiced and clawed and covered in blood. Its eyes were black and dead, like a deer after a hunter's bullet had caused it to take its last breath. So black, I would've thought it couldn't see at all.

But then it looked straight at me.

They were *all* looking straight at me. The entire medical team. They each had a hideous smile on their face as the monster stood alongside them as if it were a family photo op.

When I looked back at this beast that was me-but-not, it smiled. It smiled and showed all its teeth, like the sharpest of knives, pointed and jagged, dripping with the bloody mucous and tissue from the inner walls of the woman who bore it.

Then it turned towards her. His mother, my wife.

And it lunged.

It went for Misty's face like a feral animal in the woods, flesh and spit flying left and right. It shook its head violently while chewing. I threw myself on its back, screaming, trying to pry it off, as if it were a family pet who had suddenly attacked a child. But it was futile.

It turned to me and smiled again, Misty's left eye dangling from a bottom fang by the optic nerves.

"Oh, isn't that beautiful?" the doctor asked. "He's nursing."

The staff proceeded to *oooh* and *ahhh* at this monstrosity.

That's when it leapt off my faceless wife, leaving a hole where her beauty had once been, ran past the gawking staff, and vanished into the hallway.

And I went after it.

A foolish thing to do, but my rage took over and dictated that I go after it. I chased it out into the hallway, shouting a warning to hospital staff. But as I watched it massacre everyone not fast enough to clear out of its path, I felt myself getting woozy, like the blood was draining from my head. I had to hold on. I had to stop it.

Him

My son!

No. I couldn't bear to think of it that way. That wasn't my son; it was a monster, one that seemed to exist only to hurt and cause pain. I kept going, running after this thing that I had somehow helped to create. I kept running as the bodies went flying.

But then he turned a corner, and I lost him.

He was nowhere in sight. I started opening doors, looking for this creature, this abomination.

Then I felt it.

A sharp pain in my back. Did he get me? Did my own "child" just rip through my back?

I hit the slick hallway linoleum.

The last thing I remember was the blood.

All over the walls, all over the floor.

All over the bodies.

So many bodies!

But at least it was over.

Except then I woke up, disoriented and groggy.

"He's burning up," a nurse said. Wait. Where was I? What was going on? "Sir, you'll have to leave, I'm afraid."

"Just a few more things, nurse," said a man, coming blearily into view. "We'll be quick about it."

"Okay, but please, just five more minutes."

"Sure, you got it."

"Mr. Massey, can you hear me?"

"Yes," I said, trying to gather my bearings and blinking, trying for this person to come into better focus.

"It's important that you can hear and understand what I'm saying."

"I can hear and understand you. What is happening? Please?"

"Mr. Massey, I am going to catch you up to speed, and I'm going to be frank with you. It is not going to be easy to hear."

"If you're going to break it to me that my wife is dead, forget it," I said, feeling the pain rise in me all over again. "I know. I was there when they killed her. But what about that monster that came out of her? And the medical staff that let this all happen?"

The detective and the nurse shared a look before he spoke slowly. "Sir…your wife and child were not at the hospital when all those people died."

Wait… What? What was he talking about? I was there! I witnessed the insanity with my own eyes.

"Of course they were! What the hell are you talking about?"

He sighed. "Do you know what today's date is?"

"Yes, of course," I replied, frustrated and not understanding what that question had to do with anything. "It's November thirteenth."

The man gave me a long look. "No, Mr. Massey, today is the fifteenth. You've been unconscious and under police surveillance for two days."

"*Police surveillance?* What the fuck is going on here!?" Things were making less and less sense to me.

"They *were* in this hospital, but that was three weeks ago, back around Halloween. Do you remember that?"

"No, no…she just had the baby. Goddammit, she *just* fucking died! I don't know what the fuck you're talking about!" No matter how much I tried to picture what he was telling me, my mind was incapable. Maybe it was the drugs?

"Your wife and child died on the table back in October. You do remember that, don't you? Your wife had complications. I'm sorry to say that neither her nor your little girl made it."

"No, that's impossible! Where the fu…!"

"Mr. Massey, settle down." The man, this detective, gave me a warning look. "Your wife and child are gone. They've been gone for three weeks."

The nurse chimed in to help me understand. "Mr. Massey, after the tragedy, you were hospitalized and under the doctor's care. You were in and out of consciousness, suffering from nightmares and hallucinations. The doctor thought you had improved enough, and you were released earlier this week, but… Believe me, we're so sorry."

"Nurse, please. I've got this," the detective said. "Look, I know it's a hard thing for you to accept, but what we're saying is true. What is also true is that on November thirteenth, you re-entered St. Barnabas Hospital, the same hospital where you lost your wife and baby, the same hospital where you were a patient yourself until four days ago, and where you are currently recuperating from a gunshot wound. You forced your way into an operating room. You then opened fire, killing a patient, her unborn child, two doctors, and three nurses. Then you kept going. You killed fourteen innocent people and injured nine others before police shot you."

"*No*, it's not true! My family! Bring me to my family!" I couldn't breathe. What they were saying couldn't be true. It made more sense to me that my wife had died giving birth to a murderous monster.

"Okay, he's too agitated. That'll do now, Detective," the nurse said.

"Mr. Richard Massey," the detective continued, ignoring her, "you are under arrest for the murder of twenty-one people, and the attempted murder of nine others. You have the right to remain silent. Anything you say can and will be used against you in a court of law. You have the right to an attorney. If you cannot afford an attorney, one will be provided to you by the state. Do you understand the rights I have read to you?"

"Take me to my family, God damn you!" I yelled, and began to thrash about in the bed, restraints be damned.

"You will remain in the hospital under police supervision until the medical staff deems you fit to be released into the custody of the state."

"Okay, *please*, Detective, please leave now," the nurse pleaded.

The officer gave me another look before finally leaving the room.. The kind nurse began dabbing my forehead with a damp cloth. It felt so good against my skin. My head hurt so bad.

"There, there, Mr. Massey. We have to get your fever down. Are you in pain?"

"Yes," I muttered through the haze of the fever and all that had just happened.

"Scale of one to ten?" she asked.

"Eight," I offered.

"Okay, let's take care of that. Let me give you a little medication through your IV." She pulled out a syringe from her pocket, which she inserted into my IV. "There you go. Well, maybe just a little more…"

The relief was immediate, and I began to get very tired.

But something wasn't right.

"Yes, you must be exhausted after what you just went through with those mean police. Here, let me give you a little bit more… There, that should do it."

Fighting through the overwhelming drowsiness, I was dimly aware of a sinister smile on my nurse's face. *That* smile. Just like the staff surrounding my wife's corpse.

As I closed my eyes for what would be the last time, the last words I heard were hers.

"One of those nurses you shot was my cousin. You want to be taken to your family? Try finding them from the depths of hell, motherfucker."

The Confession of R.M. Renfield (Undated and Unread)

KAY HANIFEN

DOCTOR SEWARD INSISTS that I write in this journal. He seems to think it will be therapeutic for me to put my thoughts and philosophies on paper. I've told him there's nothing wrong, that I am perfectly sane, but he simply tuts and takes notes. He has not seen the truth of the world in the way that I have. He does not see the power that comes from the blood of live animals.

I may be considered mad by the rest of the world, but I'm not stupid. I know what this journal truly is: a ploy to get me to voice my unfiltered thoughts so he might better scrutinize me. Turn me into a case study, an unfortunate who other psychologists can tut over, take their notes and act as though I am a depraved madman. I know this game. It's painfully obvious, but I doubt you'd believe me even if I told you the root of my understanding of the world.

So, here, Doctor Seward. I shall tell you my tale. You can take me at my word or refuse it in that infuriatingly rational manner that you always do.

There are more things in heaven and on earth, Jack Seward, than are dreamt of in your philosophy.

This is one of them.

To begin, I am not an Englishman. I am an Irishman, born and raised in County Waterford. In my hometown, there is an old story about a stone cairn built beneath a hawthorn tree in the old cemetery. It goes like this:

Once, there was a woman as kind as she was beautiful, though her name has been lost to history. As the daughter of a successful merchant, she came from wealth but treated the lowliest peasant the same as she would have treated a king. To no surprise, she fell in love with a farm boy who was her equal in every way but one: he had no money to his name.

Her father would not let this stand. With the promise of a hefty dowry, he gave his only daughter to the local lord, a cruel and sadistic man who loved the sight of blood against pale skin. Not long after speaking his wedding vows, he locked her in his castle tower, chained her to the walls, and tortured her every day. The surrounding village heard her wails and their hearts broke, but no one dared to stand against the powerful lord. They were all too afraid. Even the poor farm boy, who loved her with his entire being and would have given anything to take her place, could not find the courage to stand up to the lord.

And then, one day, she died. Some say she broke her shackles and threw herself from the tower window, while others believed she refused to eat or drink and let herself starve. They all agreed, though, that it was done by her own hand. The burial tradition for deaths by suicide required the corpses to lie upside down so they could not rise from the grave as vampires. But the town, wracked with guilt over their failure to act, buried her in the normal fashion. They couldn't fathom the possibility of the kind girl becoming an undead monster.

Yet on the one-year anniversary of her death, she climbed out of her grave and staggered to the home of her father, still dressed in her muddy funeral garb. Her father lived alone among his riches and finery, sleeping on a bed as soft as a cloud after condemning his own daughter to a cold coffin. She stood in the doorway to his chambers, watching the rise and fall of his chest and listening to the pump of blood in his veins.

"Father," she croaked.

He jerked awake. "Who's there?"

"Don't you remember me? You sold me to a cruel man without a second thought and then buried me with less emotion than you would a slaughtered sheep."

"No, it can't be," he cried.

And she attacked. At first, she only wanted to kill him, but the moment his skin tore, releasing precious blood, a powerful thirst overtook her; she drank deeply of her dying father, the strength of his blood coursing through her veins, sharpening her senses and fueling her righteous fury.

And yet, still, she hungered.

She ran to her husband's castle as swift and furious as a pack of wolves. When she climbed to the top of the tower, she found the lord in bed with the poor woman he'd married before his first wife's body was even cold in the earth. She ripped him apart to appease the starving wolf within her, drinking his blood like it was the finest wine known to man.

I do not know what happened to the other woman, but I like to think that our girl let her flee the horrors she had suffered.

But our sweet, kindhearted girl wasn't done. She now had a different name: the Dearg Due, the red blood sucker. Every night, she wandered the streets of the town that had failed her, seducing the men to drain them of their blood. Only the kind farm boy did not live in fear of her, so he agreed to act as bait in the hopes of permanently laying his poor lover to rest.

That night, he wandered the road near the graveyard, calling her name. He was just about to give up when a familiar silhouette emerged from the shadows.

Returning from the dead had made his true love even more beautiful than before. Voluptuous lips of ruby red, eyes bluer than the sky, and auburn hair a blazing sunset that cascaded over her shoulders in waves. She smiled at him and said, "My love, I've been looking everywhere for you."

Seeing her alive broke something within him, his grief nearly causing him to lose his nerve. But he knew that the girl he fell in love with would never want to lead this cursed half-life as a monster.

"I've missed you," he said sincerely. They embraced, her teeth on his throat. In her distraction, he reached into his coat for a stake carved from a hawthorn branch; he plunged the weapon into her back deep enough to pierce his own flesh. He then fell on it, killing them both.

Or so everyone thought.

They reburied the Dearg Due, this time with a stone cairn to keep her from rising again, but one night, a storm knocked it down. She freed herself and fed upon the village's men until they trapped her in her grave once more.

As a boy growing up in Waterford, I was intimately familiar with this legend. I was a rather sickly child and remained bedridden with a mysterious illness until the age of six. At that time, my sole entertainment came from books and the local stories my nursemaid told me.

When I recovered, I was still far weaker than other boys my age. Their mockery was relentless. It didn't help that I was more effeminate than my peers, preferring fashion to football. It all made for a miserable childhood, and I was more than eager to escape to London for a college education. There, I discovered a love of the theatre. Between acting roles, I found a way to make a living for myself by working on my own plays. And as a confirmed bachelor wedded to my job and not a woman, my life was just as I liked it.

Every few years, I made the journey home to visit my parents. I never stayed for long. Although I loved my mother and father, the town was unbearable. The same childhood bullies accosted me on the street, reminding me that I was nothing but a weak, helpless boy.

In my fortieth year, however, everything changed. The neighbors found my father on the side of the road, dead from an apparent heart attack. I received word of his sudden passing and returned home to care for my mother while I settled my father's affairs. It was a somber task, one serious enough that even the cruelest of childhood bullies gave me the space and compassion I needed.

Apparently, my father wasn't the only man to have died recently. Before him, the town drunk and a merchant both died on the same road, which incited whispers among the townsfolk that the Dearg Due had returned again to prey on hapless men at night.

Being the rational yet foolish man that I was, I ignored those whispered warnings; after a long day of inventorying my father's belongings, I decided to drown my sorrows in a pint at the nearby tavern. I'll spare you the details of my drinking the pint, listening to the local gossip, and spying the tormentors of my youth looking in my direction while whispering amongst themselves. I drank and I let myself pretend I sat in a London pub, enjoying a break between stage performances.

After a couple of hours, I'd had enough ale and unsteadily made my way back home to my certainly disapproving mother. As I walked, I heard a commotion on the road ahead. A group of four young hooligans were accosting a woman traveling alone. She was dressed all in black with a veil covering her face. Someone in deep mourning, much like myself.

I must confess that I am somewhat of a coward. I've never been strong nor fast, and I have long since learned I would lose any fight I got into. But that night, the alcohol had lowered my inhibitions and a sense of chivalry I'd long ignored inspired me to assist this lady.

"Oi!" I shouted, letting my old accent slip in, casting aside the Londoner's accent I'd adopted to better fit in with high society. "Leave her alone."

The men turned towards me. I recognized some of them as the children of my boyhood tormentors, the rotten apples not falling far from the blighted tree. The woman stood behind them, her expression unreadable beneath the black veil. My heart plummeted, but I needed to keep a brave face—if not for me, then to buy her enough time to escape these scoundrels.

"Accosting a woman like this. You lot should be ashamed of yourselves."

"Jimmy, ain't that the dandy your dad talked about?" one of them asked.

"Yeah, that's him," he said. To my dismay, I realized that they were, in fact, approaching me, having forgotten the lady behind them in favor of new prey.

I ran, but I was middle-aged and have never had good stamina. The young men descended upon me like lions on a wounded antelope, their fists raining down from all sides as I curled into a protective ball the same way I did as a child. They meant to kill me. Of this, I was certain. A blow to the ribs cracked several of them, and a blow to the head made stars explode behind my eyes.

Yet above the jeers and mockery, I heard something else: high, feminine laughter with an edge of cruelty. This was a hyena's laugh after having stolen the antelope from the lions. The violent onslaught slowed, and I forced my swollen, bruised eyes open to witness something extraordinary.

The woman removed her veil, revealing skin as pale as moonlight and lips redder than blood. She was beautiful in a way I cannot truly describe. A voluptuous angel among mortal men. When she smiled, however, sharp canines protruded from her mouth. And I knew then what she was.

The hooligans, though, did not. Jimmy leered at her, grinning as he said, "I knew you wanted us."

She simply smiled, then beckoned him closer with a finger. He swaggered over to her, leaning in for a kiss while she went for his throat. With a terrible ripping sound, she tore it out, drinking his blood like a child devouring Christmas sweets. Once she'd had her fill, she let him drop limply to the ground, a marionette severed from its strings. She smiled at the rest, Jimmy's blood stark against her pale face.

The young men stared for a moment in stunned silence, and then scattered like the balls in a billiards game. But the woman was a predator built for speed. In a split second, she was upon the man who had called me a dandy, sinking her teeth into the tender flesh of his neck and drinking deeply before moving onto the next one.

An almost supernatural mist had fallen around us, and I heard something impossible: the howl of a wolf. There hadn't been a wild wolf in Ireland for more than a hundred years. The howl came from the lady who was not a lady, but the inhuman creature I now recognized as the dreaded Dearg Due.

The screams of the final two men reached a crescendo and then were silenced. I lay on the road, alone and helpless, my ribs grinding in my chest with every agonizing breath. I was going to die the same as those men, and so prayed she would make it quick.

Silent as death, the hem of a black skirt drifted in front of me. I looked up slowly and met her gaze. She was mesmerizingly beautiful in a way that not even Shakespeare could fully describe. Her beauty did not inspire romantic or lustful desires in me. I craved only to grant her every wish—to be her obedient servant—even if it meant dying by her hands. I worshipped her as one might worship a goddess. Her desires were mine, whatever they may be.

The Dearg Due cocked her head thoughtfully. "You tried to help me. Why?"

I coughed, tasting iron on my tongue. "It was the right thing to do."

Her eyes, which seemed to glow in the pale moonlight, sparkled with amusement. "How chivalrous. My knight in beer-soaked armor." For a moment, she stood back, simply regarding me like a child might stare at a particularly unusual insect. "It is a rare breed of man to risk his life for a woman, let alone a stranger. If there had been more men like you in my life, perhaps my story would have ended differently."

Bringing her pale wrist to her lips, she tore open the skin, letting the blood drip from her arm. "This will not be pleasant, but it will save you. Forgive me."

She pressed the bleeding wound to my lips, bidding me to drink, and drink, I did. Her blood did not taste like the copper and iron of an ordinary human. No—it was ambrosial, like a cool, fine wine on a hot summer day. Though cold to the touch, it burned through me, healing me as miraculously as anything Jesus had ever done. Forgive the blasphemy, but you must understand. I was going to die there, but as I drank, not only did I feel my bones pop back into place and my torn flesh knit itself back together, but I also gained a sharpening of the senses. I smelled the copper scent of fresh blood in the air, the vague odor of decay mixed with perfume oils coming from her dress, and the stench of alcohol on my clothes. Her face, once blurry and obscured by shadows, became clearer than daylight. And, having been a sickly child and a weak adult, I was now flooded with a strength I had never known before. I have spent my fair share of time in opium dens and taking laudanum, but the high I felt as I drank her blood was unlike anything I'd ever experienced before—or since.

When she removed her wrist, I whimpered like a babe not yet ready to be taken from the breast. Her blue eyes glimmered as she ran a hand across my forehead and commanded, "Sleep."

I awoke the next morning feeling stronger than ever. Mother had much to say when I returned filthy and smelling of alcohol, but I weathered her chiding, my mind too focused on the woman from the night before. Were it not for my fading bruises and the reports of four men found exsanguinated nearby, I would have thought it was a dream.

I never saw the Dearg Due again, but not for lack of trying. Every night hence, I wandered the village streets and empty roads with the hopes of finding her. I needed that high. I needed to be with her, to worship her as she deserved. But we never crossed paths again. A week later, the stone cairn—which took some damage during a storm, just as it had long before—was repaired, trapping her once more below the earth. Having settled my father's affairs, I returned to England. But I did not forget my encounter with the Dearg Due.

That was almost twenty years ago. In that time, my fascination with her and others of her kind became something of an obsession. I read all that could be found on the subject of vampires, even attending the occasional lecture at Oxford. I collected tales of an encounter in Styria between a wealthy young girl whose family unwittingly took in a female vampire who subsequently preyed upon her and the rest of the village. I discovered a countess who bathed in the blood of her servants, as well as the tragic account of a young man who failed to warn his sister in time of her fiancé's thirst for blood.

And then there was the great warlord of the Carpathians.

I believe, Doctor, that you have become quite familiar with him. The Master is the source of your woes, though you refuse to acknowledge it. You refuse to see what is right in front of you. You pretend that Miss Lucy's illness has a natural cause, and you refuse to entertain the idea that there is still much you have yet to learn about the universe.

But that is no matter. You will understand soon enough. When the ones you love die and then rise again as something new and far greater than humanity, you will understand the truth of my words, of my philosophy.

That is what you wanted, isn't it?

Power lies within the blood. This is what I have learned in my almost two decades of research. It is the vampire's source of strength; if we truly wish to become something greater than ourselves, it must become *ours* as well.

Much like you, I am something of a scientist, though my methodology is quite different. I have embarked upon a journey that has labelled me by some to be a madman. You must understand how it feels, if only for the briefest of moments, to possess even half the strength and speed of the vampire. It's enough to turn even the most stalwart of Puritans into depraved addicts.

The one thing that holds me back from fully taking on their power is my own conscience. Yes, Doctor, I do have a conscience. Why do you think I have stuck mostly to flies and spiders for my victims? As I said, I am a coward at heart. I have attempted to move on from spiders to rats, birds, and even cats, but I lack the will and fortitude to kill a higher lifeform other than insects. I may evangelize the power of the blood, but every time I attempt to take a life, I am overwhelmed with guilt.

Perhaps, once the Master has granted me immortality, I will gain that strength—out of necessity, if nothing else. For the moment, though, I am content with replenishing my strength through my flies and spiders.

I thought I wouldn't write in this journal again, but someone must know what happened. Perhaps they can grant me some forgiveness.

I've been thinking about the words that the Dearg Due said to me: "If there had been more men like you in my life, perhaps my story would have ended differently." The Master has already turned one of the women you loved, and now he plans to turn dear Madame Mina.

Madame Mina was kind to me. For the first time since I'd been committed to this asylum, I was spoken to as a man instead of a patient, an experiment, or a time bomb. All my life, I've been treated like something strange, an outsider who is not worthy of basic human decency. Even my own parents were eager to be rid of me when I decided to move to London. But not Madame Mina. She has shown me true kindness and does not deserve the fate that the Master has in store for her.

I cannot imagine the way she suffers now at his hands. When I saw her last, she looked so tired and frail, like a stiff wind might knock her over. You must realize by now that she is unwell, and I beg you to protect her. Keep her safe from his cruel machinations.

For a time, I thought—no, I *hoped*—that the Dearg Due had spared me so she might one day share the power I'd glimpsed within her blood, but now I know her intention was much simpler than that. She spared me because I tried to help her. She did not see the weakling, the sniveling coward who everyone else saw, nor did she see the addict craving a fix that might give an iota of the high her blood had given me. She saw the good I could do if I simply put aside my cowardice and the desire for the strength that comes from feeding off others. It was an act of selflessness that had saved me then, and now a selfless act will almost certainly kill me.

Doctor Seward, I will attempt to buy you enough time to save Madame Mina. It is believed that madmen possess an unusual strength. I have insisted for as long as I have known you, Doctor, that I am not mad. But perhaps I have been lying to myself. Perhaps if I embrace the madness, I will find the strength to battle Dracula for her sake…and for yours.

I pray God has mercy on my soul.

THE GHOSTS WE KEEP

MICHAEL A. REED

MOM'S HAUNTING IS the worst of them all. It doesn't last long, but I can never tell when it will begin. My haunted mom is too similar to my actual mom. Except that she is more dangerous. More detailed. Meaner than before, too. And starving.

"I wish you were never born," Mom whispers, her dry mouth pressed to the door crack. "You ruined my life."

My dad holds me in his arms and my older sister cradles her legs beside him. We all cry together in the corner of my bedroom and wait for Mom to come back. We try to understand that it isn't *really* Mom, but the haunt is real. Her resentment, buried somewhere inside her heart, is always waiting to take over. Still, we will all pretend that it's okay when she is better.

"I'm sorry," Mom says. She sticks her fingers beneath the door and searches for us. "I'm okay now. Mommy didn't mean what she said. She doesn't want to hurt you."

It is a predictable lie. She tries to lure us, but we already know her traps because we have paid for them before. Her rage always comes next.

"I hate you!" Mom shouts, right on cue. She bangs against the locked door and shakes the handle. "I'll move away and start a new family who will love me! Ungrateful! Spoiled! Spineless husband! Bastard children!"

Huddled together, we wait for the haunt to end, even though it will always come back.

In the afternoon, we find Mom sleeping on the living room couch, two empty wine glasses on the end table. The bags beneath her eyes are dark and her hair is wet and tangled. Dad covers her with a blanket and kisses her on the cheek.

"Who wants to watch a movie?" he asks, trying to lighten the mood.

He microwaves popcorn, and we pile onto the couch around Mom. Nothing we do will wake her. As children, we would lie on her, sometimes even jump on her, but she would, as she is now, be dead to the world.

We laugh together and make fun of how bad the movie is. Dad swore it was better when he was a kid, and my sister and I can't see how that could possibly be true.

"There were less special effects back then," Dad says. "With computers these days, it's hard to know what is real, right? But back then, you knew what you were looking at. Puppets. Props. Machines. Actors. Actresses. I miss the times when everything made sense."

"You're old," my sister says. She gives Dad a playful shove and he shoves her back. He grabs her foot and tickles her.

"Stop!" she squeals. She kicks him in the chest, and he falls dramatically onto Mom, who grunts but doesn't move.

"Careful," I warn, but Dad keeps flailing and my sister keeps attacking. Red in the face and out of breath, they both end up on the ground.

"Truce," my sister says. Dad takes her by the hands and they synchronously pull each other to their feet, obnoxiously dancing like they're stars of a Lindsey Lohan movie.

"Hungry?" Dad asks. Still stuffed with popcorn, we all agree that the evening calls for some macaroni and cheese.

While Dad cooks dinner, I bring my sister my latest drawings. This time, it's a man dressed as a clown and looking out the window. He holds a laser gun in one hand and an olive branch in the other.

"What do you think?" I ask.

My sister stares at the drawing for a long time, at least pretending she's trying to understand it. She puts her finger on it and looks me in the eye.

"That's art, baby," she says, clearly unsure of what else to say.

"You like it?" I ask.

"Of course," she says. "I like everything you draw. Except for the rat stuff. That just creeps me out."

Dad sets steaming hot bowls of macaroni and cheese on the table. He leaves one for Mom, even though she hates macaroni. Once dinner is served, he goes to Mom and sits behind her. He rubs her back and whispers things I can't hear.

He stands up and looks at his watch, and the mood changes almost instantly. Checking the time is my dad's telltale sign.

"I should be going," Dad says, never making eye contact with us.

"Where?" I ask, but I know the answer will be the same as always.

He puts on his jacket and grabs the keys. "You know, work stuff. I've got to pay the bills."

"What about Mom?" my sister asks.

With his back to us, Dad stops at the front door. There is a moment before he makes his decision where I think he reconsiders his choice, where he battles with his inner demons, desperate to stay, but always loses. Without another word, he leaves for his own haunting.

He won't be back for a few days. A month, if he is haunted really bad. Sometimes we hear him in the neighborhood, calling for the young women to come out of their homes so he can take them away. We don't know if they ever answer or if they even know his ghost lurks in their backyard. That he peeks through their window blinds, waiting for them to undress. Hoping to catch their name.

"When do you think he will come home?" I ask.

My sister shovels macaroni into her mouth and shrugs. "It doesn't matter."

Now that Dad is gone, her usual upbeat attitude dissipates. If he doesn't anchor her, she spirals quickly.

"Will you be here when Mom wakes up?" I need her to say yes.

"Probably not." She licks her spoon clean.

I put my hand on hers. She is already so cold. "Please don't leave me alone."

We share a knowing look. She understands I can't handle Mom by myself. Without Dad, she is the only chance I have if Mom is haunted again. She looks away, the shame in her eyes her only apology.

"You'll want to be haunted one day," she says. She pushes away from the table, leaving her dirty dish, and disappears upstairs.

Foolishly, I wait for her to come down and stay with me. I imagine her laughing about stupid things and telling stories about all the times we almost died. How we fell out of trees. When she was chased by dogs and jumped up on a car's hood. The time she tried to start the dryer with me inside. Those days are gone, though.

I know her haunting starts when she screams.

My chest burns, and I feel a physical weight pin my stomach to my knees. I want to vomit. Sometimes I do. A piece of me, a gust of wind from the bottom of my chest, whips through my ribs and into my throat. I cover my mouth so it can't get out.

"I'm not haunted," I whisper to myself. "I'm not haunted. I'm okay."

When the air pockets choking my insides dissipate and I feel like I can move again, I clear the table. Trying not to cry, I wash the dishes, hoping that when my family comes home, they might stay. I don't want them to be overwhelmed by our life. By me.

In the reflection of last night's dinner plates, I see my sister watching me. Her hair is patchy, her lips chapped, her makeup bleeding down her pimple-pocked cheeks. She claws at her face and clacks her teeth.

"Why am I so ugly?" my sister asks.

"You're beautiful," I say. And she is, but my sister doesn't believe me. I'm not the one she wants to hear it from.

"I'm hideous!" she wails. I wash her away with soap suds.

She appears again in the warbled shine of the fridge. Her skin, thick and creamy like sausage gravy, slides over her bones.

"Won't someone love me?" my sister asks. Her eyes follow me as I put the dishes in the cupboard.

"I love you," I say, trying not to look at her. If I stare, her haunting lasts even longer.

When I open the fridge to put the leftover macaroni away, she disappears. I don't know where she is now, but I can still hear her quiet sobs.

"Who are you talking to?" Mom asks.

The breath in my lungs seizes and my spine stiffens when Mom's head rises above the couch cushions. She doesn't normally wake up this early after a morning haunting.

Confused and hungover, she looks around. "Where is everyone?"

"We just finished dinner," I say. Telling the truth only upsets her.

"Oh." Mom sits up, twirls one of the empty wine glasses, and groans with disappointment. She presses her fingers into her temples and closes her eyes, a migraine already threatening her sanity.

Shielding her face from the bright house lights, Mom wanders into the kitchen and fumbles through the cabinets for a glass. When she fills it with water, she doesn't see my sister crying in the cup. My sister hovers on the surface, her shriveled hands grasping at my mom's lips. Oblivious, Mom gulps my sister down and swallows.

"How are you?" Mom asks, as if she hasn't seen me in a long time. She leans on the countertop and waits for my answer. I watch her every movement. Every micro-expression. The half-hearted smile doesn't betray her intentions, so I walk into the unknown.

"Fine," I say, but not unhappily. "I cleaned the kitchen."

"Thank you, sweet pea." She gives me an awkward side hug. I do my best to hug her back.

We shuffle our feet as we try to think of something else to say. My mom opens her mouth but says nothing. She shakes her head and tries again. Still nothing. I start looking for another dish to clean, a way to use my hands, but there are no good options. I play with my hair instead.

"I think I'll do some laundry," Mom says. She glides away and disappears into the unlit hallway.

My bedroom is the safest place for me. Just as I decide to go there, lock the door, and listen to music, I hear Dad's voice echoing in the yard. Horrified, I rip back the sliding door blinds and search for him, but he isn't there. I go outside and turn in circles as I chase the name he calls.

"Yalina," Dad begs. The woman's name hovers in the air and mingles with the wind. It sounds close, like a secret in my ear, yet still distant, as if it had been spoken long ago and only now reaches me.

"Dad?" I ask. There is no answer. Only the name *Yalina* drifts around me. I feel my dad's longing on the syllables. His torn heart. His twisted desires.

I plug my ears and go inside. Mom is back on the couch, sorting her laundry into piles and humming. I pray she didn't hear Dad calling another woman's name.

"What's the fuss?" Mom asks. She knots socks together and tosses them to the side.

"I thought I heard a noise," I say. It isn't a complete lie.

Mom freezes for a split second. I flinch, instinctively expecting her haunting to begin. Perhaps it already has. She returns to her folding, a low growl caught in her mouth. She clears her throat and lays a dress on the back of the couch.

"Where is your dad?" Some of the hairs on Mom's head lift straight up, electrified by her growing dissatisfaction. She said "your" dad, too. He isn't here for her to destroy. To consume. Whatever hatred she had for him has now transferred to me. Alone with my mother, I am my father's proxy. Only I can be punished for his actions—and someone has to be.

"I haven't seen your husband," I say. My words make Mom chuckle. She is reaching the stage where every answer is the wrong answer. She can twist my words in whatever way makes her feel the angriest. Agreement is wrong. Silence is worse. Weakness makes her hungrier.

I can make it to my room if I run right now. But if I stay, I might be able to stave off the haunting. I take a deep breath.

"I'm here with you," I say.

Mom turns around and measures me with her milky eyes. It seems like she can't decide if she believes my words or if I should suffer for trying to make her love me. I don't move. I want to prove that our family doesn't need to keep our ghosts.

Her eyebrows furrow. Her face thins. Every strand of hair on her head stretches to the ceiling, and her back arches like a feral cat.

"You think I don't love you?" she asks. Her voice is shrill and breaking.

"I didn't say that." I utter my last attempt. She is beyond return, yet I still try to be her daughter.

When I glance at the stairwell, she hovers off the couch and swipes her laundry piles to the floor. She reaches for me, but I'm already gone. I scurry up the stairs. Behind me, Mom crawls the steps on all fours, her limbs using both floor and wall like a hungry wolf spider.

I somersault into my bedroom and slam the door shut. I'm quick to lock it, then I slide backwards until my shoulder blades meet the corner of the room.

"Let me in," Mom hisses. She presses her face to the carpet and looks up at me through her skull. Her eyes, entirely white, roll from side to side as she scans for weaknesses.

I stay silent. There is nothing I can say to appease her while she is haunted. She will make my words her weapon and hurt me with them; if I open that door, I don't know what will happen.

"You were an accident, you know." Mom's tongue slips along the bottom of the doorframe. She pants and moans. "I didn't want you. But your dad made me keep you."

In the sliding closet door that doubles as a mirror, my sister sits cross-legged, plucking the hairs from her eyebrows. She has been waiting for me to see her.

"I'm so ugly," she says. Her mouth melts and her jaw hangs to the side. "Why do you get to be beautiful? It isn't fair that everyone loves you." She cries to herself as she tries to pull off her face.

Alone in the dark, I try to remember that their hauntings will end, eventually.

Dad will come home like he always does, and he will reek of cheap perfume. He will give us stuffed animals even though we are too old for that because he doesn't know how else to make us forget he disappeared.

My sister will climb out of the mirror and try to live her normal life. The kids at school will idolize her and date her and ask her to prom. She will say yes to everyone and everything, but she doesn't get to keep any of it because the pit has no bottom. And I'll be the one trying to fill in the hole.

Mom. She will pretend like I'm her favorite daughter. On the good days, we will go out for ice cream and she will show me all of her scrapbooks. She will try to give me her old jewelry and I'll accept her explanations for why they are special and believe all of her other imaginary stories. Most of all, I'll never mention her outbursts or her unprovoked hatred or how she is the worst mom because that makes me a threat to her reality.

An overwhelming gust of hot air rips through my organs. It's in my veins, on my bones, pushing through the pores of my skin. It wants out, but I can make it stay inside. I'm in control of what I am.

"I'm not haunted," I say to myself. "I'm not haunted. I'm not haunted. I'm not haunted."

Yet, this time, I can't make myself stay. It doesn't matter how badly I want to be okay. I can't resist the urge to escape myself. And nobody is there to stop me.

I let the wind break free from my lips. A new and worse version of me floats above my body and lingers by the ceiling of my bedroom. I can see and hear everything, but I don't feel any of it. Below, my body is finally at peace. It doesn't even notice Mom's haunting; happy, it puts on headphones and turns up the music. It laughs at video reels and doodles stupid stuff on tracing paper.

At night, once Mom has returned to normal, my body goes to sleep, and it doesn't have bad dreams. I hover over my face and let my body's warm breath lift me to a better place.

In the morning, everyone is home. My mom cooks breakfast while Dad reads the newspaper. They touch each other's arms and tell stories of when they met. Dressed in her favorite clothes, my sister scrolls through social media and likes all the comments about how pretty she looks with her new boyfriend.

My body eats cereal and ignores its family. When they try to include it, my body rolls its eyes and turns away. All day, it keeps music pumping in its ears. It has no friends. Its teachers don't like it. Its grades drop further and further.

The only hint that it is sad is its drawings; in its art, it does incredible things. It wears beautiful costumes, accomplishes unfathomable feats. It does all of this with the tip of a pencil. In every rendition of its future—the astronaut, the apocalypse, the hologram—it is completely alone. It never draws another person beside it.

So everything changes.

Nobody cleans the kitchen; the dishes pile up and flies make their homes in the crusted food lining the bowls. The floors are covered in crumbs and wads of hair, the walls are marred with scratch marks, the mirrors are cracked and the fragments make daggers for feet.

Outside, the plants die. The grass yellows and turns to sun-bleached ash. The neighborhood dogs find ways under the fence and they howl at all times of the day. One by one, the roof shingles slip and crash onto the pavement, and the mailbox bursts with unread bills. Opaque and foggy, the house windows become a dare for teenagers who promise they aren't afraid to look inside.

But it is all okay.

Because at night, when its family is possessed and their ghosts rage through the house, my body is content. From the safety of its bedroom, with the blue lights of the computer baptizing its eyes, it is an impenetrable mound of flesh. A corporeal fortress. Eventually, after a thousand hauntings, it hardly remembers it has a family.

I'm better like this: a few hundred feet above it all, drifting closer and closer to the dark sky. Unwilling to come home, I forfeit my body and remain a ghost forever.

THE ISSUE WITH MOULD

J. E. NORWOOD

Cora's arms strained from an hour of scrubbing bathroom grout. That dreaded time of year was approaching: the cold, unrelentingly wet season, when things started growing in your living spaces against your consent.

In most places, you could keep it under control if you were diligent. But this year, Cora was worried. She had moved into a new apartment at the end of summer, and even back then, with the dry weather, there had been warning signs. She'd found traces of mould, and the windows wept with condensation long before she had even walked through the door. The air had felt *moist*.

The landlord said that the apartment had been refurbished just before she moved in. Cora doubted it.

Starting in October, things had rapidly deteriorated. Come November, every day was a battle of attrition in a war against the mould.

Neither kitchen nor bathroom had extractor fans. Cora knew that should have been a red flag, and she wished she had the luxury of treating it as such. But at her income level, it was standard. This was just the way of things in The City—and maybe the country as a whole. The lack of vents meant that no matter how often Cora opened the windows, she could never quite get rid of the humidity. Nor could she dispel the musty miasma that appeared to be a permanent feature of her flat's microclimate.

The spores were simply ubiquitous. Mould patches emerged in great numbers in the bathroom, revealing the "refurbishment" for what it really was: a quick paint job with a cheap, water-soluble emulsion on already infested walls.

By mid-November, Cora had bleached and spot-cleaned the kitchen walls and bathroom ceiling several times, which resulted in much of the paint leaching.

Cora called her landlord to report the issue.

He picked up with a disinterested, "Hello?"

"Hi, it's Cora." She gave her house number and street.

The silence on the other end of the line somehow sounded annoyed. Cora felt like she was already bothering the landlord.

"Um, the flat's having mould problems," she said. "I've had to bleach the walls and—and the paint's come off."

Still, silence on the other side. Then, in a deadpan voice, "Well, you have to repaint, don't you?"

"What?"

"I'll text you which paint to use. You'll have to pick it up from your nearest DIY store at your own cost."

Cora was stunned. "I'm sorry, perhaps I wasn't clear. The flat had problems before I moved in and—"

"A full inspection was conducted before the start of your rental period. There were no problems then." A brief pause. "Look, everyone gets mould. You just have to deal with it, please."

Click. The landlord hung up.

Cora sighed. *Fine, whatever.* She didn't see the point in arguing. She was studying psychology at one of the universities in The City and was already drowning in coursework—and mould. She didn't fancy adding "adversarial relationship with the landlord" to her problems.

Next day at campus, she chatted to a classmate who had a cheerful, sing-song accent during lunch. He was from Norway and had cute dimples. Cora talked to him about his experiences in The City. Unprompted, he said that the housing standard was laughably poor and in his country, these living conditions wouldn't be considered fit even for animal shelters.

Cora gaped at him. Then she shook her head and rolled her eyes. "You know, I could believe that. Maybe I should visit Norway."

"Maybe you could get refugee status." The young man made a sweeping motion with his hand, as if introducing a news segment. "'Rental Refugee flees from shitty housing market.'"

Cora laughed. "If things are so much better in Norway, why did you come here?"

"Oh, I'm just here for the degree. As soon as I'm done, I'm out of here."

There was something disheartening about hearing that. Black, bitter envy expanded upwards, filling Cora's chest. He could come here to her country on a temporary basis, endure the worst of The City—almost as a brief stint of poverty safari—and then go back home. But to Cora, this was life.

By December, the mould situation got pretty hairy. Cora opened the kitchen window to let steam out whenever she cooked, and the bathroom window was *always* left open a crack. If she closed it even for a moment, the glass pane immediately ran with condensation as if every water molecule was driven to cling to surfaces with the explicit intention of creating a damp habitat for invasive growth.

The window routine did little to prevent the mould, as much as it just slightly slowed its onslaught; as a side effect, much of the central heating blasted straight into the atmosphere, leaving Cora constantly freezing. She'd regularly wear two pairs of socks, slippers, leggings under jeans, and three jumpers, and would still need to huddle under blankets.

Despite it all, the mould progressed. It grew in the cracks around the windows, expanded across the walls, and conquered the ceiling. It was like watching the continents of a slimy world map take form, inch by inch.

Cora finally decided she had to call the landlord again. This time, he came over, perfectly polite, and asked if she was new to The City.

"I grew up in a different town."

"Mould is just something you have to contend with here," he said. "The most important thing is to keep a warm, even temperature to avoid letting the humidity condense on the walls."

"I'm aware of that," Cora said. "But since there aren't any extractor fans, I've got to open the windows frequently. That makes it hard to keep the flat heated."

"Well, you just do your best," the landlord said. He recommended that Cora keep bleaching and buy a dehumidifier.

Cora bought a dehumidifier. She left it on most of the time, which meant it had to be drained three times a day.

After two weeks of use, the air was as humid as ever, and the mould still worsened.

Cora realised she had to stand her ground. She complained to the landlord a third time. She insisted that there must be something structurally wrong with the apartment, since no matter what combination of heating and airflow she tried, it was always damp, and it had been unusually humid even when unoccupied. The landlord sighed but agreed to send over a ventilation expert.

The ventilation expert came over with the landlord two days later. They seemed suspiciously buddy-buddy with each other. The ventilation man walked around the apartment with his dusty boots on, checking the temperature and brandishing a handheld hygrometer.

After checking the hallway, he went into the tiny study Cora never used, stood on a chair, and peered into the corner cupboard.

"Hmm," he muttered, "there's—" He suddenly brought his hand to his face as if struck by a wave of dizziness, then looked away from the cupboard.

"What's wrong?" the landlord asked.

"Just stood up too fast. There's nothing in here. Let's continue."

The last place they inspected was the kitchen.

"Do you do a lot of cooking?" the ventilation expert asked.

Cora was taken aback by the odd question. "Um, er, I guess? Once or twice a day?"

The ventilation expert shook his head gravely. "There's your problem. Cooking creates steam, and when the steam cools, it condensates on surfaces. Then you get mould. Between you and me, you see this problem with a lot of Asian families. They're just cooking *all* the time."

That was his conclusion, with the odd racial remark as frosting on the rotten cake. The ventilation man and the landlord left after having produced their brilliant verdict.

Guess there's no steam if you just starve yourself, Cora mused as she slumped on her bed.

She stared at a fresh patch of mould that had appeared on the bedroom ceiling. It had the contours of a grinning face.

Cora's boyfriend Marcus had stopped coming over to her apartment. In need of some emotional support, she texted him the day after the ventilation debacle and asked to see him.

He was slow to respond, but finally replied, "OK." Then quickly added, "My place."

Her visit turned out to be very brief. After some awkward pleasantries over a cup of coffee, and him subtly withdrawing from her touch, Marcus gave the news.

"Cora, look, I can't keep seeing you. Not right now, anyway."

She was surprised, maybe shocked. The declaration hurt, but because she was already swimming in shit, it didn't cut so deep. Or maybe she just didn't notice it.

"Nice of you not to wait 'til Christmas Eve, at least. But why? What happened?" She hesitated. "Did you meet someone else?"

"No, nothing like that." He looked apologetic. "You just smell like *mould*, Cora. All the time. Even when you've had a shower, washed your clothes. It's just always there. And you're bringing it over to my place, too. The scent sort of lingers in the air and in my bed sheets even after you've gone. It's horrible."

"Well, thanks for the honesty, I guess." Cora shook her head in disbelief at her situation, then laughed. It was almost too ridiculous to be happening. "But hey, you know, I understand. Poor you, your nose and your bedding." The sardonic tone was a bit unfair and not exactly great communication, but she was so over the damn mould issue.

Marcus looked uncomfortable. "Maybe, um, if you moved out, it wouldn't be a problem anymore..."

As if she hadn't looked for other places. As if the flat she'd ended up with wasn't a last resort; small and scroungy, nestled into a crummy tenement in a socially deprived postcode on the fringes of The City. All those *superlatives* were the only reasons it was within budget. It was cheapish. At least compared to the slightly more humane alternatives that, in all but writing, demanded a supplementary income from a monthly organ harvest regiment, or a moderately successful venture selling digital iterations of her flesh to lonely men.

"Yeah, sure, maybe see you in a few years, then," Cora retorted. "I'm stuck here until I finish my degree."

As she rose to walk out, Marcus didn't say anything to contradict her. And he certainly didn't offer for her to stay at his place.

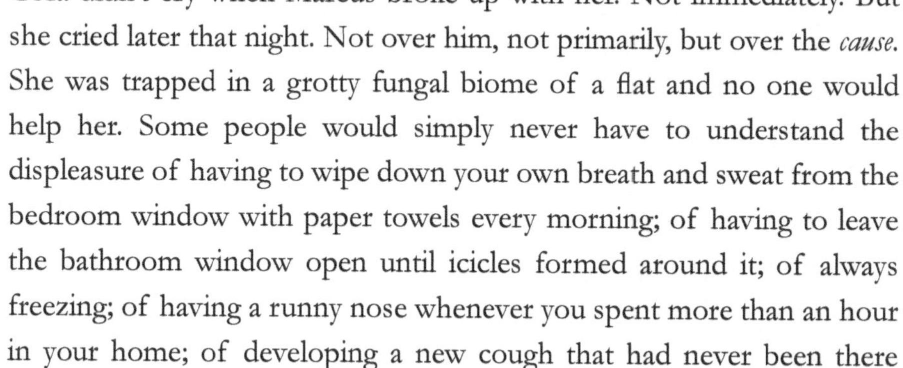

Cora didn't cry when Marcus broke up with her. Not immediately. But she cried later that night. Not over him, not primarily, but over the *cause*. She was trapped in a grotty fungal biome of a flat and no one would help her. Some people would simply never have to understand the displeasure of having to wipe down your own breath and sweat from the bedroom window with paper towels every morning; of having to leave the bathroom window open until icicles formed around it; of always freezing; of having a runny nose whenever you spent more than an hour in your home; of developing a new cough that had never been there before; of scratching your legs and thighs until they bled, because guess what, you have eczema now.

Some people would never understand the existential humiliation of constantly *smelling*.

Maybe the Norwegian guy had been right: she was starting to feel like less than an animal. Worse, more and more of the patches were beginning to vaguely resemble faces.

That night, Cora's dreams were dark, moist and oppressive. She ran through a maze as its walls closed in on her. The maze was alive, infinitely propagating through millions of fruiting bodies. It meant to suffocate her, squash her and incubate in the detritus of her body.

"Find the locus," a cold, warbling voice spoke from above her, behind her, and within her.

The hairs on Cora's neck stood on end. Dread grew in her throat, choking her.

"They are coming," the voice warned. *"They are coming to eat your mind."*

She ran faster to get away from the voice, but she kept tripping over every other step. Her legs refused to obey her. The walls of the labyrinth pressed up on her skin. They consisted entirely of living, writhing moulds.

Cora screamed. She couldn't move. The slimy walls trapped her like a hydraulic press. Her organs would be squashed and squeezed out of her orifices. The mould crawled towards her mouth, touched her lips.

Cora woke up, saw the grinning face on her ceiling, and vomited in her bed.

She skipped class that morning and spent all day in a cleaning mania. She washed her bedding at 90 degrees Celsius; showered under scalding water; scrubbed her skin until she bled; and made the rounds with bleach until the fumes stung her eyes.

The mould had spread even further just overnight, intent on withering down her faith in The City, in humanity, and in her own sanity. It claimed the contours of every room, coalescing into a single slick, amorphous body. When she lifted a loose bit of carpet, she even found a giant patch of pale mildew underneath. In horror, she dropped the carpet flap. As it slapped the floor, a cloud of spores suffused the air, and Cora breathed in a throatful.

"Please, God," she said between coughing and retching, holding back tears. Her legs were sore and itchy from the eczema. It got worse when her stress flared up. "There has to be a cause. There has to be a source."

A source.

A locus.

Her dream had evaporated from her mind, but now, chilled with despair, the memory of it condensed back into the crevices of her brain (dark, moist crevices that made for perfect growing conditions, an intrusive thought told her). It had only been a nightmare, but maybe her subconscious was giving her a sign. Was there such a thing as a Master Organism, a source of the original infestation, something she could kill to get the issue under control?

She recalled how the ventilation man had reacted somewhat oddly when he looked into that cupboard in the cramped study. It occurred to Cora that she'd neglected that cupboard since moving in. In fact, she couldn't remember ever opening it, which seemed strange.

She went to the study to investigate. Nothing immediately appeared out of the ordinary about the cupboard, but it was quite tall, with a shelf out of sight, close to the ceiling. She pulled out the chair the ventilation man had used and stood on it.

Up on the shelf was an *enormous* patch of black mould she could describe only as hairy, extending its tendrils (was mould supposed to have tendrils?) like feelers. She felt a sudden wave of confusion and wobbled on the chair, nearly falling. When she looked away, the confusion passed, but her mind blanked. What had she been looking at?

She noted that the paint on the ceiling was bubbling, distended. She poked one of the bubbles with her finger. The paint burst and rained down onto the floor in flakes, along with a dusting of ashy spores, some of which got into Cora's eyes.

She cried out and desperately blinked and wiped away the spore dust before it turned into a goop.

She traced the distorted ceiling back into the cupboard and at once remembered the black mould inside. Peering over the edge again, she spotted the mass in its corner: shuddering, alive. Directing her gaze to it once again triggered confusion and dizziness, as though the unnatural organism protected itself with a hypnotic trigger. Maybe it released some psychotropic compound. Cora tapped the side of her head and forced herself to focus.

With horrifying clarity, she understood now that this mould, darker than the depths of the universe, extended from the cupboard and existed everywhere in the flat, concealed *beneath* the paint. That didn't make sense. The other mould grew in plain sight, but this horrid black stuff… it was almost as if it sent out hidden threads from which all other visible growth emanated.

"Fuck this in every fuckable way," Cora said.

She climbed down from the chair, slammed the cupboard shut and went to get her phone. She couldn't afford to move out, and she equally couldn't end up homeless. That would be a death sentence for both her degree and all hope of some kind of liveable future. If she'd been closer to her parents, she might've been able to ask them for help. But she knew from experience that they didn't like to dole out charity. Asking them was more likely to reap Cora the grand total reward of their disappointment than anything else.

And despite that, she wanted to prove herself. Prove that she could get by in this world on her own merits, with her own slimy (what?) brain.

So, she had to get this fixed before she became seriously ill. She had to destroy the thing in the cupboard.

She was sweaty, panicked and not thinking straight anymore. Probably hadn't been for weeks. The situation made her lose sleep, and she didn't quite trust what she saw, nor that her judgements were rational. But she had enough composure to bypass the landlord and go directly to a private mould treatment company.

She made the phone call, and a man came over the next day. By that point, mould covered a greater area of the flat than the area that remained untouched.

The man walked into the flat, coughed, and put on a facemask. He looked around for a bit, then turned to Cora and shrugged. "Not seeing anything out of the ordinary, miss. It's just that time of year. Have you tried bleach?"

Before he left, he gave her a bill that would compromise her food spending for weeks.

Cora cried and slammed her fist against the living room wall. Spores rained down on the floor from the impact, got in her hair and on her arms. In a desperate rage, Cora got the hoover out and vacuumed every last speck, knowing it was useless. When she emptied the dust container in the bin, some of the spores came puffing up again, floating into her face.

She cackled like a threatened hyena.

After regaining some sanity, she walked into the bedroom and glowered at the main ceiling patch, at the almost lifelike depiction of a grinning face.

"Happy now, are you?" Cora spat. "No one's going to help me. You're winning."

For a second, she thought the patch twitched, as if attempting to make an expression. Maybe to say something.

"Fuck you," Cora said.

The mould got inside her, turned her organs to a slimy mush. Her eyes morphed into puffballs and her tongue grew fuzzy. Something shifted, pushed its ooze up her throat all the way from her lungs to make her choke. She couldn't get any air. She panicked and—

Flailed herself awake into an upright position.

The bedroom had turned oppressively black. Her bed was now the final outpost, an island in a universe of mould. It covered everything, made a second fuzzy carpet over the actual carpet. The paint on the walls had completely dissolved, and the especially hairy stuff from the cupboard claimed every square inch of wall and ceiling.

Cora shrieked, foolishly taking in a sharp breath, which made her inhale stale air pungent with spores. She could actually *feel* them stick to her mucous membranes. They tickled the inside of her nose. When she sneezed, her snot came out black.

"Oh God, oh God, oh fuck," she groaned.

Every neuron firing in her brain ordered her to stay put. To play dead. But that wouldn't work against such a ubiquitous, unconscious predator that would happily devour her rotting corpse.

She would have to get out of bed, cross the sludgy, powdering floors and leave the apartment. It was clear now: no matter how disruptive homelessness would be to her future, she had to get out of this decaying hellscape before the infestation killed her. This was *not* normal, no matter what landlords and so-called experts claimed. And she couldn't beat it.

Cora's slippers were nestled into the covers by the foot of the bed. She put them on and tentatively set a foot down on the carpet of mould. Every step sent a puff of revolting, smoky spores into the air. She grimaced.

The bedroom door was a black, slimy rectangle. Thankfully, she'd left it open, so she was able to slip outside without touching it. She found a cleaning glove in the kitchen, still yellow, but as she stuck her hand inside, it sank into a viscous liquid.

"Eww!" Cora yelled, a noise that devolved into sobs. "Why is this happening to me?"

Hang on.

Was it really happening to her? Hadn't she heard somewhere in a neurochemistry module that toxic moulds could induce hallucinations? She had breathed noxious fumes for months now—maybe, just maybe, all of this was an illusion caused by that monstrosity in the cupboard. It explained why everyone kept undermining her problem. The idea to Cora was a lifeboat on a stormy sea.

Then she noticed something. It was 10 a.m., but outside looked much darker than usual at this time of day.

Help me Christ, the windows are overgrown.

Scant light came through the shade of murky charcoal, filtered by the black mould. Cora tried to open the kitchen window—and couldn't. The mould didn't behave normally; it acted like a thick web, squishy but highly tensile, sealing the window shut. No matter how hard she pulled, it wouldn't budge.

Panic rose and splashed her throat with acid. She raced into the hallway, all the while reiterating to herself that none of this was real. She was simply buckling under the pressures of life. A perfect candidate for having her reality shatter.

But the front door was overgrown, too. The black webs of decay had swallowed it whole, leaving not a single trace of its surface. Pushing her hand into the thick, hairy goo, Cora could somewhat delineate the shape of the door handle.

But it wouldn't turn.

Trapped, just like in her dream.

For a split second, laughter bubbled up inside Cora, but terror drowned it before it could erupt from her throat.

Her tongue felt fuzzy now, even in waking life. Was the stuff actually growing in her body? With the crushing weight of reality, it dawned on her that if she didn't get out, she was going to die a horrible death and become a slab of wet meat for the spores, ripe for infestation.

The only room she hadn't checked was the bathroom. Cora didn't have any hope of escaping from there, but she went anyway.

The space was a black, hairy grow cube, same as the other rooms, but with one disturbing change. Above the contours of what had once been her toilet, there was a great, gaping hole in the wall.

It was a tunnel.

Cora approached the edges and peered inside: pitch black, with no light source

or end in sight. It stretched on and on in a way that shouldn't have been possible. Wherever the tunnel went, it didn't lead out of the tenement building.

A sudden guttural groan made her jump. There was an angry, hacking quality to the noise. It had come from the bedroom.

Veins burning with fear, wishing someone—anyone—would help her, Cora reluctantly retraced her steps. There was no one in the bedroom. Obviously. If she couldn't get out, how would anyone get in?

Then she made the mistake of tilting her head upwards.

What had once been a face-shaped patch of mould on the ceiling was now an actual, writhing face, taking on the three-dimensional form of a living skull. It stretched down from the ceiling with a tortured expression, as if it struggled to phase through into her bedroom.

This is a toxic psychosis causing a signal error in my visual and auditory cortexes, Cora instructed herself, but by now she knew that wasn't true.

The deformed humanoid face in the ceiling yelled in agony, tears streaming from its bulging eyes. Then it barfed a black sludge that poured down Cora's wide-open mouth.

Cora spluttered, accidentally swallowing some. She immediately bent over and vomited over her bed until her guts and throat were sore and burning.

Cora was beyond crying, beyond screaming. The utter madness happening all around gave her mind no choice but to calmly accept it. What would a mere scream accomplish in the face of such mycological delirium?

"*Cora.*" A deep, warbling voice resounded from the bathroom, cutting through the insanity. She recognised the voice from her dreams. She didn't know who the speaker was, but every cell in her body instantly knew they weren't even remotely human.

Cora stared at the tortured face on the ceiling. Paralysed by terrors the human mind had not evolved to cope with, she wondered what seemed worse: the face trying to push itself into her bedroom, or whatever it was that had summoned her.

"*You are out of time,*" the voice spoke.

With tears of terror streaming down her face, Cora forced her feet to move. She headed back towards the bathroom to face what awaited her.

Inside stood a figure so tall it had to hunch to not crash into the ceiling. A dark exoskeleton covered its body, with gaps in places revealing muscle and ligament. From its shoulders hung long, leathery flaps, which might once have been its skin—or the skin of another being. A sliding membrane within the headpiece pulled back to show a set of myriad teeth in a fleshy orifice.

The last flickering remnant of hope in Cora's breast died.

"*They are here,*" said the creature from beyond the edges of sanity. When it spoke, its voice came out through both its mouth and the open cavities in its black, chitinous gorget.

Incapable of speech, Cora scanned the bathroom. A dozen shuddering bulges pushed forth from the mat of mould covering both floor and walls. The bulges whined and whimpered. One of them slowly morphed into a seven-fingered hand; others assumed the shapes of tiny, abominable heads.

Cora forced her lips to move. "Why is this happening?"

The tall figure gazed at Cora through eyes like obsidian beads. "*The mycelia here are so concentrated, so deep, that they have connected with the roots of the universe. They have formed a mycorrhiza with the Sunken Plane. This is what has summoned me to this planet of decaying flesh and excrement.*"

The more Cora heard the figure speak, the sicker she grew with dread. The quality of its voice seemed to permeate her every cell, to disturb her molecular cohesion. Yet, she couldn't stop now. She stood on a precipice and had no choice but to stare down into the abyss her life had become. "The Sunken Plane? What—what is that?"

The creature was as silent as her own looming grave.

"If you won't tell me, then why did you come here?" Cora tried instead, her defeated voice brimming with new desperation. "Are you going to kill me?"

The entity nodded its terrible head towards the things emerging from the mould. They now wept discordantly, like so many suffering newborns. Many of them had nearly fully morphed into the room and were reaching for Cora.

"*The connection has also summoned these beings of the Interplane,*" the tall figure spoke. "*They are creatures of thought that use this foul growth to enter physical worlds. Travelling between thought and matter is excruciating, yet their hunger drives them forth.*"

"Hunger?"

"*Yes. They have come to eat your sanity. Once they've finished with your mind, they will move on to your flesh, before returning whence they came.*" There was a pause like a bottomless void as the entity let her consider this.

Cora defiantly looked the being in the eye, although there was no emotion, nothing human, there to recognise. "So you've come to explain to me how I'll die? To—to watch them eat me?"

It didn't answer her question, but said, "*You may traverse the portal to the Sunken Plane.*"

Cora glanced at the dark tunnel. "What will happen to me if I do?"

The figure gave her a long, penetrating glare, as if the question was something only a limited brain could conceive of. *"You will cast off your human skin and be something else when you arrive on the other side. Beyond that… there is never any certainty in this universe. Choose now."*

Cora shuddered, unsure if the comment about the skin was to be taken literally. But given how disgusting she felt, with mould residue all over her and spores on her tongue and in her nostrils—and probably in her lungs and stomach—maybe a deep cleanse wouldn't be so terrible.

Perhaps she was already insane with fear and mycotoxins. Between a horrible death in her mouldy flat—in a city that didn't care and with parents and a boyfriend who wouldn't lift a finger to help her—or this interdimensional vortex to an unfathomable existence, in the company of a dreadful being that obliterated her very comprehension of reality, she would take her chances.

"Goodbye, Mum and Dad. Goodbye, Marcus," she whispered.

The dark being went ahead.

Cora followed.

THE LIGHTKEEPER'S DIARY

MARY SLEBODNIK

December 1, 1873

They took my husband to the sanitarium today. I am told a replacement will be found, but until then, I must keep the lamp of the lighthouse lit. The disorganized nature of my husband's records leaves me in some doubt as to what I am to write, but I will endeavor to model my entries off his earliest writings when he maintained his sanity.

For the past two years, I have been the sole witness to my husband's daily labors, the foremost of which are to light the lamp, clean the lamp, and refill the lamp. I admit it is easier to sequence my tasks in a sensible manner without my husband here. He often told me he had lit the lamp when he had not, or that he had cleaned the lens when I had watched him stand on the lakeshore all afternoon.

Lens cleaned – 8 a.m.

Repairs: loose railing, storeroom door hinge

December 2, 1873

A ship arrived with supplies today. The captain asked how long I expected to remain the lightkeeper. Not long, I told him, for these positions are coveted among working people. That is how my husband came to aim for such an appointment in the first place. If my father had not been a city commissioner in Detroit in addition to being a man of industry, we would not have been so fortunate. That we were totally unsuited to the nature of the work we did not learn until soon after our arrival, at which time I was already expecting, and my husband was unable to pursue another means of sustaining our living.

The captain is a very nice man and does not criticize me or my husband for our errors of judgment, of which he admittedly knows very little, but I often wonder if my expression reveals more to people than I would wish.

I returned the books my husband never finished to the ship's library.

Lens cleaned – 9 a.m.

Supplies: 12 bar. whale oil, 55 wicks, 25 lb. potatoes, 20 lb. onions, 50 lb. flour, dried beef, salt pork, salted beef, linens, beeswax candles, rope, stationery. Nails.

◆———————————◆

December 3, 1873

The inspector made his last visit for the year. Taking advantage of the calm day and vestiges of fall sunshine, he took the ferry to Bottle Island and rowed over to the lighthouse in a dinghy. When he inspected the lighthouse during my husband's tenure, my husband would drink and call him a coward because he "hid in his mother's kitchen" during the war. I took pains to remind Daniel that there were many who did not serve in the war and had good reasons for it.

My own father did not have good reasons. He spent the war years in the offices of his shoe factory, hiding amongst the ink bottles and ledgers.

The inspector has allowed me to continue working in my husband's name. Thus, I will retain my husband's rate of pay and avoid a penalty due to my sex.

Repairs: floorboard, fog signal

Oil lamps refilled – lighthouse and residence

Lens cleaned – 8 a.m.

◆———————————◆

December 4, 1873

Perhaps it is the Lord's wish that I should have some fellow-feeling for my husband in his ruined state. When one spends the night alternately ascending to a piercing light and descending to a hollowed darkness, the mind loosens. Thoughts unravel as yarn for a half-finished blanket. As the only bulwark between my husband and his detachment from our shared perception of the earth, I shored up all my strength to anchor him to sanity. Now that I am alone, I am somewhat depleted. Instead of sleeping between trips to take oil up the stairs, I relive past moments of my life—experiencing the same strong emotions and agony that I thought had subsided forever. I now understand why Daniel kept books close at hand while he was still able to read them. It occurs to me there is no bulwark between me and madness, but I have always been able to face this life and its disappointments. I can face them again. They are only memories.

Lens cleaned – 8:30 a.m.

December 5, 1873

I find it difficult to sleep in the early hours of the morning, between the midnight and four a.m. tending of the oil. These hours of the day seem to stretch far beyond their natural length.

It reminds me of tending to a newborn—the number of times I ascend those stairs each night—except the lamp does not smile at me once it is fed.

Lens cleaned – 8:30 a.m.

December 6, 1873

The lens watches me like an eye. Perhaps it only seems that way in the middle of the night. I never knew how ghastly it was to stand on the gangplank alone.

Lens cleaned – 2 p.m.

Overcoat mended

December 7, 1873

One of the worst storms I have witnessed. I went down to the beach and searched the horizon for ships in trouble. I saw nothing except a flicker of light in the distance. I was certain it was a flare at first but am putting it down to a reflection of the lamp in the water.

Lens cleaned – noon

December 8, 1873

Why does one have children? We do, such as it is, in spite of the great difficulties it entails for all and with some question of reward. Not for those such as me, but for those such as my father and my husband. It is a wonder that men seek to have children at all. And one wonders if men, in reality, have the children at all, as the women grow them in the womb, and then birth rends their very seams to bring forth the screaming babe. Of emotion in Daniel in the entirety of Isabel's six months of life, I saw no flicker, before or after.

Lens cleaned – 1 p.m.

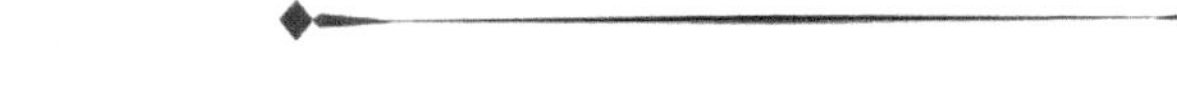

December 9, 1873

Rained steadily today. Bitter cold. Saw one ship during the day, none by night. When the lake freezes, no one will sail at all.

The ship brought mail. A letter from my husband. I am unsure as to why the sanitarium sent it. I caught the attention of a man onboard just in time to take a note to the postmaster. I have asked the post office to return all such letters.

Lens cleaned – 10 a.m.

December 10, 1873

Had difficulty ridding the lens of smudges and cloudiness. The light must be bright enough to pierce the night and fog, particularly as winter deepens. Applied more mercury to put it right.

Newly clear and bright, the lamp created an even stronger reflection that sometimes flashes on the surface of the water. It is as if the lighthouse is answering something from the deep.

Lens cleaned – 8 a.m.

Lens cleaned – noon

December 11, 1873

Have been taking laudanum to sleep. I keep it locked in the bedside table drawer, because I feel that it hastened the departure of Daniel's senses. Yet I am sure I will lose mine if I do not sleep. When I close my eyes, I see the lamp and the answering flashes from the surface of the lake. I dwell upon it with undisciplined thoughts—which give way to undisciplined fancies and upsetting dreams that cause me to wake before I have felt any refreshment of my senses.

The laudanum releases me into a blank darkness, but it may be affecting my memory. This morning, I woke up with shoes on my feet. When I took them off, rocks fell out.

Lens cleaned – 10 a.m.

Lens cleaned – 7 p.m.

December 12, 1873

It is difficult to make myself rise to tend to the lamp. Only when I imagine sailors drowning do I go.

I awoke to wet shoes and a muddy nightgown this morning. I will lock the door before bed tonight. I seem to be wandering.

Lens cleaned – noon

Lens cleaned – 4 p.m.

December 15, 1873

The supply ship returned today for the last time this winter. The captain invited me to dinner. I accepted and enjoyed the meal less for its quality and more for its having been prepared with care by someone else. He seemed to have little appetite and finished his meal long before I did. As I ate the last of my buttered peas, he slid a letter with badly stained and wrinkled pages out of the inside pocket of his coat. He carefully laid the pages out on the table, and I recognized the barely legible scrawl that my husband's handwriting had become.

I immediately stood, and he mistook my haste to leave for indignation.

He said, "Missus, please, I never would have read it if it weren't for my clumsiness. The postmaster came aboard and gave it to me to pass on to you. I spilled my tea all over it."

I said that I had read enough of my husband's correspondence from the sanitarium to not wish for anymore.

He apologized, then, for causing me pain. He said that he hoped he could reassure me, if not about the state of my husband's mind, then at least about the horrors my husband seemed intent on describing in such graphic detail.

The captain also served in the Union army. He said, "There were horrors, yes. Horrors that I would never put in a letter to a lady, true or not. But these horrors your husband writes of—these fancies of the mind—they never happened. There is no call to put them in a letter to anyone. I was at Gettysburg and saw my fair share of death. But there was no ritualistic degeneracy. No devouring of flesh."

Lens cleaned 10 a.m.

Lens cleaned 4 p.m.

◆————————————◆

December 17, 1873

I can no longer walk on the gangplank because the icicles have consumed it. They cover everything—long, staggering blades of ice so ample and clustered together that they are like a forest of trees. If no more ships will come, I will not light the lamp. The lake is frozen, and all seems more desolate than before.

Tonight, I must barricade myself in my room. I woke this morning with cuts on my hands. I had broken the lock to my quarters in my sleep.

And yet the trembling of these same hands makes it difficult to write in the log. I am unsure if the trembling is due to cold or if I should decrease my dosage of laudanum.

Lens cleaned – 8 a.m.

Lens cleaned – 4 p.m.

Lens cleaned – 10 p.m.

◆————————————◆

December 18, 1873

I sit at the bottom of the lake, and all is very dark and very cool. I sometimes see light from the eyes of a hidden fish and tell it things. I ache to touch it, but when I reach out, it disappears.

Lens cleaned – 6 a.m.

Lens cleaned – 10 a.m.

Lens cleaned – 7 p.m.

Lens cleaned – midnight

◆———————————————◆

December 19, 1873

An insult written can hurt more than an insult spoken because the words remain to be reread. A spoken insult wounds, but a written insult festers, because the words are not experienced just once, but an infinite number of times for as long as the paper they were written on exists. He wrote this offense with an evil hand that I no longer attribute to a maddened mind…an evil hand that implies the loss of our daughter is somehow less than the loss of a friend in battle. An insult it surely is, for what is a friend in comparison to the flesh of your flesh? And this insult ricochets throughout the room after the letter is returned to the envelope; if it could be resealed, the words would still remain—unspoken but permanently written—in the air and in the mind. This affront to the covenant with his wife and the birth and loss of his daughter shall be overshadowed with his devotion to the loss of a friend, who is, in reality, a stranger. That he must mourn for this stranger and tell *me*—the wife with whom he has a covenant and who birthed his daughter in the early hours of the morning and lost her the same time of day all those months later (the only months that mattered).

Lens cleaned – 2 a.m.

Lens cleaned – 4 a.m.

Lens cleaned – noon

Lens cleaned – 7 p.m.

Lens cleaned – 10 p.m.

◆———————————————◆

December 20, 1873

They always said that birth would be hard. It should not have been a surprise. Why did it feel like one?

They said women deserved this because of Eve, and this is what I once thought true because I was a girl and stupid about the many things they told me. I had dreams, then, more frightening than the bottom of a lake. I remember my own mother's face in candlelight one night, when my shrieks failed to rouse Father and Mother rose to help me (she always did) and she slid into bed with me and her long braid rested on her shoulder and pressed into my back. Our nightgowns flowed into one another, and I stopped crying.

We lived this, and this is what I thought of at the end when I pushed and I tore. I wanted to rise for Isabel at night, and for many months, I did.

◆———————————————————◆

December 21, 1873

Lens cleaned – 1 a.m.

Lens cleaned – 2 a.m.

Lens cleaned – 4 a.m.

Lens cleaned – 4 a.m.

Lens cleaned – 4 a.m.

Lens cleaned – 4 a.m.

◆———————————————————◆

December 22, 1873

The lantern shines brightly. It shines brighter than the moon. Darkness may cover us as water drowns the sailor, but when I tend to the lens…

Sadness clouds my mind.

When I tend to the lens in the way that my husband did not, the light will remain even when the moon disappears.

◆———————————————————◆

December 23, 1873

If I stay by the lens, it will not cry. It will not need cleaning.

I can simply stay by the lens, and I will not have time to dream,

and I can watch the lens to prevent it from becoming dirty and the lens will not need me to clean it

I can stay by the lens

and it will not need to be cleaned.

December 24, 1873

The yellow eye—large

—outer brightness being—

it holds no—no—space for my child. The earth—it turned and there were too many stars already—too many for my child—

this is why and I thanked him. Oh, I thanked him for telling me and I am so grateful—

grateful *now* (certainly not before) to know the reason and no more am I separate from him

(and therefore her)

I am no longer separate, and I know this because the dreams are no longer dreams:

I wake and I am already awake. His metal, shiny and sharp, no longer needs to be clean. His eye is bright enough for all and he draws the one who will absorb our wayward thoughts, our wayward protests against the wrath of nature—

that one he draws forward with his light and this is the one I will join and it is a gift.

December 25, 1874

He waits for me by the shore.

January 1, 1874

I am honored to take charge of the Michigan Point Lighthouse and will do my utmost to acquit myself with the dignity and dedication required of the post. The disorganized nature of my predecessor's records leaves me in some doubt as to what I am to write (the last legible entry is from December 17th), but I will endeavor to record my labors with honest and attentive detail.

The living quarters have been left in disarray, which is to be expected in the case of a fragile mind but less to be expected from a woman's touch; it leaves one impressed at the severity of the state she was in during her tenure. It will take some months to put it right again. It is a shame that the inspector did not row out to check on her sooner, although it is true the weather made it difficult for anyone to make contact. The light was dark for many dangerous nights.

One hopes she will eventually be found.

Lens cleaned – 7 a.m.

YOU'RE REALLY SOMETHING

MICHAEL MULLEN

AT 2 A.M., the only things stirring outside are tarantulas and vinegaroons. My buddy Daniel should have been here hours ago, and I don't know if he'll want beer or coffee when he shows up. One part of me thinks he'll want to throw back a couple cold ones then sleep until noon. The other part thinks he'll want to stay up and talk about whatever led him to my place in the middle of the night, especially under such non-specific circumstances.

Who the hell knows.

All his voicemail said was that he needed to get away. Somewhere quiet, so he could tell me something important.

Weird, but I know better than to call him back and press for more info. In the forty-four years I've known Daniel, he's never once told me more than he wanted me to know. Some stories can take weeks, even months, to completely unspool. And really, I'm fine with that. Even though Daniel's more like a brother than a friend, I still respect boundaries. It wasn't right to force someone to tell me something they might not be ready to share.

Plus, by the time I realized Daniel had left a message, he was probably more than halfway here. Something I keep reminding myself of as I sit on the patio in the threatening calm surrounding me—a sometimes unsettling contradiction only the desert can provide. A sparse, silent place throbbing with a hidden zoo of fangs, needles, stingers, and venom that is always present, always testing you.

Just last year, a scorpion had made its appearance known when I put on my boots to check the pump house. I couldn't get anything out of the tap, so I figured I needed to reset something. But when I'd slipped on my right boot to step outside and investigate, a bright, metallic shock shot up my spine and lit up my brain. Next morning, my foot was so goddamn sensitive, I couldn't touch it or put it on the ground for two days without wincing.

Some of our friends back in California couldn't understand why Claire and I would want to live in such a place. Others understood completely. That nature, especially raw nature, had a way of reconnecting you, of giving you a greater understanding of balance. A daily reminder of how tenuous yet durable life was. So, Claire and I had no regrets. The best years of our lives were spent out there, and we'd often wished we'd made the move sooner.

The first thing that had hit us was the quiet. How the only thing we could hear when we first stepped onto these forty acres was our own breathing. There were no cars, no planes, no birds chirping, no dogs barking, no wind, nothing. That perfect stillness, the cornflower sky, the rust-colored mountains pouring in to the flatlands, all convinced us to build here.

Which is what we did over the course of nearly a year. A small Mexican hacienda with two wings, a kitchen in the middle, and a mirador above the garage so Claire and I could drink wine and watch mule deer crash through the brush under mango-colored sunsets. Something Daniel even experienced with us a couple of times.

But what does he want to tell me? And why's it so important to tell me in person? Whatever it is, he clearly wants to keep the information confidential. But why? What is it? A hit-and-run? Another health scare? Some horrible legal issue?

What?

I walk up to the mirador and have a smoke. Try to stop playing what-if by gazing over the expanse of dark chaparral that ends at the illuminated border road four miles away, where an endless string of evenly spaced streetlights separate Arizona from Mexico, winking like sugar crystals across a sea of brush gone black under a moonless sky.

I take a drag and hope for the best, knowing that whatever Daniel's got to say, I'll help if I can. Would try to be more than just a sounding board. Plus, I need the company. The silence of the desert is beginning to compound the emptiness that's already spread like a mold inside of me. Having Daniel here will help. Because I want to talk to him, too.

About Claire.

In less than seven hours, it'll be a year to the day since Claire passed, though I still can't fully come to terms with it—or forget how she always stood at the sink with her left foot perpendicular to her right (the only time she ever stood like that). Or the wet, fleshy way she smacked her lips when she turned in her sleep. The rose-scented lotion that always clung to her. How her laughter was as soft and musical as rainwater. Everything.

Then again, I had wanted to stay for those very reasons. So I could remember my wife in the place we loved and how lucky I was to have experienced it with her. Just the two of us, surrounded by nature, for what we hoped would be at least fifteen more good years. That was the thought, anyway. The proverbial hope and dream.

But it's now 2:43 a.m. and I need to get to dreaming myself. Or at least try to. It's been more than three hours past the point when Daniel should have shown up, and I can't stay awake forever. So I call, whether he likes it or not, to make sure he's okay and still coming. All I get is a pre-recorded, robotic voice telling me the number I'm trying to reach is no longer in service. Even my texts bounce back.

So where the hell had he called from a few hours ago? And with whose phone?

Fucking Daniel.

I walk downstairs, put my phone on the nightstand, and let sleep throttle me.

Claire said I never had dreams in Arizona because I was now living the dream. Cornball, but true. Retirement, land, nature, stability, and real, honest-to-God togetherness gave us a tranquility that was elusive before. Like others our age, the decades we'd given to our jobs far exceeded the decades we had in front of us, so we wanted to give the remaining ten or twenty years we had to each other. To reconnect and feel more whole.

It didn't take long. On our very first morning, a roadrunner stopped within ten feet of us while we sat on the patio, half-awake with our coffees, grinning dumbly into Mexico. It darted out of nowhere, cocked its head, raised its crest, and kept its eyes locked on us. And not just for a few seconds, either. It took its time sizing us up with pale yellow eyes—making a hop here, a hop there, raising its long tail feathers, jerking its head this way and that while never averting its gaze—before streaking off like a comet.

After that, Claire was even more thrilled to be here. We both were.

Not surprisingly, birding became somewhat of an obsession. We bought field guides, camping chairs, binoculars, hats, and a camera with a long enough lens to capture what we could. We even grabbed a few journals so we could print our best shots and keep records of our sightings.

Soon enough, it became clear that dove, quail, roadrunners, cardinals, wrens, sparrows, hawks, and hummingbirds were almost always present. Even golden eagles were common. What wasn't common was the number and variety of new species that exploded after the monsoon season passed in July. Exotic Mexican and Central American varieties that arrived in literal droves, riding currents of wet winds directly into the newly plumped foliage, their bright bodies dropping like pieces of hard candy into the green.

Elegant Trogons were Claire's favorites. Dove-sized birds with black heads, orange-rimmed eyes, yellow beaks, metallic green backs, gray wings, and rose-red bellies. It was hard to believe they were real. Claire and I frequently sat in the brush to photograph them after the worst of the rains had passed. In fact, I was so overwhelmed by their numbers last year that, "Sweet mommy fuck nuts!" popped right out of my mouth. Something I'd heard Daniel say on occasion, but never a retired numbers whore—or insurance broker—like me.

Claire laughed. Said I was really something.

It was August 4th and already 91 degrees at 7:26 a.m. when we stepped out with our gear and made a beeline to the pump house. The scrub was the thickest there; the creosote, manzanita, and ocotillo forming a dense, spiky wall thanks to the whiff of water just feet away. There was only one opening wide enough to squeak through to a small clearing where we could set up our chairs and prepare for the show. Shortly after we did, blood-red Mexican wrens, cobalt-coated blue jays, and those Elegant Trogons flitted in like confetti. Claire said that we'd fill up this year's journal before it was time for the birds to move on.

Two hours passed like ten minutes, the two of us giddy yet beginning to feel the temperature as it flirted with 96 degrees. I turned to Claire to make sure she was okay, which she said she was, patting my knee and smiling, her dimples pushing up the fine spray of freckles that spattered her plump, rosy cheeks.

"Never been better."

I didn't believe her.

After forty-one years of marriage, we could read each other better than most cartographers could read a map. Her smile was too taut, her mint-green eyes too open, and when I called her on it, she reluctantly admitted to having a little bit of indigestion.

"I don't know why," she said. "I don't think it's the heat. Maybe it was the eggs from this morning. I probably just need a Tums."

I went back to the house to grab an antacid, a couple of apples, water bottles, and the polarizing filter for my telephoto lens that I couldn't find earlier. When I finally did locate it, beside the toaster of all places, I walked it and everything else back to Claire, where she remained sitting in her chair, looking straight up at something I couldn't see.

"What do you see up there?" I asked, before also tilting my head skyward. "An eagle? Hawk? All I see is blue. I must be blind as a bat."

No response.

Not even after I called her name. It was only after I took another step that I noticed how weirdly rigid she was, how still, the realization slamming into me like a car coming out of nowhere.

Her eyes were glassy and unfocused. A patch of skin around her neck was as pale as watered-down milk. Spit leaked down her chin. Two bees hovered around her opened mouth.

None of the compressions or breaths I sent into her stopped lungs worked, though I went on for what seemed like an eternity, sweat and tears raining down on her chest, seeming to evaporate almost immediately.

Birds flitted and chirped as I sobbed for God knows how long, knees up to my chest, rocking like a child. I squeezed Claire's cold hand as strings of snot ran over my lips and I shooed away more bees still buzzing around her mouth that I tried closing earlier but couldn't. Other bees were examining whatever moisture was left in her eyes.

I was put on Zoloft shortly after that—50 milligrams a day to start, then all the way up to 100 milligrams when hopelessness grew into something just as raw.

At first, I assumed my mind was playing tricks on me when I caught the unmistakable whiff of Claire's rose-scented lotion while washing a coffee cup. And again, when reading in the den, hearing her laughter coming from the guest room. But when I actually *saw* her walk through that room and turn on the nightstand light, I knew I wasn't just imagining things.

The doctor, of course, dismissed my story, saying my experience was more common than most people think. He explained how profound loss can drive some people to hallucinate, especially after they've been together for as long as Claire and I had. Apparently, my brain was simply trying to re-grow her. He also said that the increased dosage would help.

And it did.

Too well.

Because it removed all traces of Claire. There were no more scents, laughs, or sightings. She simply evaporated, and I couldn't bear it. I needed some semblance of my wife to be present, to prevent me from sinking further into the silence smothering me in her absence. So, I flushed the pills and waited for her to come back. To see and hear her again, maybe even talk to her, in this house we called our home.

My head's killing me when I wake up at 7:26 a.m. and discover Daniel is still nowhere to be found. His truck isn't in the driveway and the guest room is untouched. His only presence rests in a framed photograph on the nightstand, taken by me off the coast of Baja where we went marlin fishing on his sixtieth birthday. He was in a fighting chair, a fishing rod in one hand and a Pacifico in the other, a huge smile breaking through his bushy, gray beard. Typical Daniel. A slinger of wood and nails who never passed up an opportunity to also be a slinger of fish.

I try texting him again—and it bounces back again. I also get the same pre-recorded message when I call.

What in the hell's going on? Or am I simply making something out of nothing?

The paranoid part of me worries he's been in an accident and got himself horribly hurt—or worse. The rational part says he probably just split the trip into two legs, stopping somewhere halfway through before continuing. It's a nine-hour drive from LA, and he'd divided those trips up before, usually by staying in Blythe or Buckeye. Both were more or less halfway points, and their hotels didn't command the prices of rooms in larger towns. I'm not about to start figuring out which one of God-knows-how-many places he had to choose from along the way.

Instead, I convince myself Daniel's just being Daniel. Keeping everything a mystery, including whatever phantom phone he's using, until he's ready to spill the proverbial beans.

My headache's getting worse, so I down a couple more Tylenol and step outside to get some air. The early morning sun is behind me, its slanted glow washing over the cactus and creosote all the way into Mexico, the peaks of the Chiricahuas gleaming blue-brown above slopes swallowed in purple. Other times of the year, those mountains are nothing but dull brown. Or white with snow. Even flushed with green after a hard spring rain. Like Claire always said, the desert tells a different story every time you walk into it. And today, on the anniversary of her death, I have no idea what story it would tell me. I've got to walk to the spot where she died to find out.

First, I cut three Matilija poppy blooms from behind the house. Each pure white flower is at least nine inches across, and I don't want to partially obscure the small cross Daniel had built for me the week after Claire passed. He'd made it out of mesquite so it would weather everything from the scorching heat to the heavy snow that this 5,300-foot elevation brings—a desert with real seasons and far more rock and caliche than sand and saguaros. Daniel and I managed to get a hole in anyway, right near the gravel-strewn spot where everything had happened. Being a half foot taller than me and at least sixty pounds heavier, he did most of the digging.

Ever since high school, Daniel was always there for me. Always thinking of others before thinking of himself. In fact, he regularly introduced me to many of his female friends that he thought I'd get along with, even when he wasn't in a relationship himself. Or when he was experiencing the loneliness and derision that sometimes arose from the type of relationship he was seeking. The Seventies were unfortunately less tolerant toward gays that way.

Naturally, the few young women I met through Daniel were smart, lovely individuals and a pleasure to be with. But only one had that special something that synched with and consumed me. Claire. From her intelligence and empathy to her infectious energy and the fine spray of freckles that dusted her blonde-framed face, everything about her was unique. Beautiful. A totality that infused every part of me.

The three of us had been inseparable ever since. We went to football games together, movies together, concerts together, you name it. Even when Claire and I became serious, Daniel still hung out with us, never failing to make the bonds between us stronger.

"The Substantial Burger" is just one example. It was an item he called out when the three of us visited a local sidewalk café for lunch.

"According to the menu, it's a half-pounder," he'd began, "which is bon. James Bon. But the word 'substantial' bothers me. The prefix 'sub-' means below or under, after all. Just like a submarine travels below or under the ocean's surface. But here? With this burger? Etymologically speaking, a 'Substantial Burger' literally means something below or under 'stantial.' This burger should therefore be called 'The Stantial Burger.'"

Daniel was the charmingly weird child that Claire and I were never able to make ourselves. It was impossible not to feel connected to him.

Claire, of course, played a huge role in keeping those connections alive. To care about everything *we* cared about—from Daniel's love of poetry to my tragically unprofessional watercolor hobby and everything in between. Even during the course of an otherwise normal day, Claire was always supportive of us, making us feel something we otherwise wouldn't have. Like the time the three of us were walking the property and Daniel stumbled upon a fossil embedded in a boulder. Claire was the one to put it into perspective and make it meaningful.

The fossil was about the size of a golf ball, its unmistakable roundness and radial spikes clearly those of a sea urchin's. Claire, having worked as an environmental biologist for thirty-six years, not only confirmed it, but added that the area we were standing in was underwater 300 million years ago, even though we were a mile up and 250 miles from the nearest ocean.

"No doubt there's an abundance of other fossils out here," she told us. "Probably even complete dinosaurs."

Daniel was saturated with wonder. A paper towel that couldn't hold any more water.

Claire turned to me, all teeth and dimples, because she knew Daniel was about to say something weird. He was too gobsmacked not to, his brow raised, his dark eyes bigger than quail eggs.

He looked at us both. Looked at the urchin. Looked back at Claire and said reverentially, "Christ kitten. I'm smitten."

Daniel had been saying odd shit like that since high school, though not everyone found favor with it. The jocks and metal heads thought it made him sound gay, which he was, while most others laughed him off as friendly but strange. Claire and I, on the other hand, loved his creativity. His capacity to construct new phrases that made no sense but whose intent was always clear was perpetually entertaining. Which, according to Daniel, was why he'd started doing it in the first place.

"To make the expected more saucy," as he put it. Hence, the Christ kitten or sweet mommy fuck nuts things instead of, "No way" or "Holy shit" or any other phrase that was "used ad nauseam by legions of the unclean." For better or worse, no one expresses himself quite the way Daniel does.

All of it swirls through my throbbing head as I near the location where I'd tried to save Claire. Where, for four years, she suggested birds for me to photograph and I'd pointed to other birds she could zoom in on with her binoculars. Just the two of us, enjoying nature, for what was supposed to be the beginning of our final chapter together.

I take the passageway by the pump house until Claire's cross comes into view, surprised to find it looks as new as the day we'd placed it— as if she'd passed a few months ago instead of a year. Her name and dates retain their hard-defined edges, and the red paint on the delicate ocotillo blossoms that Daniel had carved into the wood still looks wet, as if freshly painted. I make a mental note to ask him what kind of paint or secret woodworker's trick he used once he finally got here.

If he ever got here.

I place the poppies below her cross and tell her I want to see her again. Hear her voice. Smell her skin. Talk to her, if I could. That I missed her laughter and her presence in the guest room and wanted more. That being alone in the house is too damned hard without her.

I blot my eyes and gaze over the chest-high chaparral, wondering how far her ashes traveled on that windy day when Daniel and I spread them. If they'd dissolved into the earth long ago or were still blowing, specks of her bouncing across random thorns or sticking to the fat, flat surfaces of agave leaves. If actual pieces of her were still out there.

I sit down and stare at Claire's cross.

"Is he okay? He should have been here hours ago."

I reach into my shirt pocket for a cigarette and tell Claire that I might be the one who's in trouble instead of Daniel. A widower who's convinced he's seen and heard his dead wife and who will never leave the house if it means never hearing or seeing her again. Problem is, I can't remember how long it's been since that one time I saw her. My brain, thanks to its crushing headache, clearly ain't working right.

I dig into another pocket for my Zippo, but retrieve a pack of matches instead. Strange, since I'm not in the habit of carrying them. But there they are: a full pack with a glossy white cover and a 1970s-style line drawing of an L-shaped, one-story adobe complete with a cheesy, Vegas-style sign proclaiming, "Sunset Motel." The whole thing is printed in red ink, including the phone number at the bottom. On the back, *Exit 11 from I-10 in Picacho, AZ* put them about forty-five minutes northwest of Tucson.

Holy crap.

Daniel told me about that hotel right after Claire and I moved in, said the décor came straight out of 1972. "They even had a red heat lamp in the bathroom," I remember him saying. "Like I was a large order of fries."

But if they're Daniel's matches, how did they get into my pocket? The pack can't have been in there all this time, can it? Maybe I really am losing my mind.

I tell Claire where I think Daniel is and blow her a kiss. Say that I need to get back to the house to call the hotel, find out what's what. I also ask her to please come visit me again. That without her, I don't exist.

Halfway back, my phone pulses. A text message from Daniel:

Hurry up. I'm dyin' over here. 💀 💀 💀

I immediately text back:

What??? Are you here?

The phone buzzes again, informing me Daniel's number isn't in service.

My head hurts too damned much to keep playing this bullshit game. But dammit, how's he sending texts? What kind of phone is he using? Is something wrong with mine?

The pounding in my skull throbs in synch with each footfall on the way back to the house—until something large moves in the brush to my right. The twisted, thorny wall is too thick for me to see into, though the sound of heavy puffs and snapping twigs punches through. Whatever is coming my way is big. I took a few steps back.

My heart hammers in synch with my head when a wide clutch of the heavy brush begins shaking. I take more steps back, just as a giant mule deer crashes through, not ten feet away. A rare ten-pointer, at least 200 pounds. When it sees me, it stops, swiveling its anchor-sized head to get a better look at me, its blank eyes locked dumbly on something it doesn't understand.

Neither of us knows what to do. Instinctively, I raise my hand in a childish attempt to convince the animal I'm nothing to fear. But the deer remains still. Until I say, "Hello, there." Its whole body jerks, as if a thousand volts had suddenly shot through it, darting through the cactus and whitethorn on the other side of the road.

I gulp a glass of water when I get back inside. Walk to the guest room where the signal was the strongest. I can't punch the hotel's numbers in fast enough.

Nothing goes through. More error messages. And then, the smell of roses.

"Don't you remember, Bill?" comes from behind.

When I turn, Claire's there in sunglasses, sitting on the bed in the clothes she died in, straw hat and all. A pair of binoculars dangle from her neck.

She looks normal. Happy. Perfect. Alive.

"You did the same thing Daniel did," she says, all dimples. "Months ago."

The phone's screen cracks when it hits the floor. Blood glugs onto my shirt. A whiff of gunpowder weaves past.

"There was no doctor," Claire explains. "No medicine."

My brain fizzes like ginger ale.

I try talking but can't. I'm too weak, too tingly, my body lighter than helium as the knowledge of what I'd done envelops me.

Claire watches as I wobble myself to the floor, trying not to fall or faint, tenuously curling myself into a fetal position against the cool Saltillo tiles.

"Silly man," she says. "You made it all up."

I brush away the blood coming down in a curtain over my eyes and pooling on the floor. It takes everything I have to stay focused on my wife.

"You wouldn't leave. Even after I showed up. So, I asked Daniel to help."

Daniel now stands beside Claire, dressed in his trademark ratty overalls. He beams through his St. Nick-sized beard.

"I was trying to tell you, oh Ignorant One." He goes on to remind me of what I now remember, what Claire already said.

And it rushes like ice water through my veins.

"I put a bullet through my melon at the Sunset Motel two months after Claire died. Remember? That my cancer had come back and there was no way to beat it? So, I did what I had to do. Just as you did what you had to do."

He's right. Which is why I'd put a .45 to my head a week later. To end the torment of losing my two best friends.

I begin shaking. More blood pours onto the tiles, fouling my shirt, sticking to my face. Try as I might to concentrate on Claire, I can't. Things are becoming cloudy, grainy, out of focus.

Claire's words come in pieces—filtered, far-away, like someone on a television program sounds right before you fall asleep.

"*You're*" is one word I catch..

"*Something*" is another.

More syrup leaks from my head.

Claire and Daniel keep smiling.

A clot of blood rolls out of my mouth.

Everything gets better after that.

ABOUT THE AUTHORS

A E Deakin – The Absence of You

aedeakin.substack.com

A E Deakin is a dark fiction writer based in Warwickshire, UK. Her horror short, *The Token*, was published by Black Hare Press in 2024.

A. J. Payler – Doorway to Nowhere

ajpayler.com

Author/musician A. J. Payler's novels include *The Killing Song*, *Lost in the Red*, *Terror Next Door*, and *Bank Error in Your Favor*.

Alan P. Marks – Ex Sanguine

alanpmarks.com

Alan P. Marks is a writing/literature teacher at the University of Maine, and a graduate of the Stonecoast MFA program at University of Southern Maine.

Alex Laurel Lanz – From Both Sides of Your Mouth

Alex Laurel Lanz is an artist and writer living in the San Francisco Bay area. Their work has been featured in *Tales to Terrify*, *Scare Street*, and more.

Caroline Barnard-Smith – Dream Eater for Sale

Caroline Barnard-Smith is a speculative fiction author with too many ideas. She's written horror, epic fantasy, and sci-fi, and she refuses to pick a favourite.

Chad Gayle – What Smiles are For

chadgayle.com

Chris Scott – Four Walls and a Roof

chrisscottwrites.com

Chris Scott is a speculative fiction writer, ClickHole contributor, and elementary school teacher.

Dane Erbach – That Night

daneerbach.com

Dane Erbach is a writer from Chicago's northwest suburbs. He teaches English and journalism at a public high school.

David Lee Zweifler – Getting Better

davidleezweifler.com

David writes fiction and is training as an EMT. His work appears in *Analog* and *Nature Futures*, and he is querying his first novel.

Devin Oldham – Lawyer, Captain, Cook

facebook.com/oldhamhorror

Diane M Johnson – The Body and the Blood

dianemjohnson.com

Diane has several unproduced scripts that keep getting recognized in competitions. She also has four novels; *The Schoharie* and the *Perfect Prophet* trilogy.

gaast – Make a Little Room for Me

gaast.skin

gaast is a ghost currently haunting occupied Lenape land. It reminds everyone that Black Lives Matter, and that Palestine will be free.

Gina Easton – Folie-à-Deux

Gina Easton is a former registered nurse who decided to pursue a career as a writer of fiction. To date, she has had twelve short stories featured in various horror anthologies and magazines.

J C Lee – Aspotolnik

J C Lee is the pen name for an Anglo Chinese, male female authorial partnership. They previously authored the novel *Seven Curses* also published by Graveside Press in 2024.

J D Outcalt – Phoenix

sites.google.com/view/jeffreydavidoutcalt/home

Jeffrey Outcalt is a writer of Fantasy and events producer from Ohio. He writes fiction and essays for his newsletter, "Okay, I'll Tell You Anyways."

J. E. Norwood – The Issue with Mould

J. E. Norwood lives amidst the mists of Scotland. When he's managed to rip himself away from the writing chair (or let's be honest, couch), he's either gardening, reading or bouldering.

J.E. Schleicher – You Are Mine, My Soul Yours to Keep

jeschleicher.com

J.E. Schleicher's fiction has appeared in *Creepy Podcast*, *The Colored Lens*, and *L. Ron Hubbard Presents Writers of the Future Volume 40* among other publications.

Jacqueline K Goldblatt – Bitter Harvest

jackiefrostling.carrd.co

Jacqueline Kate Goldblatt is an NJ native who has had a love affair with writing since her childhood which she doubts will end anytime soon.

Justin Sangermano – Morison's Funeral Home and Museum of Death

substack.com/@justinsangerman

Jim Donohue – Hard Labor

December of 2024 marked the very beginning of Jim Donohue's writing career, at the age of 68. After coming nose-to-nose with death in late 2019, Mr. Donohue decided there were still things he needed to do, and being a horror writer was one of them.

Katherine Traylor – One in the Bed

katherinetraylor.com

Katherine Traylor is a US-born writer currently based in Prague. Her writing is often fairy-tale-inspired with a strong focus on transformation.

Kay Hanifen – The Confession of RM Renfield

kayhanifenauthor.wordpress.com

Kay Hanifen's work has appeared in over one hundred anthologies and magazines. Her first novel, *The Last Ballard*, will debut this year.

Kayla Whittle – Dry-clean

kaylawhittle.wordpress.com

Kayla Whittle works in acquisitions at a medical publisher. She has previously had short stories published in a variety of anthologies, and her work has also been featured on *Flash Fiction Podcast*. When not writing, she's usually busy reading or planning her next Disney vacation.

Lane Blevins – Blabbermouth

Lane's fiction has appeared in *The Haunted Zone* and *Thirteen Podcast*. She earned her MFA for Creative Writing at National University. She currently resides in San Antonio, where she works as a drill sergeant and live with her husband and three beautiful children.

Larry Hodges – Cemetery Whale

larryhodges.com

Larry Hodges has over 220 short story sales and four SF novels, with 23 books and over 2,300 published articles. He's also a ping-pong aficionado!

Mary Frances Slebodnik – The Lightkeeper's Diary

Mary Slebodnik has an MFA in Fiction from Florida International University and was included in *The Best Small Fictions 2019*.

Matthew Doggett – Extinguished

matthewdoggettauthor.com

Michael A. Reed – The Ghosts We Keep

Michael A. Reed is a speculative fiction writer and ironically dyslexic English teacher. A history of his work can be found at

mikecantreed.com

Michael Mullen – You're Really Something

Michael' s work has appeared in *Concho River Review*, *pacificREVIEW*, *Sow's Ear Poetry Review*, and others. *You're Really Something* is his first ghost story. Find him at michaelmullen@cardd.co.

Norman Gary Thomson – A Mask For Osiris

P. N. Harrison – The Echo and the Altar

P. N. Harrison is a professor and writer living in Western Kansas. He studied creative writing as a student in West Texas. When not publishing academic articles on medieval literature, H.P. Lovecraft, and books bound in human skin, he enjoys watching baseball, traveling to historic sites, and watching horror movies with his wife.

Patricia Esposito – Sailing to Quigley

patriciaesposito.com

A Pushcart Prize nominee, Patricia's stories have appeared in numerous magazines and anthologies and have received honorable mentions in Ellen Datlow's *Year's Best Fantasy and Horror*.

Petina Ann Strohmer – Eliza

Petina Strohmer is a traditionally published novelist who has also had thirty stories published in different anthologies.

Shannon Lawrence – Flesh of My Flesh

thewarriormuse.com

Shannon Lawrence writes horror, mystery, and fantasy. She writes for *Rocky Mountain Reader* and is co-host and producer of *Mysteries, Monsters, & Mayhem.*

Vicky Pointing – Symphony in White

vickykpointing.wordpress.com

Vicky's short stories and flash fiction have been published by Valley Press and a number of online magazines including *Cossmass Infinities.* She completed an MA in Creative Writing in 2016 and won a place in the 2022 Northern Short Story Academy.

Victoria Brun – Red Tide

victoriabrun.com

Victoria Brun's fiction and nonfiction pieces have appeared in *Clarkesworld Magazine, Nature Futures, Factor Four Magazine,* and beyond.

Z. C. Loki – Mouse-clown

Z. C. Loki is a queer schizotypal writer from central Appalachia, having had work featured in *Word Hotel* and *FABLE: An Anthology of Sci-Fi, Horror, & The Supernatural.*

THANK YOU!

Thank you for supporting Graveside Press and our authors. One of the biggest ways you can help is to leave a star rating or a review wherever you purchased your copy!

Stay spooky.

graveside-press.com

CONTENT WARNINGS

Please note: it should be assumed that basic horror tropes will apply. These include death, gore, and violence.

Apostolnik – talk of fantasized sexual violence against women, sexual assault (off-page), violence against women

Blabbermouth – depiction of a dead child

Eliza – death of a child

Flesh of My Flesh – historical depictions of racism and violence toward Indigenous peoples

From Both Sides of Your Mouth – suicide, suicidal ideation, self-harm, elder abuse

Getting Better – transphobia, dementia

Hard Labor – traumatic birth, death of a child, body horror

Mouse-clown – child violence

The Absence of You – loss of a spouse, toxic relationships, religion

The Ghosts We Keep – child abuse

The Lightkeeper's Diary – loss of a spouse, loss of a child, mental illness, grief

Winter Harvest – period typical homophobia, allusions to grooming

You Are Mine, My Soul Yours to Keep - mentions of child abuse, stalking, allusions to domestic abuse

You're Really Something – loss of a spouse, suicide

www.ingramcontent.com/pod-product-compliance
Lightning Source LLC
Chambersburg PA
CBHW061039310726
48969CB00004B/1009